A PORTRAIT OF THE ARTIST
AS A YOUNG MAN

JAMES JOYCE was born on 2 February 1882 in Dublin, eldest of ten surviving children born to Mary Jane ('May') Murray and John Joyce. Joyce's father was then a Collector of Rates but the family, once prosperous, had just begun its slow decline into poverty. Educated first at the Jesuit Clongowes Wood and Belvedere Colleges, Joyce entered the Royal University (now University College, Dublin) in 1898. Four years later Joyce left Dublin for Paris with the intention of studying medicine but soon his reading turned more to Aristotle than physic. His mother's illness in April 1903 took him back to Dublin. Here he met and, on 16 June 1904, first stepped out with Nora Barnacle, a young woman from Galway. In October they left together for the Continent. Returning only thrice to Ireland—and never again after 1912—Joyce lived out the remainder of his life in Italy, Switzerland, and France.

The young couple went first to Pola, but soon moved to Trieste where Joyce began teaching English for the Berlitz School. Except for seven months in Rome, the Joyces stayed in Trieste for the next eleven years. Despite disputes with recalcitrant publishers, severe eye problems and the pressures of a growing family (both a son and a daughter were born), Joyce managed to write the poems that became *Chamber Music* (1907), as well as *Dubliners* (1914). He also began, abandoned, began again, and completed *A Portrait of the Artist as a Young Man* (1916), which appeared first in instalments in *The Egoist* from 2 February 1914 (Joyce's thirty-second birthday). (The first attempt, *Stephen Hero*, was published posthumously in 1944.) By the time the family moved to Zurich in July 1915, he had also begun *Ulysses*.

Over the next seven years, first in Zurich, later in Paris, *Ulysses* progressed. Partial serial publication in the *Little Review* (1917–18) brought suppression, confiscation, and finally conviction for obscenity. Sylvia Beach, proprietor of the Shakespeare and Company bookshop in Paris, offered to publish, and the first copies arrived in Joyce's hands on 2 February 1922, his fortieth birthday.

The acclaim publication brought placed Joyce at the centre of the literary movement only later known as Modernism, but he was already restlessly pushing back its borders. Within the year he had begun his next project, known only mysteriously as *Work in Progress*. This occupied him for the next sixteen years, until in 1939 it was published as *Finnegans Wake*. By this time, Europe was on the brink of war. When Germany invaded France the Joyces left Paris, first for Vichy then on to Zurich. Here Joyce died on 13 January 1941 after surgery for a perforated ulcer. He was buried in Fluntern Cemetery.

JERI JOHNSON is senior Fellow in English, Exeter College, Oxford. She has written on Joyce, textual theory, feminist literary theory, and Virginia Woolf, and edited Joyce's *Ulysses* and *Dubliners* for Oxford World's Classics.

OXFORD WORLD'S CLASSICS

*For over 100 years Oxford World's Classics have brought
readers closer to the world's great literature. Now with over 700
titles—from the 4,000-year-old myths of Mesopotamia to the
twentieth century's greatest novels—the series makes available
lesser-known as well as celebrated writing.*

*The pocket-sized hardbacks of the early years contained
introductions by Virginia Woolf, T. S. Eliot, Graham Greene,
and other literary figures which enriched the experience of reading.
Today the series is recognized for its fine scholarship and
reliability in texts that span world literature, drama and poetry,
religion, philosophy and politics. Each edition includes perceptive
commentary and essential background information to meet the
changing needs of readers.*

OXFORD WORLD'S CLASSICS

JAMES JOYCE

A Portrait of the Artist as a Young Man

Edited with an Introduction and Notes by
JERI JOHNSON

OXFORD
UNIVERSITY PRESS

OXFORD

UNIVERSITY PRESS

Great Clarendon Street, Oxford OX2 6DP

Oxford University Press is a department of the University of Oxford.
It furthers the University's objective of excellence in research, scholarship,
and education by publishing worldwide in

Oxford New York

Auckland Bangkok Buenos Aires Cape Town Chennai
Dar es Salaam Delhi Hong Kong Istanbul Karachi Kolkata
Kuala Lumpur Madrid Melbourne Mexico City Mumbai Nairobi
São Paulo Shanghai Taipei Tokyo Toronto

Oxford is a registered trade mark of Oxford University Press
in the UK and in certain other countries

Published in the United States
by Oxford University Press Inc., New York

Editorial matter © Jeri Johnson 2000
Text © Copyright 1964 by the Estate of James Joyce

Database right Oxford University Press (maker)

First published 2000
Reissued 2008

British Library Cataloguing in Publication Data

Data available

Library of Congress Cataloging in Publication Data

Joyce, James, 1882–1941.
A portrait of the artist as a young man / James Joyce; edited
with an introduction and notes by Jeri Johnson.
(Oxford world's classics)
Includes bibliographical references.
1. Dublin (Ireland)—Fiction. 2. Young men—Fiction. 3. Artists—Fiction. I. Johnson,
Jeri. II. Title. III. Oxford world's classics (Oxford University Press)
PR6019.O9 P64 2000 823'.912–dc21 00–038595

ISBN 978–0–19–953644–3

5

Typeset in Ehrhardt
by RefineCatch Limited, Bungay, Suffolk
Printed in Great Britain by
Clays Ltd, St Ives plc

CONTENTS

ABBREVIATIONS

CDD	Stanislaus Joyce, *The Complete Dublin Diary*, ed. George H. Healey (Ithaca: Cornell University Press, 1971)
E	Richard Ellmann, *James Joyce* (1959; rev. edn. 1982; corr. New York: Oxford University Press, 1983)
LI, LII, LIII	*Letters of James Joyce*, 3 vols.: vol. i ed. Stuart Gilbert; vols. ii and iii ed. Richard Ellmann (New York: Viking, 1957, 1966)

INTRODUCTION

'astounding bad manners'

WHEN *A Portrait of the Artist as a Young Man* began to appear in instalments in the English 'little magazine' the *Egoist* in 1914,[1] men of letters at least took note: Ezra Pound described it as 'damn well written'; W. B. Yeats praised its author as 'a man of genius' and 'the most remarkable new talent in Ireland to-day'.[2] With book publication two years later, the reviewers divided themselves unequally between those who found it 'extraordinarily dirty', who declared that 'no clean-minded person could possibly allow it to remain within in reach of his wife, his sons or daughters . . . is it Art? We doubt it', and those who found 'passages in this book comparable with the best in English literature'.[3] H. G. Wells famously diagnosed Joyce as in the grips of a 'cloacal obsession. He would bring back into the general picture of life aspects which modern drainage and modern decorum have taken out of ordinary intercourse and conversation. . . . If the reader is squeamish upon these matters, then there is nothing for it but to shun this book',[4] while Virginia Woolf confided to her diary that she was 'disillusioned' by reading Joyce as by 'a queasy undergraduate scratching his pimples'.[5] Against this, the young American poet Hart Crane went so far as to claim for Joyce abilities

---

[1] *Portrait* appeared in the *Egoist* in 25 instalments from 2 February 1914 (Joyce's 32nd birthday) to 1 September 1915; B. W. Huebsch published it in book form in the United States on 29 December 1916 and The Egoist Press in England on 12 February 1917 (see 'Composition and Publication History').

[2] Ezra Pound to H. L. Mencken (18 Feb. 1915), *Letters of Ezra Pound: 1907–1941*, ed. D. D. Paige (London: Faber & Faber, 1951), 94; W. B. Yeats to Edmund Gosse (24 July 1915) and to the Secretary of the Royal Literary Fund (29 July 1915), *Letters of W. B. Yeats* (London: Hart-Davis, 1954), 597, 599.

[3] All in unsigned reviews: the first, in 'A Study in Garbage', *Everyman* (23 Feb. 1917); the second, in *Irish Book Lover*, 8/9–10 (Apr.–May 1917); the third, in *New Age*, 21/11 (12 July 1917); all reprinted in Robert H. Deming (ed.), *James Joyce: The Critical Heritage*, 2 vols. (London: Routledge & Kegan Paul, 1970), i. 85, 102, 110.

[4] H. G. Wells, 'James Joyce', *Nation*, 20 (24 Feb. 1917); repr. in Deming (ed.), *Critical Heritage* i. 86.

[5] *The Diary of Virginia Woolf*, 5 vols. (1978; repr. Harmondsworth: Penguin, 1981), ii. 188–9. In fairness to Woolf, we should point out that her comment concerns her response to *Ulysses*, not to *Portrait*, and was made on 16 August 1922, though one cannot imagine her finding the earlier 'undergraduate' any less 'queasy'-making.

'common to only the greatest' writers and to declare *Portrait* 'spiritu-
ally the most inspiring book' he had ever read ('aside from Dante'): 'It
is Bunyan raised to art and then raised to the ninth power.'[6]

Everything Joyce ever published caused a commotion at least the
equal of this. *Dubliners*, the volume of short stories which itself
appeared in 1914, had been refused by scores of publishers, including two who agreed to print, then withdrew, one of whom went so far
as to destroy the proofs already pulled for fear of being prosecuted
for libel or obscenity. The stories were, he claimed, too frank, too
willing to use real names of real people (including that of a recently
dead king of England) in contexts and conversations less than
flattering. By the time *Ulysses* appeared in 1922, its serial publication
had already been thrice suppressed, twice burned, and once successfully prosecuted for obscenity.[7] And by the time Joyce's last work,
Finnegans Wake, emerged in 1939, it had already become infamous as
being synonymous with impenetrable obscurity. Today, Joyce is frequently cited as the greatest writer of prose fiction of the twentieth
century, but the mention of his name still causes a shiver of apprehension to pass through listeners. He is still rumoured to be 'dirty'
or 'difficult'.

But in 1914, Joyce was virtually unknown. Born in 1882 into a
respectable middle-class Catholic family just prior to that family's
relentless, demoralizing financial decline, Joyce grew up in an
Ireland subject to British rule on the one hand and Roman Catholic
domination on the other. And the claims of Ireland (as against
Britain) often conflicted with those of the Church. Most formatively
for Joyce, they did so when Charles Stewart Parnell, leader of the
Irish Parliamentary Party and, many thought, the man most likely to
achieve Home Rule for Ireland, was discovered to have been having
an 'affair' for ten years with a married woman, Katherine O'Shea.
First Gladstone, the Prime Minister who had formed an alliance
with Parnell at Westminster, then the Catholic bishops condemned
the adulterer as unfit for public life. He lost control of the Party and
his candidates lost the ensuing election in Ireland. Within the year

---

[6] Hart Crane, 'Joyce and Ethics', *Little Review*, 5/3 (July 1918), 65; repr. in Deming
(ed.), *Critical Heritage*, i. 124.

[7] See Jeri Johnson, 'Composition and Publication History', in James Joyce, *Ulysses:
The 1922 Text*, ed. Jeri Johnson, Oxford World's Classics (Oxford: Oxford University
Press 1993), pp. xxxviii–xlii.

Parnell died. Though only 9 at the time, Joyce would never forget what he considered the treachery of the priests and their hand in the destruction of Ireland's 'uncrowned king'.[8]

The episode provided him with material for one of the most vividly realized scenes in *Portrait*, and occasioned his earliest publication, a poem entitled 'Et Tu, Healy' in which he lionized Parnell and indicted those closest to him as traitors. In the title, he equates the Parnellite Timothy Healy's turning on Parnell with Brutus's betrayal of Caesar.[9] The precocity of the allusion (he was 9 when he wrote the poem) suggests not only imagination but a decent education. Far from being the 'self taught working man' Woolf imagined him,[10] Joyce was educated at the Jesuit Clongowes Wood and Belvedere Colleges. He attended university, though *not* Trinity College, Dublin. That institution had been founded by Elizabeth I in 1591 with the express purpose of furthering the Protestant reformation in Ireland—the express purpose, that is, of eradicating Catholicism, not educating its adherents. Until 1873 entrance was restricted to those who submitted to religious tests, effectively to those who were the offspring of Anglo-Irish Protestents, the landholding minority who for centuries had been Britain's ruling class in Ireland. By Joyce's time, Catholics could attend, though the clergy strongly urged them not to set foot in the heathen institution. He studied instead under the auspices of the Royal University (what would become University College, Dublin), an institution carrying the imprimatur of no less a Catholic than its first rector, John Henry, Cardinal Newman. Here, he made a name for himself as clever, if prone to cause a certain kind of trouble: he refused to sign a petition denouncing Yeats's *Countess Cathleen* as defaming Ireland, refused to modify a paper delivered to the college's Literary and Historical Society to include in it an insistence that drama have an 'ethical' dimension, refused to accept the non-acceptance for publication by a

[8] See notes to pp. 5, 13, 22, 25–7, 30, 33, 210, below.

[9] The poem does not survive, but Stanislaus Joyce, Richard Ellmann, Herbert Gorman, and John J. Slocum and Herbert Cahoon all give accounts of its having existed and, indeed, of James's father John Joyce having had it published (Stanislaus Joyce, *My Brother's Keeper* (1958; repr. New York: Viking, 1969), 45–6; *E* 33; Herbert Gorman, *James Joyce* (1939; repr. London: John Lane and Bodley Head, 1941), 36; John J. Slocum and Herbert Cahoon, *A Bibliography of James Joyce: 1882–1941* (1953; repr. Westport, Conn.: Greenwood Press, 1971), 3–4).

[10] Virginia Woolf, *Diary* (16 Aug. 1922), ii. 189.

college magazine of another paper in which he decried the Irish parochialism of the new Irish Literary Theatre; he published it himself instead.[11] When in April 1900 the *Fortnightly Review* printed his 'Ibsen's New Drama', Joyce (then only 18) demonstrated his belief that Ireland 'afford[ed] no literary model to the artist'; he would 'look abroad'.[12] Within four years he had left Ireland for the Continent and would return only three times to visit (in 1909 and 1912). Even then it was to wrangle with publishers over their continued refusals to publish *Dubliners* without censoring it, but by 1912 he had already written first one, then another entirely different, version of the work that would become *A Portrait of the Artist as a Young Man*.

Running clearly through this life are the two entwined threads of the history of the domination of Ireland by Britain, of Irish Catholics by British Protestants, and of those Irish Catholics themselves by the strictures of the institutionalized Catholic Church. A third, vivid thread carries the aspiring artist's refusal to submit to either authority especially in matters of art. In the fabric of the whole, all three are woven inseparably together. By the time he left Ireland, the young Joyce had already determined that he would reweave this history and create art out of the tale of their mutual entanglement. This is the tale that *Portrait* tells, a tale tracing the growth and development of a young Irish Catholic artist-to-be until, at last, he embraces 'Life' and turns to leave Ireland. Joyce, that is, determined to weave the thematic threads of his own life history into the fabric of a novel and to do so without flinching from the facts. He had formed himself in the insistence on holding out for the truth; this novel would be truthful.

Those early reviewers of *Portrait* found it so. In fact, what Joyce's antagonists, early and late, despised was what one reviewer of *Portrait* called his 'invincible honesty', another his 'intellectual integrity, his sharp eyes, and his ability to set down precisely. . . . He is a realist of the first order.'[13] Everyone, whether praising or condemning the

[11] See James Joyce, 'Drama and Life' (1900) and 'The Day of the Rabblement' (1901), *Critical Writings*, ed. Ellsworth Mason and Richard Ellmann (1959; repr. New York: Viking, 1973), 38–46, 68–72, and James Joyce, *Occasional, Critical, and Political Writing*, ed. Kevin Barry (Oxford: Oxford University Press, 2000), 23–9, 50–2.

[12] 'Ibsen's New Drama', *Critical Writings*, 47–67, and Barry (ed.), 30–49; 'The Day of the Rabblement', *Critical Writings*, 70, and Barry (ed.), 50.

[13] Francis Hackett, 'Green Sickness', *New Republic*, 10/122 (3 Mar. 1917), repr. in Deming (ed.), *Critical Heritage*, i. 94; J. C. Squire, 'Mr James Joyce', *New Statesman*, 9 (14 Apr. 1917). repr. ibid. i. 100.

novel, stood astonished at Joyce's ability to present what J. C. Squire described as 'sheer undecorated, unintensified truth'.[14] But these reviewers didn't know the man James Joyce from a bar of soap. They could not possibly be judging whether the novel was a faithful, truthful account of his own life, whether, that is, it was a faithful, true autobiography, whether Stephen Dedalus was a faithful, true portrait of James Joyce. So what, then, did these critics mean by 'truth'?

H. G. Wells gives the game away when he mentions 'decorum'. There are things that polite, decorous people do not mention in public. Nice people don't talk about religion or politics, nor do they ever on any account admit into discussion the emissions, excitations, vulnerabilities of the body. In the eyes of such decorous people, James Joyce was not a nice writer. Early critics felt they had to warn the unsuspecting public: '[O]ne distinguishing feature of the book [is] its astounding bad manners. About this one must speak frankly at the start and have done with it', wrote one. Another found 'the religious questions and the political questions . . . too roughly handled to please the incurably devout and patriotic. If they ever put up a statue of Joyce in Dublin, it will not be during his life time' (he was right on that one at least). A third critic, fronting up to the *really* vulgar issues, pointed to what he called *Portrait*'s 'improprieties—there is one on the very first page'.[15] On the very first page? 'When you wet the bed first it is warm then it gets cold' (5). In 1916, wetting the bed was not the proper stuff of fiction. Nor was sex, nor family fights about the conflicting demands of loyalty to one's religious leaders as against loyalty to one's country, nor the torments of Hell vividly and sensuously evoked by a priest attempting to scare the holy bejesus out of young boys and send them trembling to the confessional, nor those boys' irreverent banter, nor the graffiti they scrawl on toilet walls, nor the 'smugging' they get up to within those walls, nor even the simple closely and unflinchingly observed consequences of poverty—aspiring artists should not be shown picking lice off their necks, let alone visiting prostitutes or . . . wetting the bed. When publishing the novel serially, even the *Egoist*, that harbinger of artistic

---

[14] Ibid.
[15] 'A. M.', 'A Sensitivist', *Manchester Guardian*, 22,018 (2 Mar. 1917), 3, repr. in Deming (ed.), *Critical Heritage*, i. 93; John Macy, 'James Joyce', *The Dial*, 62/744 (14 June 1917), repr. ibid. 107–8; A. Clutton-Brock, 'Wild Youth', *Times Literary Supplement*, 789 (1 Mar. 1917), 103, repr. ibid. 89.

freedom, had been forced by its printers to accede to the excision of a
long paragraph at the opening of Chapter III where Stephen imagines that he will again visit 'the squalid quarter of brothels' as 'the
whores' are 'just coming out of their houses making ready for the
night' (86).[16] That kind of 'undecorated, unintensified truth' was
just too much to print.

'nature . . . expressed otherwise'

But truth-telling alone does not a great novel make. *Stephen Hero*,
Joyce's first attempt to weave the threads of his own life into fiction,
shows candour. This was not enough. Intending that the finished
work comprise sixty-three chapters, Joyce managed to complete only
twenty-five when he cast it aside. At its best *Stephen Hero* charms as
does occasionally any run-of-the-mill Edwardian novel. Despite his
brother Stanislaus's estimate at the time—'the chapters are
exceptionally well written in a style which seems to me altogether
original'[17]—one cannot imagine this book causing much more than a
ripple of notice. Its interest now is largely if not entirely as an early
Joyce misfire. It shares with *Portrait* subject matter and genre, for
though only the 'University episode' survives, we know it was meant
to follow in detail the life of a young Irish Catholic boy from infancy
to young manhood. Each is a *Bildungsroman*, a novel tracing the
growth and development of an individual to the point that he or she
walks out of the novel on the last page seemingly self-determined
and self-determining. Each is, in fact, a *Kunstlerroman*, a novel
depicting the growth and development of an artist. Both *Stephen
Hero*'s Stephen Daedalus and *Portrait*'s Stephen Dedalus live lives
similar in many respects to Joyce's own. As he told Stanislaus, he
meant the novel to be 'almost autobiographical'.[18] (And in a

[16] *Egoist* 1/15 (1 Aug. 1914), 289. The British Library holds a composite copy of
Portrait, prepared by Joyce and Harriet Weaver from *Egoist* tearsheets, proofs, and
galleys, marked by Weaver to show the printer's excisions (BL C.116.h.6, p. 29r). See
also Hans Walter Gabler, 'Towards a Critical Text of James Joyce's *A Portrait of the
Artist as a Young Man*', *Studies in Bibliography*, 27 (1974), 3; Jane Lidderdale and Mary
Nicholson, *Dear Miss Weaver: Harriet Shaw Weaver: 1876–1961* (New York: Viking,
1970), 92, 99, 103.

[17] *CDD* 20, entry for 10 March 1904; James Joyce, *Stephen Hero*, ed. Theodore
Spencer, rev. edn. John J. Slocum and Herbert Cahoon (1963; repr. St Albans: Triad,
1977).

[18] *CDD* 12 (2 Feb. 1904).

reversal that had life imitating art, when Joyce published the first versions of three stories that, revised, he included in *Dubliners*, he did so under the pseudonym 'Stephen Daedalus'.[19]) *Stephen Hero*, more obviously autobiographical than *Portrait*, takes its form from the episodic, 'one-damn-thing-after-another' school and includes events seemingly because they happened to the young Joyce and characters seemingly because Joyce met their equivalents in real life. Stephen's family plays a much larger part in *Stephen Hero*, and individuals other than Stephen are drawn independently and dramatically. And yet Joyce became frustrated with the book very early in his writing of it. As he wrote to Stanislaus, 'I am afraid I cannot finish my novel for a long time. I am discontented with a great deal of it and yet how is Stephen's nature to be expressed otherwise? Eh?'[20] In answering this question, Joyce transformed a workmanlike novel into a work of art.

The steps Joyce took were principally two: most significantly, he moved the narrative centre of consciousness from a wholly independent third-person narrator to one which exists between Stephen and the third-person narrator. Joyce's precise method represents a radical departure from previous modes of story-telling and profoundly affects the meanings of the novel (a point to which we will return). Events and characters of *Portrait* take their significance from Stephen. While there is still a third-person narrator, that narrator presents *Stephen's* perceptions: the attitudes towards others and events are his; they are 'seen' by or 'focalized' by him. And because they are viewed by him, they reflect something about him. All go to the ends of characterizing the young artist-in-the-making.

Secondly, Joyce ruthlessly exercised a principle of selection. No longer in *Portrait* do we get everything including the kitchen sink; no longer does the narrative go plodding along in a this-happened-and-then-that-happened-and-then-that-happened kind of way. Instead of sixty-three chapters there are five and those five are carefully patterned individual entities even as they play parts in the overall pattern of the whole novel. The general movement—one dictated by the demands of chronology: Stephen grows up—remains, but each

[19] Early versions of 'The Sisters', 'Eveline' and 'After the Race' appeared in George Russell's *Irish Homestead* (13 Aug., 10 Sept., and 17 Dec. 1904) under the pseudonym 'Stephen Daedalus'.

[20] James Joyce to Stanislaus Joyce, 19 November 1904, *LII* 71.

chapter displays its own pattern and movement. Each individual episode mirrors, in effect, the general movement of the whole; each is a minidrama of rising from lowliness to triumph. Unlike *Stephen Hero*, *Portrait* shows Joyce compressing, selecting the salient detail, arranging things to suit the aesthetic pattern of the novel, not to accord with the timing of his own life history. So, critics have found it impossible to match the chronology of the novel to the events in Joyce's own life. In writing *Portrait*, Joyce selected; he arranged; he did not transcribe.

In this new arrangement, each chapter represents a phase in the life of the young artist. Chapter I gives Stephen's early childhood: Stephen at Clongowes Wood College, at home with his family in Bray for the Christmas dinner fight about Parnell, back at Clongowes where he is unjustly pandied by one schoolmaster and, having pleaded this injustice before another, emerges triumphant. Chapter II traces a pattern of Stephen's burgeoning sexuality which registers in his longing to find in his own life one like the beautiful Mercedes in *The Count of Monte Cristo*, in his writing verses to E——C——, in his reeling from finding the word 'foetus' carved into the bench of the physics theatre when he visits Cork with his father, in his masturbatory fantasies, and finally in his visit to the prostitute with which the chapter ends. Counterpointing this narrative preoccupation are his family's moves. When the chapter opens Stephen has already left Clongowes and the family has moved to Blackrock; during its course, they move to first one then another address in Dublin, each less salubrious than the last. At Dublin's Belvedere College Stephen acts the part of the 'farcical pedagogue' in the Whitsuntide play and defends his unorthodox literary tastes against the philistinism of his schoolmates. Chapter III concerns itself entirely with the religious reawakening which culminates in Stephen's repentance and confession. Stephen, still in mortal sin at the chapter's outset, attends a retreat with the other Belvedere boys. There Father Arnall's harrowing, vividly detailed sermon on the torments of Hell that will visit the unrepentant sinful fills him with guilt, and with 'trembling body . . . with whimpering lips' he confesses his sins to an old priest. Chapter IV traces the slow disintegration of Stephen's religious commitment and its replacement with the secular call to art. Because of Stephen's now evident piety, the director of Belvedere asks him if he might have a vocation for the priesthood. Stephen opts instead for university. Walking on the strand, he 'seem[s] to see' Daedalus, the mythic artificer whose name he bears, then encounters a young woman whom he imagines a fabulous creature, 'one whom magic had changed into the likeness of a strange and beautiful seabird' (144). Both seem to him emblems of his calling as an artist. In the meantime, to avoid eviction, the family moves yet again. Over the course of Chapter V, Stephen sloughs off friends, family, national and religious demands in order to answer the call of art. At university he converses with the dean of studies about language and art, with his friends Davin (about Irish politics), Lynch (about his theories of art), and Cranly (about love, particularly that of a mother and son, and about his having left the Church). To Cranly, he declares, 'I will not serve' (201):

I will not serve that in which I no longer believe whether it call itself my home, my fatherland or my church: and I will try to express myself in some mode of life or art as freely as I can and as wholly as I can, using for my defence the only arms I allow myself to use—silence, exile, and cunning. (208)

In the interstices, he writes a villanelle to a 'temptress', unnamed but clearly 'E——C——'. In the final pages of the novel, we are given Stephen's 'diary' as he prepares to leave Ireland, and for the first time the narrative proceeds in the first person. In his last entry he implores Daedalus: 'Old father, old artificer, stand me now and ever in good stead' (213).

Such an account presents the novel as in the mode of the usual novel of development, and reads Stephen's life as a gradual and inevitable movement towards triumphant independence when on the final page he sets off to 'forge in the smithy of [his] soul the uncreated conscience of [his] race' (213). Within each chapter a similar pattern of rising action can be seen: each opens with Stephen in humility and ends with him triumphant. The careful selection and arrangement of events differs markedly from that episodic plodding of *Stephen Hero*.

'a mosaic of jagged fragments'

But if in standing back from the novel and examining the relations of its five chapters to its overall structure, we discern a pattern, early reviewers did not detect it. H. G. Wells typified their reactions when he described the book as 'a mosaic of jagged fragments'.[21] Open the book and look at it: it breaks repeatedly into sections within chapters. Each break marks a temporal and geographical shift. Each new section opens without any consoling narrator explaining where we are or how we got there or how much time has elapsed since the last section. Each chapter breaks even more decisively with its predecessor. Even within sections, the narrative shifts. Take the opening of Chapter III, for example. We follow Stephen's thoughts as he contemplates another visit to the prostitutes only to discover that he is actually sitting in a classroom during a mathematics lecture. Thoughts seldom follow a straight line; in following Stephen's thoughts, the narrative moves from imagined future event to the mundane present setting within which that future is contemplated. Once the maths lesson ends and the rector of the college announces the forthcoming religious retreat, the narrative breaks off. The next words are those of Father Arnall as he opens his sermon on Hell. Things have happened, we imagine (as though Stephen were a real person living an actual life), between the maths lesson and the retreat, but they are not recounted. A continuous developmental narrative only emerges when we stand far enough back and draw bold lines connecting the discrete dots that constitute individual sections and chapters.

The point here is simple: the events presented are not scrupulously faithful to every detail of Stephen's lived experience. They are selected by Joyce, who with remarkable spareness and precision provides the telling detail. Things happen in this novel because of their significance to the portrait of Stephen that Joyce wishes to draw, because they reveal something about him (and the culture in which he exists). Take as an example another small difference between *Stephen Hero* and *Portrait*. In the former, Stephen has twice the number of acquaintances he has in *Portrait*, and ten times as many conversations with them. By reducing these to the three salient conversations of Chapter V, Joyce intensifies Stephen's isolation and allows the narrative to do double duty. The three conversations represent quite specifically the claims of nation, family, and Church against which Stephen articulates his independence and elaborates his imagined escape through art. Similarly, in *Stephen Hero* Stephen is repeatedly described in terms of his 'ineradicable egoism'; he

[21] Wells, in Deming (ed.), *Critical Heritage*, i. 87.

is 'the wholehearted young egoist' who possesses an 'ingenuous arrogance': in expecting that Stephen will 'follow the path of remunerative respectability', his family 'first fulfilled him with egoism; and he rejoiced that his life had been so self-centred'.[22] Critics of *Portrait* have often remarked Stephen's callowness and his arrogance. But a striking shift in terminology from *Stephen Hero* to *Portrait* marks a precise and significant difference between the two Stephens. In the latter, he is identified not by his 'ego' but by his 'pride'. His is a 'pride of silence' (148). 'His father's whistle, his mother's mutterings, the screech of an unseen maniac were to him now so many voices offending and threatening to humble the pride of his youth' (147). 'Pride after satisfaction uplifted him like long slow waves' (139). Unlike 'arrogance' or 'egoism', 'pride' carries with it an element of justification: one is justly proud of one's accomplishments. And the Stephen of *Portrait* uses his pride to give him strength to leave family, Church, and homeland. Significantly, however, in shifting Stephen's egoistic arrogance to pride, Joyce again extracts a double meaning. 'Pride' carries another association which, in a pattern of careful repetition, Joyce points out. When Stephen declares to Cranly, 'I will not serve' (which he does twice: 201, 208), he echoes another, as Cranly calmly notes ('That remark was made before': 201). As Father Arnall (twice) tells his 'dear boys', Lucifer, a.k.a. Satan, that son of the morning who fell from heaven dragging with him a third of the hosts of heaven, committed 'the sin of pride' when he uttered '*non serviam: I will not serve*' (99). '[A]n instant of rebellious pride of the intellect made Lucifer . . . fall from . . . glory' (112–13). Stephen's pride sustains him, but the echo suggests that his pride, like its proverbial equivalent, may precede a fall.

'he confesses in a foreign language'

Joyce had a mind intrigued by the 'not-quite-samenesses' of things, by, that is, the ways in which things are at once distinctively themselves and like other things, the ways things can be themselves and still be metaphors or symbols. The habit was nurtured by the culture of that Catholic Church he left behind. There, every element of church ritual has a meaning beyond itself, whether it be the altar, the candles, the chalice, the priest's vestments or the gestures he

[22] *Stephen Hero*, 35, 114, 48.

performs. In writing *Portrait*, Joyce exploited this potential double-ness of things. So, Stephen is both like and unlike Lucifer, just as he is both like and unlike his two namesakes, St Stephen, the first Christian martyr, and Daedalus, Ovid's archetype of the artist.[23]

And he is both like and unlike James Joyce. *Portrait* is famously autobiographical. The book opens with a story of a moocow coming down the road where 'a nicens little boy named baby tuckoo' lived (5). The real, historical John Joyce told this story to his real, histori-cal son James.[24] The close resemblance of the characters within the novel to actual persons, persons with whom James Joyce was demon-strably personally acquainted (many of whom afterwards claimed such identifications[25]), and of events in the novel to those that Joyce experienced, the fact that biographies and critiques have been writ-ten taking the proximity of fictional to real persons as premiss,[26] and the fact that any novel written by any novelist about one who becomes a writer will provoke the suspicion that that novel might well be derived from the details of that novelist's own life, have led to the endlessly reiterated description of this novel as 'autobiographi-cal'. Of course it is—autobiographical, that is.[27] James Joyce shared with Stephen Dedalus a Jesuit education at Clongowes Wood, Belvedere, and University Colleges. He lived, like Stephen, in a series of decreasingly salubrious houses in Bray, Blackrock, and Dublin. He lived, like Stephen, in an Ireland dominated by the

[23] See notes to the novel's epigraph and to p. 6, line 26.

[24] John Joyce in a letter to his son James: 'I wonder do you recollect the old days in Brighton Square, when you were Babie Tuckoo, and I used to take you out in the Square and tell you all about the moo-cow that used to come down from the mountain and take little boys across?' (31 Jan. 1931, *LIII* 212).

[25] See e.g. J. F. Byrne, *Silent Years: An Autobiography with Memoirs of James Joyce and Our Ireland* (New York: Farrar, Straus and Young, 1953); C. P. Curran, *Struggle with Fortune* (Dublin: Browne and Nolan, n.d.) and *James Joyce Remembered* (Oxford: Oxford University Press, 1968); Eugene Sheehy, *May it Please the Court* (Dublin: C. J. Fallon, 1951); and Robert Scholes and Richard M. Kain (eds.), *The Workshop of Daedalus: James Joyce and the Raw Materials for 'A Portrait of the Artist as a Young Man'*, Part II: 'The Artist as a Young Man' (Evanston, Ill.: Northwestern University Press, 1965), 111–237.

[26] See e.g. *E*; Chester G. Anderson (ed.), *A Portrait of the Artist as a Young Man*, Viking Critical Edition (New York: Viking, 1968), notes *passim*; Anderson painstakingly identifies the 'real' equivalents of virtually every character in the novel.

[27] In this respect, note at least Joyce's comment to Frank Budgen: ' "Some people who read my book, *A Portrait of the Artist*, forget that it is called *A Portrait of the Artist as a Young Man*." He underlined with his voice the last four words of the title.' Budgen, himself an artist, provides a suggestive gloss on what might be meant by Joyce's com-ment and a useful comment on the art of portraiture more generally (*James Joyce and the Making of 'Ulysses'* (1934; repr. Bloomington: Indiana University Press, 1961), 60–1.

Catholic Church and occupied economically, linguistically, and governmentally by 'foreigners'. Like Stephen, he acted the part of a 'farcical pedagogue' in a school play, flirted with the idea of becoming a priest, but chose instead to become a writer. And, like Stephen, he left Ireland. He, too, passed through a phase of intense aestheticism, read Aquinas and Aristotle, and fashioned an aesthetic, but unlike Stephen he emerged the other side and wrote a novel Stephen could never have written. As Stanislaus remarked: 'Jim is thought to be very frank about himself but his style is such that it might be contended that he confesses in a foreign language—an easier confession than in the vulgar tongue.'[28] That 'foreign language', the language of art, makes Stephen something other. Hugh Kenner describes him as a Joycean 'shadow self'. Such 'shadow-selves', he argues, 'are not the author. They are potentialities contained within the author. They are what he has not become.'[29] In creating the 'portrait' that is Stephen, Joyce exploited the potential fecundity of meaning latent in the actual material history of his own life. He gave to mundane reality a shape, an aesthetic form, and squeezed out of things every last drop of metaphoric and symbolic significance.

'He sang that song. That was his song'

But if this is true, Joyce is no mere symbolist. Remember that critic who claimed 'He is a realist of the first order'? Well, he is . . . and he isn't. We've already noted the truthfulness of his including in this novel the 'improprieties' often missing from fiction. Similarly, Joyce insistently placed his characters in real space: Stephen walks through real Dublin streets, passes or enters real Dublin pubs or colleges or churches. Of his later *Ulysses* Joyce famously remarked that he wanted 'to give a picture of Dublin so complete that if the city one day suddenly disappeared from the earth it could be reconstructed out of [his] book'.[30] In trying to get his earlier *Dubliners* into print, Joyce had had to contend with publishers who thought names of real places did not belong in any fiction but certainly not in such indecorous fiction as this. In retaliation, Joyce insisted that 'he is a

[28] Stanislaus Joyce, quoted in *E* 148.

[29] Hugh Kenner, 'The Cubist *Portrait*', in Thomas Staley and Bernard Benstock (eds.), *Approaches to Joyce's 'Portrait': Ten Essays* (Pittsburgh: University of Pittsburgh Press, 1976), 178–9.

[30] Joyce to Frank Budgen, quoted in Budgen, *James Joyce and the Making of 'Ulysses'*, 67–8.

very bold man who dares to alter in the presentment, still more to deform, whatever he has seen and heard'.[31] This insistent fidelity to fact runs through all three of these works. So, in *Portrait*, if the narrative mentions the 'marbles' in the chapel at Clongowes, you can bet that the wooden columns in the chapel at Clongowes were painted to look like marble.

But unlike *Dubliners* and *Ulysses*, *A Portrait of the Artist as a Young Man* is tied intimately and inextricably to a single character. Joyce ties this knot between narrative and character by focalizing it through Stephen: the action is viewed through Stephen's eyes; what we read is what he sees, or thinks, or feels. Because of this, material details come to the reader already filtered through a particular apprehension of them, their appearance in the story requiring that Stephen has perceived them. But, in doing this, Joyce does not make the novel a first-person narrative. Until the diary entries in the last section of the book, the narrative stays insistently third person. Stephen does not narrate this novel; he is narrated by it. And yet the language of the novel seems utterly unlike the usual language deployed by omniscient third-person narrators. Look again at that first page: 'The moocow came down the road where Betty Byrne lived: she sold lemon platt' (5) or 'When you wet the bed first it is warm then it gets cold. His mother put on the oilsheet. That had the queer smell' (5). Utterly suited to an attentive, perceptive, inquisitive but naïve child, one for whom the circumambient world registers with vivid sensory immediacy, this language appears to be not that of the invisible third-person narrator, but that of Stephen. The narrator appropriates Stephen's language to narrate this tale: not only his vocabulary, but his grammar, his arrangement of words, in short, his idiolect. (By 'idiolect' we mean the *form of language* used by a particular individual, an idiosyncratic 'style', one characteristic of this person and not that, the original Greek word itself being cognate with that for 'private property',[32] as though Stephen's idiolect were

---

[31] Joyce to Grant Richards, 5 May 1906, *LII* 134.

[32] 'Idiolect'—an individual's own distinctive form of speech—derives from the Greek *idios*, meaning 'own, private', and *legein*, 'to speak', and is related to 'idiom'—the form of speech peculiar to a people or country—which itself comes from the Greek *idioma*, 'property', and *idios*, 'own, private'; so *idiomatos*: 'private property'. The etymological implication is that one's peculiar mode of speaking, the particular arrangement of these words in this order, is one's own private property (a principle upheld by, for example, copyright law).

his personal possession.) And yet the narrative stubbornly remains in the third person. This may be Stephen's idiolect but the narrator has appropriated it to his own ends.

This technique differs subtly from free indirect discourse which presents characters' words and thoughts indirectly rather than directly (as quoted by the narrator: 'he said', 'she thought'). Through free *indirect* discourse, the narrative can move surreptitiously into those thoughts while still staying grammatically strictly in the third person and without signalling that such a move has occurred. So, for example, the narrator in Jane Austen's *Emma* (1816): 'He stop[ped] again, rose again, and seemed quite embarrassed.—He was more in love with her than Emma had supposed; and who can say how it might have ended, if his father had not made his appearance?'[33] This appears to come as the omniscient narrator's objective analysis; only later do we realize that the narrator is here presenting Emma's assumptions. The technique provides great opportunities for irony, and Austen exploits them fully. Joyce, too, uses free indirect discourse in *Portrait* when the third-person narrator moves into Stephen's thoughts without signalling directly that he has done so.[34] But his use of it differs markedly from Austen's. The language of the narrative in *Emma* remains relatively stylistically consistent throughout the novel no matter what is being related or whose thoughts are being relayed. By and large, *Emma*'s style is Austen's. From the opening page of *Portrait*, the narrative proceeds in Stephen's idiom: Joyce uses language, style, idiolect not to embellish an identificative authorial signature, nor as indicators of his own cast

[33] Jane Austen, *Emma* (1816), ch. 30; ed. James Kinsley, Oxford World's Classics (Oxford: Oxford University Press, 1980), 235.

[34] *Portrait* is often described as a 'stream-of-consciousness' novel. The term is borrowed from philosophy, specifically from William James, philosopher brother of the novelist Henry, who used it to describe the workings of consciousness as experienced by the individual. When applied to literature, it remains descriptive only of fictions which share a preoccupation with representing character through pre-verbal or unspoken 'thoughts'. It is thus a generic grouping, not a technique. The term tells us nothing about how the aim of 'representing thoughts' is accomplished. See William James, *Principles of Psychology* (New York: Henry Holt, 1890), i. 239; Robert Hurley, *Stream of Consciousness in the Modern Novel* (Berkeley, Los Angeles, London: University of California Press, 1954); and for 'free indirect discourse', see Mieke Bal, *Narratology: Introduction to the Theory of Narrative* (1980), trans. Christine van Boheemen (Toronto: University of Toronto Press, 1985), 140–2; or Seymour Chatman, *Story and Discourse: Narrative Structure in Fiction and Film* (Ithaca: Cornell University Press, 1978).

of mind, or of the wisdom or folly of the narrator, but instead as markers of character.[35]

There is no high-falutin narrative term for this technique, though Hugh Kenner has dubbed it the 'Uncle Charles Principle'[36] after the character in *Portrait* the description of whom caused Wyndham Lewis to accuse Joyce of slipshod writing. Lewis, fed up with hearing what a brilliant writer Joyce was, took it upon himself to indicate precisely and locally an example of Joyce's use of hackneyed and clichéd language, in the opening of Chapter II where 'uncle Charles repaired to his outhouse' (50). Lewis opined that characters 'repair' to 'outhouses' in second-rate fiction; not in serious literature.[37] But, as Kenner points out, uncle Charles does not 'repair' to the 'outhouse' because Joyce could find no finer language. He 'repairs to the outhouse' because 'repairing' is what *characters* like uncle Charles do. With deft economy, Joyce provides an extra characterizing fillip: with no overt indication that it is doing so, the narrative appropriates a typically carolingian word, a word of the sort uncle Charles would himself use, a slightly clichéd, slightly supercilious, slightly but inaptly pretentious word, a word that overreaches its grasp by the smallest yet clumsiest of margins.[38] This 'Uncle Charles Principle' writ large is the stylistic principle of *Portrait*. The lexicon, the sentence structure, the diction, follow those of the protagonist, the 'artist' of the title. They will change as that 'artist' changes, mature as he does, grow complex, florid,

---

[35] As early as 1903, in a review of a not very good but—for Joyce's later project of writing his own novel about a rebellious 'young man'—relevant French novel (Marcelle Tinayre's *The House of Sin*), Joyce (over)praised a writer because he adapted the novel's prose style to the exigencies of the subject matter: 'The last chapters of the book . . . show an admirable adjustment of style and narrative, the prose pausing more and more frequently with every lessening of vitality, and finally expiring' (*Critical Writings*, 122, and Barry (ed.) 85–6).

[36] Hugh Kenner, 'The Uncle Charles Principle', *Joyce's Voices* (Berkeley: University of California Press, 1978), 15–38.

[37] Wyndham Lewis, quoted ibid. 17.

[38] Similarly, Lily the caretaker's daughter in the opening sentence of Joyce's *Dubliners* short story 'The Dead': 'Lily the caretaker's daughter was literally run off her feet.' That 'literally' is the giveaway. The one thing sure is that Lily is not *literally* but rather *metaphorically* run off her feet. The sentence has committed the common sin of attempting to strengthen metaphorical statements by reporting them as literal occurrences: 'I am literally dead with exhaustion.' No . . . The opening sentence of 'The Dead' adopts the language of the character being written about—'literally' is Lily's kind of word (James Joyce, *Dubliners* (1914), ed. Jeri Johnson (Oxford: Oxford University Press, 2000), 138; Kenner, *Joyce's Voices*, 15).

overwrought in parallel with the development of his mind. As the artist grows, so grows the style.

Paradoxically, by restricting the language of the narrative to the idiolect of the central character, Joyce draws a much subtler portrait than could have been achieved by allowing that narrative lexical and dictional free range. The method itself implies a conception of character quite unlike that underpinning the narrative modes employed in earlier fictions. Character here exists at an intersection between interiority and exteriority, between the idiolect of the character (that private interior language of individualism) and the third-person narrative (that exterior frame itself significant of the ostensible objectivity of the outer world), neither wholly private, nor entirely public. The central character of this novel may think that this is his story. Indeed, never before has the language of a novel been tied so intimately to the idiosyncratic viewpoint, the mental and linguistic habits of the character therein depicted. But by retaining the third-person narrative, Joyce displaces the potentially stifling narcissistic egoism that such proximity might otherwise produce.[39] A small but significant space opens up between character and narrator, not to mention character and author. And in maintaining this space Joyce avoids reinforcing those old humanist clichés of identity as wholly self-generated, of the individual existing independent of the strictures of history, culture, and ideology.

'O, the green wothe botheth'

By deploying the 'Uncle Charles Principle' Joyce provides an astonishingly 'realistic' representation of Stephen. But neither the progression of the narrative through Stephen's idiom nor its

---

[39] Not that everyone has noticed this fact. One of the oldest debates in *Portrait* criticism centres on the question of irony, which might itself be thought of as a matter of distance—between, for example, what is said (denotatively) and what is meant (connotatively). Wayne C. Booth, for example, maintained that the narrative of the novel was so irremediably tied to the attitudes of the central character that there was no space for irony to operate; it was impossible to distinguish the attitudes of the character from those of (the narrator or) the author; and the attitudes of Stephen were insufferable ('The Problem of Distance in *Portrait*', in *The Rhetoric of Fiction* (Chicago: University of Chicago Press, 1961), 323–36). Hugh Kenner, on the other hand, found the portrait of Stephen ironic throughout (first in his 'The *Portrait* in Perspective', in *James Joyce: Two Decades of Criticism*, ed. Seon Givens (New York: Vanguard, 1948), 132–74, and later in the revision of this as a chapter in *Dublin's Joyce* (1955; repr. with new introd. New York: Columbia University Press, 1987), 109–33).

focalization through him means that Stephen understands everything he sees, or everything the narrative presents. An example: on the first page of *Portrait*, a song is sung: '*O, the wild rose blossoms | On the little green place*'. Since this is Joyce, you can be guaranteed that it is a real song. And if you know the real song, you will know something that neither Joyce nor his narrator tells you directly: in the real song, the rose blossoms on a little green *grave*. That these adults have changed the word tells you something about the kind of 'truth' they allow their son to hear. That 'death' is present, if only as a repressed shadow, on the first page of the novel tells you something about the nature of this 'life' story. Stephen neither perceives nor understands these things. Joyce here remains scrupulously faithful to the real, but manages at once to make it do double duty.

Put slightly differently, we might characterize Joyce's writing as duplicitous, in the strict sense of that word as 'twofold' or 'double in action or conduct'. Take yet again that first page of the novel. It presents this small child's world through a densely economical language at once both so vividly realistic that his sensory and social worlds are evoked with exceptional precision and clarity, and so symbolically resonant that virtually every theme, leitmotif, moral, political, or aesthetic concern that will arise in the succeeding novel is here proleptically figured.[40] Notice: the world is apprehended within the space of a few paragraphs through each of the five senses: hearing (the story), sight (the hairy face of his father), taste (the lemon platt), touch (the warmth and cold of the wet bed), smell (the oilsheet). The social world unfolds: first with father (the patriarch who passes on the word, culture, history), then with mother (who tends to the body and its uncontrolled emissions); next with the extended family: first uncle Charles then 'Dante'; finally with the neighbourhood: the Vances who have a different father and mother and who live at number seven. The comparative relation of this to that, of he to she, is delineated: mother smells nicer than father; uncle Charles and Dante are older than father and mother, but uncle Charles is older than Dante. Themes that will exfoliate over the course of the novel are sounded: Irish history and politics are

---

[40] Hugh Kenner, again, first notices this: *Dublin's Joyce*, 114–15. With 'prolepsis', the rhetorical figure of anticipation (which means 'to take before'), a form or symbol or word anticipates something that will happen later.

brought into the intimacy of the extended family through Dante's keeping of two brushes, one for Michael Davitt and one for Parnell. The family's and society's inculcation of heterosexual norms is acknowledged: 'when they were grown up he was going to marry Eileen'. The expectation that moral behaviour can be elicited and enforced through the threat of punishment becomes apparent: the eagles will put out Stephen's eyes if he does not apologize (for some unnamed, even unimagined wrongdoing; guilt is induced early). The two sides of the leitmotif which will repeatedly recur—that of birds and by extension flight—are sounded first (and positively) in the epigraphic allusion to Daedalus, the 'cunning artificer' who fashions wings for himself and so flies free of the labyrinth in which he is trapped, and second (negatively) in the punitive eagles who will 'come and pull out his eyes'. Perhaps most significantly, Stephen's aesthetic predisposition shows itself. He attends carefully to, and identifies with the protagonist of, the story his father tells him: 'He was baby tuckoo.' He hears the song '*O the wild rose blossoms | On the little green place*' and 'rewrites' it in his own idiom: '*O, the green wothe botheth*', the lisping 'botheth' testifying to the realism of the account, while his transformation of the 'wild rose' into the 'green wothe' (or 'geen wothe' as Joyce actually wrote) suggests for the second time in the novel the contrary, that rather than being a faithful representation of the real world, art 'alters nature' (as the novel's epigraph suggests).[41] Finally, he transforms the material of everyday life, here society's imprecations, its threats of punishment, into a work of art:

> *Pull out his eyes,*
> *Apologise,*
> *Apologise,*
> *Pull out his eyes.*

> *Apologise,*
> *Pull out his eyes,*
> *Pull out his eyes,*
> *Apologise.*

[41] In the manuscript of *A Portrait of the Artist as a Young Man*, the line reads 'O the geen wothe botheth' (*The James Joyce Archive*, ed. Michael Groden, 63 vols. (New York: Garland, 1977–80), 9: 5). The novel's epigraph—*Et ignotas animum dimittit in artes*—comes from Ovid's *Metamorphoses* and means 'So then to unimagined arts he set his mind'; in the original poem, the line continues 'and altered nature's laws'.

This kind of symbolic realism or realistic symbolism typifies the double work of *Portrait*, a novel at once vividly 'true to life' and aesthetically finely wrought. But there is more than craftedness at issue here, and Joyce draws it quite precisely out of his realistic portrait of Stephen. Stephen aspires to be an artist, an artist whose medium will be language. Joyce makes this plausible by showing him as preoccupied with language: Stephen repeatedly ponders words, their meanings, their effects, their textures, and we are persuaded that his choice of vocation—art not the priesthood—is 'realistic'. This linguistic preoccupation, however, leads beyond the mere characterization of Stephen. In its repeated address to the nature of language, the novel itself seems to be linguistically and aesthetically self-aware. When, for example, the novel opens 'Once upon a time', it self-consciously draws attention to itself *as* a story, as a narrative. The phrase itself has become utterly clichéd: it no longer means anything except 'what is about to follow will be a story'. Because of this, that 'once upon a time' metatextually signifies—it comments on the novel's status as a text, as a narrative (and not, say, as a transcription of reality). At its most innocent interpretation, the novel begins with story-telling because Stephen will leave the last page hoping to become a writer, and the narrative's saturation in the idiom of the character elicits this tale-telling opening as a symbolic prefiguration of that future vocation. That's its realistic function; its metatextual effect is to say 'pay attention; this is a novel that knows it's a novel, one wise to the ways of art'.

Over the course of the novel, Stephen's understanding of language grows more sophisticated, but it never quite catches up with the conceptions of language and of the nature of art possessed by the Joyce who wrote the novel in which Stephen finds himself. But what does Stephen understand and how does this differ from what the novel displays?

'God's real name was God'

The opening pages of this novel lay a firm foundation for the plausibility of Stephen's final decision to become 'an artist'. His pre-occupation with language begins early, matures, remains. So at Clongowes, with all the precocity of the future artist, he contemplates the meaning of 'belt':

[H]is hands were bluish with cold. He kept his hands in the sidepockets of his belted grey suit. That was a belt round his pocket.[42] And belt was also to give a fellow a belt. One day a fellow had said to Cantwell:

—I'd give you such a belt in a second.

Cantwell had answered:

—Go and fight your match. Give Cecil Thunder a belt. I'd like to see you. He'd give you a toe in the rump for yourself.

That was not a nice expression. His mother had told him not to speak with the rough boys in the college. Nice mother!   (6–7)

The narrative's description of Stephen's being cold, of his keeping his hands in the pockets of his 'belted' suit, slides unremarked into Stephen's contemplation of the name of the thing itself: 'That was a belt'. But the second the word is applied to the thing, the meaning of the word splits in two: 'And belt was also to give a fellow a belt.' If the first meaning of the word sits firmly in a conception of language as nominative, denotative—language and the world coexist in a mutually confirming alliance—the second meaning pulls against this. In this arena, words have multiple meanings derived from and conveyed through the unofficial, extracurricular realm of verbal threat and schoolboy banter. Not surprisingly in this context, Stephen's thoughts slip on to even less sanctioned words: 'He'd give you a toe in the rump for yourself' and 'rump' is 'not a nice expression'. As so often in this first chapter, Stephen retreats from the 'not nice' by thinking of 'nice mother', who we will remember has a 'nice smell' and who plays the piano for him to dance. But this retreat is temporary; the fascination with language persists:

—You are McGlade's suck.

Suck was a queer word. The fellow called Simon Moonan that name because Simon Moonan used to tie the prefect's false sleeves behind his back and the prefect used to let on to be angry. But the sound was ugly. Once he had washed his hands in the lavatory of the Wicklow Hotel and his father pulled the stopper up by the chain after and the dirty water went down through the hole in the basin. And when it had all gone down slowly the hole in the basin had made a sound like that: suck. Only louder.

To remember that and the white look of the lavatory made him feel cold and then hot. There were two cocks that you turned and water came out: cold and hot. He felt cold and then a little hot: and he could see the names printed on the cocks. That was a very queer thing.   (8–9)

[42] The manuscript has 'jacket' for 'pocket'. Groden (ed.), *James Joyce Archive*, 9: 13.

If Stephen could be said to have a theory of language at this point, it would be the bow-wow or onomatopoeic theory: the word for the thing imitates its actual acoustic equivalent in reality: 'suck' has its name because things that 'suck' make 'sucky' sounds—like the water in the basin going down the hole: 'suck. Only louder'. 'Only louder': even in this profoundly mimetic theory, words don't quite match the real thing. And again, oddly, the contemplation of language brings Stephen into the realm of the 'not nice'. Partly this is verisimilitude: children ponder the meanings of words they don't quite understand; most often the words they don't quite understand are words that are 'not nice', words that are 'queer'. The entire first chapter depicts with extraordinary vividness the uneasiness (even powerlessness) that children feel when 'others' know something they do not (compare the incident where Stephen is asked whether or not he kisses his mother goodnight (11)).

But something more is going on here. If 'suck' is a 'queer word', so is 'queer'. Until recently it meant (as an adjective) 'peculiar, eccentric' or (in slang) 'drunk' or (in thieves' cant) 'bad, worthless'; or (as a verb) 'to puzzle, to cheat, to spoil'. The *Shorter Oxford English Dictionary* is too polite to record its more 'eccentric' meaning of 'homosexual', let alone its most recent swerve into a prideful self-appellation of that very group whose ugly taunters spat it out to shame them into hiding or conforming. This late history means that no reader can now read this passage without noting the uncanny proximity in this naïve text of so many 'not nice', indeed 'queer' words: 'suck', 'queer', 'cocks'. But then we ourselves begin to slide into the perverse, the eccentric, the peculiar. Or do we? Later, some boys will be caught 'smugging' in the 'square' for which they will face the option either of being flogged on the 'rump', that 'vital spot', or of being expelled—forced outside the circle of the community (of communion and communication). Unruly bodies must be policed either corporally or verbally. But the unruly body is quite precisely what obtrudes into Stephen's ruminations about language, both about 'belts' and about 'sucks'. In the latter case, the chain of associations—from 'suck' to 'water' to 'lavatory' to 'cocks' on which words are written: 'hot' and 'cold'—seems to produce in Stephen a somatic or bodily response: 'To remember that and the white look of the lavatory made him feel cold and then hot. There were two cocks that you turned and water came out: cold and hot. He felt cold and then a little hot.' 'Cold and hot', 'cold and hot', 'cold and hot'. A rhythm establishes itself, a rhythm like that noted by Stephen when trains pass telegraph poles or go in and out of tunnels or when he opens and closes the flaps of his ears. And with rhythm the body again enters: the most primitive rhythms come in inhaling and exhaling, in eating and excreting, in a ceaseless movement of in and out.[43] '[T]he train went on, roaring and then stopping; roaring again, stopping. It was nice to hear it roar and stop and then roar out of the tunnel again and then stop' (10). Of course on the level of the mimetic, of realistic representation, Stephen's body is even more literally present than we at first suspect. He feels 'cold and hot' because, as we will soon discover, he has a fever contracted when he was 'shouldered' into 'the square ditch', that cesspit or drainage trough from the school's lavatory (8). But all these words circle back upon themselves and we end up where we began with words and the body mutually invoking one another at every turn. Language comes to be more associated with effluent than fluency. These are 'queer words' indeed, and while Stephen senses their peculiarity, he does not fully understand their reverberating effects and meanings. He tries to master their waywardness by delineating clearly his own location, and the ultimate end of all meaning in the final great wordsmith, God:

He turned to the flyleaf of the geography and read what he had written there: himself, his name and where he was.

> *Stephen Dedalus*
> *Class of Elements*
> *Clongowes Wood College*
> *Sallins*
> *County Kildare*
> *Ireland*
> *Europe*
> *The World*
> *The Universe*

That was in his writing: and Fleming one night for a cod had written on the opposite page:

---

[43] This rhythmic aspect of language Julia Kristeva describes as analogous to the *semiotic chora*, the persistence of which within symbolic language disrupts and undermines denotation and coherent meaning (*Revolution in Poetic Language*, trans. Margaret Waller (New York: Columbia University Press, 1984), 25–30, 58).

> *Stephen Dedalus is my name,*
> *Ireland is my nation.*
> *Clongowes is my dwellingplace*
> *And heaven my expectation.*

He read the verses backwards but then they were not poetry. Then he read the flyleaf from the bottom to the top till he came to his own name. That was he: and he read down the page again. What was after the universe? Nothing. But was there anything round the universe to show where it stopped before the nothing place began? It could not be a wall but there could be a thin thin line there all round everything. It was very big to think about everything and everywhere. Only God could do that. He tried to think what a big thought that must be but he could think only of God. God was God's name just as his name was Stephen. *Dieu* was the French for God and that was God's name too; and when anyone prayed to God and said *Dieu* then God knew at once that it was a French person that was praying. But though there were different names for God in all the different languages in the world and God understood what all the people who prayed said in their different languages still God remained always the same God and God's real name was God.   (12–13)

A great deal happens here (and don't miss the quiet comment about poetic form). Stephen attempts to place himself: I am I; I live here; here is a particular place even if it exists within 'a very big' place called 'everywhere' or 'the universe'; even that 'very big place' must be situated somewhere: 'what was after the universe?' 'Nothing', a 'nothing' which must itself begin somewhere, must be placed: 'was there anything round the universe to show where it stopped before the nothing place began?' (A belt, perhaps?) Each placing becomes a displacing as the finite slowly moves to the infinite: God. And thinking of 'only God' Stephen again ponders the name of the thing. Contemplation of the world to the ends of understanding is for Stephen invariably an act of attempted linguistic mastery, of belting in and containing the thing by voicing its totemic name. But thinkng of 'God's name'—the one name which, according to Judaic law, must never be spoken—only gets him into trouble again, for God has more than one name: '*Dieu* was the French for God and that was God's name too'; indeed 'there were different names for God in all the different languages in the world'. And the vertiginous bigness of 'everything and everywhere' yawns. But Stephen reaches to control the splintering through 'all the different languages in the world' of the whatness of this thing, this place, this God: 'God remained always the same God and God's real name was God'. God's *real* name? There is language and then there is *real* language, and the latter resides in God.

'good old blunt English'

We as readers are charmed by this passage: charmed because of Stephen's ingenuous innocence, his fledgling attempts to master the incomprehensibility of God, his easy, guileless acceptance; charmed because we know more than he about these things. Our sophistication reads his simplicity and smiles. He will learn better, we think. And he does. By the time he has learned to divert his religious instructors from the serious matters of education by putting to them 'curious questions' about the catechism (89), has suffered the fires and stench of Hell in Father Arnall's sermon (Chapter III), has survived the attempted seduction of him into the priesthood by the Church (Chapter IV) and encountered his 'envoy from the fair courts of life' (145), the young woman on the strand, he also understands a great deal more about the ways and weight of language. Walking the streets of Dublin,

he found himself glancing from one casual word to another on his right or left in stolid wonder that they had been so silently emptied of instantaneous sense until every mean shop legend bound his mind like the words of a spell and his soul shrivelled up, sighing with age as he walked on in a lane among heaps of dead language. His own consciousness of language was ebbing from his brain and trickling into the very words themselves which set to band and disband themselves in wayward rhythms:

> The ivy whines upon the wall
> And whines and twines upon the wall
> The ivy whines upon the wall
> The yellow ivy on the wall
> Ivy, ivy up the wall.

Did any one ever hear such drivel? Lord Almighty! Who ever heard of ivy whining on a wall? Yellow ivy: that was all right. Yellow ivory also. And what about ivory ivy?

The word now shone in his brain, clearer and brighter than any ivory sawn from the mottled tusks of elephants. *Ivory, ivoire, avorio, ebur.* (150)

By this point words have floated free of the real world—or almost: 'Who ever heard of ivy whining on a wall?' They remain a source of 'wonder' but are 'emptied of instantaneous sense' and spellbind his mind. The words 'band and disband *themselves* in *wayward* rhythms'. It is their history *as words*, words independent of actual 'mottled tusks of elephants', that enchants: '*Ivory, ivoire, avorio, ebur.*' You can almost hear him intoning quietly to himself. Stephen experiences here a pleasure both intellectual and somatic: 'intellectual' in his mastery of four linguistically distinct 'ivories' and 'somatic' in the trance they induce, the 'word' shining in his brain. This pleasure in multiplicity, in plenitude, in the splitting and splintering of the word into words, is a far cry from the anxiety Stephen felt as a child and for which he sought comfort in 'God's real name'.

And Stephen has learned too that 'heaps of dead language' come freighted with history, and that history is never anodyne. As he later bandies words with the dean of studies, he points to the difficulty arising in 'esthetic discussion' from the fact that meanings of words depend on context; unless one knows 'whether words are being used according to the literary tradition or according to the tradition of the marketplace' (157) confusion results. At this point the dean is just about following Stephen's argument. The conversation that follows is a small ironic masterpiece, and Stephen knows it. In attempting to illustrate his point, he remarks a use of the word 'detain' by Newman, that crafter of 'cloistral silverveined prose' (147–8), who

says of the Blessed Virgin that she was detained in the full company of the saints. The use of the word in the marketplace is quite different. *I hope I am not detaining you.*

—Not in the least, said the dean politely.

—No, no, said Stephen, smiling, I mean . . .

—Yes, yes: I see, said the dean quickly, I quite catch the point: *detain.*

He thrust forward his under jaw and uttered a dry short cough.   (157–8)

Stephen's mastery of the language, the dean, and the entire situation marks him as already a clever, linguistically deft young man, but the dean yet has something to teach him if only by virtue of his own failure to comprehend. The dean is English. Stephen has been pondering this fact in the interstices of their exchange. The dean has been struggling to gain a foothold in this conversation about the virtues of hard work, about literal and metaphoric lamps, and even (and most foolishly on his part) about art. Stephen runs circles round him, as above. In trying to recover from his embarrassment, the dean returns to the (metaphoric) lamp in the hope of imparting at least a nugget of wisdom:

—To return to the lamp, he said, the feeding of it is also a nice problem. You must choose the pure oil and you must be careful when you pour it in not to overflow it, not to pour in more than the funnel can hold.
—What funnel? asked Stephen.
—The funnel through which you pour the oil into your lamp.
—That? said Stephen. Is that called a funnel? Is it not a tundish?
—What is a tundish?
—That. The . . . the funnel.
—Is that called a tundish in Ireland? asked the dean. I never heard the word in my life.
—It is called a tundish in Lower Drumcondra, said Stephen laughing, where they speak the best English.
—A tundish, said the dean reflectively. That is a most interesting word. I must look that word up. Upon my word I must.   (158)

Stephen, of course, does look it up: '13 *April*: That tundish has been on my mind for a long time. I looked it up and find it English and good old blunt English too. Damn the dean of studies and his funnel! What did he come here for to teach us his own language or to learn it from us? Damn him one way or the other!' (212). By this point, Stephen's linguistic understanding has sufficiently advanced that he willingly, if implicitly, acknowledges that there is no tether binding word to object in a one-to-one correspondence: the battle here is not over which word is the real word for the object under discussion. The verbal gesturing—'That?' 'That'—may make it appear as though an object were present: it is not. The indicative pronouns point not at any 'real' funnel or tundish but back and forth at one another, at the two words 'funnel' and 'tundish' freed from their objective referential function. But they none the less enter this discussion with hundreds of years of a very material history trailing in their wake. As Stephen thinks:

—The language in which we are speaking is his before it is mine. How different are the words *home*, *Christ*, *ale*, *master*, on his lips and on mine! I cannot speak or write these words without unrest of spirit. His language, so familiar and so foreign, will always be for me an acquired speech. I have not made or accepted its words. My voice holds them at bay. My soul frets in the shadow of his language.   (159)

'His language' not 'mine'. England colonized Ireland and with it attempted to suppress and supplant the indigenous culture; English remains 'foreign', 'an acquired speech' for this Irishman. But the fight being fought between funnels and tundishes is not a fight between an English and an Irish word. Both are English, though 'tundish' more 'solidly' so, deriving as it does from the two Old English words *tunne* and *disć* while 'funnel' only arrives into English in the late medieval period having probably at that point crossed the channel from France. The ironies abound: the Irishman uses the older and more solidly English word, the Englishman the French *arriviste*; Ireland, having suffered occupation by the English, has preserved an English culture now absent from England; the dean of studies, having attempted to teach, ends up being taught his own language by one whose 'soul frets in [its] shadow'.

If Stephen acknowledges that language is the site of historical and political contestation, he harbours no sentimental ideas that an indigenous Irish language and culture might be superior to, more authentic or less 'foreign' than, the English of the invaders. During the late nineteenth century there sprang up in Ireland various movements devoted to re-establishing 'authentic' Irish culture (as against the invidious invaders' imported version), most notably the Gaelic League. Its effects can everywhere be seen in *Portrait*, from Emma's attending 'league classes' (where she would be learning Gaelic), to Davin's enthusiasm for hurley (a genuinely Irish sport). But it is a movement with which Stephen will have no truck:

—This race and this country and this life produced me, [Stephen] said. I shall express myself as I am.
—Try to be one of us, repeated Davin. In your heart you are an Irishman but your pride is too powerful.
—My ancestors threw off their language and took another, Stephen said. They allowed a handful of foreigners to subject them. Do you fancy I am going to pay in my own life and person debts they made? What for?
—For our freedom, said Davin.
—No honourable and sincere man, said Stephen, has given up to you his life and his youth and his affections from the days of Tone to those of Parnell but you sold him to the enemy or failed him in need or reviled him and left him for another. And you invite me to be one of you. I'd see you damned first. (170)

'Damned.' That's pretty strong language for one who has so recently recovered from the devastating effects of his own contemplation of damnation. (He damns one other in the novel, the dean of studies: 'Damn him one way or the other!') And there is little doubt that in part the strength of Stephen's reaction comes because he still harbours an intense (sentimental?) resentment at Parnell's treatment by his fellow countrymen, especially the devoutly Catholic who would not tolerate his adultery, a resentment he has learned at his father's knee on Christmas Day. Stephen's anger arises here too partly at the claim being made on him to play a part in a drama he seeks to avoid, fancying instead his own alternative romantic myth of the proud, individual man of artistic genius who flies free of the shackles with which others would bind him. As he continues with Davin:

—The soul is born, he said vaguely, first in those moments I told you of. It has a slow and dark birth, more mysterious than the birth of the body. When the soul of a man is born in this country there are nets flung at it to hold it back from flight. You talk to me of nationality, language, religion. I shall try to fly by those nets. (171)

By the end of the novel, Stephen will assert that 'the shortest way to Tara [is] *via* Holyhead'[44] (211): to encounter (or even engender) Irish culture one must leave Ireland. But what Stephen does not recognize is his very indebtedness, indeed inevitably inextricable indebtedness to that culture he wishes to leave behind. His own words betray him: 'I shall try to fly by those nets.' Prepositions are tricky things, and the small one here is duplicitous: 'by' can mean either 'past, beyond' (I shall fly beyond, fly past and so escape those nets) or (and this meaning is the older of the two) 'through the agency, means or instrumentality of' (Those nets will be the very means whereby I shall fly). Far from escaping nationality, language, religion, Stephen will carry them everywhere with him. Despite all Stephen's sophisticated understanding of the waywardness of words, he imagines still that he is master of his own.

'a winged form flying'

He similarly presumes that he can assume the mantle of the 'cunning artificer' whose name he bears. His last words in the novel—'Old

---

[44] 'Tara' was the ancient seat of Irish kings; Holyhead, the port in north Wales where ships heading east from Dublin landed (see notes).

father, old artificer, stand me now and ever in good stead' (213)—
signal his aspiration to soar with Daedalus, whose self-fashioned
wings allowed him to escape that labyrinth of his own making.
Earlier in the novel, before its epiphanic crisis[45] in which he
encounters his 'envoy from the fair courts of life', Stephen has been
wandering on the strand in self-absorbed reverie. In the water,
school friends taunt and tease, calling in schoolboy Greek various
versions of his oddly Greek name—'Stephanos Dedalos! Bous
Stephanoumenos! Bous Stephaneforos!' Stephen attempts to take
the mention of 'his strange name' as 'a prophecy':

[A]t the name of the fabulous artificer, he seemed to hear the noise of dim
waves and to see a winged form flying above the waves and slowly climbing the air. What did it mean? Was it a quaint device opening a page of
some medieval book of prophecies and symbols, a hawklike man flying
sunward above the sea, a prophecy of the end he had been born to serve
and had been following through the mists of childhood and boyhood, a
symbol of the artist forging anew in his workshop out of the sluggish
matter of the earth a new soaring impalpable imperishable being?   (142)

The contemplation of such a possibility, that his name might pre-
figure his future as artist, 'the end he had been born to serve', stirs his
blood: 'His heart trembled in an ecstasy of fear and his soul was in
flight'. 'An ecstasy of flight made radiant his eyes and wild his breath
and tremulous and wild and radiant his windswept limbs' (142). It is
the intensely self-absorbed, repetitious, precious self-consciousness
of these lines as Stephen whips himself into 'an ecstasy' that gives
one sympathy for those early critics who maintained that the narrator's adoption of the idiolect of the character allowed no room for

---

[45] 'Epiphany': a word which Joyce appropriates from the lexicon of the sacred to
that of the profane. The Feast of the Epiphany in the Christian calendar celebrates
the arrival of the Magi at the scene of Christ's birth (the point at which God incarnate
(or the Word made flesh) is shown forth to the wise men of the world). Joyce turns it
to his own ends. In *Stephen Hero*, Stephen Daedalus explains to Cranly: 'By an
epiphany he meant a sudden spiritual manifestation, whether in the vulgarity of speech
or of gesture or in a memorable phase of the mind itself.' It represents a moment in
which the radiant whatness and full significance of a thing suddenly become apparent.
It has now entered the general critical vocabulary. Joyce himself wrote a series of
what are called by Joyce critics 'Epiphanies' and these have now been published. It
is perhaps significant that the word itself does not appear in *Portrait*. *Stephen Hero*,
188; 'Epiphanies', *Poems and Shorter Writings*, ed. Richard Ellmann, A. Walton Litz, and
John Whittier-Ferguson (London: Faber & Faber, 1991), 161–200.

irony to breathe.[46] But irony there most assuredly is, for Stephen's words are followed immediately by shouts from the boys: '—One! Two! ... Look out! —O, Cripes, I'm drownded!' (142). Stephen ignores them and continues his reverie. But the reader notes the proximity of 'drowning' to Daedalus's soaring flight. In placing Stephen's self-absorbed fantasy cheek-by-jowl with the boys' banter, the narrative ironically metamorphoses Stephen from Daedalus, the father, into Icarus, the son, who drowned. Icarus's arrogant, ecstatic pleasure at being able to fly caused him to soar too close to the sun; the wax from which his wings were made melted, and he fell into the sea. Stephen struggles to control his self-image and to weave his words so that they will bring about the future he longs for. And the narrative in deploying Stephen's euphoric language capitulates, but only so far. 'He' is subject to other readings than his own, not least that which the narrative suggests here: in his youthful, egoistic arrogance he overreaches his grasp.

Here we see an instance of the narrative structure of this tale pulling against, even as it at times colludes with, Stephen's desires. There are others. For example, as a *Bildungsroman*, this novel delineates the growth and development of Stephen to the point that he walks out of the novel on the last page seemingly self-determined and self-determining. To a certain extent, the appearance of Stephen as independent is an effect of the fact that walking out of the novel at the end is the last thing he does.[47] Nothing narratively happens after the last page, and the final picture of the protagonist asserting his independence reaches into that final emptiness. This novel's ending with Stephen's invocation of Daedalus leaves the 'artist' not yet having flown, not yet having created very much,[48] but aspiring to a great deal. It is a powerful ending and how we read it will tell us much about ourselves. The momentum produced by the *Bildungsroman* form might well sweep us up in its force and sweep Stephen into flight. But another rhythm has already been set up in *Portrait*,

[46] See n. 15, above.

[47] Compare Roland Barthes's analysis of the 'hermeneutic code' in literature, that through which the merely formal arrangement of a text produces the sense that 'truth' has been revealed (*S/Z* (1970), trans. Richard Miller (New York: Hill and Wang, 1974), 19, 209–10).

[48] Though the poem (the 'villanelle') he does write is one Joyce himself wrote many years before *Portrait* had even been conceived in its final form (see Robert Scholes, 'Stephen Dedalus: Poet or Esthete?', *PMLA* 79 (Sept. 1964), 484–9).

one which undermines the plausibility of Stephen's soaring successfully. The structural rhythm of the novel, established in the five discrete and tightly formed chapters, pulls against the consistently rising action that the novel of development requires. As we have seen, the movement of each chapter mimics the rising action of the novel as a whole: each begins with Stephen in humility and ends with him triumphant. And then the next opens again in humility.[49] A rhythmic movement of repeated rise and fall emerges which counters the supposed single movement of an insistent and inexorable rise. This rhythm presents not rising action culminating in triumph, but rising action followed invariably by a fall, followed by rising action followed by a fall, and so on. The reader's expectation ought, therefore, to be that Stephen's final cry will go unheard, that he will fall, not soar, that when next seen he will have again been humbled and that, far from having become Daedalus, he will have plunged instead like Icarus.[50]

However sophisticated Stephen's aesthetic may be by the end of the novel, that aesthetic will not account for these kinds of multiple meanings, for the symbolic realism of the novel, for its duplicitous language. He has not even yet come to a recognition of the extent of his own implication in the structures—linguistic, cultural, historical, familial, religious, even mythic—he wishes to flee. Just prior to his Daedalean invocation, Stephen provides his ultimate statement of his artistic intentions: 'Welcome, O life! I go to encounter for the millionth time the reality of experience and to forge in the smithy of my soul the uncreated conscience of my race' (213). Stephen shows no signs of recognizing that 'forge' means two things at once: 'to beat into shape, to frame or fashion' *and* 'to make something in fraudulent imitation of something else, to counterfeit'. The narrative knows this; Joyce knows this. Joyce has forged a vivid, evocative, plausible, sincere, even at times ironic portrait of Stephen, a portrait which in teasing out the duplicities of language exploits the potential meanings latent in the actual history of his own life. In this Joyce

[49] Kenner, *Dublin's Joyce*, 129: 'Each chapter closes with a synthesis of triumph which the next destroys.'

[50] And if we cheat and go outside the bounds of this novel, we can argue that fall he does, for by the opening of *Ulysses* he has flown to the Continent only to return to Dublin and to show no signs of being able once again to attempt flight. But by that time, Joyce was to say of Stephen that he had a shape that couldn't be changed (to Frank Budgen, quoted in Budgen, *James Joyce and the Making of 'Ulysses'*, 105).

becomes an artist or a poet in Aristotle's terms, not a historian: the poet presents 'a kind of thing that *might* be', the historian 'the thing that has been'.[51] Joyce, the artist, creates in *A Portrait of the Artist as a Young Man* a genuine forgery.

[51] Aristotle, *Poetics*, VIII.1451ᵃ38–1451ᵇ4; *Complete Works of Aristotle: The Revised Oxford Translation*, ed. Jonathan Barnes, 2 vols. (Princeton: Princeton University Press, 1984), ii. 2322–3.

COMPOSITION AND
PUBLICATION HISTORY

JAMES JOYCE had several tries at writing *A Portrait of the Artist as a Young Man* before it finally emerged serially in the *Egoist* in 1914. Ten years earlier (7 January 1904), he had written an 'autobiographical essay' in the third person, titled it 'A Portrait of the Artist',[1] and submitted it to Fred Ryan and W. K. Magee, then editors of *Dana, a magazine of independent thought*. But *Dana* was insufficiently 'independent' in its 'thought' to publish Joyce's piece, which Stanislaus Joyce claims, was 'because of the sexual experiences narrated in it'. The refusal, according to Stanislaus, spurred the young artist into action:

Jim . . . has decided to turn his paper into a novel, and having come to that decision is just as glad, he says, that it was rejected . . . Jim is beginning his novel, as he usually begins things, half in anger, to show that in writing about himself he has a subject of more interest than their aimless discussion.[2]

That novel, to be called *Stephen Hero*[3] after, seemingly, the English ballad *Turpin Hero*, had as its central character a young man named Stephen Daedalus who, in the way of the protagonists of many first novels, resembled his creator in many respects. It was written in the third person, in a style not particularly remarkable (though Stanislaus, never blindly uncritical of his brother's work, thought it 'exceptionally well written in a style which seems to me altogether original' (*CDD* 20)), and was planned to have sixty-three chapters

---

[1] The holograph survives; it is written in Joyce's hand, bears the date '7/1/1904', and shows signs of having been pillaged for other writings; a photoreproduction can be found in *The James Joyce Archive*, ed. Michael Groden, 63 vols. (New York: Garland, 1977–80), 7: 70–85; it has been published in *Poems and Shorter Writings*, 211–18. For an alternative account of the origins of *Portrait*, see Hans Walter Gabler, 'Introduction', *A Portrait of the Artist as a Young Man*, ed. Hans Walter Gabler with Walter Hettche (New York and London: Garland, 1993), 1–2.

[2] *CDD* 11–12, entry for 2 February 1904 (James Joyce's 22nd birthday).

[3] It has been published: James Joyce, *Stephen Hero*, ed. Theodore Spencer, rev. edn. John J. Slocum and Herbert Cahoon (1963; repr. St Albans: Triad, 1977).

(*LII* 83). All that survives are eleven chapters[4] comprising what Joyce referred to as the 'University episode'. He had begun writing at speed (Ellmann claims that the first chapter was written in eight days: *E* 148); by March he had completed eleven chapters (*CDD* 19–20). However, by the time he left Ireland on 8 October, he had made it only part way through Chapter XII (which he completed in Zurich later that month: *LII* 67). The work thereafter continued steadily (his progress can be traced through his letters to Stanislaus) until by July 1905 he had sent to his brother the text up to at least Chapter XXIV (*LII* 91). Joyce set it to one side to work on *Dubliners* and never returned to complete it.

When he began again in 1907, it was with an entirely new conception: a novel covering the whole of the span of *Stephen Hero*, but in five chapters instead of sixty-three. Between 8 September 1907 and 7 April 1908, three chapters were completed (*E* 264). Again Joyce stopped. He started again under the encouragement of Ettore Schmitz (an Italian novelist who published under the name Italo Svevo), who wrote on 8 February 1909 in response to reading the first three chapters.[5] Sometime in 1911 Joyce threw one of these manuscripts—either that of *Stephen Hero* or that of *Portrait* as completed to this stage—into the fire; it had to be 'rescued by a family fire brigade', as Joyce wrote to Harriet Weaver (*LI* 136).[6] Whether *Stephen Hero* or *Portrait*, Joyce's frustration seems clear: 'the "original" original I tore up and threw into the stove about eight years ago in a fit of rage on account of the trouble over *Dubliners*' (6 January 1920: *LI* 136). The trouble? Getting anyone to publish the stories on which he had been working without excising so much that they were left in shreds. But persist he did (Gabler gives a detailed account of the full progress of this process)[7] until he was ready to

---

[4] Though as edited it comprises 12 episodes, marked XV to XXVI; as Gabler has shown, the chapter entitled in the edition 'XIX' is actually a continuation of 'XVIII'; this makes the chapter marked 'XX' really 'XIX', and so on (Gabler, 'The Seven Lost Years of *A Portrait of the Artist as a Young Man*', in Thomas F. Staley and Bernard Benstock (eds), *Approaches to Joyce's 'Portrait': Ten Essays* (Pittsburgh: University of Pittsburgh Press, 1976), 55.

[5] Quoted in full in *E* 273–4.

[6] Stories as to exactly which manuscript it was diverge, and in the absence of any manuscript remains showing signs of having been at least scorched, textual criticism has had to read carefully between the lines of Joyce's letters to try and decipher what he means by 'the "original" original' (*LI* 136). Gabler argues strongly that it was *Portrait* and not, as legend would have it, *Stephen Hero* (Gabler, 'Introduction', 4).

[7] Gabler, 'The Seven Lost Years'.

consign the novel entire for publication serially in the *Egoist*, beginning with the 2 February 1914 issue. The date marked his thirty-second birthday.

Almost three years later, on 29 December 1916, B. W. Huebsch brought *Portrait* out in book form in the United States (set from the *Egoist* proofsheets). Harriet Weaver imported the American sheets and published the book in England on 12 February 1917 under the *Egoist* imprint (dated 1916). The second (though first true English) edition, printed in Southport and published by the *Egoist*, appeared in March 1918 (though dated 1917; corrections were made for this edition from Joyce's lists of errata compiled by Harriet Weaver). Another printing, using imported American sheets and issued under the *Egoist* imprint, appeared in 1921. The text was entirely reset with corrections and published by Jonathan Cape in 1924 (Joyce himself having carefully read proofs for this, the third edition). After this, Joyce's attention was taken up with other matters.

In 1964, the 'definitive' text was published in the United States by Viking (and in England in 1968 by Jonathan Cape). This text was established by Chester G. Anderson comparing the holograph manuscript with all editions published in the USA and England during Joyce's lifetime and with lists of corrections and changes noted by Joyce, and then submitting his suggested corrections to Richard Ellmann, who accepted some and rejected others.[8] As Anderson himself has said, 'there were errors', some of which he tried in 1971 to correct, but these were 'vetoed' by Ellmann.[9] He did manage to get them into print in 1993.[10] That same year, Hans Walter Gabler produced the first truly critical edition, fully corrected using the fair-copy manuscript (held by the National Library of Ireland)[11] as copy-text and collating this against the proofs and published text of the *Egoist* serialization, the New York first edition (1916), the second edition (English first edition, 1918), the third edition (Jonathan

---

[8] James Joyce, *A Portrait of the Artist as a Young Man*, corrected by Chester G. Anderson, ed. by Richard Ellmann (New York: Viking, 1964); this text was reprinted by Jonathan Cape in London, 1968. The same year the text was also reprinted in the Viking Critical Library: James Joyce, *A Portrait of the Artist as a Young Man: Text, Criticism and Notes*, ed. Chester G. Anderson (New York: Viking, 1968).

[9] Chester G. Anderson, 'About this Text', in *A Portrait of the Artist as a Young Man*, ed. R. B. Kershner (Boston: Bedford Books, 1993), pp. ix–x, ix.

[10] In the edition cited in n. 9.

[11] And photoreproduced in *The James Joyce Archive*, vols. 9 and 10.

Cape, 1924), and the Viking edition of 1964. He includes a full list of emendations of accidentals and a historical collation of variants.[12] I recommend it to everyone interested in the full history of Joyce's attempts to get a correct edition of *Portrait* into print.

The aim of this edition is more modest. The text is the 1968 Jonathan Cape printing of the 1964 'definitive text' published by Viking and edited by Chester Anderson. Corrections marked by Joyce and collated by Harriet Weaver, some of which were made only to the English 1918 and 1924 editions, have been entered. Errors that crept into the 1968 Cape printing have been silently corrected. One late change, sent by Joyce to Harriet Weaver separately in 1917, has been entered. The chapter titles have been changed back from the Cape arabic numerals to the roman numerals of every other printing. All these are listed in the list of selected variants in the Appendix, which also notes selected departures in substantives of this text from the manuscript, the *Egoist*, 1916, 1918, 1924, 1964, and 1968 printings. Most of these mark differences between this text and the original manuscript. Finally, the three asterisks at section breaks (rather than Cape's one) have been restored, and the practice of starting each chapter on a new page has been reinstated.

[12] James Joyce, *A Portrait of the Artist as a Young Man*, ed. Hans Walter Gabler with Walter Hettche (New York and London: Garland, 1993).

SELECT BIBLIOGRAPHY

Bibliography/Textual History

Anderson, Chester G., 'About this Text', in R. B. Kershner (ed.), *James Joyce, A Portrait of the Artist as a Young Man': Case Studies in Contemporary Criticism* (Boston: Bedford Books, 1993), pp. ix–x.

—— 'The Text of James Joyce's *A Portrait of the Artist as a YoungMan'*, *Neuphilologische Mitteilungen*, 65 (Spring 1964), 160–200.

Cohn, Alan M., and Kain, Richard M. (comps.), 'Supplemental James Joyce Checklist' (now 'Current James Joyce Checklist'), *James Joyce Quarterly*, 1– (1964–).

Deming, Robert H. (ed.), *A Bibliography of James Joyce Studies*, 2nd edn. (Boston: Hall, 1977).

Gabler, Hans Walter, 'Introduction' to James Joyce, *A Portrait of the Artist as a Young Man*, ed. Hans Walter Gabler with Walter Hettche (New York: Garland Publishing, 1993), 1–18.

—— 'The Seven Lost Years of *A Portrait of the Artist as a Young Man'*, in Thomas F. Staley and Bernard Benstock (eds.), *Approaches to Joyce's 'Portrait': Ten Essays* (Pittsburgh: University of Pittsburgh Press, 1976), 25–60.

—— 'Towards a Critical Text of James Joyce's *A Portrait of the Artist as a Young Man'*, *Studies in Bibliography*, 27 (1974), 1–53.

Rice, Thomas Jackson, *James Joyce: A Guide to Research* (New York and London: Garland, 1982).

Scholes, Robert, and Kain, Richard M. (eds), *The Workshop of Daedalus: James Joyce and the Raw Materials for 'A Portrait of the Artist as a Young Man'* (Evanston, Ill.: Northwestern University Press, 1965).

Slocum, John J., and Cahoon, Herbert, *A Bibliography of James Joyce [1882–1941]* (1953; repr. Westport, Conn.: Greenwood Press, 1971).

Biography

Ellmann, Richard, *James Joyce* (1959; rev. edn. 1982; corr. New York: Oxford University Press, 1983).

Beach, Sylvia, *Shakespeare and Company* (New York: Harcourt Brace, 1959).

Byrne, J. F., *Silent Years: An Autobiography with Memoirs of James Joyce and Our Ireland* (New York: Farrar, Straus and Young, 1953).

Curran, C. P., *James Joyce Remembered* (Oxford: Oxford University Press, 1968).

—— *Struggle with Fortune* (Dublin: Browne and Nolan, n.d.).

Gorman, Herbert, *James Joyce* (1939; repr. London: John Lane and Bodley Head, 1941).

Joyce, Stanislaus, *Complete Dublin Diary of Stanislaus Joyce*, ed. George H. Healey (Ithaca: Cornell University Press, 1971).

—— *My Brother's Keeper: James Joyce's Early Years*, ed. Richard Ellmann (1958; repr. New York: Viking, 1969).

Lidderdale, Jane, and Nicholson, Mary, *Dear Miss Weaver: Harriet Shaw Weaver, 1876–1961* (New York: Viking, 1970).

Maddox, Brenda, *Nora: A Biography of Nora Joyce* (London: Hamish Hamilton, 1988).

Potts, Willard, (ed.), *Portraits of the Artist in Exile: Recollections of James Joyce by Europeans* (1979; repr. New York: Harcourt Brace, 1986).

Pound, Ezra, *Pound/Joyce: The Letters of Ezra Pound to James Joyce, with Pound's Essays on Joyce*, ed. Forrest Read (London: Faber & Faber, 1968).

Power, Arthur, *Conversations with James Joyce*, ed. Clive Hart (1974; repr. Chicago: University of Chicago Press, 1982).

Sheehy, Eugene, *May it Please the Court* (Dublin: C. J. Fallon, 1951).

Editions and Other Works

The Critical Writings of James Joyce, ed. Ellsworth Mason and Richard Ellmann (1959; repr. New York: Viking, 1973).

The James Joyce Archive, ed. Michael Groden, 63 vols. (New York and London: Garland, 1977–80), vols. 7–10: *Portrait* materials; Michael Groden (ed.), *James Joyce's Manuscripts: An Index to the James Joyce Archive* (New York and London: Garland, 1980).

Joyce and Hauptmann: Before Sunrise: James Joyce's Translation, ed. Jill Perkins (San Marino, Calif.: Huntington Library, 1978).

Letters of James Joyce, 3 vols.: vol. i ed. Stuart Gilbert; vols. ii and iii ed. Richard Ellmann (New York: Viking, 1957, 1966).

Occasional, Critical, and Political Writing, ed. Kevin Barry (Oxford: Oxford University Press, 2000).

Poems and Shorter Writings, ed. Richard Ellmann, A. Walton Litz, and John Whittier-Ferguson (London: Faber & Faber, 1991), especially 'A Portrait of the Artist' (1904), 211–18.

A Portrait of the Artist as a Young Man, Viking Critical Edition, ed. Chester G. Anderson (New York: Viking, 1968).

A Portrait of the Artist as a Young Man, ed. J. S. Atherton, 2nd edn. (London: Heinemann Educational Books, 1973).

A Portrait of the Artist as a Young Man, ed. Hans Walter Gabler with Walter Hettche (New York: Garland, 1993).

Selected Letters of James Joyce, ed. Richard Ellmann (New York: Viking, 1975).

Stephen Hero, ed. Theodore Spencer, rev. edn. John J. Slocum and Herbert Cahoon (1963; repr. St Albans: Triad, 1977).

'Ulysses': The 1922 Text, ed. Jeri Johnson, Oxford World's Classics (Oxford: Oxford University Press, 1993).

'Ulysses': A Critical and Synoptic Edition, ed. Hans Walter Gabler with Wolfhard Steppe and Claus Melchior, 3 vols. (New York and London: Garland, 1984; rev. pbk. edn., 1986).

The Workshop of Daedalus: James Joyce and the Raw Materials for 'A Portrait of the Artist as a Young Man' (Evanston, Ill.: Northwestern University Press, 1965).

General Criticism

Attridge, Derek, *Peculiar Language: Literature as Difference from the Renaissance to James Joyce* (London: Methuen, 1988).

—— (ed.), *The Cambridge Companion to James Joyce* (Cambridge: Cambridge University Press, 1990).

—— and Ferrer, Daniel (eds.), *Post-Structuralist Joyce: Essays from the French* (Cambridge: Cambridge University Press, 1984).

Aubert, Jacques, *The Aesthetics of James Joyce* (1973; rev. edn. Baltimore: Johns Hopkins University Press, 1992).

Beja, Morris, *et al.* (eds.), *James Joyce: The Centennial Symposium* (Urbana and Chicago: University of Illinois Press, 1986).

Borach, Georges, 'Conversations with James Joyce', trans. and ed. Joseph Prescott, *College English*, 15 (Mar. 1954), 325–7.

Bowen, Zack, and Carens, James F. (eds.), *A Companion to Joyce Studies* (Westport, Conn. and London: Greenwood Press, 1984).

Brown, Richard, *Joyce and Sexuality* (Cambridge: Cambridge University Press, 1985).

Budgen, Frank, *James Joyce and the Making of 'Ulysses'* (1934; repr. Bloomington: Indiana University Press, 1961).

Cixous, Hélène, *The Exile of James Joyce* (1968), trans. Sally A. J. Purcell (New York: David Lewis, 1972).

Deming, Robert H. (ed.), *James Joyce: The Critical Heritage*, 2 vols. (London: Routledge & Kegan Paul, 1970).

Ellmann, Richard, *The Consciousness of Joyce* (New York: Oxford University Press, 1977).

Givens, Seon (ed.), *Two Decades of Joyce Criticism* (1948; rev. ed. New York: Vanguard, 1963).

Goldman, Arnold, *The Joyce Paradox: Form and Freedom in His Fiction* (London: Routledge & Kegan Paul, 1966).

Herr, Cheryl, *Joyce's Anatomy of Culture* (Urbana and Chicago: University of Illinois Press, 1986).

Kenner, Hugh, *Dublin's Joyce* (1955; repr. with new introd. New York: Columbia University Press, 1987).

—— *Joyce's Voices* (Berkeley and Los Angeles: University of California Press, 1978).

Levin, Harry, *James Joyce: A Critical Introduction* (1941; rev. edn. New York: New Directions, 1960).

MacCabe, Colin, *James Joyce and the Revolution of the Word* (London: Macmillan, 1978).

—— (ed.) *James Joyce: New Perspectives* (Brighton: Harvester Press, 1982).

Mahaffey, Vicki, *Reauthorizing Joyce* (Cambridge: Cambridge University Press, 1988).

Manganiello, Dominic, *Joyce's Politics* (London: Routledge & Kegan Paul, 1980).

Noon, William T., *Joyce and Aquinas* (1957; repr. New Haven: Yale University Press, 1963).

Parrinder, Patrick, *James Joyce* (Cambridge: Cambridge University Press, 1984).

Peake, C. H., *James Joyce: The Citizen and the Artist* (London: Edward Arnold, 1977).

Rabaté, Jean-Michel, *James Joyce, Authorized Reader* (Baltimore: Johns Hopkins University Press, 1991).

—— *Joyce Upon the Void: The Genesis of Doubt* (New York: St Martin's Press, 1991).

Riquelme, John Paul, *Teller and Tale in Joyce's Fiction: Oscillating Perspectives* (Baltimore: Johns Hopkins University Press, 1983).

Scott, Bonnie Kime, *Joyce and Feminism* (Brighton: Harvester, 1984).

Senn, Fritz, *Nichts Gegen Joyce: Joyce Against Nothing* (Zurich: Haffmans Verlag, 1983).

—— *Joyce's Dislocations: Essays on Reading as Translation* (Baltimore: Johns Hopkins University Press, 1984).

Sullivan, Kevin, *Joyce Among the Jesuits* (New York: Columbia University Press, 1958).

On A Portrait of the Artist as a Young Man

Beja, Morris, *James Joyce: 'Dubliners' and 'A Portrait': A Casebook* (London: Macmillan, 1973).

Booth, Wayne C., 'The Problem of Distance in *A Portrait*', in *The Rhetoric of Fiction* (Chicago: University of Chicago Press, 1961), 323–36.

Burke, Kenneth, 'Fact, Inference and Proof in the Analysis of Literary

Symbolism', *Terms for Order* ed. Stanley E. Hyman (Bloomington: Indiana University Press, 1964), 145–72.

Ellmann, Maud, 'Disremembering Dedalus: *A Portrait of the Artist as a Young Man*', in Robert Young (ed.), *Untying the Text: A Post-Structuralist Reader* (London: Routledge, 1981), 189–206.

Froula, Christine, *Modernism's Body: Sex, Culture and Joyce* (New York: Columbia University Press, 1996).

Gifford, Don, *Joyce Annotated: Notes for 'Dubliners' and 'A Portrait of the Artist as a Young Man'*, 2nd edn. (Berkeley: University of California Press, 1982).

Hayman, David, 'Daedalian Imagery in *A Portrait of the Artist as a Young Man*', in Frederick Will (ed.), *Heriditas: Seven Essays on the Modern Experience of the Classical* (Austin: University of Texas Press, 1964), 33–54.

—— '*A Portrait of the Artist as a Young Man* and *L'Éducation Sentimentale*: The Structural Affinities', *Orbis Litterarum*, 19 (1964), 161–75.

Levenson, Michael, 'Stephen's Diary in Joyce's *Portrait*—The Shape of Life', *ELH* 52 (1985), 1017–35.

Rabaté, Jean-Michel, 'A Portrait of the Artist as Bogeyman', in Bernard Benstock (ed.), *James Joyce: The Augmented Ninth* (Syracuse: Syracuse University Press, 1988), 103–34.

Riquelme, John Paul, 'The Preposterous Shape of Portraiture: *Portrait*', in Harold Bloom (ed.), *James Joyce's 'Portrait': Modern Critical Interpretations* (New York: Chelsea House, 1988), 87–101.

—— '*Stephen Hero, Dubliners*, and *A Portrait of the Artist as a Young Man*', in Derek Attridge (ed.), *The Cambridge Companion to James Joyce* (Cambridge: Cambridge University Press, 1990), 103–30.

Schutte, William (ed.), *Twentieth-Century Interpretations of 'A Portrait of the Artist as a Young Man'* (Englewood Cliffs, NJ: Prentice Hall, 1968).

Staley, Thomas F., and Benstock, Bernard (eds), *Approaches to Joyce's 'Portrait': Ten Essays* (Pittsburgh, University of Pittsburgh Press, 1976).

Thrane, James R., 'Joyce's Sermon on Hell: Its Source and its Backgrounds', *Modern Philology*, 57 (Feb. 1960), 172–98.

Further Reading in Oxford World's Classics

Joyce, James, *Occasional, Critical, and Political Writing*, ed. Kevin Barry.

—— *Ulysses: The 1922 Text*, ed. Jeri Johnson.

—— *Dubliners*, ed. Jeri Johnson.

A CHRONOLOGY OF JAMES JOYCE

1882 (2 Feb.) Born James Augustine Joyce, eldest surviving son of John Stanislaus Joyce ('John'), a Collector of Rates, and Mary Jane ('May') Joyce née Murray, at 41 Brighton Square West, Rathgar, Dublin. (May) Phoenix Park murders.

1884 First of many family moves, to 23 Castlewood Avenue, Rathmines, Dublin. (17 Dec.) John Stanislaus Joyce ('Stanislaus') born.

1886 Gladstone's Home Rule bill defeated.

1887 Family (now four children: three boys, one girl) moves to 1 Martello Terrace, Bray, south of Kingstown (now Dun Laoghaire). JJ's uncle, William O'Connell, moves in with family, as does Mrs 'Dante' Hearn Conway, who is to act as a governess.

1888 (1 Sept.) JJ enrols at Clongowes Wood College, near Sallins, County Kildare, a Jesuit boys' school.

1889 After his first communion, JJ becomes altar boy. (At his later confirmation, also at Clongowes, JJ takes 'Aloysius' as his saint's name.) Given four strikes on the back of the hand with a pandybat for use of 'vulgar language'. (24 Dec.) Captain O'Shea files for divorce from Katherine ('Kitty') O'Shea on grounds of her adultery with Charles Stewart Parnell, MP, leader of the Irish Home Rule Party.

1890 Parnell ousted as leader of Home Rule Party.

1891 (June) JJ removed from Clongowes as family finances fade. John Joyce loses job as Rates Collector (pensioned off at age of 42). (6 Oct.) Parnell dies. JJ writes 'Et Tu, Healy', identifying Tim Healy, Parnell's lieutenant, with Brutus and indicting Ireland's rejection of Parnell as treachery.

1892 Family (now eight children: four boys, four girls) move to Blackrock, then into central Dublin.

1893 Children sent to the Christian Brothers School on North Richmond Street. (6 Apr.) JJ and his brothers enter Belvedere College, Jesuit boys' day-school, fees having been waived. Last Joyce child born (family now four boys, six girls). Gaelic League founded.

1894 JJ travels to Cork with John Joyce, who is disposing of the last of the family's Cork properties. Family moves to Drumcondra. JJ wins first of many Exhibitions for excellence in state examinations. (Summer) Trip to Glasgow with John Joyce. Family moves again, to

North Richmond Street. JJ reads Lamb's *Adventures of Ulysses* and writes theme on Ulysses as 'My Favourite Hero'.

1895 JJ enters the Sodality of the Blessed Virgin Mary.

1896 JJ chosen prefect of the Sodality, attends retreat, later claims to have begun his 'sexual life' in this, his fourteenth year.

1897 JJ wins prize for best English composition in Ireland for his age group.

1898 JJ begins to read Ibsen, attends and reviews plays. Leaves Belvedere. (Sept.) Enters Royal University (now University College, Dublin). Family continues to move from house to house.

1899 (8 May) JJ attends première of Yeats's *The Countess Cathleen*, refuses to sign students' letter of protest to the *Freeman's Journal* against the play.

1900 (20 Jan.) JJ delivers paper 'Drama and Life' before the university Literary and Historical Society, defending the attention paid to mundane life in contemporary drama (especially Ibsen's); outraged protest from students. (1 Apr.) JJ's review of Ibsen's *When We Dead Awaken*, 'Ibsen's New Drama', published in *Fortnightly Review*. Ibsen responds with pleasure. JJ visits London, attends Music Hall, writes prose and verse plays, poems, begins to keep 'epiphany' notebook.

1901 JJ writes 'The Day of the Rabblement', an attack on the Irish Literary Theatre and its narrow nationalism, and publishes it privately in a pamphlet with Francis Skeffington's essay arguing for equality for women.

1902 (1 Feb.) JJ delivers paper to Literary and Historical Society praising the Irish poet James Clarence Mangan and advocating literature as 'the continual affirmation of the spirit'. (Mar.) JJ's brother George dies. JJ leaves university and registers for the Royal University Medical School. (Oct.) Meets Yeats and, later, Lady Gregory. Leaves Medical School and (1 Dec.) departs for Paris, ostensibly to study medicine. Passes through London where Yeats introduces him to Arthur Symons. Reviews books for Dublin *Daily Express*. (23 Dec.) Returns to Dublin for Christmas.

1903 JJ meets Oliver St John Gogarty. (17 Jan.) Returns to Paris by way of London. Giving up on medical school, spends days in Bibliothèque Nationale, nights in Bibliothèque Sainte-Geneviève. (Mar.) Meets Synge. (11 Apr.) Returns to Dublin due to mother's illness; she dies (13 Aug.). JJ continues to write reviews.

1904 JJ writes essay 'A Portrait of the Artist', first seeds of later novel

A Portrait of the Artist as a Young Man. Begins writing stories, which will become *Dubliners*, and publishes three in the *Irish Homestead*. Begins work on *Stephen Hero*. Writes and publishes poems which will be collected later as *Chamber Music*. Leaves the family home, takes rooms in Dublin, teaches at Clifton School, Dalkey. Writes 'The Holy Office', a satirical poem about the contemporary Dublin literary scene. (10 June) Meets Nora Barnacle and on 16 June first goes out with her. Joins Gogarty (for one week) in the Martello Tower, Sandycove. (8 Oct.) JJ and Nora leave Dublin together for the Continent, first to Zurich, then to job with the Berlitz School in Pola where JJ will teach English.

1905   JJ and Nora move to Trieste, where JJ teaches English for Berlitz School. (27 July) Son, Giorgio, born. *Chamber Music* submitted to (and refused by) four publishers in Dublin and London. First version of *Dubliners* submitted to Grant Richards, Dublin publisher, who contracts to publish it, but later withdraws. Stanislaus moves to Trieste (where he stays until his death in 1955).

1906   (July) Family moves to Rome where JJ accepts abortive job in bank. (30 Sept.) JJ writes to Stanislaus, 'I have a new story for *Dubliners* in my head. It deals with Mr. Hunter'; later (13 Nov.) identifies it: 'I thought of beginning my story *Ulysses*.' Begins 'The Dead' instead.

1907   (Jan.) Riots at the Abbey Theatre over J. M. Synge's *The Playboy of the Western World*. (7 Feb.) JJ writes to Stanislaus: '*Ulysses* never got any forrader than the title.' (Mar.) Family returns to Trieste. JJ writes three articles for *Il Piccolo della Sera* on Ireland. (Apr.) Lectures on 'Ireland, Island of Saints and Sages', at the Università del Popolo in Trieste. (May) Elkin Matthews (London) publishes *Chamber Music*. (July) JJ contracts rheumatic fever and is hospitalized; beginnings of his eye troubles. (26 July) Daughter, Lucia, born. Scraps the 26 chapters of *Stephen Hero* and begins to rework entirely as *Portrait*. (Nov.) JJ tells Stanislaus that he will 'expand his story "Ulysses" into a short book and make a Dublin "Peer Gynt" of it'. Completes 'The Dead'.

1908   JJ completes first three chapters of *Portrait*, but then sets them aside. Family troubles and continued poverty.

1909   Friendship with Ettore Schmitz (Italian author 'Italo Svevo'), whose high opinion of *Portrait* fragments spurs Joyce to revise and continue. (Mar.) JJ writes article on Oscar Wilde for *Piccolo della Sera*. (Apr.) Revised *Dubliners* sent to Maunsel & Co. in Dublin.

(July) JJ and Giorgio go to Dublin and Galway. JJ signs contract with Maunsel & Co. and meets old acquaintances. One, Vincent Cosgrave, who had also wooed Nora, claimed that she had been unfaithful to JJ with him. JJ's '1909 Letters' to Nora written as result, first, of his doubting and, later, of his reconciliation with, her. (Sept.) JJ, Giorgio, and JJ's sister Eva return to Trieste. (Oct.) JJ returns to Dublin as agent for Triestine consortium to open first cinema in Dublin. (20 Dec.) The 'Volta' cinema opens.

1910 (2 Jan.) JJ returns to Trieste with another sister, Eileen. 'Volta' fails. Publication of *Dubliners* delayed.

1911 Continuing delay of *Dubliners*. JJ writes open letter, published in Arthur Griffiths's *Sinn Féin*, complaining of his mistreatment at the hands of his publishers.

1912 JJ lectures on Blake and Defoe at the Università, writes article '*L'Ombra di Parnell*' for *Piccolo della Sera*, sits Italian state examinations to become a teacher. Nora and Lucia travel to Ireland, followed quickly by JJ and Giorgio. (JJ's last trip to Ireland.) Negotiations with Maunsel & Co. finally fail; proofs destroyed. JJ writes broadside 'Gas from a Burner' in response and publishes it on his return to Trieste (15 Sept.). JJ begins his (twelve) *Hamlet* lectures at the Università. Begins writing poetry again.

1913 JJ continues *Hamlet* lectures. Grant Richards again shows interest in *Dubliners*. Ezra Pound writes (having been told by Yeats of JJ).

1914 JJ revises *Portrait*, sends first chapter and *Dubliners* to Pound. Pound asks to publish poem ('I Hear an Army') in Imagist anthology in USA, and begins serialization of *Portrait* (beginning 2 Feb.) in the *Egoist* (originally called the *New Freewoman* and edited by Dora Marsden and Rebecca West). Under demand of publishing, JJ finishes last two chapters. (June) Harriet Shaw Weaver takes over editorship of *Egoist*. (15 June) Grant Richards publishes *Dubliners*. (Aug.) World War I begins. JJ writes *Giacomo Joyce*. (Nov.) JJ drafts notes for *Exiles*. Begins *Ulysses*.

1915 (9 Jan.) Stanislaus arrested, interned in Austrian detention centre for remainder of war. *Exiles* completed. (15 May) Italy enters war. (June) In return for a pledge of neutrality, Joyce family allowed to leave Austrian Trieste and move to neutral Swiss Zurich. Through the intercession of Yeats and Pound, JJ awarded a grant (£75) from the Royal Literary Fund. *Ulysses* in progress.

1916 Easter Rising in Dublin. (Aug.) JJ granted £100 from the British Civil List (again at Pound's instigation). (Dec.) B. W. Huebsch

(New York) publishes *Dubliners* and *Portrait*. JJ writes 'A Notebook of Dreams'—'record' of Nora's dreams with JJ's interpretations.

1917 (Feb.) English edition of *Portrait* published by Egoist Press. JJ suffers eye troubles which lead to his first eye operation (Aug.). (Feb.) Harriet Shaw Weaver begins anonymous benefaction to JJ; her financial support will continue until (and beyond) JJ's death (when she pays for his funeral). (Oct.) Family goes to Locarno for winter. *Ulysses* continues; first three chapters ('Telemachia') written and sent to Pound. JJ contracts with Weaver to publish *Ulysses* serially in the *Egoist*.

1918 (Jan.) Family returns to Zurich. Pound sends 'Telemachia' to Jane Heap and Margaret Anderson, editors of the *Little Review*. Serial publication begins with March issue. Under pressure of serialization, JJ continues writing. (May) *Exiles* published by Grant Richards. JJ receives financial gift from Mrs Harold McCormick. JJ forms theatrical group, the English Players, with Claud Sykes. First performance: *The Importance of Being Earnest*. JJ meets Frank Budgen. Further eye troubles. (11 Nov.) Armistice signed. By New Year's Eve, *Ulysses* drafted through episode 9, 'Scylla and Charybdis'.

1919 (Jan.) Irish War of Independence begins. Publication of *Ulysses* continues in *Little Review*. January (first part of 'Lestrygonians') and May (first half of 'Scylla and Charybdis') issues confiscated and burned by US Postal Authorities. *Egoist* publishes edited versions of four episodes (2, 3, 6, and 10). (7 Aug.) *Exiles* performed (unsuccessfully) in Munich. Mrs McCormick discontinues financial support, ostensibly because JJ refused to be psychoanalysed by her analyst, Carl Jung. (Oct.) Family returns to Trieste.

1920 (June) JJ and Pound meet for the first time. (July) Family moves to Paris. JJ meets Adrienne Monnier and Sylvia Beach, later T. S. Eliot and Wyndham Lewis and, later still, Valery Larbaud. (Sept.) JJ sends first *Ulysses* 'schema' to Carlo Linati. *Ulysses* composition and serialization continue. January (second half of 'Cyclops') and July–August (second half of 'Nausicaa') issues of the *Little Review* confiscated by US Postal Authorities. (20 Sept.) Complaint lodged by the New York Society for the Suppression of Vice, specifically citing 'Nausicaa' issue. What was to be the final *Little Review* instalment of *Ulysses* (first part of 'Oxen of the Sun') published in Sept.–Dec. issue.

1921 (Feb.) Editors of *Little Review* convicted of publishing obscenity; publication ceases. Sylvia Beach offers to publish *Ulysses* under the imprint of Shakespeare and Company (her Paris bookshop), to be printed in Dijon by Maurice Darantière, to be funded by advance subscription. JJ agrees. Episodes sent seriatim to printers; JJ continues to compose while also adding to and correcting returned proofs. Manuscript of episode 15, 'Circe', thrown in fire by typist's outraged husband. (29 Oct.) JJ 'completes' 'Ithaca' (last episode to be drafted), continues correction and addition. (7 Dec.) Valery Larbaud delivers lecture on *Ulysses* at Shakespeare and Company; uses another 'schema' of the book provided by Joyce (the 'Gilbert schema'). (Dec.) Treaty granting southern Ireland dominion status signed, the war having ended in July.

1922 (2 Feb.) First two copies of *Ulysses* delivered by express train from Dijon in time for celebration of JJ's fortieth birthday. Irish Civil War. (1 Apr.) Nora and children visit Ireland where their train is fired upon by troops. Return to Paris. JJ's eye troubles recur. (Aug.) Family travels to England where JJ meets Harriet Weaver for the first time. (Sept.) Return to Paris and trip to Côte d'Azure.

1923 JJ begins *Work in Progress* (working title of *Finnegans Wake*). Irish Civil War ends.

1924 (Apr.) First fragments from *Work in Progress* published in *transatlantic review*. French translation of *Portrait* published.

1927 (June) Instalments of *Work in Progress* begin to be published in Eugene Jolas's *transition*. (July) *Pomes Penyeach* published by Shakespeare and Company.

1928 *Anna Livia Plurabelle* published in New York.

1929 (Feb.) French translation of *Ulysses* published by Adrienne Monnier's *La Maison des Amis des Livres*. Samuel Beckett *et al.* publish *Our Exagmination Round his Factification . . .* as *aide d'explication* and defence of *Work in Progress*. *Tales Told of Shem and Shaun* published in Paris. Roth's pirated edition of *Ulysses* published in New York.

1930 Publication of Stuart Gilbert's *James Joyce's 'Ulysses'*, critical study of *Ulysses*, written with JJ's assistance. *Haveth Childers Everywhere* published in Paris and New York.

1931 (May) French translation (completed with JJ's assistance) of *Anna Livia Plurabelle* published in *Nouvelle Revue*. (4 July) JJ and Nora Barnacle married in London to ensure the inheritance of their children. (29 Dec.) John Joyce dies.

1932 (15 Feb.) Son, Stephen James Joyce, born to Giorgio and Helen Joyce. JJ writes 'Ecce Puer'. Lucia's first breakdown and stay in

Maillard clinic. The Odyssey Press edition of *Ulysses*, 'specially revised . . . by Stuart Gilbert', published in Hamburg.

1933 Lucia's initial hospitalization in Nyon, Switzerland. (6 Dec.) Judge John M. Woolsey, US District Court, delivers opinion that *Ulysses* is not obscene and can be published in the USA.

1934 Random House publishes US edition of *Ulysses*. Lucia again hospitalized. JJ returns to *Work in Progress*. *The Mime of Mick Nick and the Maggies* published in The Hague. Frank Budgen's *James Joyce and the Making of 'Ulysses'* (written with JJ's assistance) published in London. Lucia under the care of Carl Jung.

1935 Publication of Limited Editions Club edition of *Ulysses* with illustrations by Henri Matisse.

1936 (Oct.) Bodley Head publishes *Ulysses* in London. (Dec.) *Collected Poems* published in New York.

1937 (Oct.) *Storiella She is Syung* published in London.

1938 (13 Nov.) Finishes *Finnegans Wake*. Douglas Hyde becomes Eire's first president.

1939 (Jan.) Yeats dies. (4 May) *Finnegans Wake* is published in London and New York, though advance copy reaches JJ in time for his fifty-seventh birthday on 2 Feb. (1 Sept.) Germany invades Poland; two days later France and Great Britain declare war on Germany. Family leaves Paris for St Gérard-le-Puy, near Vichy. Herbert Gorman's biography, commissioned and abetted by JJ, published in New York.

1940 France falls to the Nazis. Family moves to Zurich.

1941 (13 Jan.) JJ dies after surgery on a perforated ulcer, buried in Fluntern cemetery, Zurich, without the last rites of the Catholic Church. Nora dies in 1951, buried separately in Fluntern, though both bodies were reburied together in 1966.

A PORTRAIT
OF THE ARTIST AS
A YOUNG MAN

Et ignotas animum dimittit in artes.
Ovid, *Metamorphoses*, VIII, 188

ONCE upon a time and a very good time it was there was a moocow coming down along the road and this moocow that was coming down along the road met a nicens little boy named baby tuckoo. . . .

His father told him that story: his father looked at him through a glass: he had a hairy face.

He was baby tuckoo. The moocow came down the road where Betty Byrne lived: she sold lemon platt.

> *O, the wild rose blossoms*
> *On the little green place.*

He sang that song. That was his song.

> *O, the green wothe botheth.*

When you wet the bed first it is warm then it gets cold. His mother put on the oilsheet. That had the queer smell.

His mother had a nicer smell than his father. She played on the piano the sailor's hornpipe for him to dance. He danced:

> *Tralala lala*
> *Tralala tralaladdy*
> *Tralala lala*
> *Tralala lala.*

Uncle Charles and Dante clapped. They were older than his father and mother but uncle Charles was older than Dante.

Dante had two brushes in her press. The brush with the maroon velvet back was for Michael Davitt and the brush with the green velvet back was for Parnell. Dante gave him a cachou every time he brought her a piece of tissue paper.

The Vances lived in number seven. They had a different father and mother. They were Eileen's father and mother. When they were grown up he was going to marry Eileen. He hid under the table. His mother said:

—O, Stephen will apologise.

Dante said:

—O, if not, the eagles will come and pull out his eyes.

> *Pull out his eyes,*
> *Apologise,*
> *Apologise,*
> *Pull out his eyes.*
>
> *Apologise,*
> *Pull out his eyes,*
> *Pull out his eyes,*
> *Apologise.*

* * *

The wide playgrounds were swarming with boys. All were shouting and the prefects urged them on with strong cries. The evening air was pale and chilly and after every charge and thud of the footballers the greasy leather orb flew like a heavy bird through the grey light. He kept on the fringe of his line, out of sight of his prefect, out of the reach of the rude feet, feigning to run now and then. He felt his body small and weak amid the throng of players and his eyes were weak and watery. Rody Kickham was not like that: he would be captain of the third line all the fellows said.

Rody Kickham was a decent fellow but Nasty Roche was a stink. Rody Kickham had greaves in his number and a hamper in the refectory. Nasty Roche had big hands. He called the Friday pudding dog-in-the-blanket. And one day he had asked:

—What is your name?

Stephen had answered:

—Stephen Dedalus.

—What kind of a name is that?

And when Stephen had not been able to answer Nasty had asked:

—What is your father?

Stephen had answered:

—A gentleman.

Then Nasty Roche had asked:

—Is he a magistrate?

He crept about from point to point on the fringe of his line, making little runs now and then. But his hands were bluish with cold. He kept his hands in the sidepockets of his belted grey suit.

That was a belt round his pocket. And belt was also to give a fellow a belt. One day a fellow had said to Cantwell:

—I'd give you such a belt in a second.

Cantwell had answered:

—Go and fight your match. Give Cecil Thunder a belt. I'd like to see you. He'd give you a toe in the rump for yourself.

That was not a nice expression. His mother had told him not to speak with the rough boys in the college. Nice mother! The first day in the hall of the castle when she had said goodbye she had put up her veil double to her nose to kiss him: and her nose and eyes were red. But he had pretended not to see that she was going to cry. She was a nice mother but she was not so nice when she cried. And his father had given him two fiveshilling pieces for pocket money. And his father had told him if he wanted anything to write home to him and, whatever he did, never to peach on a fellow. Then at the door of the castle the rector had shaken hands with his father and mother, his soutane fluttering in the breeze, and the car had driven off with his father and mother on it. They had cried to him from the car, waving their hands:

—Goodbye, Stephen, goodbye!

—Goodbye, Stephen, goodbye!

He was caught in the whirl of a scrimmage and, fearful of the flashing eyes and muddy boots, bent down to look through the legs. The fellows were struggling and groaning and their legs were rubbing and kicking and stamping. Then Jack Lawton's yellow boots dodged out the ball and all the other boots and legs ran after. He ran after them a little way and then stopped. It was useless to run on. Soon they would be going home for the holidays. After supper in the studyhall he would change the number pasted up inside his desk from seventyseven to seventysix.

It would be better to be in the studyhall than out there in the cold. The sky was pale and cold but there were lights in the castle. He wondered from which window Hamilton Rowan had thrown his hat on the haha and had there been flowerbeds at that time under the windows. One day when he had been called to the castle the butler had shown him the marks of the soldiers' slugs in the wood of the door and had given him a piece of shortbread that the community ate. It was nice and warm to see the lights in the castle. It was like something in a book. Perhaps Leicester Abbey was like that. And there were nice sentences in Doctor Cornwell's Spelling Book. They were like poetry but they were only sentences to learn the spelling from.

> *Wolsey died in Leicester Abbey*
> *Where the abbots buried him.*
> *Canker is a disease of plants,*
> *Cancer one of animals.*

It would be nice to lie on the hearthrug before the fire, leaning his head upon his hands, and think on those sentences. He shivered as if he had cold slimy water next his skin. That was mean of Wells to shoulder him into the square ditch because he would not swop his little snuff box for Wells's seasoned hacking chestnut, the conqueror of forty. How cold and slimy the water had been! A fellow had once seen a big rat jump into the scum. Mother was sitting at the fire with Dante waiting for Brigid to bring in the tea. She had her feet on the fender and her jewelly slippers were so hot and they had such a lovely warm smell! Dante knew a lot of things. She had taught him where the Mozambique Channel was and what was the longest river in America and what was the name of the highest mountain in the moon. Father Arnall knew more than Dante because he was a priest but both his father and uncle Charles said that Dante was a clever woman and a wellread woman. And when Dante made that noise after dinner and then put up her hand to her mouth: that was heartburn.

A voice cried far out on the playground:
—All in!
Then other voices cried from the lower and third lines:
—All in! All in!
The players closed around, flushed and muddy, and he went among them, glad to go in. Rody Kickham held the ball by its greasy lace. A fellow asked him to give it one last: but he walked on without even answering the fellow. Simon Moonan told him not to because the prefect was looking. The fellow turned to Simon Moon and said:
—We all know why you speak. You are McGlade's suck.
Suck was a queer word. The fellow called Simon Moonan that name because Simon Moonan used to tie the prefect's false sleeves behind his back and the prefect used to let on to be angry. But the sound was ugly. Once he had washed his hands in the lavatory of the Wicklow Hotel and his father pulled the stopper up by the chain after and the dirty water went down through the hole in the basin.

And when it had all gone down slowly the hole in the basin had made a sound like that: suck. Only louder.

To remember that and the white look of the lavatory made him feel cold and then hot. There were two cocks that you turned and water came out: cold and hot. He felt cold and then a little hot: and he could see the names printed on the cocks. That was a very queer thing.

And the air in the corridor chilled him too. It was queer and wettish. But soon the gas would be lit and in burning it made a light noise like a little song. Always the same: and when the fellows stopped talking in the playroom you could hear it.

It was the hour for sums. Father Arnall wrote a hard sum on the board and then said:

—Now then, who will win? Go ahead, York! Go ahead, Lancaster!

Stephen tried his best but the sum was too hard and he felt confused. The little silk badge with the white rose on it that was pinned on the breast of his jacket began to flutter. He was no good at sums but he tried his best so that York might not lose. Father Arnall's face looked very black but he was not in a wax: he was laughing. Then Jack Lawton cracked his fingers and Father Arnall looked at his copybook and said:

—Right. Bravo Lancaster! The red rose wins. Come on now, York! Forge ahead!

Jack Lawton looked over from his side. The little silk badge with the red rose on it looked very rich because he had a blue sailor top on. Stephen felt his own face red too, thinking of all the bets about who would get first place in elements, Jack Lawton or he. Some weeks Jack Lawton got the card for first and some weeks he got the card for first. His white silk badge fluttered and fluttered as he worked at the next sum and heard Father Arnall's voice. Then all his eagerness passed away and he felt his face quite cool. He thought his face must be white because it felt so cool. He could not get out the answer for the sum but it did not matter. White roses and red roses: those were beautiful colours to think of. And the cards for first place and second place and third place were beautiful colours too: pink and cream and lavender. Lavender and cream and pink roses were beautiful to think of. Perhaps a wild rose might be like those colours and he remembered the song about the wild rose blossoms on the little green place. But you could not have a green rose. But perhaps somewhere in the world you could.

The bell rang and then the classes began to file out of the rooms and along the corridors towards the refectory. He sat looking at the two prints of butter on his plate but could not eat the damp bread. The tablecloth was damp and limp. But he drank off the hot weak tea which the clumsy scullion, girt with a white apron, poured into his cup. He wondered whether the scullion's apron was damp too or whether all white things were cold and damp. Nasty Roche and Saurin drank cocoa that their people sent them in tins. They said they could not drink the tea; that it was hogwash. Their fathers were magistrates, the fellows said.

All the boys seemed to him very strange. They had all fathers and mothers and different clothes and voices. He longed to be at home and lay his head on his mother's lap. But he could not: and so he longed for the play and study and prayers to be over and to be in bed.

He drank another cup of hot tea and Fleming said:

—What's up? Have you a pain or what's up with you?

—I don't know, Stephen said.

—Sick in your breadbasket, Fleming said, because your face looks white. It will go away.

—O yes, Stephen said.

But he was not sick there. He thought that he was sick in his heart if you could be sick in that place. Fleming was very decent to ask him. He wanted to cry. He leaned his elbows on the table and shut and opened the flaps of his ears. Then he heard the noise of the refectory every time he opened the flaps of his ears. It made a roar like a train at night. And when he closed the flaps the roar was shut off like a train going into a tunnel. That night at Dalkey the train had roared like that and then, when it went into the tunnel, the roar stopped. He closed his eyes and the train went on, roaring and then stopping; roaring again, stopping. It was nice to hear it roar and stop and then roar out of the tunnel again and then stop.

Then the higher line fellows began to come down along the matting in the middle of the refectory, Paddy Rath and Jimmy Magee and the Spaniard who was allowed to smoke cigars and the little Portuguese who wore the woolly cap. And then the lower line tables and the tables of the third line. And every single fellow had a different way of walking.

He sat in a corner of the playroom pretending to watch a game of dominos and once or twice he was able to hear for an instant the little song of the gas. The prefect was at the door with some boys and Simon Moonan was knotting his false sleeves. He was telling them something about Tullabeg.

Then he went away from the door and Wells came over to Stephen and said:

—Tell us, Dedalus, do you kiss your mother before you go to bed?

Stephen answered:

—I do.

Wells turned to the other fellows and said:

—O, I say, here's a fellow says he kisses his mother every night before he goes to bed.

The other fellows stopped their game and turned round, laughing. Stephen blushed under their eyes and said:

—I do not.

Wells said:

—O, I say, here's a fellow says he doesn't kiss his mother before he goes to bed.

They all laughed again. Stephen tried to laugh with them. He felt his whole body hot and confused in a moment. What was the right answer to the question? He had given two and still Wells laughed. But Wells must know the right answer for he was in third of grammar. He tried to think of Wells's mother but he did not dare to raise his eyes to Wells's face. He did not like Wells's face. It was Wells who had shouldered him into the square ditch the day before because he would not swop his little snuffbox for Wells's seasoned hacking chestnut, the conqueror of forty. It was a mean thing to do; all the fellows said it was. And how cold and slimy the water had been! And a fellow had once seen a big rat jump plop into the scum.

The cold slime of the ditch covered his whole body; and, when the bell rang for study and the lines filed out of the playrooms, he felt the cold air of the corridor and staircase inside his clothes. He still tried to think what was the right answer. Was it right to kiss his mother or wrong to kiss his mother? What did that mean, to kiss? You put your face up like that to say goodnight and then his mother put her face down. That was to kiss. His mother put her lips on his cheek; her lips were soft and they wetted his cheek; and they made a tiny little noise: kiss. Why did people do that with their two faces?

Sitting in the studyhall he opened the lid of his desk and changed the number pasted up inside from seventyseven to seventysix. But the Christmas vacation was very far away: but one time it would come because the earth moved round always.

There was a picture of the earth on the first page of his geography: a big ball in the middle of clouds. Fleming had a box of crayons and one night during free study he had coloured the earth green and the clouds maroon. That was like the two brushes in Dante's press, the brush with the green velvet back for Parnell and the brush with the maroon velvet back for Michael Davitt. But he had not told Fleming to colour them those colours. Fleming had done it himself.

He opened the geography to study the lesson; but he could not learn the names of places in America. Still they were all different places that had those different names. They were all in different countries and the countries were in continents and the continents were in the world and the world was in the universe.

He turned to the flyleaf of the geography and read what he had written there: himself, his name and where he was.

> *Stephen Dedalus*
> *Class of Elements*
> *Clongowes Wood College*
> *Sallins*
> *County Kildare*
> *Ireland*
> *Europe*
> *The World*
> *The Universe*

That was in his writing: and Fleming one night for a cod had written on the opposite page:

> *Stephen Dedalus is my name,*
> *Ireland is my nation.*
> *Clongowes is my dwellingplace*
> *And heaven my expectation.*

He read the verses backwards but then they were not poetry. Then he read the flyleaf from the bottom to the top till he came to his own name. That was he: and he read down the page again. What was after the universe? Nothing. But was there anything round the universe to show where it stopped before the nothing place began? It could not be a wall but there could be a thin thin line there all round everything. It was very big to think about everything and everywhere. Only God could do that. He tried to think what a big thought that must be but he could think only of God. God was God's name just as his name was Stephen. *Dieu* was the French for God and that was God's name too; and when anyone prayed to God and said *Dieu* then God knew at once that it was a French person that was praying. But though there were different names for God in all the different languages in the world and God understood what all the people who prayed said in their different languages still God remained always the same God and God's real name was God.

It made him very tired to think that way. It made him feel his head very big. He turned over the flyleaf and looked wearily at the green round earth in the middle of the maroon clouds. He wondered which was right, to be for the green or for the maroon, because Dante had ripped the green velvet back off the brush that was for Parnell one day with her scissors and had told him that Parnell was a bad man. He wondered if they were arguing at home about that. That was called politics. There were two sides in it: Dante was on one side and his father and Mr Casey were on the other side but his mother and uncle Charles were on no side. Every day there was something in the paper about it.

It pained him that he did not know well what politics meant and that he did not know where the universe ended. He felt small and weak. When would he be like the fellows in poetry and rhetoric? They had big voices and big boots and they studied trigonometry. That was very far away. First came the vacation and then the next term and then vacation again and then again another term and then again the vacation. It was like a train going in and out of tunnels and that was like the noise of the boys eating in the refectory when you opened and closed the flaps of the ears. Term, vacation; tunnel, out; noise, stop. How far away it was! It was better to go to bed to sleep. Only prayers in the chapel and then bed. He shivered and yawned. It would be lovely in bed after the sheets got a bit hot. First they were so cold to get into. He shivered to think how cold they were first. But then they got hot and then he could sleep. It was lovely to be tired. He yawned again. Night prayers and then bed: he shivered and wanted to yawn. It would be lovely in a few minutes. He felt a warm glow creeping up from the cold shivering sheets, warmer and warmer till he felt warm all over, ever so warm; ever so warm and yet he shivered a little and still wanted to yawn.

The bell rang for night prayers and he filed out of the studyhall after the others and down the staircase and along the corridors to the chapel. The corridors were darkly lit and the chapel was darkly lit. Soon all would be dark and sleeping. There was cold night air in the chapel and the marbles were the colour the sea was at night. The sea was cold day and night: but it was colder at night. It was cold and dark under the seawall beside his father's house. But the kettle would be on the hob to make punch.

The prefect of the chapel prayed above his head and his memory knew the responses:

> *O Lord, open our lips*
> *And our mouth shall announce Thy praise.*
> *Incline unto our aid, O God!*
> *O Lord, make haste to help us!*

There was a cold night smell in the chapel. But it was a holy smell. It was not like the smell of old peasants who knelt at the back of the chapel at Sunday mass. That was a smell of air and rain and turf and corduroy. But they were very holy peasants. They breathed behind him on his neck and sighed as they prayed. They lived in Clane, a fellow said: there were little cottages there and he had seen a woman standing at the halfdoor of a cottage with a child in her arms, as the cars had come past from Sallins. It would be lovely to sleep for one night in that cottage before the fire of smoking turf, in the dark lit by the fire, in the warm dark, breathing the smell of the peasants, air and rain and turf and corduroy. But, O, the road there between the trees was dark! You would be lost in the dark. It made him afraid to think of how it was.

He heard the voice of the prefect of the chapel saying the last prayer. He prayed it too against the dark outside under the trees.

Visit, we beseech Thee, O Lord, this habitation and drive away from it all the snares of the enemy. May Thy holy angels dwell herein to preserve us in peace and may Thy blessing be always upon us through Christ, Our Lord. Amen.

His fingers trembled as he undressed himself in the dormitory. He told his fingers to hurry up. He had to undress and then kneel and say his own prayers and be in bed before the gas was lowered so that he might not go to hell when he died. He rolled his stockings off and put on his nightshirt quickly and knelt trembling at his bedside and repeated his prayers quickly quickly, fearing that the gas would go down. He felt his shoulders shaking as he murmured:

> *God bless my father and my mother and spare them to me!*
> *God bless my little brothers and sisters and spare them to me!*
> *God bless Dante and uncle Charles and spare them to me!*

He blessed himself and climbed quickly into bed and, tucking the end of the nightshirt under his feet, curled himself together under the cold white sheets, shaking and trembling. But he would not go to hell when he died; and the shaking would stop. A voice bade the boys in the dormitory goodnight. He peered out for an instant over the coverlet and saw the yellow curtains round and before his bed that shut him off on all sides. The light was lowered quietly.

The prefect's shoes went away. Where? Down the staircase and along the corridors or to his room at the end? He saw the dark. Was it true about the black dog that walked there at night with eyes as big as carriagelamps? They said it was the ghost of a murderer. A long shiver of fear flowed over his body. He saw the dark entrance hall of the castle. Old servants in old dress were in the ironingroom above the staircase. It was long ago. The old servants were quiet. There was a fire there but the hall was still dark. A figure came up the staircase from the hall. He wore the white cloak of a marshal; his face was pale and strange; he held his hand pressed to his side. He looked out of strange eyes at the old servants. They looked at him and saw their master's face and cloak and knew that he had received his death-wound. But only the dark was where they looked: only dark silent air. Their master had received his deathwound on the battlefield of Prague far away over the sea. He was standing on the field; his hand was pressed to his side; his face was pale and strange and he wore the white cloak of a marshal.

O how cold and strange it was to think of that! All the dark was cold and strange. There were pale strange faces there, great eyes like carriagelamps. They were the ghosts of murderers, the figures of marshals who had received their deathwound on battlefields far away over the sea. What did they wish to say that their faces were so strange?

Visit, we beseech Thee, O Lord, this habitation and drive away from it all . . .

Going home for the holidays! That would be lovely: the fellows had told him. Getting up on the cars in the early wintry morning outside the door of the castle. The cars were rolling on the gravel. Cheers for the rector!

Hurray! Hurray! Hurray!

The cars drove past the chapel and all caps were raised. They drove merrily along the country roads. The drivers pointed with their whips to Bodenstown. The fellows cheered. They passed the farmhouse of the Jolly Farmer. Cheer after cheer after cheer. Through Clane they drove, cheering and cheered. The peasant women stood at the halfdoors, the men stood here and there. The lovely smell there was in the wintry air: the smell of Clane: rain and wintry air and turf smouldering and corduroy.

The train was full of fellows: a long long chocolate train with cream facings. The guards went to and fro opening, closing, locking, unlocking the doors. They were men in dark blue and silver; they had silvery whistles and their keys made a quick music: click, click: click, click.

And the train raced on over the flat lands and past the Hill of Allen. The telegraphpoles were passing, passing. The train went on and on. It knew. There were coloured lanterns in the hall of his father's house and ropes of green branches. There were holly and ivy round the pierglass and holly and ivy, green and red, twined round the chandeliers. There were red holly and green ivy round the old portraits on the walls. Holly and ivy for him and for Christmas.

Lovely . . .

All the people. Welcome home, Stephen! Noises of welcome. His mother kissed him. Was that right? His father was a marshal now: higher than a magistrate. Welcome home, Stephen!

Noises . . .

There was a noise of curtainrings running back along the rods, of water being splashed in the basins. There was a noise of rising and dressing and washing in the dormitory: a noise of clapping of hands as the prefect went up and down telling the fellows to look sharp. A pale sunlight showed the yellow curtains drawn back, the tossed beds. His bed was very hot and his face and body were very hot.

He got up and sat on the side of his bed. He was weak. He tried to pull on his stocking. It had a horrid rough feel. The sunlight was queer and cold.

Fleming said:

—Are you not well?

He did not know: and Fleming said:

—Get back into bed. I'll tell McGlade you're not well.

—He's sick.

—Who is?

—Tell McGlade.

—Get back into bed.

—Is he sick?

A fellow held his arms while he loosened the stocking clinging to his foot and climbed back into the hot bed.

He crouched down between the sheets, glad of their tepid glow. He heard the fellows talk among themselves about him as they dressed for mass. It was a mean thing to do, to shoulder him into the square ditch, they were saying.

Then their voices ceased; they had gone. A voice at his bed said:

—Dedalus, don't spy on us, sure you won't?

Wells's face was there. He looked at it and saw that Wells was afraid.

—I didn't mean to. Sure you won't?

His father had told him, whatever he did, never to peach on a fellow. He shook his head and answered no and felt glad. Wells said:

—I didn't mean to, honour bright. It was only for cod. I'm sorry.

The face and the voice went away. Sorry because he was afraid. Afraid that it was some disease. Canker was a disease of plants and cancer one of animals: or another different. That was a long time ago then out on the playgrounds in the evening light, creeping from point to point on the fringe of his line, a heavy bird flying low through the grey light. Leicester Abbey lit up. Wolsey died there, The abbots buried him themselves.

It was not Wells's face, it was the prefect's. He was not foxing. No, no: he was sick really. He was not foxing. And he felt the prefect's hand on his forehead; and he felt his forehead warm and damp against the prefect's cold damp hand. That was the way a rat felt, slimy and damp and cold. Every rat had two eyes to look out of. Sleek slimy coats, little little feet tucked up to jump, black shiny eyes to look out of. They could understand how to jump. But the minds of rats could not understand trigonometry. When they were dead they lay on their sides. Their coats dried then. They were only dead things.

The prefect was there again and it was his voice that was saying that he was to get up, that Father Minister had said he was to get up and dress and go to the infirmary. And while he was dressing himself as quickly as he could the prefect said:

—We must pack off to Brother Michael because we have the collywobbles! Terrible thing to have the collywobbles! How we wobble when we have the collywobbles!

He was very decent to say that. That was all to make him laugh. But he could not laugh because his cheeks and lips were all shivery: and then the prefect had to laugh by himself.

The prefect cried:

—Quick march! Hayfoot! Strawfoot!

They went together down the staircase and along the corridor and past the bath. As he passed the door he remembered with a vague fear the warm turfcoloured bogwater, the warm moist air, the noise of plunges, the smell of the towels, like medicine.

Brother Michael was standing at the door of the infirmary and from the door of the dark cabinet on his right came a smell like medicine. That came from the bottles on the shelves. The prefect spoke to Brother Michael and Brother Michael answered and called the prefect sir. He had reddish hair mixed with grey and a queer look. It was queer that he would always be a brother. It was queer too that you could not call him sir because he was a brother and had a different kind of look. Was he not holy enough or why could he not catch up on the others?

There were two beds in the room and in one bed there was a fellow: and when they went in he called out:

—Hello! It's young Dedalus! What's up?

—The sky is up, Brother Michael said.

He was a fellow out of the third of grammar and, while Stephen was undressing, he asked Brother Michael to bring him a round of buttered toast.

—Ah, do! he said.

—Butter you up! said Brother Michael. You'll get your walking papers in the morning when the doctor comes.

—Will I? the fellow said. I'm not well yet.

Brother Michael repeated:

—You'll get your walking papers, I tell you.

He bent down to rake the fire. He had a long back like the long back of a tramhorse. He shook the poker gravely and nodded his head at the fellow out of third of grammar.

Then Brother Michael went away and after a while the fellow out of third of grammar turned in towards the wall and fell asleep.

That was the infirmary. He was sick then. Had they written home to tell his mother and father? But it would be quicker for one of the priests to go himself to tell them. Or he would write a letter for the priest to bring.

Dear Mother

I am sick. I want to go home. Please come and take me home. I am in the infirmary.

Your fond son,
Stephen

How far away they were! There was cold sunlight outside the window. He wondered if he would die. You could die just the same on a sunny day. He might die before his mother came. Then he would have a dead mass in the chapel like the way the fellows had told him it was when Little had died. All the fellows would be at the mass, dressed in black, all with sad faces. Wells too would be there but no fellow would look at him. The rector would be there in a cope of black and gold and there would be tall yellow candles on the altar and round the catafalque. And they would carry the coffin out of the chapel slowly and he would be buried in the little graveyard of the community off the main avenue of limes. And Wells would be sorry then for what he had done. And the bell would toll slowly.

He could hear the tolling. He said over to himself the song that Brigid had taught him.

> *Dingdong! The castle bell!*
> *Farewell, my mother!*
> *Bury me in the old churchyard*
> *Beside my eldest brother.*
> *My coffin shall be black,*
> *Six angels at my back,*
> *Two to sing and two to pray*
> *And two to carry my soul away.*

How beautiful and sad that was! How beautiful the words were where they said *Bury me in the old churchyard!* A tremor passed over his body. How sad and how beautiful! He wanted to cry quietly but not for himself: for the words, so beautiful and sad, like music. The bell! The bell! Farewell! O farewell!

The cold sunlight was weaker and Brother Michael was standing at his bedside with a bowl of beeftea. He was glad for his mouth was hot and dry. He could hear them playing on the playgrounds. And the day was going on in the college just as if he were there.

Then Brother Michael was going away and the fellow out of third of grammar told him to be sure and come back and tell him all the news in the paper. He told Stephen that his name was Athy and that his father kept a lot of racehorses that were spiffing jumpers and that his father would give a good tip to Brother Michael any time he wanted it because Brother Michael was very decent and always told him the news out of the paper they got every day up in the castle. There was every kind of news in the paper: accidents, shipwrecks, sports and politics.

—Now it is all about politics in the paper, he said. Do your people talk about that too?

—Yes, Stephen said.

—Mine too, he said.

Then he thought for a moment and said:

—You have a queer name, Dedalus, and I have a queer name too, Athy. My name is the name of a town. Your name is like Latin.

Then he asked:

—Are you good at riddles?

Stephen answered:

—Not very good.

Then he said:

—Can you answer me this one? Why is the county Kildare like the leg of a fellow's breeches?

Stephen thought what could be the answer and then said:

—I give it up.

—Because there is a thigh in it, he said. Do you see the joke? Athy is the town in the county Kildare and a thigh is the other thigh.

—O, I see, Stephen said.

—That's an old riddle, he said.

After a moment he said:

—I say!

—What? asked Stephen.

—You know, he said, you can ask that riddle another way?

—Can you? said Stephen.

—The same riddle, he said. Do you know the other way to ask it?

—No, said Stephen.

—Can you not think of the other way? he said.

He looked at Stephen over the bedclothes as he spoke. Then he lay back on the pillow and said:

—There is another way but I won't tell you what it is.

Why did he not tell it? His father, who kept the racehorses, must be a magistrate too like Saurin's father and Nasty Roche's father. He thought of his own father, of how he sang songs while his mother played and of how he always gave him a shilling when he asked for sixpence and he felt sorry for him that he was not a magistrate like the other boys' fathers. Then why was he sent to that place with them? But his father had told him that he would be no stranger there because his granduncle had presented an address to the liberator there fifty years before. You could know the people of that time by their old dress. It seemed to him a solemn time: and he wondered if that was the time when the fellows in Clongowes wore blue coats with brass buttons and yellow waistcoats and caps of rabbitskin and drank beer like grownup people and kept greyhounds of their own to course the hares with.

He looked at the window and saw that the daylight had grown weaker. There would be cloudy grey light over the playgrounds. There was no noise on the playgrounds. The class must be doing the themes or perhaps Father Arnall was reading a legend out of the book.

It was queer that they had not given him any medicine. Perhaps Brother Michael would bring it back when he came. They said you got stinking stuff to drink when you were in the infirmary. But he felt better now than before. It would be nice getting better slowly. You could get a book then. There was a book in the library about Holland. There were lovely foreign names in it and pictures of strangelooking cities and ships. It made you feel so happy.

How pale the light was at the window! But that was nice. The fire rose and fell on the wall. It was like waves. Someone had put coal on and he heard voices. They were talking. It was the noise of the waves. Or the waves were talking among themselves as they rose and fell.

He saw the sea of waves, long dark waves rising and falling, dark under the moonless night. A tiny light twinkled at the pierhead where the ship was entering: and he saw a multitude of people gathered by the waters' edge to see the ship that was entering their harbour. A tall man stood on the deck, looking out towards the flat dark land: and by the light at the pierhead he saw his face, the sorrowful face of Brother Michael.

He saw him lift his hand towards the people and heard him say in a loud voice of sorrow over the waters:

—He is dead. We saw him lying upon the catafalque.

A wail of sorrow went up from the people.

—Parnell! Parnell! He is dead!

They fell upon their knees, moaning in sorrow.

And he saw Dante in a maroon velvet dress and with a green velvet mantle hanging from her shoulders walking proudly and silently past the people who knelt by the waters' edge.

*   *   *

A great fire, banked high and red, flamed in the grate and under the ivytwined branches of the chandelier the Christmas table was spread. They had come home a little late and still dinner was not ready: but it would be ready in a jiffy, his mother had said. They were waiting for the door to open and for the servants to come in, holding the big dishes covered with their heavy metal covers.

All were waiting: uncle Charles, who sat far away in the shadow of the window, Dante and Mr Casey, who sat in the easychairs at either side of the hearth, Stephen, seated on a chair between them, his feet resting on the toasted boss. Mr Dedalus looked at himself in the pierglass above the mantel-piece, waxed out his moustache-ends and then, parting his coattails, stood with his back to the glowing fire: and still, from time to time, he withdrew a hand from his coattail to wax out one of his moustache-ends. Mr Casey leaned his head to one side and, smiling, tapped the gland of his neck with his fingers. And Stephen smiled too for he knew now that it was not true that Mr Casey had a purse of silver in his throat. He smiled to think how the silvery noise which Mr Casey used to make had deceived him. And when he had tried to open Mr Casey's hand to see if the purse of silver was hidden there he had seen that the fingers could not be straightened out: and Mr Casey had told him that he had got those three cramped fingers making a birthday present for Queen Victoria.

Mr Casey tapped the gland of his neck and smiled at Stephen with sleepy eyes: and Mr Dedalus said to him:

—Yes. Well now, that's all right. O, we had a good walk, hadn't we, John? Yes . . . I wonder if there's any likelihood of dinner this evening. Yes. . . . O, well now, we got a good breath of ozone round the Head today. Ay, bedad.

He turned to Dante and said:

—You didn't stir out at all, Mrs Riordan?

Dante frowned and said shortly:

—No.

Mr Dedalus dropped his coattails and went over to the sideboard. He brought forth a great stone jar of whisky from the locker and filled the decanter slowly, bending now and then to see how much he had poured in. Then replacing the jar in the locker he poured a little of the whisky into two glasses, added a little water and came back with them to the fireplace.

—A thimbleful, John, he said, just to whet your appetite.

Mr Casey took the glass, drank, and placed it near him on the mantelpiece. Then he said:

—Well, I can't help thinking of our friend Christopher manufacturing . . .

He broke into a fit of laughter and coughing and added: —. . . manufacturing that champagne for those fellows.

Mr Dedalus laughed loudly.

—Is it Christy? he said. There's more cunning in one of those warts on his bald head than in a pack of jack foxes.

He inclined his head, closed his eyes, and, licking his lips profusely, began to speak with the voice of the hotelkeeper.

—And he has such a soft mouth when he's speaking to you, don't you know. He's very moist and watery about the dewlaps, God bless him.

Mr Casey was still struggling through his fit of coughing and laughter. Stephen, seeing and hearing the hotelkeeper through his father's face and voice, laughed.

Mr Dedalus put up his eyeglass and, staring down at him, said quietly and kindly:

—What are you laughing at, you little puppy, you?

The servants entered and placed the dishes on the table. Mrs Dedalus followed and the places were arranged.

—Sit over, she said.

Mr Dedalus went to the end of the table and said:

—Now, Mrs Riordan, sit over. John, sit you down, my hearty.

He looked round to where uncle Charles sat and said:

—Now then, sir, there's a bird here waiting for you.

When all had taken their seats he laid his hand on the cover and then said quickly, withdrawing it:

—Now, Stephen.

Stephen stood up in his place to say the grace before meals:

Bless us, O Lord, and these Thy gifts which through Thy bounty we are about to receive through Christ Our Lord. Amen.

All blessed themselves and Mr Dedalus with a sigh of pleasure lifted from the dish the heavy cover pearled around the edge with glistening drops.

Stephen looked at the plump turkey which had lain, trussed and skewered, on the kitchen table. He knew that his father had paid a guinea for it in Dunn's of D'Olier Street and that the man had prodded it often at the breastbone to show how good it was: and he remembered the man's voice when he had said:

—Take that one, sir. That's the real Ally Daly.

Why did Mr Barrett in Clongowes call his pandybat a turkey? But Clongowes was far away: and the warm heavy smell of turkey and ham and celery rose from the plates and dishes and the great fire was banked high and red in the grate and the green ivy and red holly made you feel so happy and when dinner was ended the big plumpudding would be carried in, studded with peeled almonds and sprigs of holly, with bluish fire running around it and a little green flag flying from the top.

It was his first Christmas dinner and he thought of his little brothers and sisters who were waiting in the nursery, as he had often waited, till the pudding came. The deep low collar and the Eton jacket made him feel queer and oldish: and that morning when his mother had brought him down to the parlour, dressed for mass, his father had cried. That was because he was thinking of his own father. And uncle Charles had said so too.

Mr Dedalus covered the dish and began to eat hungrily. Then he said:

—Poor old Christy, he's nearly lopsided now with roguery.

—Simon, said Mrs Dedalus, you haven't given Mrs Riordan any sauce.

Mr Dedalus seized the sauceboat.

—Haven't I? he cried. Mrs Riordan, pity the poor blind.

Dante covered her plate with her hands and said:

—No, thanks.

Mr Dedalus turned to uncle Charles.

—How are you off, sir?

—Right as the mail, Simon.

—You, John?

—I'm all right. Go on yourself.

—Mary? Here, Stephen, here's something to make your hair curl.

He poured sauce freely over Stephen's plate and set the boat again on the table. Then he asked uncle Charles was it tender. Uncle Charles could not speak because his mouth was full but he nodded that it was.

—That was a good answer our friend made to the canon. What? said Mr Dedalus.

—I didn't think he had that much in him, said Mr Casey.

—*I'll pay you your dues, father, when you cease turning the house of God into a pollingbooth.*

—A nice answer, said Dante, for any man calling himself a catholic to give to his priest.

—They have only themselves to blame, said Mr Dedalus suavely. If they took a fool's advice they would confine their attention to religion.

—It is religion, Dante said. They are doing their duty in warning the people.

—We go to the house of God, Mr Casey said, in all humility to pray to our Maker and not to hear election addresses.

—It is religion, Dante said again. They are right. They must direct their flocks.

—And preach politics from the altar, is it? asked Mr Dedalus.

—Certainly, said Dante. It is a question of public morality. A priest would not be a priest if he did not tell his flock what is right and what is wrong.

Mrs Dedalus laid down her knife and fork, saying:

—For pity's sake and for pity sake let us have no political discussion on this day of all days in the year.

—Quite right, ma'am, said uncle Charles. Now, Simon, that's quite enough now. Not another word now.

—Yes, yes, said Mr Dedalus quickly.

He uncovered the dish boldly and said:

—Now then, who's for more turkey?

Nobody answered. Dante said:

—Nice language for any catholic to use!

—Mrs Riordan, I appeal to you, said Mrs Dedalus, to let the matter drop now.

Dante turned on her and said:

—And am I to sit here and listen to the pastors of my church being flouted?

—Nobody is saying a word against them, said Mr Dedalus, so long as they don't meddle in politics.

—The bishops and priests of Ireland have spoken, said Dante, and they must be obeyed.

—Let them leave politics alone, said Mr Casey, or the people may leave their church alone.

—You hear? said Dante turning to Mrs Dedalus.

—Mr Casey! Simon! said Mrs Dedalus. Let it end now.

—Too bad! Too bad! said uncle Charles.

—What? cried Mr Dedalus. Were we to desert him at the bidding of the English people?

—He was no longer worthy to lead, said Dante. He was a public sinner.

—We are all sinners and black sinners, said Mr Casey coldly.

—*Woe be to the man by whom the scandal cometh!* said Mrs Riordan. *It would be better for him that a millstone were tied about his neck and that he were cast into the depths of the sea rather than that he should scandalise one of these, my least little ones.* That is the language of the Holy Ghost.

—And very bad language if you ask me, said Mr Dedalus coolly.

—Simon! Simon! said uncle Charles. The boy.

—Yes, yes, said Mr Dedalus. I meant about the . . . I was thinking about the bad language of that railway porter. Well now, that's all right. Here, Stephen, show me your plate, old chap. Eat away now. Here.

He heaped up the food on Stephen's plate and served uncle Charles and Mr Casey to large pieces of turkey and splashes of sauce. Mrs Dedalus was eating little and Dante sat with her hands in her lap. She was red in the face. Mr Dedalus rooted with the carvers at the end of the dish and said:

—There's a tasty bit here we call the pope's nose. If any lady or gentleman . . .

He held a piece of fowl up on the prong of the carvingfork. Nobody spoke. He put it on his own plate, saying:

—Well, you can't say but you were asked. I think I had better eat it myself because I'm not well in my health lately.

He winked at Stephen and, replacing the dishcover, began to eat again.

There was a silence while he ate. Then he said:

—Well now, the day kept up fine after all. There were plenty of strangers down too.

Nobody spoke. He said again:

—I think there were more strangers down than last Christmas.

He looked round at the others whose faces were bent towards their plates and, receiving no reply, waited for a moment and said bitterly:

—Well, my Christmas dinner has been spoiled anyhow.

—There could be neither luck nor grace, Dante said, in a house where there is no respect for the pastors of the church.

Mr Dedalus threw his knife and fork noisily on his plate.

—Respect! he said. Is it for Billy with the lip or for the tub of guts up in Armagh? Respect!

—Princes of the church, said Mr Casey with slow scorn.

—Lord Leitrim's coachman, yes, said Mr Dedalus.

—They are the Lord's anointed, Dante said. They are an honour to their country.

—Tub of guts, said Mr Dedalus coarsely. He has a handsome face, mind you, in repose. You should see that fellow lapping up his bacon and cabbage of a cold winter's day. O Johnny!

He twisted his features into a grimace of heavy bestiality and made a lapping noise with his lips.

—Really, Simon, said Mrs Dedalus, you should not speak that way before Stephen. It's not right.

—O, he'll remember all this when he grows up, said Dante hotly—the language he heard against God and religion and priests in his own home.

—Let him remember too, cried Mr Casey to her from across the table, the language with which the priests and the priests' pawns broke Parnell's heart and hounded him into his grave. Let him remember that too when he grows up.

—Sons of bitches! cried Mr Dedalus. When he was down they turned on him to betray him and rend him like rats in a sewer. Lowlived dogs! And they look it! By Christ, they look it!

—They behaved rightly, cried Dante. They obeyed their bishops and their priests. Honour to them!

—Well, it is perfectly dreadful to say that not even for one day in the year, said Mrs Dedalus, can we be free from these dreadful disputes!

Uncle Charles raised his hands mildly and said:

—Come now, come now, come now! Can we not have our opinions whatever they are without this bad temper and this bad language? It is too bad surely.

Mrs Dedalus spoke to Dante in a low voice but Dante said loudly:

—I will not say nothing. I will defend my church and my religion when it is insulted and spit on by renegade catholics.

Mr Casey pushed his plate rudely into the middle of the table and, resting his elbows before him, said in a hoarse voice to his host:

—Tell me, did I tell you that story about a very famous spit?

—You did not, John, said Mr Dedalus.

—Why then, said Mr Casey, it is a most instructive story. It happened not long ago in the county Wicklow where we are now.

He broke off and, turning towards Dante, said with quiet indignation:

—And I may tell you, ma'am, that I, if you mean me, am no renegade catholic. I am a catholic as my father was and his father before him and his father before him again when we gave up our lives rather than sell our faith.

—The more shame to you now, Dante said, to speak as you do.

—The story, John, said Mr Dedalus smiling. Let us have the story anyhow.

—Catholic indeed! repeated Dante ironically. The blackest

protestant in the land would not speak the language I have heard this evening.

Mr Dedalus began to sway his head to and fro, crooning like a country singer.

—I am no protestant, I tell you again, said Mr Casey flushing.

Mr Dedalus, still crooning and swaying his head, began to sing in a grunting nasal tone:

> *O, come all you Roman catholics*
> *That never went to mass.*

He took up his knife and fork again in good humour and set to eating, saying to Mr Casey:

—Let us have the story, John. It will help us to digest.

Stephen looked with affection at Mr Casey's face which stared across the table over his joined hands. He liked to sit near him at the fire, looking up at his dark fierce face. But his dark eyes were never fierce and his slow voice was good to listen to. But why was he then against the priests? Because Dante must be right then. But he had heard his father say that she was a spoiled nun and that she had come out of the convent in the Alleghanies when her brother had got the money from the savages for the trinkets and the chainies. Perhaps that made her severe against Parnell. And she did not like him to play with Eileen because Eileen was a protestant and when she was young she knew children that used to play with protestants and the protestants used to make fun of the litany of the Blessed Virgin. *Tower of Ivory*, they used to say, *House of Gold!* How could a woman be a tower of ivory or a house of gold? Who was right then? And he remembered the evening in the infirmary in Clongowes, the dark waters, the light at the pierhead and the moan of sorrow from the people when they had heard.

Eileen had long white hands. One evening when playing tig she had put her hands over his eyes: long and white and thin and cold and soft. That was ivory: a cold white thing. That was the meaning of *Tower of Ivory*.

—The story is very short and sweet, Mr Casey said. It was one day down in Arklow, a cold bitter day, not long before the chief died. May God have mercy on him!

He closed his eyes wearily and paused. Mr Dedalus took a bone from his plate and tore some meat from it with his teeth, saying:

—Before he was killed, you mean.

Mr Casey opened his eyes, sighed and went on:

—It was down in Arklow one day. We were down there at a meeting and after the meeting was over we had to make our way to the railway station through the crowd. Such booing and baaing, man, you never heard. They called us all the names in the world. Well there was one old lady, and a drunken old harridan she was surely, that paid all her attention to me. She kept dancing along beside me in the mud bawling and screaming into my face: *Priesthunter! The Paris Funds! Mr Fox! Kitty O'Shea!*

—And what did you do, John? asked Mr Dedalus.

—I let her bawl away, said Mr Casey. It was a cold day and to keep up my heart I had (saving your presence, ma'am) a quid of Tullamore in my mouth and sure I couldn't say a word in any case because my mouth was full of tobacco juice.

—Well, John?

—Well. I let her bawl away, to her heart's content, *Kitty O'Shea* and the rest of it till at last she called that lady a name that I won't sully this Christmas board nor your ears, ma'am, nor my own lips by repeating.

He paused. Mr Dedalus, lifting his head from the bone, asked:

—And what did you do, John?

—Do! said Mr Casey. She stuck her ugly old face up at me when she said it and I had my mouth full of tobacco juice. I bent down to her and *Phth!* says I to her like that.

He turned aside and made the act of spitting.

—*Phth!* says I to her like that, right into her eye.

He clapped a hand to his eye and gave a hoarse scream of pain.

—*O Jesus, Mary and Joseph!* says she. *I'm blinded! I'm blinded and drownded!*

He stopped in a fit of coughing and laughter, repeating:

—*I'm blinded entirely.*

Mr Dedalus laughed loudly and lay back in his chair while uncle Charles swayed his head to and fro.

Dante looked terribly angry and repeated while they laughed:

—Very nice! Ha! Very nice!

It was not nice about the spit in the woman's eye. But what was the name the woman had called Kitty O'Shea that Mr Casey would not repeat? He thought of Mr Casey walking through the crowds of people and making speeches from a wagonette. That was what he had been in prison for and he remembered that one night Sergeant O'Neill had come to the house and had stood in the hall, talking in a low voice with his father and chewing nervously at the chinstrap of his cap. And that night Mr Casey had not gone to Dublin by train but a car had come to the door and he had heard his father say something about the Cabinteely road.

He was for Ireland and Parnell and so was his father: and so was Dante too for one night at the band on the esplanade she had hit a gentleman on the head with her umbrella because he had taken off his hat when the band played *God save the Queen* at the end.

Mr Dedalus gave a snort of contempt.

—Ah, John, he said. It is true for them. We are an unfortunate priestridden race and always were and always will be till the end of the chapter.

Uncle Charles shook his head, saying:

—A bad business! A bad business!

Mr Dedalus repeated:

—A priestridden Godforsaken race!

He pointed to the portrait of his grandfather on the wall to his right.

—Do you see that old chap up there, John? he said. He was a good Irishman when there was no money in the job. He was condemned to death as a whiteboy. But he had a saying about our clerical friends, that he would never let one of them put his two feet under his mahogany.

Dante broke in angrily:

—If we are a priestridden race we ought to be proud of it! They are the apple of God's eye. *Touch them not*, says Christ, *for they are the apple of My eye.*

—And can we not love our country then? asked Mr Casey. Are we not to follow the man that was born to lead us?

—A traitor to his country! replied Dante, A traitor, an adulterer! The priests were right to abandon him. The priests were always the true friends of Ireland.

—Were they, faith? said Mr Casey.

He threw his fist on the table and, frowning angrily, protruded one finger after another.

—Didn't the bishops of Ireland betray us in the time of the union when bishop Lanigan presented an address of loyalty to the Marquess Cornwallis? Didn't the bishops and priests sell the aspirations of their country in 1829 in return for catholic emancipation? Didn't they denounce the fenian movement from the pulpit and in the confessionbox? And didn't they dishonour the ashes of Terence Bellew MacManus?

His face was glowing with anger and Stephen felt the glow rise to his own cheek as the spoken words thrilled him. Mr Dedalus uttered a guffaw of coarse scorn.

—O, by God, he cried, I forgot little old Paul Cullen! Another apple of God's eye!

Dante bent across the table and cried to Mr Casey:

—Right! Right! They were always right! God and morality and religion come first.

Mrs Dedalus, seeing her excitement, said to her:

—Mrs Riordan, don't excite yourself answering them.

—God and religion before everything! Dante cried. God and religion before the world!

Mr Casey raised his clenched fist and brought it down on the table with a crash.

—Very well, then, he shouted hoarsely, if it comes to that, no God for Ireland!

—John! John! cried Mr Dedalus, seizing his guest by the coatsleeve.

Dante stared across the table, her cheeks shaking. Mr Casey struggled up from his chair and bent across the table towards her, scraping the air from before his eyes with one hand as though he were tearing aside a cobweb.

—No God for Ireland! he cried. We have had too much God in Ireland. Away with God!

—Blasphemer! Devil! screamed Dante, starting to her feet and almost spitting in his face.

Uncle Charles and Mr Dedalus pulled Mr Casey back into his chair again, talking to him from both sides reasonably. He stared before him out of his dark flaming eyes, repeating:

—Away with God, I say!

Dante shoved her chair violently aside and left the table, upsetting her napkinring which rolled slowly along the carpet and came to rest against the foot of an easychair. Mrs Dedalus rose quickly and followed her towards the door. At the door Dante turned round violently and shouted down the room, her cheeks flushed and quivering with rage:

—Devil out of hell! We won! We crushed him to death! Fiend!

The door slammed behind her.

Mr Casey, freeing his arms from his holders, suddenly bowed his head on his hands with a sob of pain.

—Poor Parnell! he cried loudly. My dead king!

He sobbed loudly and bitterly.

Stephen, raising his terrorstricken face, saw that his father's eyes were full of tears.

* * *

The fellows talked together in little groups.

One fellow said:

—They were caught near the Hill of Lyons.

—Who caught them?

—Mr Gleeson and the minister. They were on a car.

The same fellow added:

—A fellow in the higher line told me.

Fleming asked:

—But why did they run away, tell us?

—I know why, Cecil Thunder said. Because they had fecked cash out of the rector's room.

—Who fecked it?

—Kickham's brother. And they all went shares in it.

But that was stealing. How could they have done that?

—A fat lot you know about it, Thunder! Wells said. I know why they scut.

—Tell us why.

—I was told not to, Wells said.

—O, go on, Wells, all said. You might tell us. We won't let it out.

Stephen bent forward his head to hear. Wells looked round to see if anyone was coming. Then he said secretly:

—You know the altar wine they keep in the press in the sacristy?

—Yes.

—Well, they drank that and it was found out who did it by the smell. And that's why they ran away, if you want to know.

And the fellow who had spoken first said:

—Yes, that's what I heard too from the fellow in the higher line.

The fellows were all silent. Stephen stood among them, afraid to speak, listening. A faint sickness of awe made him feel weak. How could they have done that? He thought of the dark silent sacristy. There were dark wooden presses there where the crimped surplices lay quietly folded. It was not the chapel but still you had to speak under your breath. It was a holy place. He remembered the summer evening he had been there to be dressed as boatbearer, the evening of the procession to the little altar in the wood. A strange and holy place. The boy that held the censer had swung it gently to and fro near the door with the silvery cap lifted by the middle chain to keep the coals lighting. That was called charcoal: and it had burned quietly as the fellow had swung it gently and had given off a weak sour smell. And then when all were vested he had stood holding out the boat to the rector and the rector had put a spoonful of incense in it and it had hissed on the red coals.

The fellows were talking together in little groups here and there on the playground. The fellows seemed to him to have grown smaller: that was because a sprinter had knocked him down the day before, a fellow out of second of grammar. He had been thrown by the fellow's machine lightly on the cinderpath and his spectacles had been broken in three pieces and some of the grit of the cinders had gone into his mouth.

That was why the fellows seemed to him smaller and farther away and the goalposts so thin and far and the soft grey sky so high up. But there was no play on the football grounds for cricket was coming: and some said that Barnes would be the prof and some said it would be Flowers. And all over the playgrounds they were playing rounders and bowling twisters and lobs. And from here and from there came the sounds of the cricketbats through the soft grey air. They said: pick, pack, pock, puck: like drops of water in a fountain slowly falling in the brimming bowl.

Athy, who had been silent, said quietly:

—You are all wrong.

All turned towards him eagerly.

—Why?

—Do you know?

—Who told you?

—Tell us, Athy.

Athy pointed across the playground to where Simon Moonan was walking by himself kicking a stone before him.

—Ask him, he said.

The fellows looked there and then said:

—Why him?

—Is he in it?

—Tell us, Athy. Go on. You might if you know.

Athy lowered his voice and said:

—Do you know why those fellows scut? I will tell you but you must not let on you know.

He paused for a moment and then said mysteriously:

—They were caught with Simon Moonan and Tusker Boyle in the square one night.

The fellows looked at him and asked:

—Caught?

—What doing?

Athy said:

—Smugging.

All the fellows were silent: and Athy said:

—And that's why.

Stephen looked at the faces of the fellows but they were all looking across the playground. He wanted to ask somebody about it. What did that mean about the smugging in the square? Why did the five fellows out of the higher line run away for that? It was a joke, he thought. Simon Moonan had nice clothes and one night he had shown him a ball of creamy sweets that the fellows of the football fifteen had rolled down to him along the carpet in the middle of the refectory when he was at the door. It was the night of the match against the Bective Rangers and the ball was made just like a red and green apple only it opened and it was full of the creamy sweets. And one day Boyle had said that an elephant had two tuskers instead of two tusks and that was why he was called Tusker Boyle but some fellows called him Lady Boyle because he was always at his nails, paring them.

Eileen had long thin cool white hands too because she was a girl. They were like ivory; only soft. That was the meaning of *Tower of Ivory* but protestants could not understand it and made fun of it. One day he had stood beside her looking into the hotel grounds. A waiter was running up a trail of bunting on the flagstaff and a fox terrier was scampering to and fro on the sunny lawn. She had put her hand into his pocket where his hand was and he had felt how cool and thin and soft her hand was. She had said that pockets were funny things to have: and then all of a sudden she had broken away and had run laughing down the sloping curve of the path. Her fair hair had streamed out behind her like gold in the sun. *Tower of Ivory. House of Gold.* By thinking of things you could understand them.

But why in the square? You went there when you wanted to do something. It was all thick slabs of slate and water trickled all day out of tiny pinholes and there was a queer smell of stale water there. And behind the door of one of the closets there was a drawing in red pencil of a bearded man in a Roman dress with a brick in each hand and underneath was the name of the drawing:

Balbus was building a wall.

Some fellows had drawn it there for a cod. It had a funny face but it was very like a man with a beard. And on the wall of another closet there was written in backhand in beautiful writing:

Julius Cæsar wrote The Calico Belly.

Perhaps that was why they were there because it was a place where some fellows wrote things for cod. But all the same it was queer what Athy said and the way he said it. It was not a cod because they had run away. He looked with the others in silence across the playground and began to feel afraid.

At last Fleming said:

—And we are all to be punished for what other fellows did?

—I won't come back, see if I do, Cecil Thunder said. Three days' silence in the refectory and sending us up for six and eight every minute.

—Yes, said Wells. And old Barrett has a new way of twisting the note so that you can't open it and fold it again to see how many ferulæ you are to get. I won't come back too.

—Yes, said Cecil Thunder, and the prefect of studies was in second of grammar this morning.

—Let us get up a rebellion, Fleming said. Will we?

All the fellows were silent. The air was very silent and you could hear the cricketbats but more slowly than before: pick, pock.

Wells asked:

—What is going to be done to them?

—Simon Moonan and Tusker are going to be flogged, Athy said, and the fellows in the higher line got their choice of flogging or being expelled.

—And which are they taking? asked the fellow who had spoken first.

—All are taking expulsion except Corrigan, Athy answered. He's going to be flogged by Mr Gleeson.

—Is it Corrigan that big fellow? said Fleming. Why, he'd be able for two of Gleeson!

—I know why, Cecil Thunder said. He is right and the other fellows are wrong because a flogging wears off after a bit but a fellow that has been expelled from college is known all his life on account of it. Besides Gleeson won't flog him hard.

—It's best of his play not to, Fleming said.

—I wouldn't like to be Simon Moonan and Tusker, Cecil Thunder said. But I don't believe they will be flogged. Perhaps they will be sent up for twice nine.

—No, no, said Athy. They'll both get it on the vital spot.

Wells rubbed himself and said in a crying voice:

—Please, sir, let me off!

Athy grinned and turned up the sleeves of his jacket, saying:

> *It can't be helped;*
> *It must be done.*
> *So down with your breeches*
> *And out with your bum.*

The fellows laughed; but he felt that they were a little afraid. In the silence of the soft grey air he heard the cricketbats from here and from there: pock. That was a sound to hear but if you were hit then you would feel a pain. The pandybat made a sound too but not like that. The fellows said it was made of whalebone and leather with lead inside: and he wondered what was the pain like. There were different kinds of pains for all the different kinds of sounds. A long thin cane would have a high whistling sound and he wondered what was that pain like. It made him shivery to think of it and cold: and what Athy said too. But what was there to laugh at in it? It made him shivery: but that was because you always felt like a shiver when you let down your trousers. It was the same in the bath when you undressed yourself. He wondered who had to let them down, the master or the boy himself. O how could they laugh about it that way?

He looked at Athy's rolledup sleeves and knuckly inky hands. He had rolled up his sleeves to show how Mr Gleeson would roll up his sleeves. But Mr Gleeson had round shiny cuffs and clean white wrists and fattish white hands and the nails of them were long and pointed. Perhaps he pared them too like Lady Boyle. But they were terribly long and pointed nails. So long and cruel they were though the white fattish hands were not cruel but gentle. And though he trembled with cold and fright to think of the cruel long nails and of the high whistling sound of the cane and of the chill you felt at the end of your shirt when you undressed yourself yet he felt a feeling of queer quiet pleasure inside him to think of the white fattish hands, clean and strong and gentle. And he thought of what Cecil Thunder had said; that Mr Gleeson would not flog Corrigan hard. And Fleming had said he would not because it was best of his play not to. But that was not why.

A voice from far out on the playground cried:

—All in!

And other voices cried:

—All in! All in!

During the writing lesson he sat with his arms folded, listening to the slow scraping of the pens. Mr Harford went to and fro making little signs in red pencil and sometimes sitting beside the boy to show him how to hold the pen. He had tried to spell out the headline for himself though he knew already what it was for it was the last of the book. *Zeal without prudence is like a ship adrift.* But the lines of the letters were like fine invisible threads and it was only by closing his right eye tight tight and staring out of the left eye that he could make out the full curves of the capital.

But Mr Harford was very decent and never got into a wax. All the other masters got into dreadful waxes. But why were they to suffer for what fellows in the higher line did? Wells had said that they had drunk some of the altar wine out of the press in the sacristy and that it had been found out who had done it by the smell. Perhaps they had stolen a monstrance to run away with it and sell it somewhere. That must have been a terrible sin, to go in there quietly at night, to open the dark press and steal the flashing gold thing into which God was put on the altar in the middle of flowers and candles at benediction while the incense went up in clouds at both sides as the fellow swung the censer and Dominic Kelly sang the first part by himself in the choir. But God was not in it of course when they stole it. But still it was a strange and a great sin even to touch it. He thought of it with deep awe; a terrible and strange sin: it thrilled him to think of it in the silence when the pens scraped lightly. But to drink the altar wine out of the press and be found out by the smell was a sin too: but it was not terrible and strange. It only made you feel a little sickish on account of the smell of the wine. Because on the day when he had made his first holy communion in the chapel he had shut his eyes and opened his mouth and put out his tongue a little: and when the rector had stooped down to give him the holy communion he had smelt a faint winy smell off the rector's breath after the wine of the mass. The word was beautiful: wine. It made you think of dark purple because the grapes were dark purple that grew in Greece outside houses like white temples. But the faint smell off the rector's breath had made him feel a sick feeling on the morning of his first communion. The day of your first communion was the happiest day of your life. And once a lot of generals had asked Napoleon what was the happiest day of his life. They thought he would say the day he won some great battle or the day he was made an emperor. But he said:

—Gentlemen, the happiest day of my life was the day on which I made my first holy communion.

Father Arnall came in and the Latin lesson began and he remained still, leaning on the desk with his arms folded. Father Arnall gave out the themebooks and he said that they were scandalous and that they were all to be written out again with the corrections at once. But the worst of all was Fleming's theme because the pages were stuck together by a blot: and Father Arnall held it up by a corner and said it was an insult to any master to send him up such a theme. Then he asked Jack Lawton to decline the noun *mare* and Jack Lawton stopped at the ablative singular and could not go on with the plural.

—You should be ashamed of yourself, said Father Arnall sternly. You, the leader of the class!

Then he asked the next boy and the next and the next. Nobody knew. Father Arnall became very quiet, more and more quiet as each boy tried to answer and could not. But his face was blacklooking and his eyes were staring though his voice was so quiet. Then he asked Fleming and Fleming said that that word had no plural. Father Arnall suddenly shut the book and shouted at him:

—Kneel out there in the middle of the class. You are one of the idlest boys I ever met. Copy out your themes again the rest of you.

Fleming moved heavily out of his place and knelt between the two last benches. The other boys bent over their themebooks and began to write. A silence filled the classroom and Stephen, glancing timidly at Father Arnall's dark face, saw that it was a little red from the wax he was in.

Was that a sin for Father Arnall to be in a wax or was he allowed to get into a wax when the boys were idle because that made them study better or was he only letting on to be in a wax? It was because he was allowed because a priest would know what a sin was and would not do it. But if he did it one time by mistake what would he do to go to confession? Perhaps he would go to confession to the minister. And if the minister did it he would go to the rector: and the rector to the provincial: and the provincial to the general of the jesuits. That was called the order: and he had heard his father say that they were all clever men. They could all have become highup people in the world if they had not become jesuits. And he wondered what Father Arnall and Paddy Barrett would have become and what Mr McGlade and Mr Gleeson would have become if they had not become jesuits. It was hard to think what because you would have to think of them in a different way with different coloured coats and trousers and with beards and moustaches and different kinds of hats.

The door opened quietly and closed. A quick whisper ran through the class: the prefect of studies. There was an instant of dead silence and then the loud crack of a pandybat on the last desk. Stephen's heart leapt up in fear.

—Any boys want flogging here, Father Arnall? cried the prefect of studies. Any lazy idle loafers that want flogging in this class?

He came to the middle of the class and saw Fleming on his knees.

—Hoho! he cried. Who is this boy? Why is he on his knees? What is your name, boy?

—Fleming, sir.

—Hoho, Fleming! An idler of course. I can see it in your eye. Why is he on his knees, Father Arnall?

—He wrote a bad Latin theme, Father Arnall said, and he missed all the questions in grammar.

—Of course he did! cried the prefect of studies. Of course he did! A born idler! I can see it in the corner of his eye.

He banged his pandybat down on the desk and cried:

—Up, Fleming! Up, my boy!

Fleming stood up slowly.

—Hold out! cried the prefect of studies.

Fleming held out his hand. The pandybat came down on it with a loud smacking sound: one, two, three, four, five, six.

—Other hand!

The pandybat came down again in six loud quick smacks.

—Kneel down! cried the prefect of studies.

Fleming knelt down squeezing his hands under his armpits, his face contorted with pain, but Stephen knew how hard his hands were because Fleming was always rubbing rosin into them. But perhaps he was in great pain for the noise of the pandies was terrible. Stephen's heart was beating and fluttering.

—At your work, all of you! shouted the prefect of studies. We want no lazy idle loafers here, lazy idle little schemers. At your work, I tell you. Father Dolan will be in to see you every day. Father Dolan will be in tomorrow.

He poked one of the boys in the side with the pandybat, saying:

—You, boy! When will Father Dolan be in again?

—Tomorrow, sir, said Tom Furlong's voice.

—Tomorrow and tomorrow and tomorrow, said the prefect of studies. Make up your minds for that. Every day Father Dolan. Write away. You, boy, who are you?

Stephen's heart jumped suddenly.

—Dedalus, sir.

—Why are you not writing like the others?

—I . . . my . . .

He could not speak with fright.

—Why is he not writing, Father Arnall?

—He broke his glasses, said Father Arnall, and I exempted him from work.

—Broke? What is this I hear? What is this your name is? said the prefect of studies.

—Dedalus, sir.

—Out here, Dedalus. Lazy little schemer. I see schemer in your face. Where did you break your glasses?

Stephen stumbled into the middle of the class, blinded by fear and haste.

—Where did you break your glasses? repeated the prefect of studies.

—The cinderpath, sir.

—Hoho! The cinderpath! cried the prefect of studies. I know that trick.

Stephen lifted his eyes in wonder and saw for a moment Father Dolan's whitegrey not young face, his baldy whitegrey head with fluff at the sides of it, the steel rims of his spectacles and his nocoloured eyes looking through the glasses. Why did he say he knew that trick?

—Lazy idle little loafer! cried the prefect of studies. Broke my glasses! An old schoolboy trick! Out with your hand this moment!

Stephen closed his eyes and held out in the air his trembling hand with the palm upwards. He felt the prefect of studies touch it for a moment at the fingers to straighten it and then the swish of the sleeve of the soutane as the pandybat was lifted to strike. A hot burning stinging tingling blow like the loud crack of a broken stick made his trembling hand crumple together like a leaf in the fire: and at the sound and the pain scalding tears were driven into his eyes. His whole body was shaking with fright, his arm was shaking and his crumpled burning livid hand shook like a loose leaf in the air. A cry sprang to his lips, a prayer to be let off. But though the tears scalded his eyes and his limbs quivered with pain and fright he held back the hot tears and the cry that scalded his throat.

—Other hand! shouted the prefect of studies.

Stephen drew back his maimed and quivering right arm and held out his left hand. The soutane sleeve swished again as the pandybat was lifted and a loud crashing sound and a fierce maddening tingling burning pain made his hand shrink together with the palms and fingers in a livid quivering mass. The scalding water burst forth from his eyes and, burning with shame and agony and fear, he drew back his shaking arm in terror and burst out into a whine of pain. His body shook with a palsy of fright and in shame and rage he felt the scalding cry come from his throat and the scalding tears falling out of his eyes and down his flaming cheeks.

—Kneel down! cried the prefect of studies.

Stephen knelt down quickly pressing his beaten hands to his sides. To think of them beaten and swollen with pain all in a moment made him feel so sorry for them as if they were not his own but someone else's that he felt sorry for. And as he knelt, calming the last sobs in his throat and feeling the burning tingling pain pressed in to his sides, he thought of the hands which he had held out in the air with the palms up and of the firm touch of the prefect of studies when he had steadied the shaking fingers and of the beaten swollen reddened mass of palm and fingers that shook helplessly in the air.

—Get at your work, all of you, cried the prefect of studies from the door. Father Dolan will be in every day to see if any boy, any lazy idle little loafer wants flogging. Every day. Every day.

The door closed behind him.

The hushed class continued to copy out the themes. Father Arnall rose from his seat and went among them helping the boys with gentle words and telling them the mistakes they had made. His voice was very gentle and soft. Then he returned to his seat and said to Fleming and Stephen:

—You may return to your places, you two.

Fleming and Stephen rose and, walking to their seats, sat down. Stephen, scarlet with shame, opened a book quickly with one weak hand and bent down upon it, his face close to the page.

It was unfair and cruel because the doctor had told him not to read without glasses and he had written home to his father that morning to send him a new pair. And Father Arnall had said that he need not study till the new glasses came. Then to be called a schemer before the class and to be pandied when he always got the card for first or second and was the leader of the Yorkists! How could the prefect of studies know that it was a trick? He felt the touch of the prefect's fingers as they had steadied his hand and at first he had thought he was going to shake hands with him because the fingers were soft and firm: but then in an instant he had heard the swish of the soutane sleeve and the crash. It was cruel and unfair to make him kneel in the middle of the class then: and Father Arnall had told them both that they might return to their places without making any difference between them. He listened to Father Arnall's low and gentle voice as he corrected the themes. Perhaps he was sorry now and wanted to be decent. But it was unfair and cruel. The prefect of studies was a priest but that was cruel and unfair. And his whitegrey face and the nocoloured eyes behind the steelrimmed spectacles were cruel looking because he had steadied the hand first with his firm soft fingers and that was to hit it better and louder.

—It's a stinking mean thing, that's what it is, said Fleming in the corridor as the classes were passing out in file to the refectory, to pandy a fellow for what is not his fault.

—You really broke your glasses by accident, didn't you? Nasty Roche asked.

Stephen felt his heart filled by Fleming's words and did not answer.

—Of course he did! said Fleming. I wouldn't stand it. I'd go up and tell the rector on him.

—Yes, said Cecil Thunder eagerly, and I saw him lift the pandybat over his shoulder and he's not allowed to do that.

—Did they hurt much? Nasty Roche asked.

—Very much, Stephen said.

—I wouldn't stand it, Fleming repeated, from Baldyhead or any other Baldyhead. It's a stinking mean low trick, that's what it is. I'd go straight up to the rector and tell him about it after dinner.

—Yes, do. Yes, do, said Cecil Thunder.

—Yes, do. Yes, go up and tell the rector on him, Dedalus, said Nasty Roche, because he said that he'd come in tomorrow again to pandy you.

—Yes, yes. Tell the rector, all said.

And there were some fellows out of second of grammar listening and one of them said:

—The senate and the Roman people declared that Dedalus had been wrongly punished.

It was wrong; it was unfair and cruel: and, as he sat in the refectory, he suffered time after time in memory the same humiliation until he began to wonder whether it might not really be that there was something in his face which made him look like a schemer and he wished he had a little mirror to see. But there could not be; and it was unjust and cruel and unfair.

He could not eat the blackish fish fritters they got on Wednesdays in lent and one of his potatoes had the mark of the spade in it. Yes, he would do what the fellows had told him. He would go up and tell the rector that he had been wrongly punished. A thing like that had been done before by somebody in history, by some great person whose head was in the books of history. And the rector would declare that he had been wrongly punished because the senate and the Roman people always declared that the men who did that had been wrongly punished. Those were the great men whose names were in Richmal Magnall's Questions. History was all about those men and what they did and that was what Peter Parley's Tales about Greece and Rome were all about. Peter Parley himself was on the first page in a picture. There was a road over a heath with grass at the side and little bushes: and Peter Parley had a broad hat like a protestant minister and a big stick and he was walking fast along the road to Greece and Rome.

It was easy what he had to do. All he had to do was when the dinner was over and he came out in his turn to go on walking but not out to the corridor but up the staircase on the right that led to the castle. He had nothing to do but that: to turn to the right and walk fast up the staircase and in half a minute he would be in the low dark narrow corridor that led through the castle to the rector's room. And every fellow had said that it was unfair, even the fellow out of second of grammar who had said that about the senate and the Roman people.

What would happen? He heard the fellows of the higher line stand up at the top of the refectory and heard their steps as they came down the matting: Paddy Rath and Jimmy Magee and the Spaniard and the Portuguese and the fifth was big Corrigan who was going to be flogged by Mr Gleeson. That was why the prefect of studies had called him a schemer and pandied him for nothing: and, straining his weak eyes, tired with the tears, he watched big Corrigan's broad shoulders and big hanging black head passing in the file. But he had done something and besides Mr Gleeson would not flog him hard: and he remembered how big Corrigan looked in the bath. He had skin the same colour as the turfcoloured bogwater in the shallow end of the bath and when he walked along the side his feet slapped loudly on the wet tiles and at every step his thighs shook a little because he was fat.

The refectory was half empty and the fellows were still passing out in file. He could go up the staircase because there was never a priest or a prefect outside the refectory door. But he could not go. The rector would side with the prefect of studies and think it was a schoolboy trick and then the prefect of studies would come in every day the same only it would be worse because he would be dreadfully waxy at any fellow going up to the rector about him. The fellows had told him to go but they would not go themselves. They had forgotten all about it. No, it was best to forget all about it and perhaps the prefect of studies had only said he would come in. No, it was best to hide out of the way because when you were small and young you could often escape that way.

The fellows at his table stood up. He stood up and passed out among them in the file. He had to decide. He was coming near the door. If he went on with the fellows he could never go up to the rector because he could not leave the playground for that. And if he went and was pandied all the same all the fellows would make fun and talk about young Dedalus going up to the rector to tell on the prefect of studies.

He was walking down along the matting and he saw the door before him. It was impossible: he could not. He thought of the baldy head of the prefect of studies with the cruel nocoloured eyes looking at him and he heard the voice of prefect of studies asking him twice what his name was. Why could he not remember the name when he was told the first time? Was he not listening the first time or was it to make fun out of the name? The great men in the history had names like that and nobody made fun of them. It was his own name that he should have made fun of if he wanted to make fun. Dolan: it was like the name of a woman that washed clothes.

He had reached the door and, turning quickly up to the right, walked up the stairs and, before he could make up his mind to come back, he had entered the low dark narrow corridor that led to the castle. And as he crossed the threshold of the door of the corridor he saw, without turning his head to look, that all the fellows were looking after him as they went filing by.

He passed along the narrow dark corridor, passing little doors that were the doors of the rooms of the community. He peered in front of him and right and left through the gloom and thought that those must be portraits. It was dark and silent and his eyes were weak and tired with tears so that he could not see. But he thought they were the portraits of the saints and great men of the order who were looking down on him silently as he passed: saint Ignatius Loyola holding an open book and pointing to the words *Ad Majorem Dei Gloriam* in it, saint Francis Xavier pointing to his chest, Lorenzo Ricci with his berretta on his head like one of the prefects of the lines, the three patrons of holy youth, saint Stanislaus Kostka, saint Aloysius Gonzaga and blessed John Berchmans, all with young faces because they died when they were young, and Father Peter Kenny sitting in a chair wrapped in a big cloak.

He came out on the landing above the entrance hall and looked about him. That was where Hamilton Rowan had passed and the marks of the soldiers' slugs were there. And it was there that the old servants had seen the ghost in the white cloak of a marshal.

An old servant was sweeping at the end of the landing. He asked him where was the rector's room and the old servant pointed to the door at the far end and looked after him as he went on to it and knocked.

There was no answer. He knocked again more loudly and his heart jumped when he heard a muffled voice say:

—Come in!

He turned the handle and opened the door and fumbled for the handle of the green baize door inside. He found it and pushed it open and went in.

He saw the rector sitting at a desk writing. There was a skull on the desk and a strange solemn smell in the room like the old leather of chairs.

His heart was beating fast on account of the solemn place he was in and the silence of the room: and he looked at the skull and at the rector's kindlooking face.

—Well, my little man, said the rector, what is it?

Stephen swallowed down the thing in his throat and said:

—I broke my glasses, sir.

The rector opened his mouth and said:

—O!

Then he smiled and said:

—Well, if we broke our glasses we must write home for a new pair.

—I wrote home, sir, said Stephen, and Father Arnall said I am not to study till they come.

—Quite right! said the rector.

Stephen swallowed down the thing again and tried to keep his legs and his voice from shaking.

—But, sir . . .

—Yes?

—Father Dolan came in today and pandied me because I was not writing my theme.

The rector looked at him in silence and he could feel the blood rising to his face and the tears about to rise to his eyes.

The rector said:

—Your name is Dedalus, isn't it?

—Yes, sir.

—And where did you break your glasses?

—On the cinderpath, sir. A fellow was coming out of the bicycle house and I fell and they got broken. I don't know the fellow's name.

The rector looked at him again in silence. Then he smiled and said:

—O, well, it was a mistake; I am sure Father Dolan did not know.

—But I told him I broke them, sir, and he pandied me.

—Did you tell him that you had written home for a new pair? the rector asked.

—No, sir.

—O well then, said the rector, Father Dolan did not understand. You can say that I excuse you from your lessons for a few days.

Stephen said quickly for fear his trembling would prevent him:

—Yes, sir, but Father Dolan said he will come in tomorrow to pandy me again for it.

—Very well, the rector said, it is a mistake and I shall speak to Father Dolan myself. Will that do now?

Stephen felt the tears wetting his eyes and murmured:

—O yes sir, thanks.

The rector held his hand across the side of the desk where the skull was and Stephen, placing his hand in it for a moment, felt a cool moist palm.

—Good day now, said the rector, withdrawing his hand and bowing.

—Good day, sir, said Stephen.

He bowed and walked quietly out of the room, closing the doors carefully and slowly.

But when he had passed the old servant on the landing and was again in the low narrow dark corridor he began to walk faster and faster. Faster and faster he hurried on through the gloom excitedly. He bumped his elbow against the door at the end and, hurrying down the staircase, walked quickly through the two corridors and out into the air.

He could hear the cries of the fellows on the playgrounds. He broke into a run and, running quicker and quicker, ran across the cinderpath and reached the third line playground, panting.

The fellows had seen him running. They closed round him in a ring, pushing one against another to hear.

—Tell us! Tell us!

—What did he say?

—Did you go in?

—What did he say?

—Tell us! Tell us!

He told them what he had said and what the rector had said and, when he had told them, all the fellows flung their caps spinning up into the air and cried:

—Hurroo!

They caught their caps and sent them up again spinning skyhigh and cried again:

—Hurroo! Hurroo!

They made a cradle of their locked hands and hoisted him up among them and carried him along till he struggled to get free. And when he had escaped from them they broke away in all directions, flinging their caps again into the air and whistling as they went spinning up and crying:

—Hurroo!

And they gave three groans for Baldyhead Dolan and three cheers for Conmee and they said he was the decentest rector that was ever in Clongowes.

The cheers died away in the soft grey air. He was alone. He was happy and free: but he would not be anyway proud with Father Dolan. He would he very quiet and obedient: and he wished that he could do something kind for him to show him that he was not proud.

The air was soft and grey and mild and evening was coming. There was the smell of evening in the air, the smell of the fields in the country where they digged up turnips to peel them and eat them when they went out for a walk to Major Barton's, the smell there was in the little wood beyond the pavilion where the gallnuts were.

The fellows were practising long shies and bowling lobs and slow twisters. In the soft grey silence he could hear the bump of the balls: and from here and from there through the quiet air the sound of the cricketbats: pick, pack, pock, puck: like drops of water in a fountain falling softly in the brimming bowl.

II

UNCLE CHARLES smoked such black twist that at last his nephew suggested to him to enjoy his morning smoke in a little outhouse at the end of the garden.

—Very good, Simon. All serene, Simon, said the old man tranquilly. Anywhere you like. The outhouse will do me nicely: it will be more salubrious.

—Damn me, said Mr Dedalus frankly, if I know how you can smoke such villainous awful tobacco. It's like gunpowder, by God.

—It's very nice, Simon, replied the old man. Very cool and mollifying.

Every morning, therefore, uncle Charles repaired to his outhouse but not before he had creased and brushed scrupulously his back hair and brushed and put on his tall hat. While he smoked the brim of his tall hat and the bowl of his pipe were just visible beyond the jambs of the outhouse door. His arbour, as he called the reeking outhouse which he shared with the cat and the garden tools, served him also as a soundingbox: and every morning he hummed contentedly one of his favourite songs: *O, twine me a bower* or *Blue eyes and golden hair* or *The Groves of Blarney* while the grey and blue coils of smoke rose slowly from his pipe and vanished in the pure air.

During the first part of the summer in Blackrock uncle Charles was Stephen's constant companion. Uncle Charles was a hale old man with a welltanned skin, rugged features and white side whiskers. On week days he did messages between the house in Carysfort Avenue and those shops in the main street of the town with which the family dealt. Stephen was glad to go with him on these errands for uncle Charles helped him very liberally to handfuls of whatever was exposed in open boxes and barrels outside the counter. He would seize a handful of grapes and sawdust or three or four American apples and thrust them generously into his grandnephew's hand while the shopman smiled uneasily; and, on Stephen's feigning reluctance to take them, he would frown and say:

—Take them, sir. Do you hear me, sir? They're good for your bowels.

When the order list had been booked the two would go on to the park where an old friend of Stephen's father, Mike Flynn, would be found seated on a bench, waiting for them. Then would begin Stephen's run round the park. Mike Flynn would stand at the gate near the railway station, watch in hand, while Stephen ran round the track in the style Mike Flynn favoured, his head high lifted, his knees well lifted and his hands held straight down by his sides. When the morning practice was over the trainer would make his comments and sometimes illustrate them by shuffling along for a yard or so comically in an old pair of blue canvas shoes. A small ring of wonderstruck children and nursemaids would gather to watch him and linger even when he and uncle Charles had sat down again and were talking athletics and politics. Though he had heard his father say that Mike Flynn had put some of the best runners of modern times through his hands Stephen often glanced with mistrust at his trainer's flabby stubblecovered face, as it bent over the long stained fingers through which he rolled his cigarette, and with pity at the mild lustreless blue eyes which would look up suddenly from the task and gaze vaguely into the blue distance while the long swollen fingers ceased their rolling and grains and fibres of tobacco fell back into the pouch.

On the way home uncle Charles would often pay a visit to the chapel and, as the font was above Stephen's reach, the old man would dip his hand and then sprinkle the water briskly about Stephen's clothes and on the floor of the porch. While he prayed he knelt on his red handkerchief and read above his breath from a thumbblackened prayerbook wherein catchwords were printed at the foot of every page. Stephen knelt at his side respecting, though he did not share, his piety. He often wondered what his granduncle prayed for so seriously. Perhaps he prayed for the souls in purgatory or for the grace of a happy death or perhaps he prayed that God might send him back a part of the big fortune he had squandered in Cork.

On Sundays Stephen with his father and his granduncle took their constitutional. The old man was a nimble walker in spite of his corns and often ten or twelve miles of the road were covered. The little village of Stillorgan was the parting of the ways. Either they went to the left towards the Dublin mountains or along the Goatstown road and thence into Dundrum, coming home by Sandyford. Trudging along the road or standing in some grimy wayside publichouse his elders spoke constantly of the subjects nearer their hearts, of Irish politics, of Munster and of the legends of their own family, to all of which Stephen lent an avid ear. Words which he did not understand he said over and over to himself till he had learned them by heart: and through them he had glimpses of the real world about him. The hour when he too would take part in the life of that world seemed drawing near and in secret he began to make ready for the great part which he felt awaited him the nature of which he only dimly apprehended.

His evenings were his own; and he pored over a ragged translation of *The Count of Monte Cristo*. The figure of that dark avenger stood forth in his mind for whatever he had heard or divined in childhood of the strange and terrible. At night he built up on the parlour table an image of the wonderful island cave out of transfers and paper flowers and coloured tissue paper and strips of the silver and golden paper in which chocolate is wrapped. When he had broken up this scenery, weary of its tinsel, there would come to his mind the bright picture of Marseilles, of sunny trellisses and of Mercedes. Outside Blackrock, on the road that led to the mountains, stood a small whitewashed house in the garden of which grew many rosebushes: and in this house, he told himself, another Mercedes lived. Both on the outward and on the homeward journey he measured distance by this landmark: and in his imagination he lived through a long train of adventures, marvellous as those in the book itself, towards the close of which there appeared an image of himself, grown older and sadder, standing in a moonlit garden with Mercedes who had so many years before slighted his love, and with a sadly proud gesture of refusal, saying:

—Madam, I never eat muscatel grapes.

He became the ally of a boy named Aubrey Mills and founded with him a gang of adventurers in the avenue. Aubrey carried a whistle dangling from his buttonhole and a bicycle lamp attached to his belt while the others had short sticks thrust daggerwise through theirs. Stephen, who had read of Napoleon's plain style of dress, chose to remain unadorned and thereby heightened for himself the pleasure of taking counsel with his lieutenant before giving orders. The gang made forays into the gardens of old maids or went down to the castle and fought a battle on the shaggy weedgrown rocks, coming home after it weary stragglers with the stale odours of the foreshore in their nostrils and the rank oils of the seawrack upon their hands and in their hair.

Aubrey and Stephen had a common milkman and often they drove out in the milkcar to Carrickmines where the cows were at grass. While the men were milking the boys would take turns in riding the tractable mare round the field. But when autumn came the cows were driven home from the grass: and the first sight of the filthy cowyard at Stradbrooke with its foul green puddles and clots of liquid dung and steaming brantroughs sickened Stephen's heart. The cattle which had seemed so beautiful in the country on sunny days revolted him and he could not even look at the milk they yielded.

The coming of September did not trouble him this year for he was not to be sent back to Clongowes. The practice in the park came to an end when Mike Flynn went into hospital. Aubrey was at school and had only an hour or two free in the evening. The gang fell asunder and there were no more nightly forays or battles on the rocks. Stephen sometimes went round with the car which delivered the evening milk: and these chilly drives blew away his memory of the filth of the cowyard and he felt no repugnance at seeing the cowhairs and hayseeds on the milkman's coat. Whenever the car drew up before a house he waited to catch a glimpse of a well-scrubbed kitchen or of a softlylighted hall and to see how the servant would hold the jug and how she would close the door. He thought it should be a pleasant life enough, driving along the roads every evening to deliver milk, if he had warm gloves and a fat bag of gingernuts in his pocket to eat from. But the same foreknowledge which had sickened his heart and made his legs sag suddenly as he raced round the park, the same intuition which had made him glance with mistrust at his trainer's flabby stubblecovered face as it bent heavily over his long stained fingers, dissipated any vision of the future. In a vague way he understood that his father was in trouble and that this was the reason why he himself had not been sent back to Clongowes. For some time he had felt the slight changes in his house; and these changes in what he had deemed unchangeable were so many slight shocks to his boyish conception of the world. The ambition which he felt astir at times in the darkness of his soul sought no outlet. A dusk like that of the outer world obscured his mind as he heard the mare's hoofs clattering along the tramtrack on the Rock Road and the great can swaying and rattling behind him.

He returned to Mercedes and, as he brooded upon her image, a strange unrest crept into his blood. Sometimes a fever gathered within him and led him to rove alone in the evening along the quiet avenue. The peace of the gardens and the kindly lights in the windows poured a tender influence into his restless heart. The noise of children at play annoyed him and their silly voices made him feel, even more keenly than he had felt at Clongowes, that he was different from others. He did not want to play. He wanted to meet in the real world the unsubstantial image which his soul so constantly beheld. He did not know where to seek it or how: but a premonition which led him on told him that this image would, without any overt act of his, encounter him. They would meet quietly as if they had known each other and had made their tryst, perhaps at one of the gates or in some more secret place. They would be alone, surrounded by darkness and silence: and in that moment of supreme tenderness he would be transfigured. He would fade into something impalpable under her eyes and then in a moment, he would be transfigured. Weakness and timidity and inexperience would fall from him in that magic moment.

* * *

Two great yellow caravans had halted one morning before the door and men had come tramping into the house to dismantle it. The furniture had been hustled out through the front garden which was strewn with wisps of straw and rope ends and into the huge vans at the gate. When all had been safely stowed the vans had set off noisily down the avenue: and from the window of the railway carriage, in which he had sat with his redeyed mother, Stephen had seen them lumbering heavily along the Merrion Road.

The parlour fire would not draw that evening and Mr Dedalus rested the poker against the bars of the grate to attract the flame. Uncle Charles dozed in a corner of the half furnished uncarpeted room and near him the family portraits leaned against the wall. The lamp on the table shed a weak light over the boarded floor, muddied by the feet of the vanmen. Stephen sat on a footstool beside his father listening to a long and incoherent monologue. He understood little or nothing of it at first but he became slowly aware that his father had enemies and that some fight was going to take place. He felt too that he was being enlisted for the fight, that some duty was being laid upon his shoulders. The sudden flight from the comfort and revery of Blackrock, the passage through the gloomy foggy city, the thought of the bare cheerless house in which they were now to live made his heart heavy: and again an intuition or foreknowledge of the future came to him. He understood also why the servants had often whispered together in the hall and why his father had often stood on the hearthrug, with his back to the fire, talking loudly to uncle Charles who urged him to sit down and eat his dinner.

—There's a crack of the whip left in me yet, Stephen, old chap, said Mr Dedalus, poking at the dull fire with fierce energy. We're not dead yet, sonny. No, by the Lord Jesus (God forgive me) nor half dead.

Dublin was a new and complex sensation. Uncle Charles had grown so witless that he could no longer be sent out on errands and the disorder in settling in the new house left Stephen freer than he had been in Blackrock. In the beginning he contented himself with circling timidly round the neighbouring square or, at most, going half way down one of the side streets: but when he had made a skeleton map of the city in his mind he followed boldly one of its central lines until he reached the customhouse. He passed unchallenged among the docks and along the quays wondering at the multitude of corks that lay bobbing on the surface of the water in a thick yellow scum, at the crowds of quay porters and the rumbling carts and the illdressed bearded policeman. The vastness and strangeness of the life suggested to him by the bales of merchandise stocked along the walls or swung aloft out of the holds of steamers wakened again in him the unrest which had sent him wandering in the evening from garden to garden in search of Mercedes. And amid this new bustling life he might have fancied himself in another Marseilles but that he missed the bright sky and the sunwarmed trellisses of the wineshops. A vague dissatisfaction grew up within him as he looked on the quays and on the river and on the lowering skies and yet he continued to wander up and down day after day as if he really sought someone that eluded him.

He went once or twice with his mother to visit their relatives: and, though they passed a jovial array of shops lit up and adorned for Christmas, his mood of embittered silence did not leave him. The causes of his embitterment were many, remote and near. He was angry with himself for being young and the prey of restless foolish impulses, angry also with the change of fortune which was reshaping the world about him into a vision of squalor and insincerity. Yet his anger lent nothing to the vision. He chronicled with patience what he saw, detaching himself from it and testing its mortifying flavour in secret.

He was sitting on the backless chair in his aunt's kitchen. A lamp with a reflector hung on the japanned wall of the fireplace and by its light his aunt was reading the evening paper that lay on her knees. She looked a long time at a smiling picture that was set in it and said musingly:

—The beautiful Mabel Hunter!

A ringletted girl stood on tiptoe to peer at the picture and said softly:

—What is she in, mud?

—In the pantomime, love.

The child leaned her ringletted head against her mother's sleeve, gazing on the picture, and murmured as if fascinated:

—The beautiful Mabel Hunter!

As if fascinated, her eyes rested long upon those demurely taunting eyes and she murmured again devotedly:

—Isn't she an exquisite creature?

And the boy who came in from the street, stamping crookedly under his stone of coal, heard her words. He dropped his load promptly on the floor and hurried to her side to see. But she did not raise her easeful head to let him see. He mauled the edges of the paper with his reddened and blackened hands, shouldering her aside and complaining that he could not see.

He was sitting in the narrow breakfast room high up in the old darkwindowed house. The firelight flickered on the wall and beyond the window a spectral dusk was gathering upon the river. Before the fire an old woman was busy making tea and, as she bustled at her task, she told in a low voice of what the priest and the doctor had said. She told too of certain changes she had seen in her of late and of her odd ways and sayings. He sat listening to the words and following the ways of adventure that lay open in the coals, arches and vaults and winding galleries and jagged caverns.

Suddenly he became aware of something in the doorway. A skull

appeared suspended in the gloom of the doorway. A feeble creature
like a monkey was there, drawn thither by the sound of voices at the
fire. A whining voice came from the door, asking:

—Is that Josephine?

The old bustling woman answered cheerily from the fireplace:

—No, Ellen. It's Stephen.

—O . . . O, good evening, Stephen.

He answered the greeting and saw a silly smile break over the face
in the doorway.

—Do you want anything, Ellen? asked the old woman at the fire.

But she did not answer the question and said:

—I thought it was Josephine. I thought you were Josephine,
Stephen.

And, repeating this several times, she fell to laughing feebly.

He was sitting in the midst of a children's party at Harold's Cross.
His silent watchful manner had grown upon him and he took little
part in the games. The children, wearing the spoils of their crackers,
danced and romped noisily and, though he tried to share their mer-
riment, he felt himself a gloomy figure amid the gay cocked hats and
sunbonnets.

But when he had sung his song and withdrawn into a snug corner
of the room he began to taste the joy of his loneliness. The mirth,
which in the beginning of the evening had seemed to him false and
trivial, was like a soothing air to him, passing gaily by his senses,
hiding from other eyes the feverish agitation of his blood while
through the circling of the dancers and amid the music and laughter
her glance travelled to his corner, flattering, taunting, searching,
exciting his heart. In the hall the children who had stayed latest were
putting on their things: the party was over. She had thrown a shawl
about her and, as they went together towards the tram, sprays of her
fresh warm breath flew gaily above her cowled head and her shoes
tapped blithely on the glassy road.

It was the last tram. The lank brown horses knew it and shook
their bells to the clear night in admonition. The conductor talked
with the driver, both nodding often in the green light of the lamp. On
the empty seats of the tram were scattered a few coloured tickets. No
sound of footsteps came up or down the road. No sound broke the
peace of the night save when the lank brown horses rubbed their
noses together and shook their bells.

They seemed to listen, he on the upper step and she on the lower. She came up to his step many times and went down to hers again between their phrases and once or twice stood close beside him for some moments on the upper step, forgetting to go down, and then went down. His heart danced upon her movements like a cork upon a tide. He heard what her eyes said to him from beneath their cowl and knew that in some dim past, whether in life or in revery, he had heard their tale before. He saw her urge her vanities, her fine dress and sash and long black stockings, and knew that he had yielded to them a thousand times. Yet a voice within him spoke above the noise of his dancing heart, asking him would he take her gift to which he had only to stretch out his hand. And he remembered the day when he and Eileen had stood looking into the hotel grounds, watching the waiters running up a trail of bunting on the flagstaff and the fox terrier scampering to and fro on the sunny lawn, and how, all of a sudden, she had broken out into a peal of laughter and had run down the sloping curve of the path. Now, as then, he stood listlessly in his place, seemingly a tranquil watcher of the scene before him.

—She too wants me to catch hold of her, he thought. That's why she came with me to the tram. I could easily catch hold of her when she comes up to my step: nobody is looking. I could hold her and kiss her.

But he did neither: and, when he was sitting alone in the deserted tram, he tore his ticket into shreds and stared gloomily at the corrugated footboard.

The next day he sat at his table in the bare upper room for many hours. Before him lay a new pen, a new bottle of ink and a new emerald exercise. From force of habit he had written at the top of the first page the initial letters of the jesuit motto: A.M.D.G. On the first line of the page appeared the title of the verses he was trying to write: To E—— C——. He knew it was right to begin so for he had seen similar titles in the collected poems of Lord Byron. When he had written this title and drawn an ornamental line underneath he fell into a daydream and began to draw diagrams on the cover of the book. He saw himself sitting at his table in Bray the morning after the discussion at the Christmas dinnertable, trying to write a poem about Parnell on the back of one of his father's second moiety notices. But his brain had then refused to grapple with the theme and, desisting, he had covered the page with the names and addresses of certain of his classmates:

Roderick Kickham
John Lawton
Anthony MacSwiney
Simon Moonan

Now it seemed as if he would fail again but, by dint of brooding on the incident, he thought himself into confidence. During this process all those elements which he deemed common and insignificant fell out of the scene. There remained no trace of the tram itself nor of the trammen nor of the horses: nor did he and she appear vividly. The verses told only of the night and the balmy breeze and the maiden lustre of the moon. Some undefined sorrow was hidden in the hearts of the protagonists as they stood in silence beneath the leafless trees and when the moment of farewell had come the kiss, which had been withheld by one, was given by both. After this the letters L.D.S. were written at the foot of the page and, having hidden the book, he went into his mother's bedroom and gazed at his face for a long time in the mirror of her dressingtable.

But his long spell of leisure and liberty was drawing to its end. One evening his father came home full of news which kept his tongue busy all through dinner. Stephen had been awaiting his father's return for there had been mutton hash that day and he knew that his father would make him dip his bread in the gravy. But he did not relish the hash for the mention of Clongowes had coated his palate with a scum of disgust.

—I walked bang into him, said Mr Dedalus for the fourth time, just at the corner of the square.

—Then I suppose, said Mrs Dedalus, he will be able to arrange it. I mean about Belvedere.

—Of course he will, said Mr Dedalus. Don't I tell you he's provincial of the order now?

—I never liked the idea of sending him to the christian brothers myself, said Mrs Dedalus.

—Christian brothers be damned! said Mr Dedalus. Is it with Paddy Stink and Mickey Mud? No, let him stick to the jesuits in God's name since he began with them. They'll be of service to him in after years. Those are the fellows that can get you a position.

—And they're a very rich order, aren't they, Simon?

—Rather. They live well, I tell you. You saw their table at Clongowes. Fed up, by God, like gamecocks.

Mr Dedalus pushed his plate over to Stephen and bade him finish what was on it.

—Now then, Stephen, he said, you must put your shoulder to the wheel, old chap. You've had a fine long holiday.

—O, I'm sure he'll work very hard now, said Mrs Dedalus, especially when he has Maurice with him.

—O, Holy Paul, I forgot about Maurice, said Mr Dedalus. Here, Maurice! Come here, you thickheaded ruffian! Do you know I'm going to send you to a college where they'll teach you to spell c.a.t. cat. And I'll buy you a nice little penny handkerchief to keep your nose dry. Won't that be grand fun?

Maurice grinned at his father and then at his brother. Mr Dedalus screwed his glass into his eye and stared hard at both his sons. Stephen mumbled his bread without answering his father's gaze.

—By the bye, said Mr Dedalus at length, the rector, or provincial, rather, was telling me that story about you and Father Dolan. You're an impudent thief, he said.

—O, he didn't, Simon!

—Not he! said Mr Dedalus. But he gave me a great account of the whole affair. We were chatting, you know, and one word borrowed another. And, by the way, who do you think he told me will get that job in the corporation? But I'll tell you that after. Well, as I was saying, we were chatting away quite friendly and he asked me did our friend here wear glasses still and then he told me the whole story.

—And was he annoyed, Simon?

—Annoyed! Not he! *Manly little chap!* he said.

Mr Dedalus imitated the mincing nasal tone of the provincial.

—Father Dolan and I, when I told them all at dinner about it, Father Dolan and I had a great laugh over it. *You better mind yourself Father Dolan*, said I, *or young Dedalus will send you up for twice nine*. We had a famous laugh together over it. Ha! Ha! Ha!

Mr Dedalus turned to his wife and interjected in his natural voice:

—Shows you the spirit in which they take the boys there. O, a jesuit for your life, for diplomacy!

He reassumed the provincial's voice and repeated:

—I told them all at dinner about it and Father Dolan and I and all of us we all had a hearty laugh together over it. Ha! Ha! Ha!

*   *   *

The night of the Whitsuntide play had come and Stephen from the window of the dressingroom looked out on the small grassplot across which lines of Chinese lanterns were stretched. He watched the visitors come down the steps from the house and pass into the theatre. Stewards in evening dress, old Belvedereans, loitered in groups about the entrance to the theatre and ushered in the visitors with ceremony. Under the sudden glow of a lantern he could recognise the smiling face of a priest.

The Blessed Sacrament had been removed from the tabernacle and the first benches had been driven back so as to leave the dais of the altar and the space before it free. Against the walls stood companies of barbells and Indian clubs; the dumbbells were piled in one corner: and in the midst of countless hillocks of gymnasium shoes and sweaters and singlets in untidy brown parcels there stood the stout leatherjacketed vaulting horse waiting its turn to be carried up on the stage. A large bronze shield, tipped with silver, leaned against the panel of the altar also waiting its turn to be carried up on the stage and set in the middle of the winning team at the end of the gymnastic display.

Stephen, though in deference to his reputation for essaywriting he had been elected secretary to the gymnasium, had had no part in the first section or the programme but in the play which formed the second section he had the chief part, that of a farcical pedagogue. He had been cast for it on account of his stature and grave manners for he was now at the end of his second year at Belvedere and in number two.

A score of the younger boys in white knickers and singlets came pattering down from the stage, through the vestry and into the chapel. The vestry and chapel were peopled with eager masters and boys. The plump bald sergeantmajor was testing with his foot the springboard of the vaulting horse. The lean young man in a long overcoat, who was to give a special display of intricate club swinging, stood near watching with interest, his silvercoated clubs peeping out of his deep sidepockets. The hollow rattle of the wooden dumbbells was heard as another team made ready to go up on the stage: and in another moment the excited prefect was hustling the boys through the vestry like a flock of geese, flapping the wings of his soutane nervously and crying to the laggards to make haste. A little troop of Neapolitan peasants were practising their steps at the end of the chapel, some circling their arms above their heads, some swaying their baskets of paper violets and curtseying. In a dark corner of the chapel at the gospel side of the altar a stout old lady knelt amid her copious black skirts. When she stood up a pinkdressed figure, wearing a curly golden wig and an oldfashioned straw sunbonnet, with black pencilled eyebrows and cheeks delicately rouged and powdered, was discovered. A low murmur of curiosity ran round the chapel at the discovery of this girlish figure. One of the prefects, smiling and nodding his head, approached the dark corner and, having bowed to the stout old lady, said pleasantly:

—Is this a beautiful young lady or a doll that you have here, Mrs Tallon?

Then, bending down to peer at the smiling painted face under the leaf of the bonnet, he exclaimed:

—No! Upon my word I believe it's little Bertie Tallon after all!

Stephen at his post by the window heard the old lady and the priest laugh together and heard the boys' murmur of admiration behind him as they passed forward to see the little boy who had to dance the sunbonnet dance by himself. A movement of impatience escaped him. He let the edge of the blind fall and, stepping down from the bench on which he had been standing, walked out of the chapel.

He passed out of the schoolhouse and halted under the shed that flanked the garden. From the theatre opposite came the muffled noise of the audience and sudden brazen clashes of the soldiers' band. The light spread upwards from the glass roof making the theatre seem a festive ark, anchored among the hulks of houses, her frail cables of lanterns looping her to her moorings. A sidedoor of the theatre opened suddenly and a shaft of light flew across the grass-plots. A sudden burst of music issued from the ark, the prelude of a waltz: and when the sidedoor closed again the listener could hear the faint rhythm of the music. The sentiment of the opening bars, their languor and supple movement, evoked the incommunicable emotion which had been the cause of all his day's unrest and of his impatient movement of a moment before. His unrest issued from him like a wave of sound: and on the tide of flowing music the ark was journeying, trailing her cables of lanterns in her wake. Then a noise like dwarf artillery broke the movement. It was the clapping that greeted the entry of the dumbbell team on the stage.

At the far end of the shed near the street a speck of pink light showed in the darkness and as he walked towards it he became aware of a faint aromatic odour. Two boys were standing in the shelter of a doorway, smoking, and before he reached them he had recognised Heron by his voice.

—Here comes the noble Dedalus! cried a high throaty voice. Welcome to our trusty friend!

This welcome ended in a soft peal of mirthless laughter as Heron salaamed and then began to poke the ground with his cane.

—Here I am, said Stephen, halting and glancing from Heron to his friend.

The latter was a stranger to him but in the darkness, by the aid of the glowing cigarettetips, he could make out a pale dandyish face, over which a smile was travelling slowly, a tall overcoated figure and a hard hat. Heron did not trouble himself about an introduction but said instead:

—I was just telling my friend Willis what lark it would be tonight if you took off the rector in the part of the schoolmaster. It would be a ripping good joke.

Heron made a poor attempt to imitate for his friend Wallis the rector's pedantic bass and then, laughing at his failure, asked Stephen to do it.

—Go on, Dedalus, he urged, you can take him off rippingly. *He that will not hear the churcha let him be to theea as the heathena and the publicana.*

The imitation was prevented by a mild expression of anger from Wallis in whose mouthpiece the cigarette had become too tightly wedged.

—Damn this blankety blank holder, he said, taking it from his mouth and smiling and frowning upon it tolerantly. It's always getting stuck like that. Do you use a holder?

—I don't smoke, answered Stephen.

—No, said Heron, Dedalus is a model youth. He doesn't smoke and he doesn't go to bazaars and he doesn't flirt and he doesn't damn anything or damn all.

Stephen shook his head and smiled in his rival's flushed and mobile face, beaked like a bird's. He had often thought it strange that Vincent Heron had a bird's face as well as a bird's name. A shock of pale hair lay on the forehead like a ruffled crest: the forehead was narrow and bony and a thin hooked nose stood out between the closeset prominent eyes which were light and inexpressive. The rivals were school friends. They sat together in class, knelt together in the chapel, talked together after beads over their lunches. As the fellows in number one were undistinguished dullards Stephen and Heron had been during the year the virtual heads of the school. It was they who went up to the rector together to ask for a free day or to get a fellow off.

—O by the way, said Heron suddenly, I saw your governor going in.

The smile waned on Stephen's face. Any allusion made to his father by a fellow or by a master put his calm to rout in a moment. He waited in timorous silence to hear what Heron might say next. Heron, however, nudged him expressively with his elbow and said:

—You're a sly dog, Dedalus!

—Why so? said Stephen.

—You'd think butter wouldn't melt in your mouth, said Heron. But I'm afraid you're a sly dog.

—Might I ask you what you are talking about? said Stephen urbanely.

—Indeed you might, answered Heron. We saw her, Wallis, didn't we? And deucedly pretty she is too. And so inquisitive! *And what part does Stephen take, Mr Dedalus? And will Stephen not sing, Mr Dedalus?* Your governor was staring at her through that eyeglass of his for all he was worth so that I think the old man has found you out too. I wouldn't care a bit, by Jove. She's ripping, isn't she, Wallis?

—Not half bad, answered Wallis quietly as he placed his holder once more in a corner of his mouth.

A shaft of momentary anger flew through Stephen's mind at these indelicate allusions in the hearing of a stranger. For him there was nothing amusing in a girl's interest and regard. All day he had thought of nothing but their leavetaking on the steps of the tram at Harold's Cross, the stream of moody emotions it had made to course through him and the poem he had written about it. All day he had imagined a new meeting with her for he knew that she was to come to the play. The old restless moodiness had again filled his breast as it had done on the night of the party but had not found an outlet in verse. The growth and knowledge of two years of boyhood stood between then and now, forbidding such an outlet: and all day the stream of gloomy tenderness within him had started forth and returned upon itself in dark courses and eddies, wearying him in the end until the pleasantry of the prefect and the painted little boy had drawn from him a movement of impatience.

—So you may as well admit, Heron went on, that we've fairly found you out this time. You can't play the saint on me any more, that's one sure five.

A soft peal of mirthless laughter escaped from his lips and, bending down as before, he struck Stephen lightly across the calf of the leg with his cane, as if in jesting reproof.

Stephen's movement of anger had already passed. He was neither flattered nor confused but simply wished the banter to end. He scarcely resented what had seemed to him at first a silly indelicateness for he knew that the adventure in his mind stood in no danger from their words: and his face mirrored his rival's false smile.

—Admit! repeated Heron, striking him again with his cane across the calf of the leg.

The stroke was playful but not so lightly given as the first one had been. Stephen felt the skin tingle and glow slightly and almost painlessly; and bowing submissively, as if to meet his companion's jesting mood, began to recite the *Confiteor*. The episode ended well for both Heron and Wallis laughed indulgently at the irreverence.

The confession came only from Stephen's lips and, while they spoke the words, a sudden memory had carried him to another scene called up, as if by magic, at the moment when he had noted the faint cruel dimples at the corners of Heron's smiling lips and had felt the familiar stroke of the cane against his calf and had heard the familiar word of admonition:

—Admit.

It was towards the close of his first term in the college when he was in number six. His sensitive nature was still smarting under the lashes of an undivined and squalid way of life. His soul was still disquieted and cast down by the dull phenomenon of Dublin. He had emerged from a two years' spell of revery to find himself in the midst of a new scene, every event and figure of which affected him

intimately, disheartened him or allured and, whether alluring or disheartening, filled him always with unrest and bitter thoughts. All the
leisure which his school life left him was passed in the company of
subversive writers whose gibes and violence of speech set up a
ferment in his brain before they passed out of it into his crude
writings.

The essay was for him the chief labour of his week and every
Tuesday, as he marched from home to the school, he read his fate in
the incidents of the way, pitting himself against some figure ahead of
him and quickening his pace to outstrip it before a certain goal was
reached or planting his steps scrupulously in the spaces of the
patchwork of the footpath and telling himself that he would be first
and not first in the weekly essay.

On a certain Tuesday the course of his triumphs was rudely
broken. Mr Tate, the English master, pointed his finger at him and
said bluntly:

—This fellow has heresy in his essay.

A hush fell on the class. Mr Tate did not break it but dug with his
hand between his crossed thighs while his heavily starched linen
creaked about his neck and wrists. Stephen did not look up. It was a
raw spring morning and his eyes were still smarting and weak. He
was conscious of failure and of detection, of the squalor of his own
mind and home, and felt against his neck the raw edge of his turned
and jagged collar.

A short loud laugh from Mr Tate set the class more at ease.

—Perhaps you didn't know that, he said.

—Where? asked Stephen.

Mr Tate withdrew his delving hand and spread out the essay.

—Here. It's about the Creator and the soul. Rrm . . . rrm . . .
rrm. . . . Ah! *without a possibility of ever approaching nearer*. That's
heresy.

Stephen murmured:

—I meant *without a possibility of ever reaching*.

It was a submission and Mr Tate, appeased, folded up the essay
and passed it across to him, saying:

—O . . . Ah! *ever reaching*. That's another story.

But the class was not so soon appeased. Though nobody spoke to
him of the affair after class he could feel about him a vague general
malignant joy.

A few nights after this public chiding he was walking with a letter along the Drumcondra Road when he heard a voice cry:

—Halt!

He turned and saw three boys of his own class coming towards him in the dusk. It was Heron who had called out and, as he marched forward between his two attendants, he cleft the air before him with a thin cane, in time to their steps. Boland, his friend, marched beside him, a large grin on his face, while Nash came on a few steps behind, blowing from the pace and wagging his great red head.

As soon as the boys had turned into Clonliffe Road together they began to speak about books and writers, saying what books they were reading and how many books there were in their fathers' bookcases at home. Stephen listened to them in some wonderment for Boland was the dunce and Nash the idler of the class. In fact after some talk about their favourite writers Nash declared for Captain Marryat who, he said, was the greatest writer.

—Fudge! said Heron. Ask Dedalus. Who is the greatest writer, Dedalus?

Stephen noted the mockery in the question and said:

—Of prose do you mean?

—Yes.

—Newman, I think.

—Is it Cardinal Newman? asked Boland.

—Yes, answered Stephen.

The grin broadened on Nash's freckled face as he turned to Stephen and said:

—And do you like Cardinal Newman, Dedalus?

—O, many say that Newman has the best prose style, Heron said to the other two in explanation. Of course he's not a poet.

—And who is the best poet, Heron? asked Boland.

—Lord Tennyson, of course, answered Heron.

—O, yes, Lord Tennyson, said Nash. We have all his poetry at home in a book.

At this Stephen forgot the silent vows he had been making and burst out:

—Tennyson a poet! Why, he's only a rhymester!

—O, get out! said Heron. Everyone knows that Tennyson is the greatest poet.

—And who do you think is the greatest poet? asked Boland, nudging his neighbour.

—Byron, of course, answered Stephen.

Heron gave the lead and all three joined in a scornful laugh.

—What are you laughing at? asked Stephen.

—You, said Heron. Byron the greatest poet! He's only a poet for uneducated people.

—He must be a fine poet! said Boland.

—You may keep your mouth shut, said Stephen, turning on him boldly. All you know about poetry is what you wrote up on the slates in the yard and were going to be sent to the loft for.

Boland, in fact, was said to have written on the slates in the yard a couplet about a classmate of his who often rode home from the college on a pony:

> As Tyson was riding into Jerusalem
> He fell and hurt his Alec Kafoozelum.

This thrust put the two lieutenants to silence but Heron went on:

—In any case Byron was a heretic and immoral too.

—I don't care what he was, cried Stephen hotly.

—You don't care whether he was a heretic or not? said Nash.

—What do you know about it? shouted Stephen. You never read a line of anything in your life except a trans or Boland either.

—I know that Byron was a bad man, said Boland.

—Here, catch hold of this heretic, Heron called out.

In a moment Stephen was a prisoner.

—Tate made you buck up the other day, Heron went on, about the heresy in your essay.

—I'll tell him tomorrow, said Boland.

—Will you? said Stephen. You'd be afraid to open your lips.

—Afraid?

—Ay. Afraid of your life.

—Behave yourself! cried Heron, cutting at Stephen's legs with his cane.

It was the signal for their onset. Nash pinioned his arms behind while Boland seized a long cabbage stump which was lying in the gutter. Struggling and kicking under the cuts of the cane and the blows of the knotty stump Stephen was borne back against a barbed wire fence.

—Admit that Byron was no good.

—No.

—Admit.

—No.

—Admit.

—No. No.

At last after a fury of plunges he wrenched himself free. His tormentors set off towards Jones's Road, laughing and jeering at him, while he, torn and flushed and panting, stumbled after them half blinded with tears, clenching his fists madly and sobbing.

While he was still repeating the *Confiteor* amid the indulgent laughter of his hearers and while the scenes of that malignant episode were still passing sharply and swiftly before his mind he wondered why he bore no malice now to those who had tormented him. He had not forgotten a whit of their cowardice and cruelty but the memory of it called forth no anger from him. All the descriptions of fierce love and hatred which he had met in books had seemed to him therefore unreal. Even that night as he stumbled homewards along Jones's Road he had felt that some power was divesting him of that suddenwoven anger as easily as a fruit is divested of its soft ripe peel.

He remained standing with his two companions at the end of the shed, listening idly to their talk or to the bursts of applause in the theatre. She was sitting there among the others perhaps waiting for him to appear. He tried to recall her appearance but could not. He could remember only that she had worn a shawl about her head like a cowl and that her dark eyes had invited and unnerved him. He wondered had he been in her thoughts as she had been in his. Then in the dark and unseen by the other two he rested the tips of the fingers of one hand upon the palm of the other hand, scarcely touching it and yet pressing upon it lightly. But the pressure of her fingers had been lighter and steadier: and suddenly the memory of their touch traversed his brain and body like an invisible warm wave.

A boy came towards them, running along under the shed. He was excited and breathless.

—O, Dedalus, he cried, Doyle is in a great bake about you. You're to go in at once and get dressed for the play. Hurry up, you better.

—He's coming now, said Heron to the messenger with a haughty drawl, when he wants to.

The boy turned to Heron and repeated:

—But Doyle is in an awful bake.

—Will you tell Doyle with my best compliments that I damned his eyes? answered Heron.

—Well, I must go now, said Stephen, who cared little for such points of honour.

—I wouldn't, said Heron, damn me if I would. That's no way to send for one of the senior boys. In a bake, indeed! I think it's quite enough that you're taking a part in his bally old play.

This spirit of quarrelsome comradeship which he had observed lately in his rival had not seduced Stephen from his habits of quiet obedience. He mistrusted the turbulence and doubted the sincerity of such comradeship which seemed to him a sorry anticipation of manhood. The question of honour here raised was, like all such questions, trivial to him. While his mind had been pursuing its intangible phantoms and turning in irresolution from such pursuit he had heard about him the constant voices of his father and of his masters, urging him to be a gentleman above all things and urging him to be a good catholic above all things. These voices had now come to be hollowsounding in his ears. When the gymnasium had been opened he had heard another voice urging him to be strong and manly and healthy and when the movement towards national revival had begun to be felt in the college yet another voice had bidden him be true to his country and help to raise up her fallen language and tradition. In the profane world, as he foresaw, a worldly voice would bid him raise up his father's fallen state by his labours and, meanwhile, the voice of his schoolcomrades urged him to be a decent fellow, to shield others from blame or to beg them off and to do his best to get free days for the school. And it was the din of all these hollowsounding voices that made him halt irresolutely in the pursuit of phantoms. He gave them ear only for a time but he was happy only when he was far from them, beyond their call, alone or in the company of phantasmal comrades.

In the vestry a plump freshfaced jesuit and an elderly man, in shabby blue clothes, were dabbling in a case of paints and chalks. The boys who had been painted walked about or stood still awkwardly, touching their faces in a gingerly fashion with their furtive fingertips. In the middle of the vestry a young jesuit, who was then on a visit to the college, stood rocking himself rhythmically from the tips of his toes to his heels and back again, his hands thrust well forward into his sidepockets. His small head set off with glossy red curls and his newly shaven face agreed well with the spotless decency of his soutane and with his spotless shoes.

As he watched this swaying form and tried to read for himself the legend of the priest's mocking smile there came into Stephen's memory a saying which he had heard from his father before he had been sent to Clongowes, that you could always tell a jesuit by the style of his clothes. At the same moment he thought he saw a likeness between his father's mind and that of this smiling welldressed priest: and he was aware of some desecration of the priest's office or of the vestry itself, whose silence was now routed by loud talk and joking and its air pungent with the smells of the gasjets and the grease.

While his forehead was being wrinkled and his jaws painted black and blue by the elderly man he listened distractedly to the voice of the plump young jesuit which bade him speak up and make his points clearly. He could hear the band playing *The Lily of Killarney* and knew that in a few moments the curtain would go up. He felt no stage fright but the thought of the part he had to play humiliated him. A remembrance of some of his lines made a sudden flush rise to his painted cheeks. He saw her serious alluring eyes watching him from among the audience and their image at once swept away his scruples, leaving his will compact. Another nature seemed to have been lent him: the infection of the excitement and youth about him entered into and transformed his moody mistrustfulness. For one rare moment he seemed to be clothed in the real apparel of boyhood: and, as he stood in the wings among the other players, he shared the common mirth amid which the drop scene was hauled upwards by two ablebodied priests with violent jerks and all awry.

A few moments after he found himself on the stage amid the garish gas and the dim scenery, acting before the innumerable faces of the void. It surprised him to see that the play which he had known at rehearsals for a disjointed lifeless thing had suddenly assumed a life of its own. It seemed now to play itself, he and his fellow actors aiding it with their parts. When the curtain fell on the last scene he heard the void filled with applause and, through a rift in the side scene, saw the simple body before which he had acted magically deformed, the void of faces breaking at all points and falling asunder into busy groups.

He left the stage quickly and rid himself of his mummery and passed out through the chapel into the college garden. Now that the play was over his nerves cried for some further adventure. He hurried onwards as if to overtake it. The doors of the theatre were all open and the audience had emptied out. On the lines which he had fancied the moorings of an ark a few lanterns swung in the night breeze, flickering cheerlessly. He mounted the steps from the garden in haste, eager that some prey should not elude him, and forced his way through the crowd in the hall and past the two jesuits who stood watching the exodus and bowing and shaking hands with the visitors. He pushed onward nervously, feigning a still greater haste and faintly conscious of the smiles and stares and nudges which his powdered head left in its wake.

When he came out on the steps he saw his family waiting for him at the first lamp. In a glance he noted that every figure of the group was familiar and ran down the steps angrily.

—I have to leave a message down in George's Street, he said to his father quickly. I'll be home after you.

Without waiting for his father's questions he ran across the road and began to walk at breakneck speed down the hill. He hardly knew where he was walking. Pride and hope and desire like crushed herbs in his heart sent up vapours of maddening incense before the eyes of his mind. He strode down the hill amid the tumult of suddenrisen vapours of wounded pride and fallen hope and baffled desire. They streamed upwards before his anguished eyes in dense and maddening fumes and passed away above him till at last the air was clear and cold again.

A film still veiled his eyes but they burned no longer. A power, akin to that which had often made anger or resentment fall from him, brought his steps to rest. He stood still and gazed up at the sombre porch of the morgue and from that to the dark cobbled laneway at its side. He saw the word *Lotts* on the wall of the lane and breathed slowly the rank heavy air.

—That is horse piss and rotted straw, he thought. It is a good odour to breathe. It will calm my heart. My heart is quite calm now. I will go back.

*   *   *

Stephen was once again seated beside his father in the corner of a railway carriage at Kingsbridge. He was travelling with his father by the night mail to Cork. As the train steamed out of the station he recalled his childish wonder of years before and every event of his first day at Clongowes. But he felt no wonder now. He saw the darkening lands slipping past him, the silent telegraphpoles passing his window swiftly every four seconds, the little glimmering stations, manned by a few silent sentries, flung by the mail behind her and twinkling for a moment in the darkness like fiery grains flung backwards by a runner.

He listened without sympathy to his father's evocation of Cork and of scenes of his youth, a tale broken by sighs or draughts from his pocketflask whenever the image of some dead friend appeared in it or whenever the evoker remembered suddenly the purpose of his actual visit. Stephen heard but could feel no pity. The images of the dead were all strange to him save that of uncle Charles, an image which had lately been fading out of memory. He knew, however, that his father's property was going to be sold by auction and in the manner of his own dispossession he felt the world give the lie rudely to his phantasy.

At Maryborough he fell asleep. When he awoke the train had passed out of Mallow and his father was stretched asleep on the other seat. The cold light of the dawn lay over the country, over the unpeopled fields and the closed cottages. The terror of sleep fascinated his mind as he watched the silent country or heard from time to time his father's deep breath or sudden sleepy movement. The neighbourhood of unseen sleepers filled him with strange dread as though they could harm him; and he prayed that the day might come quickly. His prayer, addressed neither to God nor saint, began with a shiver, as the chilly morning breeze crept through the chink of the carriage door to his feet, and ended in a trail of foolish words which he made to fit the insistent rhythm of the train; and silently, at intervals of four seconds, the telegraphpoles held the galloping notes of the music between punctual bars. This furious music allayed his dread and, leaning against the windowledge, he let his eyelids close again.

They drove in a jingle across Cork while it was still early morning and Stephen finished his sleep in a bedroom of the Victoria Hotel. The bright warm sunlight was streaming through the window and he could hear the din of traffic. His father was standing before the dressingtable, examining his hair and face and moustache with great care, craning his neck across the waterjug and drawing it back sideways to see the better. While he did so he sang softly to himself with quaint accent and phrasing:

> 'Tis youth and folly
> Makes young men marry,
> So here, my love, I'll
>   No longer stay.
> What can't be cured, sure,
> Must be injured, sure,
>   So I'll go to
>   Amerikay.
>
> My love she's handsome,
> My love she's bonny:
> She's like good whisky
>   When it is new;
> But when 'tis old
> And growing cold
> It fades and dies like
>   The mountain dew.

The consciousness of the warm sunny city outside his window and the tender tremors with which his father's voice festooned the strange sad happy air, drove off all the mists of the night's ill humour from Stephen's brain. He got up quickly to dress and, when the song had ended, said:

—That's much prettier than any of your other *come-all-yous.*

—Do you think so? asked Mr Dedalus.

—I like it, said Stephen.

—It's a pretty old air, said Mr Dedalus, twirling the points of his moustache. Ah, but you should have heard Mick Lacy sing it! Poor Mick Lacy! He had little turns for it, grace notes he used to put in that I haven't got. That was the boy who could sing a *come-all-you,* if you like.

Mr Dedalus had ordered drisheens for breakfast and during the meal he crossexamined the waiter for local news. For the most part they spoke at crosspurposes when a name was mentioned, the waiter having in mind the present holder and Mr Dedalus his father or perhaps his grandfather.

—Well, I hope they haven't moved the Queen's College anyhow, said Mr Dedalus, for I want to show it to this youngster of mine.

Along the Mardyke the trees were in bloom. They entered the grounds of the college and were led by the garrulous porter across the quadrangle. But their progress across the gravel was brought to a halt after every dozen or so paces by some reply of the porter's.

—Ah, do you tell me so? And is poor Pottlebelly dead?

—Yes, sir. Dead, sir.

During these halts Stephen stood awkwardly behind the two men, weary of the subject and waiting restlessly for the slow march to begin again. By the time they had crossed the quadrangle his restlessness had risen to fever. He wondered how his father, whom he knew for a shrewd suspicious man, could be duped by the servile manners of the porter; and the lively southern speech which had entertained him all the morning now irritated his ears.

They passed into the anatomy theatre where Mr Dedalus, the porter aiding him, searched the desks for his initials. Stephen remained in the background, depressed more than ever by the darkness and silence of the theatre and by the air it wore of jaded and formal study. On the desk before him he read the word *Fœtus* cut several times in the dark stained wood. The sudden legend startled his blood: he seemed to feel the absent students of the college about him and to shrink from their company. A vision of their life, which his father's words had been powerless to evoke, sprang up before him out of the word cut in the desk. A broadshouldered student with a moustache was cutting in the letters with a jackknife, seriously. Other students stood or sat near him laughing at his handiwork. One jogged his elbow. The big student turned on him, frowning. He was dressed in loose grey clothes and had tan boots.

Stephen's name was called. He hurried down the steps of the theatre so as to be as far away from the vision as he could be and, peering closely at his father's initials, hid his flushed face.

But the word and the vision capered before his eyes as he walked back across the quadrangle and towards the college gate. It shocked him to find in the outer world a trace of what he had deemed till then a brutish and individual malady of his own mind. His recent monstrous reveries came thronging into his memory. They too had sprung up before him, suddenly and furiously, out of mere words. He had soon given in to them and allowed them to sweep across and abase his intellect, wondering always where they came from, from what den of monstrous images, and always weak and humble towards others, restless and sickened of himself when they had swept over him.

—Ay, bedad! And there's the Groceries sure enough! cried Mr Dedalus. You often heard me speak of the Groceries, didn't you, Stephen. Many's the time we went down there when our names had been marked, a crowd of us, Harry Peard and little Jack Mountain and Bob Dyas and Maurice Moriarty, the Frenchman, and Tom O'Grady and Mick Lacy that I told you of this morning and Joey Corbet and poor little good hearted Johnny Keevers of the Tantiles.

The leaves of the trees along the Mardyke were astir and whispering in the sunlight. A team of cricketers passed, agile young men in flannels and blazers, one of them carrying the long green wicketbag. In a quiet bystreet a German band of five players in faded uniforms and with battered brass instruments was playing to an audience of street arabs and leisurely messenger boys. A maid in a white cap and apron was watering a box of plants on a sill which shone like a slab of limestone in the warm glare. From another window open to the air came the sound of a piano, scale after scale rising into the treble.

Stephen walked on at his father's side, listening to stories he had heard before, hearing again the names of the scattered and dead revellers who had been the companions of his father's youth. And a faint sickness sighed in his heart. He recalled his own equivocal position in Belvedere, a free boy, a leader afraid of his own authority, proud and sensitive and suspicious, battling against the squalor of his life and against the riot of his mind. The letters cut in the stained wood of the desk stared upon him, mocking his bodily weakness and futile enthusiasms and making him loathe himself for his own mad and filthy orgies. The spittle in his throat grew bitter and foul to swallow and the faint sickness climbed to his brain so that for a moment he closed his eyes and walked on in darkness.

He could still hear his father's voice.

—When you kick out for yourself, Stephen—as I daresay you will one of these days—remember, whatever you do, to mix with gentlemen. When I was a young fellow I tell you I enjoyed myself. I mixed with fine decent fellows. Everyone of us could do something. One fellow had a good voice, another fellow was a good actor, another could sing a good comic song, another was a good oarsman or a good racketplayer, another could tell a good story and so on. We kept the ball rolling anyhow and enjoyed ourselves and saw a bit of life and we were none the worse of it either. But we were all gentlemen, Stephen—at least I hope we were—and bloody good honest Irishmen too. That's the kind of fellows I want you to associate with, fellows of the right kidney. I'm talking to you as a friend, Stephen. I don't believe in playing the stern father. I don't believe a son should be afraid of his father. No, I treat you as your grandfather treated me when I was a young chap. We were more like brothers than father and son. I'll never forget the first day he caught me smoking. I was standing at the end of the South Terrace one day with some maneens like myself and sure we thought we were grand fellows because we had pipes stuck in the corners of our mouths. Suddenly the governor passed. He didn't say a word, or stop even. But the next day, Sunday, we were out for a walk together and when we were coming home he took out his cigar case and said: *By the bye, Simon, I didn't know you smoked:* or something like that. Of course I tried to carry it off as best I could. *If you want a good smoke*, he said, *try one of these cigars. An American captain made me a present of them last night in Queenstown.*

Stephen heard his father's voice break into a laugh which was almost a sob.

—He was the handsomest man in Cork at that time, by God he was! The women used to stand to look after him in the street.

He heard the sob passing loudly down his father's throat and opened his eyes with a nervous impulse. The sunlight breaking suddenly on his sight turned the sky and clouds into a fantastic world of sombre masses with lakelike spaces of dark rosy light. His very brain was sick and powerless. He could scarcely interpret the letters of the signboards of the shops. By his monstrous way of life he seemed to have put himself beyond the limits of reality. Nothing moved him or spoke to him from the real world unless he heard in it an echo of the infuriated cries within him. He could respond to no earthly or human appeal, dumb and insensible to the call of summer and gladness and companionship, wearied and dejected by his father's voice. He could scarcely recognise as his his own thoughts, and repeated slowly to himself:

—I am Stephen Dedalus. I am walking beside my father whose name is Simon Dedalus. We are in Cork, in Ireland. Cork is a city.

Our room is in the Victoria Hotel. Victoria and Stephen and Simon. Simon and Stephen and Victoria. Names.

The memory of his childhood suddenly grew dim. He tried to call forth some of its vivid moments but could not. He recalled only names: Dante, Parnell, Clane, Clongowes. A little boy had been taught geography by an old woman who kept two brushes in her wardrobe. Then he had been sent away from home to a college. In the college he had made his first communion and eaten slim jim out of his cricketcap and watched the firelight leaping and dancing on the wall of a little bedroom in the infirmary and dreamed of being dead, of mass being said for him by the rector in a black and gold cope, of being buried then in the little graveyard of the community off the main avenue of limes. But he had not died then. Parnell had died. There had been no mass for the dead in the chapel and no procession. He had not died but he had faded out like a film in the sun. He had been lost or had wandered out of existence for he no longer existed. How strange to think of him passing out of existence in such a way, not by death but by fading out in the sun or by being lost and forgotten somewhere in the universe! It was strange to see his small body appear again for a moment: a little boy in a grey belted suit. His hands were in his sidepockets and his trousers were tucked in at the knees by elastic bands.

On the evening of the day on which the property was sold Stephen followed his father meekly about the city from bar to bar. To the sellers in the market, to the barmen and barmaids, to the beggars who importuned him for a lob Mr Dedalus told the same tale, that he was an old Corkonian, that he had been trying for thirty years to get rid of his Cork accent up in Dublin and that Peter Pickackafax beside him was his eldest son but that he was only a Dublin jackeen.

They had set out early in the morning from Newcombe's coffeehouse, where Mr Dedalus' cup had rattled noisily against its saucer, and Stephen had tried to cover that shameful sign of his father's drinkingbout of the night before by moving his chair and coughing. One humiliation had succeeded another: the false smiles of the market sellers, the curvettings and oglings of the barmaids with whom his father flirted, the compliments and encouraging words of his father's friends. They had told him that he had a great look of his grandfather and Mr Dedalus had agreed that he was an ugly likeness. They had unearthed traces of a Cork accent in his speech and made him admit that the Lee was a much finer river than the Liffey. One of them in order to put his Latin to the proof had made him translate short passages from Dilectus and asked him whether it was correct to say: *Tempora mutantur nos et mutamur in illis* or *Tempora mutantur et nos mutamur in illis*. Another, a brisk old man, whom Mr Dedalus called Johnny Cashman, had covered him with confusion by asking him to say which were prettier, the Dublin girls or the Cork girls.

—He's not that way built, said Mr Dedalus. Leave him alone. He's a levelheaded thinking boy who doesn't bother his head about that kind of nonsense.

—Then he's not his father's son, said the little old man.

—I don't know, I'm sure, said Mr Dedalus, smiling complacently.

—Your father, said the little old man to Stephen, was the boldest flirt in the city of Cork in his day. Do you know that?

Stephen looked down and studied the tiled floor of the bar into which they had drifted.

—Now don't be putting ideas into his head, said Mr Dedalus. Leave him to his Maker.

—Yerra, sure I wouldn't put any ideas into his head. I'm old enough to be his grandfather. And I am a grandfather, said the little old man to Stephen. Do you know that?

—Are you? asked Stephen.

—Bedad I am, said the little old man. I have two bouncing grandchildren out at Sunday's Well. Now then! What age do you think I am? And I remember seeing your grandfather in his red coat riding out to hounds. That was before you were born.

—Ay, or thought of, said Mr Dedalus.

—Bedad I did, repeated the little old man. And, more than that, I can remember even your greatgrandfather, old John Stephen Dedalus, and a fierce old fireeater he was. Now then! There's a memory for you!

—That's three generations—four generations, said another of the company. Why, Johnny Cashman, you must be nearing the century.

—Well, I'll tell you the truth, said the little old man. I'm just twentyseven years of age.

—We're as old as we feel, Johnny, said Mr Dedalus. And just finish what you have there and we'll have another. Here, Tim or

Tom or whatever your name is, give us the same again here. By God, I don't feel more than eighteen myself. There's that son of mine there not half my age and I'm a better man than he is any day of the week.

—Draw it mild now, Dedalus. I think it's time for you to take a back seat, said the gentleman who had spoken before.

—No, by God! asserted Mr Dedalus. I'll sing a tenor song against him or I'll vault a fivebarred gate against him or I'll run with him after the hounds across the country as I did thirty years ago along with the Kerry Boy and the best man for it.

—But he'll beat you here, said the little old man, tapping his forehead and raising his glass to drain it.

—Well, I hope he'll be as good a man as his father. That's all I can say, said Mr Dedalus.

—If he is, he'll do, said the little old man.

—And thanks be to God, Johnny, said Mr Dedalus, that we lived so long and did so little harm.

—But did so much good, Simon, said the little old man gravely. Thanks be to God we lived so long and did so much good.

Stephen watched the three glasses being raised from the counter as his father and his two cronies drank to the memory of their past. An abyss of fortune or of temperament sundered him from them. His mind seemed older than theirs: it shone coldly on their strifes and happiness and regrets like a moon upon a younger earth. No life or youth stirred in him as it had stirred in them. He had known neither the pleasure of companionship with others nor the vigour of rude male health nor filial piety. Nothing stirred within his soul but a cold and cruel and loveless lust. His childhood was dead or lost and with it his soul capable of simple joys, and he was drifting amid life like the barren shell of the moon.

> *Art thou pale for weariness*
> *Of climbing heaven and gazing on the earth,*
> *Wandering companionless . . .?*

He repeated to himself the lines of Shelley's fragment. Its alternation of sad human ineffectualness with vast inhuman cycles of activity chilled him and he forgot his own human and ineffectual grieving.

*   *   *

Stephen's mother and his brother and one of his cousins waited at the corner of quiet Foster Place while he and his father went up the steps and along the colonnade where the highland sentry was parading. When they had passed into the great hall and stood at the counter Stephen drew forth his orders on the governor of the bank of Ireland for thirty and three pounds; and these sums, the moneys of his exhibition and essay prize, were paid over to him rapidly by the teller in notes and in coin respectively. He bestowed them in his pockets with feigned composure and suffered the friendly teller, to whom his father chatted, to take his hand across the broad counter and wish him a brilliant career in after life. He was impatient of their voices and could not keep his feet at rest. But the teller still deferred the serving of others to say he was living in changed times and that there was nothing like giving a boy the best education that money could buy. Mr Dedalus lingered in the hall gazing about him and up at the roof and telling Stephen, who urged him to come out, that they were standing in the house of commons of the old Irish parliament.

—God help us! he said piously, to think of the men of those times, Stephen, Hely Hutchinson and Flood and Henry Grattan and Charles Kendal Bushe, and the noblemen we have now, leaders of the Irish people at home and abroad. Why, by God, they wouldn't be seen dead in a tenacre field with them. No, Stephen, old chap, I'm sorry to say that they are only as I roved out one fine May morning in the merry month of sweet July.

A keen October wind was blowing round the bank. The three figures standing at the edge of the muddy path had pinched cheeks and watery eyes. Stephen looked at his thinly clad mother and remembered that a few days before he had seen a mantle priced at twenty guineas in the windows of Barnardo's.

—Well that's done, said Mr Dedalus.

—We had better go to dinner, said Stephen. Where?

—Dinner? said Mr Dedalus. Well, I suppose we had better, what?

—Some place that's not too dear, said Mrs Dedalus.

—Underdone's?

—Yes. Some quiet place.

—Come along, said Stephen quickly. It doesn't matter about the dearness.

He walked on before them with short nervous steps, smiling. They tried to keep up with him, smiling also at his eagerness.

—Take it easy like a good young fellow, said his father. We're not out for the half mile, are we?

For a swift season of merrymaking the money of his prizes ran through Stephen's fingers. Great parcels of groceries and delicacies and dried fruits arrived from the city. Every day he drew up a bill of fare for the family and every night led a party of three or four to the theatre to see *Ingomar* or *The Lady of Lyons*. In his coat pockets he carried squares of Vienna chocolate for his guests while his trousers' pockets bulged with masses of silver and copper coins. He bought presents for everyone, overhauled his room, wrote out resolutions, marshalled his books up and down their shelves, pored upon all kinds of price lists, drew up a form of commonwealth for the household by which every member of it held some office, opened a loan bank for his family and pressed loans on willing borrowers so that he might have the pleasure of making out receipts and reckoning the interests on the sums lent. When he could do no more he drove up and down the city in trams. Then the season of pleasure came to an end. The pot of pink enamel paint gave out and the wainscot of his bedroom remained with its unfinished and illplastered coat.

His household returned to its usual way of life. His mother had no further occasion to upbraid him for squandering his money. He too returned to his old life at school and all his novel enterprises fell to pieces. The commonwealth fell, the loan bank closed its coffers and its books on a sensible loss, the rules of life which he had drawn about himself fell into desuetude.

How foolish his aim had been! He had tried to build a breakwater of order and elegance against the sordid tide of life without him and to dam up, by rules of conduct and active interests and new filial relations, the powerful recurrence of the tides within him. Useless. From without as from within the water had flowed over his barriers: their tides began once more to jostle fiercely above the crumbled mole.

He saw clearly too his own futile isolation. He had not gone one step nearer the lives he had sought to approach nor bridged the restless shame and rancour that divided him from mother and brother and sister. He felt that he was hardly of the one blood with them but stood to them rather in the mystical kinship of fosterage, fosterchild and fosterbrother.

He burned to appease the fierce longings of his heart before which everything else was idle and alien. He cared little that he was in mortal sin, that his life had grown to be a tissue of subterfuge and falsehood. Beside the savage desire within him to realise the enormities which he brooded on nothing was sacred. He bore cynically with the shameful details of his secret riots in which he exulted to defile with patience whatever image had attracted his eyes. By day and by night he moved among distorted images of the outer world. A figure that had seemed to him by day demure and innocent came towards him by night through the winding darkness of sleep, her face transfigured by a lecherous cunning, her eyes bright with brutish joy. Only the morning pained him with its dim memory of dark orgiastic riot, its keen and humiliating sense of transgression.

He returned to his wanderings. The veiled autumnal evenings led him from street to street as they had led him years before along the quiet avenues of Blackrock. But no vision of trim front gardens or of kindly lights in the windows poured a tender influence upon him now. Only at times, in the pauses of his desire, when the luxury that was wasting him gave room to a softer languor, the image of Mercedes traversed the background of his memory. He saw again the small white house and the garden of rosebushes on the road that led to the mountains and he remembered the sadly proud gesture of refusal which he was to make there, standing with her in the moonlit garden after years of estrangement and adventure. At those moments the soft speeches of Claude Melnotte rose to his lips and eased his unrest. A tender premonition touched him of the tryst he had then looked forward to and, in spite of the horrible reality which lay between his hope of then and now, of the holy encounter he had then imagined at which weakness and timidity and inexperience were to fall from him.

Such moments passed and the wasting fires of lust sprang up again. The verses passed from his lips and the inarticulate cries and the unspoken brutal words rushed forth from his brain to force a passage. His blood was in revolt. He wandered up and down the dark slimy streets peering into the gloom of lanes and doorways, listening eagerly for any sound. He moaned to himself like some baffled prowling beast. He wanted to sin with another of his kind, to force another being to sin with him and to exult with her in sin. He felt some dark presence moving irresistibly upon him from the darkness, a presence subtle and murmurous as a flood filling him wholly with itself. Its murmur besieged his ears like the murmur of some multitude in sleep; its subtle streams penetrated his being. His hands clenched convulsively and his teeth set together as he suffered the agony of its penetration. He stretched out his arms in the street to hold fast the frail swooning form that eluded him and incited him: and the cry that he had strangled for so long in his throat issued from his lips. It broke from him like a wail of despair from a hell of sufferers and died in a wail of furious entreaty, a cry for an iniquitous abandonment, a cry which was but the echo of an obscene scrawl which he had read on the oozing wall of a urinal.

He had wandered into a maze of narrow and dirty streets. From the foul laneways he heard bursts of hoarse riot and wrangling and the drawling of drunken singers. He walked onward, undismayed, wondering whether he had strayed into the quarter of the jews. Women and girls dressed in long vivid gowns traversed the street from house to house. They were leisurely and perfumed. A trembling seized him and his eyes grew dim. The yellow gasflames arose before his troubled vision against the vapoury sky, burning as if before an altar. Before the doors and in the lighted halls groups were gathered arrayed as for some rite. He was in another world: he had awakened from a slumber of centuries.

He stood still in the middle of the roadway, his heart clamouring against his bosom in a tumult. A young woman dressed in a long pink gown laid her hand on his arm to detain him and gazed into his face. She said gaily:

—Goodnight, Willie dear!

Her room was warm and lightsome. A huge doll sat with her legs apart in the copious easychair beside the bed. He tried to bid his tongue speak that he might seem at ease, watching her as she undid her gown, noting the proud conscious movements of her perfumed head.

As he stood silent in the middle of the room she came over to him and embraced him gaily and gravely. Her round arms held him firmly to her and he, seeing her face lifted to him in serious calm and feeling the warm calm rise and fall of her breast, all but burst into hysterical weeping. Tears of joy and relief shone in his delighted eyes and his lips parted though they would not speak.

She passed her tinkling hand through his hair, calling him a little rascal.

—Give me a kiss, she said.

His lips would not bend to kiss her. He wanted to be held firmly in her arms, to be caressed slowly, slowly, slowly. In her arms he felt that he had suddenly become strong and fearless and sure of himself. But his lips would not bend to kiss her.

With a sudden movement she bowed his head and joined her lips to his and he read the meaning of her movements in her frank uplifted eyes. It was too much for him. He closed his eyes, surrendering himself to her, body and mind, conscious of nothing in the world but the dark pressure of her softly parting lips. They pressed upon his brain as upon his lips as though they were the vehicle of a vague speech; and between them he felt an unknown and timid pressure, darker than the swoon of sin, softer than sound or odour.

THE swift December dusk had come tumbling clownishly after its dull day and, as he stared through the dull square of the window of the schoolroom, he felt his belly crave for its food. He hoped there would be stew for dinner, turnips and carrots and bruised potatoes and fat mutton pieces to be ladled out in thick peppered flour-fattened sauce. Stuff it into you, his belly counselled him.

It would be a gloomy secret night. After early nightfall the yellow lamps would light up, here and there, the squalid quarter of the brothels. He would follow a devious course up and down the streets, circling always nearer and nearer in a tremor of fear and joy, until his feet led him suddenly round a dark corner. The whores would be just coming out of their houses making ready for the night, yawning lazily after their sleep and settling the hairpins in their clusters of hair. He would pass by them calmly waiting for a sudden movement of his own will or a sudden call to his sinloving soul from their soft perfumed flesh. Yet as he prowled in quest of that call, his senses, stultified only by his desire, would note keenly all that wounded or shamed them; his eyes, a ring of porter froth on a clothless table or a photograph of two soldiers standing to attention or a gaudy playbill; his ears, the drawling jargon of greeting:

—Hello, Bertie, any good in your mind?

—Is that you, pigeon?

—Number ten. Fresh Nelly is waiting on you.

—Goodnight, husband! Coming in to have a short time?

The equation on the page of his scribbler began to spread out a widening tail, eyed and starred like a peacock's; and, when the eyes and stars of its indices had been eliminated, began slowly to fold itself together again. The indices appearing and disappearing were eyes opening and closing; the eyes opening and closing were stars being born and being quenched. The vast cycle of starry life bore his weary mind outward to its verge and inward to its centre, a distant music accompanying him outward and inward. What music? The music came nearer and he recalled the words, the words of Shelley's fragment upon the moon wandering companionless, pale for weariness. The stars began to crumble and a cloud of fine stardust fell through space.

The dull light fell more faintly upon the page whereon another equation began to unfold itself slowly and to spread abroad its widening tail. It was his own soul going forth to experience, unfolding itself sin by sin, spreading abroad the balefire of its burning stars and folding back upon itself, fading slowly, quenching its own lights and fires. They were quenched: and the cold darkness filled chaos.

A cold lucid indifference reigned in his soul. At his first violent sin he had felt a wave of vitality pass out of him and had feared to find his body or his soul maimed by the excess. Instead the vital wave had carried him on its bosom out of himself and back again when it receded: and no part of body or soul had been maimed but a dark peace had been established between them. The chaos in which his ardour extinguished itself was a cold indifferent knowledge of himself. He had sinned mortally not once but many times and he knew that, while he stood in danger of eternal damnation for the first sin alone, by every succeeding sin he multiplied his guilt and his punishment. His days and works and thoughts could make no atonement for him, the fountains of sanctifying grace having ceased to refresh his soul. At most, by an alms given to a beggar whose blessing he fled from, he might hope wearily to win for himself some measure of actual grace. Devotion had gone by the board. What did it avail to pray when he knew that his soul lusted after its own destruction? A certain pride, a certain awe, withheld him from offering to God even one prayer at night though he knew it was in God's power to take away his life while he slept and hurl his soul hellward ere he could beg for mercy. His pride in his own sin, his loveless awe of God, told him that his offence was too grievous to be atoned for in whole or in part by a false homage to the Allseeing and Allknowing.

—Well now, Ennis, I declare you have a head and so has my stick! Do you mean to say that you are not able to tell me what a surd is?

The blundering answer stirred the embers of his contempt of his fellows. Towards others he felt neither shame nor fear. On Sunday mornings as he passed the churchdoor he glanced coldly at the worshippers who stood bareheaded, four deep, outside the church, morally present at the mass which they could neither see nor near. Their dull piety and the sickly smell of the cheap hairoil with which they had anointed their heads repelled him from the altar they prayed at. He stooped to the evil of hypocrisy with others, sceptical of their innocence which he could cajole so easily.

On the wall of his bedroom hung an illuminated scroll, the certificate of his prefecture in the college of the sodality of the Blessed Virgin Mary. On Saturday mornings when the sodality met in the chapel to recite the little office his place was a cushioned kneelingdesk at the right of the altar from which he led his wing of boys through the responses. The falsehood of his position did not pain him. If at moments he felt an impulse to rise from his post of honour and, confessing before them all his unworthiness, to leave the chapel, a glance at their faces restrained him. The imagery of the psalms of prophecy soothed his barren pride. The glories of Mary held his soul captive: spikenard and myrrh and frankincense, symbolising the preciousness of God's gifts to her soul, rich garments, symbolising her royal lineage, her emblems, the lateflowering plant and lateblossoming tree, symbolising the agelong gradual growth of her cultus among men. When it fell to him to read the lesson towards the close of the office he read it in a veiled voice, lulling his conscience to its music.

Quasi cedrus exaltata sum in Libanon et quasi cupressus in monte Sion. Quasi palma exaltata sum in Gades et quasi plantatio rosae in Jericho. Quasi uliva speciosa in campis et quasi platanus exaltata sum juxta aquam in plateis. Sicut cinnamomum et balsamum aromatizans odorem dedi et quasi myrrha electa dedi suavitatem odoris.

His sin, which had covered him from the sight of God, had led him nearer to the refuge of sinners. Her eyes seemed to regard him with mild pity; her holiness, a strange light glowing faintly upon her frail flesh, did not humiliate the sinner who approached her. If ever he was impelled to cast sin from him and to repent the impulse that moved him was the wish to be her knight. If ever his soul, reentering her dwelling shyly after the frenzy of his body's lust had spent itself, was turned towards her whose emblem is the morning star, *bright and musical, telling of heaven and infusing peace*, it was when her names were murmured softly by lips whereon there still lingered foul and shameful words, the savour itself of a lewd kiss.

That was strange. He tried to think how it could be but the dusk, deepening in the schoolroom, covered over his thoughts. The bell rang. The master marked the sums and cuts to be done for the next lesson and went out. Heron, beside Stephen, began to hum tunelessly.

My excellent friend Bombados.

Ennis, who had gone to the yard, came back, saying:

— The boy from the house is coming up for the rector.

A tall boy behind Stephen rubbed his hands and said:

— That's game ball. We can scut the whole hour. He won't be in till after half two. Then you can ask him questions on the catechism, Dedalus.

Stephen, leaning back and drawing idly on his scribbler, listened to the talk about him which Heron checked from time to time by saying:

— Shut up, will you. Don't make such a bally racket!

It was strange too that he found an arid pleasure in following up to the end the rigid lines of the doctrines of the church and penetrating into obscure silences only to hear and feel the more deeply his own condemnation. The sentence of saint James which says that he who offends against one commandment becomes guilty of all had seemed to him first a swollen phrase until he had begun to grope in the darkness of his own state. From the evil seed of lust all other deadly sins had sprung forth: pride in himself and contempt of others, covetousness in using money for the purchase of unlawful pleasure, envy of those whose vices he could not reach to and calumnious murmuring against the pious, gluttonous enjoyment of food, the dull glowering anger amid which he brooded upon his longing, the swamp of spiritual and bodily sloth in which his whole being had sunk.

As he sat in his bench gazing calmly at the rector's shrewd harsh face his mind wound itself in and out of the curious questions proposed to it. If a man had stolen a pound in his youth and had used that pound to amass a huge fortune how much was he obliged to give back, the pound he had stolen only or the pound together with the compound interest accruing upon it or all his huge fortune? If a layman in giving baptism pour the water before saying the words is the child baptised? Is baptism with a mineral water valid? How comes it that while the first beatitude promises the kingdom of heaven to the poor of heart the second beatitude promises also to the meek that they shall possess the land? Why was the sacrament of the eucharist instituted under the two species of bread and wine if Jesus Christ be present body and blood, soul and divinity, in the bread alone and in the wine alone? Does a tiny particle of the consecrated bread contain all the body and blood of Jesus Christ or a part only of the body and blood? If the wine change into vinegar and the host crumble into corruption after they have been consecrated is Jesus Christ still present under their species as God and as man?

—Here he is! Here he is!

A boy from his post at the window had seen the rector come from the house. All the catechisms were opened and all heads bent upon them silently. The rector entered and took his seat on the dais. A gentle kick from the tall boy in the bench behind urged Stephen to ask a difficult question.

The rector did not ask for a catechism to hear the lesson from. He clasped his hands on the desk and said:

—The retreat will begin on Wednesday afternoon in honour of saint Francis Xavier whose feast day is Saturday. The retreat will go on from Wednesday to Friday. On Friday confession will be heard all the afternoon after beads. If any boys have special confessors perhaps it will be better for them not to change. Mass will be on Saturday morning at nine o'clock and general communion for the whole college. Saturday will be a free day. Sunday of course. But Saturday and Sunday being free days some boys might be inclined to think that Monday is a free day also. Beware of making that mistake. I think you, Lawless, are likely to make that mistake.

—I, sir? Why, sir?

A little wave of quiet mirth broke forth over the class of boys from the rector's grim smile. Stephen's heart began slowly to fold and fade with fear like a withering flower.

The rector went on gravely

—You are all familiar with the story of the life of saint Francis Xavier, I suppose, the patron of your college. He came of an old and illustrious Spanish family and you remember that he was one of the first followers of saint Ignatius. They met in Paris where Francis Xavier was professor of philosophy at the university. This young and brilliant nobleman and man of letters entered heart and soul into the ideas of our glorious founder and you know that he, at his own desire, was sent by saint Ignatius to preach to the Indians. He is called, as you know, the apostle of the Indies. He went from country to country in the east, from Africa to India, from India to Japan, baptising the people. He is said to have baptised as many as ten thousand idolaters in one month. It is said that his right arm had grown powerless from having been raised so often over the heads of those whom he baptised. He wished then to go to China to win still more souls for God but he died of fever on the island of Sancian. A great saint, saint Francis Xavier! A great soldier of God!

The rector paused and then, shaking his clasped hands before him, went on:

—He had the faith in him that moves mountains. Ten thousand souls won for God in a single month! That is a true conqueror, true to the motto of our order: *ad majorem Dei gloriam*! A saint who has great power in heaven, remember: power to intercede for us in our grief, power to obtain whatever we pray for if it be for the good of our souls, power above all to obtain for us the grace to repent if we be in sin. A great saint, saint Francis Xavier! A great fisher of souls!

He ceased to shake his clasped hands and, resting them against his forehead, looked right and left of them keenly at his listeners out of his dark stern eyes.

In the silence their dark fire kindled the dusk into a tawny glow. Stephen's heart had withered up like a flower of the desert that feels the simoom coming from afar.

* * *

—*Remember only thy last things and thou shalt not sin for ever*— words taken, my dear little brothers in Christ, from the book of Ecclesiastes, seventh chapter, fortieth verse. In the name of the Father and of the Son and of the Holy Ghost. Amen.

Stephen sat in the front bench of the chapel. Father Arnall sat at a table to the left of the altar. He wore about his shoulders a heavy cloak; his pale face was drawn and his voice broken with rheum. The figure of his old master, so strangely rearisen, brought back to Stephen's mind his life at Clongowes: the wide playgrounds, swarming with boys, the square ditch, the little cemetery off the main avenue of limes where he had dreamed of being buried, the firelight on the wall of the infirmary where he lay sick, the sorrowful face of Brother Michael. His soul, as these memories came back to him, became again a child's soul.

—We are assembled here today, my dear little brothers in Christ, for one brief moment far away from the busy bustle of the outer world to celebrate and to honour one of the greatest of saints, the apostle of the Indies, the patron saint also of your college, saint Francis Xavier. Year after year for much longer than any of you, my dear little boys, can remember or than I can remember the boys of this college have met in this very chapel to make their annual retreat before the feast day of their patron saint. Time has gone on and brought with it its changes. Even in the last few years what changes can most of you not remember? Many of the boys who sat in those front benches a few years ago are perhaps now in distant lands, in the burning tropics or immersed in professional duties or in seminaries or voyaging over the vast expanse of the deep or, it may be, already called by the great God to another life and to the rendering up of their stewardship. And still as the years roll by, bringing with them changes for good and bad, the memory of the great saint is honoured by the boys of his college who make every year their annual retreat on the days preceding the feast day set apart by our holy mother the church to transmit to all the ages the name and fame of one of the greatest sons of catholic Spain.

—Now what is the meaning of this word *retreat* and why is it allowed on all hands to be a most salutary practice for all who desire to lead before God and in the eyes of men a truly christian life? A retreat, my dear boys, signifies a withdrawal for a while from the cares of our life, the cares of this workaday world, in order to examine the state of our conscience, to reflect on the mysteries of holy religion and to understand better why we are here in this world. During these few days I intend to put before you some thoughts concerning the four last things. They are, as you know from your catechism, death, judgment, hell and heaven. We shall try to understand them fully during these few days so that we may derive from the understanding of them a lasting benefit to our souls. And remember, my dear boys, that we have been sent into this world for one thing and for one thing alone: to do God's holy will and to save our immortal souls. All else is worthless. One thing alone is needful, the salvation of one's soul. What doth it profit a man to gain the whole world if he suffer the loss of his immortal soul? Ah, my dear boys, believe me there is nothing in this wretched world that can make up for such a loss.

—I will ask you therefore, my dear boys, to put away from your minds during these few days all worldly thoughts, whether of study or pleasure or ambition, and to give all your attention to the state of your souls. I need hardly remind you that during the days of the retreat all boys are expected to preserve a quiet and pious demeanour and to shun all loud unseemly pleasure. The elder boys, of course, will see that this custom is not infringed and I look especially to the prefects and officers of the sodality of Our Blessed Lady and of the sodality of the holy angels to set a good example to their fellowstudents.

—Let us try, therefore, to make this retreat in honour of saint Francis with our whole heart and our whole mind. God's blessing will then be upon all your year's studies. But, above and beyond all, let this retreat be one to which you can look back in after years when maybe you are far from this college and among very different surroundings, to which you call look back with joy and thankfulness and give thanks to God for having granted you this occasion of laying the first foundation of a pious honourable zealous christian life. And if, as may so happen, there be at this moment in these benches any poor soul who has had the unutterable misfortune to lose God's holy grace and to fall into grievous sin I fervently trust and pray that this retreat may be the turningpoint in the life of that soul. I pray to God through the merits of its zealous servant Francis Xavier that such a soul may be led to sincere repentance and that the holy communion on saint Francis' day of this year may be a lasting covenant between God and that soul. For just and unjust, for saint and sinner alike, may this retreat be a memorable one.

—Help me, my dear little brothers in Christ. Help me by your pious attention, by your own devotion, by your outward demeanour. Banish from your minds all worldly thoughts and think only of the last things, death, judgment, hell and heaven. He who remembers these things, says Ecclesiastes, shall not sin for ever. He who remembers the last things will act and think with them always before his eyes. He will live a good life and die a good death, believing and knowing that, if he has sacrificed much in this earthly life, it will be given to him a hundredfold and a thousandfold more in the life to come, in the kingdom without end—a blessing, my dear boys, which I wish you from my heart, one and all, in the name of the Father and of the Son and of the Holy Ghost. Amen.

As he walked home with silent companions a thick fog seemed to compass his mind. He waited in stupor of mind till it should lift and reveal what it had hidden. He ate his dinner with surly appetite and, when the meal was over and the greasestrewn plates lay abandoned on the table, he rose and went to the window, clearing the thick scum from his mouth with his tongue and licking it from his lips. So he had sunk to the state of a beast that licks his chaps after meat. This was the end; and a faint glimmer of fear began to pierce the fog of his mind. He pressed his face against the pane of the window and gazed out into the darkening street. Forms passed this way and that through the dull light. And that was life. The letters of the name of Dublin lay heavily upon his mind, pushing one another surlily hither and thither with slow boorish insistence. His soul was fattening and congealing into a gross grease, plunging ever deeper in its dull fear into a sombre threatening dusk, while the body that was his stood, listless and dishonoured, gazing out of darkened eyes, helpless, perturbed and human for a bovine god to stare upon.

The next day brought death and judgment stirring his soul slowly from its listless despair. The faint glimmer of fear became a terror of spirit as the hoarse voice of the preacher blew death into his soul. He suffered its agony. He felt the deathchill touch the extremities and creep onward towards the heart, the film of death veiling the eyes, the bright centres of the brain extinguished one by one like lamps, the last sweat oozing upon the skin, the powerlessness of the dying limbs, the speech thickening and wandering and failing, the heart throbbing faintly and more faintly, all but vanquished, the breath, the poor breath, the poor helpless human spirit, sobbing and sighing, gurgling and rattling in the throat. No help! No help! He, he himself, his body to which he had yielded was dying. Into the grave with it! Nail it down into a wooden box, the corpse. Carry it out of the house on the shoulders of hirelings. Thrust it out of men's sight into a long hole in the ground, into the grave, to rot, to feed the mass of its creeping worms and to be devoured by scuttling plumpbellied rats.

And while the friends were still standing in tears by the bedside the soul of the sinner was judged. At the last moment of consciousness the whole earthly life passed before the vision of the soul and, ere it had time to reflect, the body had died and the soul stood terrified before the judgmentseat. God, who had long been merciful, would then be just. He had long been patient, pleading with the sinful soul, giving it time to repent, sparing it yet awhile. But that time had gone. Time was to sin and to enjoy, time was to scoff at God and at the warnings of His holy church, time was to defy His majesty, to disobey His commands, to hoodwink one's fellow men, to commit sin after sin and sin after sin and to hide one's corruption from the sight of men. But that time was over. Now it was God's turn: and He was not to be hoodwinked or deceived. Every sin would then come forth from its lurkingplace, the most rebellious against the divine will and the most degrading to our poor corrupt nature, the tiniest imperfection and the most heinous atrocity. What did it avail then to have been a great emperor, a great general, a marvellous inventor, the most learned of the learned? All were as one before the judgmentseat of God. He would reward the good and punish the wicked. One single instant was enough for the trial of a man's soul. One single instant after the body's death, the soul had been weighed in the balance. The particular judgment was over and the soul had passed to the abode of bliss or to the prison of purgatory or had been hurled howling into hell.

Nor was that all. God's justice had still to be vindicated before men: after the particular there still remained the general judgment. The last day had come. Doomsday was at hand. The stars of heaven were falling upon the earth like the figs cast by the figtree which the wind has shaken. The sun, the great luminary of the universe, had become as sackcloth of hair. The moon was bloodred. The firmament was as a scroll rolled away. The archangel Michael, the prince of the heavenly host, appeared glorious and terrible against the sky. With one foot on the sea and one foot on the land he blew from the archangelical trumpet the brazen death of time. The three blasts of the angel filled all the universe. Time is, time was but time shall be no more. At the last blast the souls of universal humanity throng towards the valley of Jehoshaphat, rich and poor, gentle and simple, wise and foolish, good and wicked. The soul of every human being that has ever existed, the souls of all those who shall yet be born, all the sons and daughters of Adam, all are assembled on that supreme day. And lo the supreme judge is coming! No longer the lowly Lamb of God, no longer the meek Jesus of Nazareth, no longer the Man of Sorrows, no longer the Good Shepherd, He is seen now coming upon the clouds, in great power and majesty, attended by nine choirs of angels, angels and archangels, principalities, powers and virtues, thrones and dominations, cherubim and seraphim, God

Omnipotent, God Everlasting. He speaks: and His voice is heard even at the farthest limits of space, even in the bottomless abyss. Supreme Judge, from His sentence there will be and can be no appeal. He calls the just to His side, bidding them enter into the kingdom, the eternity of bliss, prepared for them. The unjust He casts from Him, crying in His offended majesty: *Depart from me, ye cursed, into everlasting fire which was prepared for the devil and his angels.* O what agony then for the miserable sinners! Friend is torn apart from friend, children are torn from their parents, husbands from their wives. The poor sinner holds out his arms to those who were dear to him in this earthly world, to those whose simple piety perhaps he made a mock of, to those who counselled him and tried to lead him on the right path, to a kind brother, to a loving sister, to the mother and father who loved him so dearly. But it is too late: the just turn away from the wretched damned souls which now appear before the eyes of all in their hideous and evil character. O you hypocrites, O you whited sepulchres, O you who present a smooth smiling face to the world while your soul within is a foul swamp of sin, how will it fare with you in that terrible day?

And this day will come, shall come, must come; the day of death and the day of judgment. It is appointed unto man to die and after death the judgment. Death is certain. The time and manner are uncertain, whether from long disease or from some unexpected accident; the Son of God cometh at an hour when you little expect Him. Be therefore ready every moment, seeing that you may die at any moment. Death is the end of us all. Death and judgment, brought into the world by the sin of our first parents, are the dark portals that close our earthly existence, the portals that open into the unknown and the unseen, portals through which every soul must pass, alone, unaided save by its good works, without friend or brother or parent or master to help it, alone and trembling. Let that thought be ever before our minds and then we cannot sin. Death, a cause of terror to the sinner, is a blessed moment for him who has walked in the right path, fulfilling the duties of his station in life, attending to his morning and evening prayers, approaching the holy sacrament frequently and performing good and merciful works. For the pious and believing catholic, for the just man, death is no cause of terror. Was it not Addison, the great English writer, who, when on his deathbed, sent for the wicked young earl of Warwick to let him see how a christian can meet his end. He it is and he alone, the pious and believing christian, who can say in his heart:

> *O grave, where is thy victory?*
> *O death, where is thy sting?*

Every word of it was for him. Against his sin, foul and secret, the whole wrath of God was aimed. The preacher's knife had probed deeply into his diseased conscience and he felt now that his soul was festering in sin. Yes, the preacher was right. God's turn had come. Like a beast in its lair his soul had lain down in its own filth but the blasts of the angel's trumpet had driven him forth from the darkness of sin into the light. The words of doom cried by the angel shattered in an instant his presumptuous peace. The wind of the last day blew through his mind; his sins, the jeweleyed harlots of his imagination, fled before the hurricane, squeaking like mice in their terror and huddled under a mane of hair.

As he crossed the square, walking homeward, the light laughter of a girl reached his burning ear. The frail gay sound smote his heart more strongly than a trumpetblast, and, not daring to lift his eyes, he turned aside and gazed, as he walked, into the shadow of the tangled shrubs. Shame rose from his smitten heart and flooded his whole being. The image of Emma appeared before him and, under her eyes, the flood of shame rushed forth anew from his heart. If she knew to what his mind had subjected her or how his brutelike lust had torn and trampled upon her innocence! Was that boyish love? Was that chivalry? Was that poetry? The sordid details of his orgies stank under his very nostrils: the sootcoated packet of pictures which he had hidden in the flue of the fireplace and in the presence of whose shameless or bashful wantonness he lay for hours sinning in thought and deed; his monstrous dreams, peopled by apelike creatures and by harlots with gleaming jewel eyes; the foul long letters he had written in the joy of guilty confession and carried secretly for days and days only to throw them under cover of night among the grass in the corner of a field or beneath some hingeless door or in some niche in the hedges where a girl might come upon them as she walked by and read them secretly. Mad! Mad! Was it possible he had done these things? A cold sweat broke out upon his forehead as the foul memories condensed within his brain.

When the agony of shame had passed from him he tried to raise his soul from its abject powerlessness. God and the Blessed Virgin were too far from him: God was too great and stern and the Blessed Virgin too pure and holy. But he imagined that he stood near Emma in a wide land and, humbly and in tears, bent and kissed the elbow of her sleeve.

In the wide land under a tender lucid evening sky, a cloud drifting westward amid a pale green sea of heaven, they stood together, children that had erred. Their error had offended deeply God's majesty though it was the error of two children, but it had not offended her whose beauty *is not like earthly beauty, dangerous to look upon, but like the morning star which is its emblem, bright and musical*. The eyes were not offended which she turned upon them nor reproachful. She placed their hands together, hand in hand, and said, speaking to their hearts:

—Take hands, Stephen and Emma. It is a beautiful evening now in heaven. You have erred but you are always my children. It is one heart that loves another heart. Take hands together, my dear children, and you will be happy together and your hearts will love each other.

The chapel was flooded by the dull scarlet light that filtered through the lowered blinds; and through the fissure between the last blind and the sash a shaft of wan light entered like a spear and touched the embossed brasses of the candlesticks upon the altar that gleamed like the battleworn mail armour of angels.

Rain was falling on the chapel, on the garden, on the college. It would rain for ever, noiselessly. The water would rise inch by inch, covering the grass and shrubs, covering the trees and houses, covering the monuments and the mountain tops. All life would be choked off, noiselessly: birds, men, elephants, pigs, children: noiselessly floating corpses amid the litter of the wreckage of the world. Forty days and forty nights the rain would fall till the waters covered the face of the earth.

It might be. Why not?

—*Hell has enlarged its soul and opened its mouth without any limits*—words taken, my dear little brothers in Christ Jesus, from the book of Isaias, fifth chapter, fourteenth verse. In the name of the Father and of the Son and of the Holy Ghost. Amen.

The preacher took a chainless watch from a pocket within his soutane and, having considered its dial for a moment in silence, placed it silently before him on the table.

He began to speak in a quiet tone.

—Adam and Eve, my dear boys, were, as you know, our first parents and you will remember that they were created by God in order that the seats in heaven left vacant by the fall of Lucifer and his rebellious angel might be filled again. Lucifer, we are told, was a son of the morning, a radiant and mighty angel; yet he fell: he fell and there fell with him a third part of the host of heaven: he fell and was hurled with his rebellious angels into hell. What his sin was we cannot say. Theologians consider that it was the sin of pride, the sinful thought conceived in an instant: *non serviam: I will not serve.* That instant was his ruin. He offended the majesty of God by the sinful thought of one instant and God cast him out of heaven into hell for ever.

—Adam and Eve were then created by God and placed in Eden, in the plain of Damascus, that lovely garden resplendent with sunlight and colour, teeming with luxuriant vegetation. The fruitful earth gave them her bounty: beasts and birds were their willing servants: they knew not the ills our flesh is heir to, disease and poverty and death: all that a great and generous God could do for them was done. But there was one condition imposed on them by God: obedience to His word. They were not to eat of the fruit of the forbidden tree.

—Alas, my dear little boys, they too fell. The devil, once a shining angel, a son of the morning, now a foul fiend, came in the shape of a serpent, the subtlest of all the beasts of the field. He envied them. He, the fallen great one, could not bear to think that man, a being of clay, should possess the inheritance which he by his sin had forfeited for ever. He came to the woman, the weaker vessel, and poured the poison of his eloquence into her ear, promising her—O, the blasphemy of that promise!—that if she and Adam ate of the forbidden fruit they would become as gods, nay as God Himself. Eve yielded to the wiles of the archtempter. She ate the apple and gave it also to Adam who had not the moral courage to resist her. The poison tongue of Satan had done its work. They fell.

—And then the voice of God was heard in that garden, calling His creature man to account: and Michael, prince of the heavenly host, with a sword of flame in his hand appeared before the guilty pair and drove them forth from Eden into the world, the world of sickness and striving, of cruelty and disappointment, of labour and hardship, to earn their bread in the sweat of their brow. But even then how merciful was God! He took pity on our poor degraded parents and promised that in the fulness of time He would send down from heaven One who would redeem them, make them once more children of God and heirs to the kingdom of heaven: and that One, that Redeemer of fallen man, was to be God's only begotten Son, the Second Person of the Most Blessed Trinity, the Eternal Word.

—He came. He was born of a virgin pure, Mary the virgin mother. He was born in a poor cowhouse in Judea and lived as a humble carpenter for thirty years until the hour of His mission had come. And then, filled with love for men, He went forth and called to men to hear the new gospel.

—Did they listen? Yes, they listened but would not hear. He was seized and bound like a common criminal, mocked at as a fool, set aside to give place to a public robber, scourged with five thousand lashes, crowned with a crown of thorns, hustled through the streets by the jewish rabble and the Roman soldiery, stripped of His garments and hanged upon a gibbet and His side was pierced with a lance and from the wounded body of Our Lord water and blood issued continually.

—Yet even then, in that hour of supreme agony, Our Merciful Redeemer had pity for mankind. Yet even there, on the hill of Calvary, He founded the holy catholic church against which, it is promised, the gates of hell shall not prevail. He founded it upon the rock of ages and endowed it with His grace, with sacraments and sacrifice, and promised that if men would obey the word of His church they would still enter into eternal life but if, after all that had been done for them, they still persisted in their wickedness there remained for them an eternity of torment: hell.

The preacher's voice sank. He paused, joined his palms for an instant, parted them. Then he resumed:

—Now let us try for a moment to realise, as far as we can, the nature of that abode of the damned which the justice of an offended God has called into existence for the eternal punishment of sinners. Hell is a strait and dark and foulsmelling prison, an abode of demons and lost souls, filled with fire and smoke. The straitness of this prisonhouse is expressly designed by God to punish those who refused to be bound by His laws. In earthly prisons the poor captive has at least some liberty of movement, were it only within the four walls of his cell or in the gloomy yard of his prison. Not so in hell. There, by reason of the great number of the damned, the prisoners are heaped together in their awful prison, the walls of which are said to be four thousand miles thick: and the damned are so utterly bound and helpless that, as a blessed saint, saint Anselm, writes in his book on similitudes, they are not even able to remove from the eye a worm that gnaws it.

—They lie in exterior darkness. For, remember, the fire of hell gives forth no light. As, at the command of God, the fire of the Babylonian furnace lost its heat but not its light so, at the command of God, the fire of hell, while retaining the intensity of its heat, burns eternally in darkness. It is a neverending storm of darkness, dark flames and dark smoke of burning brimstone, amid which the bodies are heaped one upon another without even a glimpse of air. Of all the plagues with which the land of the Pharaohs was smitten one plague alone, that of darkness, was called horrible. What name, then, shall we give to the darkness of hell which is to last not for three days alone but for all eternity?

—The horror of this strait and dark prison is increased by its awful stench. All the filth of the world, all the offal and scum of the world, we are told, shall run there as to a vast reeking sewer when the terrible conflagration of the last day has purged the world. The brimstone too which burns there in such prodigious quantity fills all hell with its intolerable stench; and the bodies of the damned themselves exhale such a pestilential odour that as saint Bonaventure says, one of them alone would suffice to infect the whole world. The very air of this world, that pure element, becomes foul and unbreathable when it has been long enclosed. Consider then what must be the foulness of the air of hell. Imagine some foul and putrid corpse that has lain rotting and decomposing in the grave, a jellylike mass of liquid corruption. Imagine such a corpse a prey to flames, devoured by the fire of burning brimstone and giving off dense choking fumes of nauseous loathsome decomposition. And then imagine this sickening stench, multiplied a millionfold and a millionfold again from the millions upon millions of fetid carcasses massed together in the reeking darkness, a huge and rotting human fungus. Imagine all this and you will have some idea of the horror of the stench of hell.

—But this stench is not, horrible though it is, the greatest physical torment to which the damned are subjected. The torment of fire is the greatest torment to which the tyrant has ever subjected his fellowcreatures. Place your finger for a moment in the flame of a candle and you will feel the pain of fire. But our earthly fire was created by God for the benefit of man, to maintain in him the spark of life and to help him in the useful arts whereas the fire of hell is of another quality and was created by God to torture and punish the unrepentant sinner. Our earthly fire also consumes more or less rapidly according as the object which it attacks is more or less combustible so that human ingenuity has even succeeded in inventing chemical preparations to check or frustrate its action. But the sulphurous brimstone which burns in hell is a substance which is specially designed to burn for ever and for ever with unspeakable fury. Moreover our earthly fire destroys at the same time as it burns so that the more intense it is the shorter is its duration: but the fire of hell has this property that it preserves that which it burns and though it rages with incredible intensity it rages for ever.

—Our earthly fire again, no matter how fierce or widespread it may be, is always of a limited extent: but the lake of fire in hell is boundless, shoreless and bottomless, it is on record that the devil himself, when asked the question by a certain soldier, was obliged to confess that if a whole mountain were thrown into the burning ocean of hell it would be burned up in an instant like a piece of wax. And this terrible fire will not afflict the bodies of the damned only from without but each lost soul will be a hell unto itself, the boundless fire raging in its very vitals. O, how terrible is the lot of those wretched beings! The blood seethes and boils in the veins, the brains are boiling in the skull, the heart in the breast glowing and bursting, the bowels a redhot mass of burning pulp, the tender eyes flaming like molten balls.

—And yet what I have said as to the strength and quality and boundlessness of this fire is as nothing when compared to its intensity, an intensity which it has as being the instrument chosen by divine design for the punishment of soul and body alike. It is a fire which proceeds directly from the ire of God, working not of its own activity but as an instrument of divine vengeance. As the waters of baptism cleanse the soul with the body so do the fires of punishment torture the spirit with the flesh. Every sense of the flesh is tortured and every faculty of the soul therewith: the eyes with impenetrable utter darkness, the nose with noisome odours, the ears with yells and howls and execrations, the taste with foul matter, leprous corruption, nameless suffocating filth, the touch with redhot goads and spikes, with cruel tongues of flame. And through the several torments of the senses the immortal soul is tortured eternally in its very essence amid the leagues upon leagues of glowing fires kindled in the abyss by the offended majesty of the Omnipotent God and fanned into everlasting and ever increasing fury by the breath of the anger of the Godhead.

—Consider finally that the torment of this infernal prison is increased by the company of the damned themselves. Evil company on earth is so noxious that even the plants, as if by instinct, withdraw from the company of whatsoever is deadly or hurtful to them. In hell all laws are overturned: there is no thought of family or country, of ties, of relationships. The damned howl and scream at one another, their torture and rage intensified by the presence of beings tortured and raging like themselves. All sense of humanity is forgotten. The yells of the suffering sinners fill the remotest corners of the vast abyss. The mouths of the damned are full of blasphemies against God and of hatred for their fellowsufferers and of curses against those souls which were their accomplices in sin. In olden times it was the custom to punish the parricide, the man who had raised his murderous hand against his father, by casting him into the depths of the sea in a sack in which were placed a cock, a monkey and a serpent. The intention of those lawgivers who framed such a law, which seems cruel in our times, was to punish the criminal by the company of hateful and hurtful beasts. But what is the fury of those dumb beasts compared with the fury of execration which bursts from the parched lips and aching throats of the damned in hell when they behold in their companions in misery those who aided and abetted them in sin, those whose words sowed the first seeds of evil thinking and evil living in their minds, those whose immodest suggestions led them on to sin, those whose eyes tempted and lured them from the path of virtue. They turn upon those accomplices and upbraid them and curse them. But they are helpless and hopeless: it is too late now for repentance.

—Last of all consider the frightful torment to those damned souls, tempters and tempted alike, of the company of the devils. These devils will afflict the damned in two ways, by their presence and by their reproaches. We can have no idea of how horrible these devils are. Saint Catherine of Siena once saw a devil and she has written that, rather than look again for one single instant on such a frightful monster, she would prefer to walk until the end of her life along a track of red coals. These devils, who were once beautiful angels, have become as hideous and ugly as they once were beautiful. They mock and jeer at the lost souls whom they dragged down to ruin. It is they, the foul demons, who are made in hell the voices of conscience. Why did you sin? Why did you lend an ear to the temptings of fiends? Why did you turn aside from your pious practices and good works? Why did you not shun the occasions of sin? Why did you not leave that evil companion? Why did you not give up that lewd habit, that impure habit? Why did you not listen to the counsels of your confessor? Why did you not, even after you had fallen the first or the second or the third or the fourth or the hundredth time, repent of your evil ways and turn to God who only waited for your repentance to absolve you of your sins? Now the time for repentance has gone by. Time is, time was, but time shall be no more! Time was to sin in secrecy, to indulge in that sloth and pride, to covet the unlawful, to yield to the promptings of your lower nature, to live like the beasts of the field, nay worse than the beasts of the field for they, at least, are but brutes and have not reason to guide them: time was but time shall be no more. God spoke to you by so many voices but you would not hear. You would not crush out that pride and anger in your heart, you would not restore those illgotten goods, you would not obey the precepts of your holy church nor attend to your religious duties, you would not abandon those wicked companions, you would not avoid those dangerous temptations. Such is the language of those fiendish tormentors, words of taunting and of reproach, of hatred and of disgust. Of disgust, yes! For even they, the very devils, when they sinned sinned by such a sin as alone was compatible with such angelical natures, a rebellion of the intellect: and they, even they, the foul devils must turn away, revolted and disgusted, from the contemplation of those unspeakable sins by which degraded man outrages and defiles the temple of the Holy Ghost, defiles and pollutes himself.

—O, my dear little brothers in Christ, may it never be our lot to hear that language! May it never be our lot, I say! In the last day of terrible reckoning I pray fervently to God that not a single soul of those who are in this chapel today may be found among those miserable beings whom the Great Judge shall command to depart for ever from His sight, that not one of us may ever hear ringing in his ears the awful sentence of rejection: *Depart from me, ye cursed, into everlasting fire which was prepared for the devil and his angels!*

He came down the aisle of the chapel, his legs shaking and the scalp of his head trembling as though it had been touched by ghostly fingers. He passed up the staircase and into the corridor along the walls of which the overcoats and waterproofs hung like gibbeted malefactors, headless and dripping and shapeless. And at every step he feared that he had already died, that his soul had been wrenched forth of the sheath of his body, that he was plunging headlong through space.

He could not grip the floor with his feet and sat heavily at his desk, opening one of his books at random and poring over it. Every word for him! It was true. God was almighty. God could call him now, call him as he sat at his desk, before he had time to be conscious of the summons. God had called him. Yes? What? Yes? His flesh shrank together as it felt the approach of the ravenous tongues of flames, dried up as it felt about it the swirl of stifling air. He had died. Yes. He was judged. A wave of fire swept through his body: the first. Again a wave. His brain began to glow. Another. His brain was simmering and bubbling within the cracking tenement of the skull. Flames burst forth from his skull like a corolla, shrieking like voices:

—Hell! Hell! Hell! Hell! Hell!

Voices spoke near him:

—On hell.

—I suppose he rubbed it into you well.

—You bet he did. He put us all into a blue funk.

—That's what you fellows want: and plenty of it to make you work.

He leaned back weakly in his desk. He had not died. God had spared him still. He was still in the familiar world of the school. Mr Tate and Vincent Heron stood at the window, talking, jesting, gazing out at the bleak rain, moving their heads.

—I wish it would clear up. I had arranged to go for a spin on the bike with some fellows out by Malahide. But the roads must be kneedeep.

—It might clear up, sir.

The voices that he knew so well, the common words, the quiet of the classroom when the voices paused and the silence was filled by the sound of softly browsing cattle as the other boys munched their lunches tranquilly, lulled his aching soul.

There was still time. O Mary, refuge of sinners, intercede for him! O Virgin Undefiled, save him from the gulf of death!

The English lesson began with the hearing of the history. Royal persons, favourites, intriguers, bishops, passed like mute phantoms behind their veil of names. All had died: all had been judged. What did it profit a man to gain the whole world if he lost his soul? At last he had understood: and human life lay around him, a plain of peace whereon antlike men laboured in brotherhood, their dead sleeping under quiet mounds. The elbow of his companion touched him and his heart was touched: and when he spoke to answer a question of his master he heard his own voice full of the quietude of humility and contrition.

His soul sank back deeper into depths of contrite peace, no longer able to suffer the pain of dread, and sending forth, as she sank, a faint prayer. Ah yes, he would still be spared; he would repent in his heart and be forgiven; and then those above, those in heaven, would see what he would do to make up for the past: a whole life, every hour of life. Only wait.

—All, God! All, all!

A messenger came to the door to say that confessions were being heard in the chapel. Four boys left the room; and he heard others passing down the corridor. A tremulous chill blew round his heart, no stronger than a little wind, and yet, listening and suffering silently, he seemed to have laid an ear against the muscle of his own heart, feeling it close and quail, listening to the flutter of its ventricles.

No escape. He had to confess, to speak out in words what he had done and thought, sin after sin. How? How?

—Father, I . . .

The thought slid like a cold shining rapier into his tender flesh: confession. But not there in the chapel of the college. He would confess all, every sin of deed and thought, sincerely: but not there among his school companions. Far away from there in some dark place he would murmur out his own shame: and he besought God humbly not to he offended with him if he did not dare to confess in the college chapel: and in utter abjection of spirit he craved forgiveness mutely of the boyish hearts about him.

Time passed.

He sat again in the front bench of the chapel. The daylight without was already failing and, as it fell slowly through the dull red blinds, it seemed that the sun of the last day was going down and that all souls were being gathered for the judgment.

—*I am cast away from the sight of Thine eyes*: words taken, my dear little brothers in Christ, from the Book of Psalms, thirtieth chapter, twentythird verse. In the name of the Father and of the Son and of the Holy Ghost. Amen.

The preacher began to speak in a quiet friendly tone. His face was kind and he joined gently the fingers of each hand, forming a frail cage by the union of their tips.

—This morning we endeavoured, in our reflection upon hell, to make what our holy founder calls in his book of spiritual exercises, the composition of place. We endeavoured, that is, to imagine with the senses of the mind, in our imagination, the material character of that awful place and of the physical torments which all who are in hell endure. This evening we shall consider for a few moments the nature of the spiritual torments of hell.

—Sin, remember, is a twofold enormity. It is a base consent to the promptings of our corrupt nature to the lowest instincts, to that which is gross and beastlike; and it is also a turning away from the counsel of our higher nature, from all that is pure and holy, from the Holy God Himself. For this reason mortal sin is punished in hell by two different forms of punishment, physical and spiritual.

—Now of all these spiritual pains by far the greatest is the pain of loss, so great, in fact, that in itself it is a torment greater than all the others. Saint Thomas, the greatest doctor of the church, the angelic doctor, as he is called, says that the worst damnation consists in this that the understanding of man is totally deprived of divine light and his affection obstinately turned away from the goodness of God. God, remember, is a being infinitely good and therefore the loss of such a being must be a loss infinitely painful. In this life we have not a very clear idea of what such a loss must be but the damned in hell, for their greater torment, have a full understanding of that which they have lost and understand that they have lost it through their own sins and have lost it for ever. At the very instant of death the bonds of the flesh are broken asunder and the soul at once flies towards God. The soul tends towards God as towards the centre of her existence. Remember, my dear little boys, our souls long to be with God. We come from God, we live by God, we belong to God: we are His, inalienably His. God loves with a divine love every human soul and every human soul lives in that love. How could it be otherwise? Every breath that we draw, every thought of our brain, every instant of life proceed from God's inexhaustible goodness. And if it be pain for a mother to be parted from her child, for a man to be exiled from hearth and home, for friend to be sundered from friend, O think what pain, what anguish, it must be for the poor soul to be spurned from the presence of the supremely good and loving Creator Who has called that soul into existence from nothingness and sustained it in life and loved it with an immeasurable love. This, then, to be separated for ever from its greatest good, from God, and to feel the anguish of that separation, knowing full well that it is unchangeable, this is the greatest torment which the created soul is capable of bearing, *pœna damni*, the pain of loss.

—The second pain which will afflict the souls of the damned in hell is the pain of conscience. Just as in dead bodies worms are engendered by putrefaction so in the souls of the lost there arises a perpetual remorse from the putrefaction of sin, the sting of conscience, the worm, as Pope Innocent the Third calls it, of the triple sting. The first sting inflicted by this cruel worm will be the memory of past pleasures. O what a dreadful memory will that be! In the lake of alldevouring flame the proud king will remember the pomps of his court, the wise but wicked man his libraries and instruments of research, the lover of artistic pleasures his marbles and pictures and other art treasures, he who delighted in the pleasures of the table his gorgeous feasts, his dishes prepared with such delicacy, his choice wines; the miser will remember his hoard of gold, the robber his illgotten wealth, the angry and revengeful and merciless murderers their deeds of blood and violence in which they revelled, the impure and adulterous the unspeakable and filthy pleasures in which they delighted. They will remember all this and loathe themselves and their sins. For how miserable will all those pleasures seem to the soul condemned to suffer in hellfire for ages and ages. How they will rage and fume to think that they have lost the bliss of heaven for the dross of earth, for a few pieces of metal, for vain honours, for bodily comforts, for a tingling of the nerves. They will repent indeed: and this is the second sting of the worm of conscience, a late and fruitless sorrow for sins committed. Divine justice insists that the understanding of those miserable wretches be fixed continually on the sins of which they were guilty and moreover, as saint Augustine points out, God will impart to them His own knowledge of sin so that sin will appear to them in all its hideous malice as it appears to the eyes of God Himself. They will behold their sins in all their foulness and repent but it will be too late and then they will bewail the good occasions which they neglected. This is the last and deepest and most cruel sting of the worm or conscience. The conscience will say: You had time and opportunity to repent and would not. You were brought up religiously by your parents. You had the sacraments and graces and indulgences of the church to aid you. You had the minister of God to preach to you, to call you back when you had strayed, to forgive you your sins, no matter how many, how abominable, if only you had confessed and repented. No. You would not. You flouted the ministers of holy religion, you turned your back on the confessional, you wallowed deeper and deeper in the mire of sin. God appealed to you, threatened you, entreated you to return to Him. O what shame, what misery! The Ruler of the universe entreated you, a creature of clay, to love Him Who made you and to keep His law. No. You would not. And now, though you were to flood all hell with your tears if you could still weep, all that sea of repentance would not gain for you what a single tear of true repentance shed during your mortal life would have gained for you. You implore now a moment of earthly life wherein to repent: in vain. That time is gone: gone for ever.

—Such is the threefold sting of conscience, the viper which gnaws the very heart's core of the wretches in hell so that filled with hellish fury they curse themselves for their folly and curse the evil companions who have brought them to such ruin and curse the devils who tempted them in life and now mock them and torture them in eternity and even revile and curse the Supreme Being Whose goodness and patience they scorned and slighted but Whose justice and power they cannot evade.

—The next spiritual pain to which the damned are subjected is the pain of extension. Man, in this earthly life, though he be capable of many evils, is not capable of them all at once inasmuch as one evil corrects and counteracts another just as one poison frequently corrects another. In hell, on the contrary, one torment, instead of counteracting another, lends it still greater force: and moreover as the internal faculties are more perfect than the external senses, so are they more capable of suffering. Just as every sense is afflicted with a fitting torment so is every spiritual faculty; the fancy with horrible images, the sensitive faculty with alternate longing and rage, the mind and understanding with an interior darkness more terrible even than the exterior darkness which reigns in that dreadful prison. The malice, impotent though it be, which possesses these demon souls is an evil of boundless extension, of limitless duration, a frightful state of wickedness which we can scarcely realise unless we bear in mind the enormity of sin and the hatred God bears to it.

—Opposed to this pain of extension and yet coexistent with it we have the pain of intensity. Hell is the centre of evils and, as you know, things are more intense at their centres than at their remotest points. There are no contraries or admixtures of any kind to temper or soften in the least the pains of hell. Nay, things which are good in themselves become evil in hell. Company, elsewhere a source of comfort to the afflicted, will be there a continual torment: knowledge, so much longed for as the chief good of the intellect, will there be hated worse than ignorance: light, so much coveted by all creatures from the lord of creation down to the humblest plant in the forest, will be loathed intensely. In this life our sorrows are either not very long or not very great because nature either overcomes them by habits or puts an end to them by sinking under their weight. But in hell the torments cannot be overcome by habit for while they are of terrible intensity they are at the same time of continual variety, each pain, so to speak, taking fire from another and reendowing that which has enkindled it with a still fiercer flame. Nor can nature escape from these intense and various tortures by succumbing to them for the soul is sustained and maintained in evil so that its suffering may be the greater. Boundless extension of torment, incredible intensity of suffering, unceasing variety of torture—this is what the divine majesty, so outraged by sinners, demands, this is what the holiness of heaven, slighted and set aside for the lustful and low pleasures of the corrupt flesh, requires, this is what the blood of the innocent Lamb of God, shed for the redemption of sinners, trampled upon by the vilest of the vile, insists upon.

—Last and crowning torture of all the tortures of that awful place is the eternity of hell. Eternity! O, dread and dire word. Eternity! What mind of man can understand it? And remember, it is an eternity of pain. Even though the pains of hell were not so terrible as they are yet they would become infinite as they are destined to last for ever. But while they are everlasting they are at the same time, as you know, intolerably intense, unbearably extensive. To bear even the sting of an insect for all eternity would be a dreadful torment. What must it be, then, to bear the manifold tortures of hell for ever? For ever! For all eternity! Not for a year or for an age but for ever. Try to imagine the awful meaning of this. You have often seen the sand on the seashore. How fine are its tiny grains! And how many of those tiny little grains go to make up the small handful which a child grasps in its play. Now imagine a mountain of that sand, a million miles high, reaching from the earth to the farthest heavens, and million miles broad, extending to remotest space, and a million miles in thickness: and imagine such an enormous mass of countless particles of sand multiplied as often as there are leaves in the forest, drops of water in the mighty ocean, feathers on birds, scales on fish, hairs on animals, atoms in the vast expanse of the air: and imagine that at the end of every million years a little bird came to that mountain and carried away in its beak a tiny grain of that sand. How many millions upon millions of centuries would pass before that bird had carried away even a square foot of that mountain, how many eons upon eons of ages before it had carried away all. Yet at the end of that immense stretch of time not even one instant of eternity could be said to have ended. At the end of all those billions and trillions of years eternity would have scarcely begun. And if that mountain rose again after it had been all carried away and if the bird came again and carried it all away again grain by grain: and if it so rose and sank as many times as there are stars in the sky, atoms in the air, drops of water in the sea, leaves on the trees, feathers upon birds, scales upon fish, hairs upon animals, at the end of all those innumerable risings and sinkings of that immeasurably vast mountain not one single instant of eternity could be said to have ended; even then, at the end of such a period, after that eon of time the mere thought of which makes our very brain reel dizzily, eternity would have scarcely begun.

—A holy saint (one of our own fathers I believe it was) was once vouchsafed a vision of hell. It seemed to him that he stood in the midst of a great hall, dark and silent save for the ticking of a great clock. The ticking went on unceasingly; and it seemed to this saint that the sound of the ticking was the ceaseless repetition of the words: ever, never; ever, never. Ever to be in hell, never to be in heaven; ever to be shut off from the presence of God, never to enjoy the beatific vision; ever to be eaten with flames, gnawed by vermin, goaded with burning spikes, never to be free from those pains; ever to have the conscience upbraid one, the memory enrage, the mind filled with darkness and despair, never to escape; ever to curse and revile the foul demons who gloat fiendishly over the misery of their dupes, never to behold the shining raiment of the blessed spirits; ever to cry out of the abyss of fire to God for an instant, a single instant, of respite from such awful agony, never to receive, even for an instant, God's pardon; ever to suffer, never to enjoy; ever to be damned, never to be saved; ever, never; ever, never. O what a dreadful punishment! An eternity of endless agony, of endless bodily and spiritual torment, without one ray of hope, without one moment of cessation, of agony limitless in extent, limitless in intensity, of torment infinitely lasting, infinitely varied, of torture that sustains eternally that which it eternally devours, of anguish that everlastingly preys upon the spirit while it racks the flesh, an eternity, every instant of which is itself an eternity, and that eternity an eternity of woe. Such is the terrible punishment decreed for those who die in mortal sin by an almighty and a just God.

—Yes, a just God! Men, reasoning always as men, are astonished that God should mete out an everlasting and infinite punishment in the fires of hell for a single grievous sin. They reason thus because, blinded by the gross illusion of the flesh and the darkness of human understanding, they are unable to comprehend the hideous malice of mortal sin. They reason thus because they are unable to comprehend that even venial sin is of such a foul and hideous nature that even if the omnipotent Creator could end all the evil and misery in the world the wars, the diseases, the robberies, the crimes, the deaths, the murders, on condition that He allowed a single venial sin to pass unpunished, a single venial sin, a lie, an angry look, a moment of wilful sloth, He, the great omnipotent God, could not do so because sin, be it in thought or deed, is a transgression of His law and God would not be God if He did not punish the transgressor.

—A sin, an instant of rebellious pride of the intellect, made

Lucifer and a third part of the cohorts of angels fall from their glory. A sin, an instant of folly and weakness, drove Adam and Eve out of Eden and brought death and suffering into the world. To retrieve the consequences of that sin the Only Begotten Son of God came down to earth, lived and suffered and died a most painful death, hanging for three hours on the cross.

—O, my dear little brethren in Christ Jesus, will we then offend that good Redeemer and provoke His anger? Will we trample again upon that torn and mangled corpse? Will we spit upon that face so full of sorrow and love? Will we too, like the cruel jews and the brutal soldiers, mock that gentle and compassionate Saviour Who trod alone for our sake the awful winepress of sorrow? Every word of sin is a wound in His tender side. Every sinful act is a thorn piercing His head. Every impure thought, deliberately yielded to, is a keen lance transfixing that sacred and loving heart. No, no. It is impossible for any human being to do that which offends so deeply the divine majesty, that which is punished by an eternity of agony, that which crucifies again the Son of God and makes a mockery of Him.

—I pray to God that my poor words may have availed today to confirm in holiness those who are in a state of grace, to strengthen the wavering, to lead back to the state of grace the poor soul that has strayed if any such be among you. I pray to God, and do you pray with me, that we may repent of our sins. I will ask you now, all of you, to repeat after me the act of contrition, kneeling here in this humble chapel in the presence of God. He is there in the tabernacle burning with love for mankind, ready to comfort the afflicted. Be not afraid. No matter how many or how foul the sins if only you repent of them they will be forgiven you. Let no worldly shame hold you back. God is still the merciful Lord Who wishes not the eternal death of the sinner but rather that he be converted and live.

—He calls you to Him. You are His. He made you out of nothing. He loved you as only a God can love. His arms are open to receive you even though you have sinned against Him. Come to Him, poor sinner, poor vain and erring sinner. Now is the acceptable time. Now is the hour.

The priest rose and, turning towards the altar, knelt upon the step before the tabernacle in the fallen gloom. He waited till all in the chapel had knelt and every least noise was still. Then, raising his head, he repeated the act of contrition, phrase by phrase, with fervour. The boys answered him phrase by phrase. Stephen, his tongue cleaving to his palate, bowed his head, praying with his heart.

> —*O my God!*—
> —*O my God!*—
> —*I am heartily sorry*—
> —*I am heartily sorry*—
> —*for having offended Thee*—
> —*for having offended Thee*—
> —*and I detest my sins*—
> —*and I detest my sins*—
> —*above every other evil*—
> —*above every other evil*—
> —*because they displease Thee, my God*—
> —*because they displease Thee, my God*—
> —*Who art so deserving*—
> —*Who art so deserving*—
> —*of all my love*—
> —*of all my love*—
> —*and I firmly purpose*—
> —*and I firmly purpose*—
> —*by Thy holy grace*—
> —*by Thy holy grace*—
> —*never more to offend Thee*—
> —*never more to offend Thee*—
> —*and to amend my life*—
> —*and to amend my life*—

* * *

He went up to his room after dinner in order to be alone with his soul: and at every step his soul seemed to sigh: at every step his soul mounted with his feet, sighing in the ascent, through a region of viscid gloom.

He halted on the landing before the door and then, grasping the porcelain knob, opened the door quickly. He waited in fear, his soul pining within him, praying silently that death might not touch his brow as he passed over the threshold, that the fiends that inhabit darkness might not be given power over him. He waited still at the threshold as at the entrance to some dark cave. Faces were there; eyes: they waited and watched.

—We knew perfectly well of course that though it was bound to come to the light he would find considerable difficulty in endeavouring to try to induce himself to try to endeavour to ascertain the spiritual plenipotentiary and so we knew of course perfectly well—

Murmuring faces waited and watched; murmurous voices filled the dark shell of the cave. He feared intensely in spirit and in flesh but, raising his head bravely, he strode into the room firmly. A doorway, a room, the same room, same window. He told himself calmly that those words had absolutely no sense which had seemed to rise murmurously from the dark. He told himself that it was simply his room with the door open.

He closed the door and, walking swiftly to the bed, knelt beside it and covered his face with his hands. His hands were cold and damp and his limbs ached with chill. Bodily unrest and chill and weariness beset him, routing his thoughts. Why was he kneeling there like a child saying his evening prayers? To be alone with his soul, to examine his conscience, to meet his sins face to face, to recall their times and manners and circumstances, to weep over them. He could not weep. He could not summon them to his memory. He felt only an ache of soul and body, his whole being, memory, will, understanding, flesh, benumbed and weary.

That was the work of devils, to scatter his thoughts and overcloud his conscience, assailing him at the gates of the cowardly and sincorrupted flesh: and, praying God timidly to forgive him his weakness, he crawled up on to the bed and, wrapping the blankets closely about him, covered his face again with his hands. He had sinned. He had sinned so deeply against heaven and before God that he was not worthy to be called God's child.

Could it be that he, Stephen Dedalus, had done those things? His conscience sighed in answer. Yes, he had done them, secretly, filthily, time after time, and, hardened in sinful impenitence, he had dared to wear the mask of holiness before the tabernacle itself while his soul within was a living mass of corruption. How came it that God had not struck him dead? The leprous company of his sins closed about him, breathing upon him, bending over him from all sides. He strove to forget them in an act of prayer, huddling his limbs closer together and binding down his eyelids: but the senses of his soul would not be bound and, though his eyes were shut fast, he saw the places where he had sinned and, though his ears were tightly covered, he heard.

He desired with all his will not to hear or see. He desired till his frame shook under the strain of his desire and until the senses of his soul closed. They closed for an instant and then opened. He saw.

A field of stiff weeds and thistles and tufted nettlebunches. Thick among the tufts of rank stiff growth lay battered canisters and clots and coils of solid excrement. A faint marshlight struggled upwards from all the ordure through the bristling greygreen weeds. An evil smell, faint and foul as the light, curled upwards sluggishly out of the canisters and from the stale crusted dung.

Creatures were in the field; one, three, six: creatures were moving in the field, hither and thither. Goatish creatures with human faces, hornybrowed, lightly bearded and grey as indiarubber. The malice of evil glittered in their hard eyes, as they moved hither and thither, trailing their long tails behind them. A rictus of cruel malignity lit up greyly their old bony faces. One was clasping about his ribs a torn flannel waistcoat, another complained monotonously as his beard stuck in the tufted weeds. Soft language issued from their spittleless lips as they swished in slow circles round and round the field, winding hither and thither through the weeds, dragging their long tails amid the rattling canisters. They moved in slow circles, circling closer and closer to enclose, to enclose, soft language issuing from their lips, their long swishing tails besmeared with stale shite, thrusting upwards their terrific faces . . .

Help!

He flung the blankets from him madly to free his face and neck. That was his hell. God had allowed him to see the hell reserved for his sins: stinking, bestial, malignant, a hell of lecherous goatish fiends. For him! For him!

He sprang from the bed, the reeking odour pouring down his throat, clogging and revolting his entrails. Air! The air of heaven! He stumbled towards the window, groaning and almost fainting with sickness. At the washstand a convulsion seized him within; and, clasping his cold forehead wildly, he vomited profusely in agony.

When the fit had spent itself he walked weakly to the window and, lifting the sash, sat in a corner of the embrasure and leaned his elbow upon the sill. The rain had drawn off; and amid the moving vapours from point to point of light the city was spinning about herself a soft cocoon of yellowish haze. Heaven was still and faintly luminous and the air sweet to breathe, as in a thicket drenched with showers: and amid peace and shimmering lights and quiet fragrance he made a covenant with his heart.

He prayed:

—He once had meant to come on earth in heavenly glory but we sinned: and then He could not safely visit us but with a shrouded majesty and a bedimmed radiance for He was God. So He came Himself in weakness not in power and He sent thee, a creature in His stead, with a creature's comeliness and lustre suited to our state. And now thy very face and form, dear mother, speak to us of the Eternal; not like earthly beauty, dangerous to look upon, but like the morning star which is thy emblem, bright and musical, breathing purity, telling of heaven and infusing peace. O harbinger of day! O light of the pilgrim! Lead us still as thou hast led. In the dark night, across the bleak wilderness guide us on to our Lord Jesus, guide us home.

His eyes were dimmed with tears and, looking humbly up to heaven, he wept for the innocence he had lost.

When evening had fallen he left the house and the first touch of the damp dark air and the noise of the door as it closed behind him made ache again his conscience, lulled by prayer and tears. Confess! Confess! It was not enough to lull the conscience with a tear and a prayer. He had to kneel before the minister of the Holy Ghost and tell over his hidden sins truly and repentantly. Before he heard again the footboard of the housedoor trail over the threshold as it opened to let him in, before he saw again the table in the kitchen set for supper he would have knelt and confessed. It was quite simple.

The ache of conscience ceased and he walked onward swiftly through the dark streets. There were so many flagstones on the footpath of that street and so many streets in that city and so many cities in the world. Yet eternity had no end. He was in mortal sin. Even once was a mortal sin. It could happen in an instant. But how so quickly? By seeing or by thinking of seeing. The eyes see the thing, without having wished first to see. Then in an instant it happens. But does that part of the body understand or what? The serpent, the most subtle beast of the field. It must understand when it desires in one instant and then prolongs its own desire instant after instant, sinfully. It feels and understands and desires. What a horrible thing! Who made it to be like that, a bestial part of the body able to understand bestially and desire bestially? Was that then he or an inhuman thing moved by a lower soul than his soul? His soul sickened at the thought of a torpid snaky life feeding itself out of the tender marrow of his life and fattening upon the slime of lust. O why was that so? O why?

He cowered in the shadow of the thought, abasing himself in the awe of God Who had made all things and all men. Madness. Who could think such a thought? And, cowering in darkness and abject, he prayed mutely to his angel guardian to drive away with his sword the demon that was whispering to his brain.

The whisper ceased and he knew then clearly that his own soul had sinned in thought and word and deed wilfully through his own body. Confess! He had to confess every sin. How could he utter in words to the priest what he had done? Must, must. Or how could he explain without dying of shame? Or how could he have done such things without shame? A madman, a loathsome madman! Confess! O he would indeed to be free and sinless again! Perhaps the priest would know. O dear God!

He walked on and on through illlit streets, fearing to stand still for a moment lest it might seem that he held back from what awaited him, fearing to arrive at that towards which he still turned with longing. How beautiful must be a soul in the state of grace when God looked upon it with love!

Frowsy girls sat along the curbstones before their baskets. Their dank hair hung trailed over their brows. They were not beautiful to see as they crouched in the mire. But their souls were seen by God; and if their souls were in a state of grace they were radiant to see: and God loved them, seeing them.

A wasting breath of humiliation blew bleakly over his soul to think of how he had fallen, to feel that those souls were dearer to God than his. The wind blew over him and passed on to the myriads and myriads of other souls on whom God's favour shone now more and now less, stars now brighter and now dimmer, sustained and failing. And the glimmering souls passed away, sustained and failing, merged in a moving breath. One soul was lost; a tiny soul: his. It flickered once and went out, forgotten, lost. The end: black cold void waste.

Consciousness of place came ebbing back to him slowly over a vast tract of time unlit, unfelt, unlived. The squalid scene composed itself around him; the common accents, the burning gasjets in the shops, odours of fish and spirits and wet sawdust, moving men and women. An old woman was about to cross the street, an oilcan in her hand. He bent down and asked her was there a chapel near.

—A chapel, sir? Yes, sir. Church Street chapel.

—Church?

She shifted the can to her other hand and directed him and, as she held out her reeking withered right hand under its fringe of shawl, he bent lower towards her, saddened and soothed by her voice.

—Thank you.

—You are quite welcome, sir.

The candles on the high altar had been extinguished but the fragrance of incense still floated down the dim nave. Bearded workmen with pious faces were guiding a canopy out through a sidedoor, the sacristan aiding them with quiet gestures and words. A few of the faithful still lingered, praying before one of the sidealtars or kneeling in the benches near the confessionals. He approached timidly and knelt at the last bench in the body, thankful for the peace and silence and fragrant shadow of the church. The board on which he knelt was narrow and worn and those who knelt near him were humble followers of Jesus. Jesus too had been born in poverty and had worked in the shop of a carpenter, cutting boards and planing them, and had first spoken of the kingdom of God to poor fishermen, teaching all men to be meek and humble of heart.

He bowed his head upon his hands, bidding his heart be meek and humble that he might be like those who knelt beside him and his prayer as acceptable as theirs. He prayed beside them but it was hard. His soul was foul with sin and he dared not ask forgiveness with the simple trust of those whom Jesus, in the mysterious ways of God, had called first to His side, the carpenters, the fishermen, poor and simple people following a lowly trade, handling and shaping the wood of trees, mending their nets with patience.

A tall figure came down the aisle and the penitents stirred: and at the last moment, glancing up swiftly, he saw a long grey beard and the brown habit of a capuchin. The priest entered the box and was hidden. Two penitents rose and entered the confessional at either side. The wooden slide was drawn back and the faint murmur of a voice troubled the silence.

His blood began to murmur in his veins, murmuring like a sinful city summoned from its sleep to hear its doom. Little flakes of fire fell and powdery ashes fell softly, alighting on the houses of men. They stirred, waking from sleep, troubled by the heated air.

The slide was shot back. The penitent emerged from the side of the box. The farther slide was drawn. A woman entered quietly and deftly where the first penitent had knelt. The faint murmur began again.

He could still leave the chapel. He could stand up, put one foot before the other and walk out softly and then run, run, run swiftly through the dark streets. He could still escape from the shame. Had it been any terrible crime but that one sin! Had it been murder! Little fiery flakes fell and touched him at all points, shameful thoughts, shameful words, shameful acts. Shame covered him wholly like fine glowing ashes falling continually. To say it in words! His soul, stifling and helpless, would cease to be.

The slide was shot back. A penitent emerged from the farther side of the box. The near slide was drawn. A penitent entered where the other penitent had come out. A soft whispering noise floated in vaporous cloudlets out of the box. It was the woman: soft whispering cloudlets, soft whispering vapour, whispering and vanishing.

He beat his breast with his fist humbly, secretly under cover of the wooden armrest. He would be at one with others and with God. He would love his neighbour. He would love God Who had made and loved him. He would kneel and pray with others and be happy. God would look down on him and on them and would love them all.

It was easy to be good. God's yoke was sweet and light. It was better never to have sinned, to have remained always a child, for God loved little children and suffered them to come to Him. It was a terrible and a sad thing to sin. But God was merciful to poor sinners who were truly sorry. How true that was! That was indeed goodness.

The slide was shot to suddenly. The penitent came out. He was next. He stood up in terror and walked blindly into the box.

At last it had come. He knelt in the silent gloom and raised his eyes to the white crucifix suspended above him. God could see that he was sorry. He would tell all his sins. His confession would be long, long. Everybody in the chapel would know then what a sinner he had been. Let them know. It was true. But God had promised to forgive him if he was sorry. He was sorry. He clasped his hands and raised them towards the white form, praying with his darkened eyes, praying with all his trembling body, swaying his head to and fro like a lost creature, praying with whimpering lips.

—Sorry! Sorry! O sorry!

The slide clicked back and his heart bounded in his breast. The face of an old priest was at the grating, averted from him, leaning upon a hand. He made the sign of the cross and prayed of the priest to bless him for he had sinned. Then, bowing his head, he repeated the *Confiteor* in fright. At the words *my most grievous fault* he ceased, breathless.

—How long is it since your last confession, my child?

—A long time, father.

—A month, my child?

—Longer, father.

—Three months, my child?

—Longer, father.

—Six months?

—Eight months, father.

He had begun. The priest asked:

—And what do you remember since that time?

He began to confess his sins: masses missed, prayers not said, lies.

—Anything else, my child?

Sins of anger, envy of others, gluttony, vanity, disobedience.

—Anything else, my child?

—Sloth.

—Anything else, my child?

There was no help. He murmured:

—I . . . committed sins of impurity, father.

The priest did not turn his head.

—With yourself, my child?

—And . . . with others.

—With women, my child?

—Yes, father.

—Were they married women, my child?

He did not know. His sins trickled from his lips, one by one, trickled in shameful drops from his soul festering and oozing like a sore, a squalid stream of vice. The last sins oozed forth, sluggish, filthy. There was no more to tell. He bowed his head, overcome.

The priest was silent. Then he asked:

—How old are you, my child?

—Sixteen, father.

The priest passed his hand several times over his face. Then, resting his forehead against his hand, he leaned towards the grating and, with eyes still averted, spoke slowly. His voice was weary and old.

—You are very young, my child, he said, and let me implore of you to give up that sin. It is a terrible sin. It kills the body and it kills the soul. It is the cause of many crimes and misfortunes. Give it up, my child, for God's sake. It is dishonourable and unmanly. You cannot know where that wretched habit will lead you or where it will come against you. As long as you commit that sin, my poor child, you will never be worth one farthing to God. Pray to our mother Mary to help you. She will help you, my child. Pray to Our Blessed Lady when that sin comes into your mind. I am sure you will do that, will you not? You repent of all those sins. I am sure you do. And you will promise God now that by His holy grace you will never offend Him any more by that wicked sin. You will make that solemn promise to God, will you not?

—Yes, father.

The old and weary voice fell like sweet rain upon his quaking parching heart. How sweet and sad!

—Do so, my poor child. The devil has led you astray. Drive him back to hell when he tempts you to dishonour your body in that way—the foul spirit who hates Our Lord. Promise God now that you will give up that sin, that wretched wretched sin.

Blinded by his tears and by the light of God's mercifulness he bent his head and heard the grave words of absolution spoken and saw the priest's hand raised above him in token of forgiveness.

—God bless you, my child. Pray for me.

He knelt to say his penance, praying in a corner of the dark nave: and his prayers ascended to heaven from his purified heart like perfume streaming upwards from a heart of white rose.

The muddy streets were gay. He strode homeward, conscious of an invisible grace pervading and making light his limbs. In spite of all he had done it. He had confessed and God had pardoned him. His soul was made fair and holy once more, holy and happy.

It would be beautiful to die if God so willed. It was beautiful to live if God so willed, to live in grace a life of peace and virtue and forbearance with others.

He sat by the fire in the kitchen, not daring to speak for happiness. Till that moment he had not known how beautiful and peaceful life could be. The green square of paper pinned round the lamp cast down a tender shade. On the dresser was a plate of sausages and white pudding and on the shelf there were eggs. They would be for the breakfast in the morning after the communion in the college chapel. White pudding and eggs and sausages and cups of tea. How simple and beautiful was life after all! And life lay all before him.

In a dream he fell asleep. In a dream he rose and saw that it was morning. In a waking dream he went through the quiet morning towards the college.

The boys were all there, kneeling in their places. He knelt among them, happy and shy. The altar was heaped with fragrant masses of white flowers: and in the morning light the pale flames of the candles among the white flowers were clear and silent as his own soul.

He knelt before the altar with his classmates, holding the altar cloth with them over a living rail of hands. His hands were trembling, and his soul trembled as he heard the priest pass with the ciborium from communicant to communicant.

—*Corpus Domini nostri.*

Could it be? He knelt there sinless and timid: and he would hold upon his tongue the host and God would enter his purified body.

—*In vitam eternam. Amen.*

Another life! A life of grace and virtue and happiness! It was true. It was not a dream from which he would wake. The past was past.

—*Corpus Domini nostri.*

The ciborium had come to him.

IV

SUNDAY was dedicated to the mystery of the Holy Trinity, Monday to the Holy Ghost, Tuesday to the Guardian Angels, Wednesday to saint Joseph, Thursday to the Most Blessed Sacrament of the Altar, Friday to the Suffering Jesus, Saturday to the Blessed Virgin Mary.

Every morning he hallowed himself anew in the presence of some holy image or mystery. His day began with an heroic offering of its every moment of thought or action for the intentions of the sovereign pontiff and with an early mass. The raw morning air whetted his resolute piety; and often as he knelt among the few worshippers at the sidealtar, following with his interleaved prayerbook the murmur of the priest, he glanced up for an instant towards the vested figure standing in the gloom between the two candles which were the old and the new testaments and imagined that he was kneeling at mass in the catacombs.

His daily life was laid out in devotional areas. By means of ejaculations and prayers he stored up ungrudgingly for the souls in purgatory centuries of days and quarantines and years; yet the spiritual triumph which he felt in achieving with ease so many fabulous ages of canonical penances did not wholly reward his zeal of prayer since he could never know how much temporal punishment he had remitted by way of suffrage for the agonising souls: and, fearful lest in the midst of the purgatorial fire, which differed from the infernal only in that it was not everlasting, his penance might avail no more than a drop of moisture, he drove his soul daily through an increasing circle of works of supererogation.

Every part of his day, divided by what he regarded now as the duties of his station in life, circled about its own centre of spiritual energy. His life seemed to have drawn near to eternity; every thought, word and deed, every instance of consciousness could be made to revibrate radiantly in heaven: and at times his sense of such immediate repercussion was so lively that he seemed to feel his soul in devotion pressing like fingers the keyboard of a great cash register and to see the amount of his purchase start forth immediately in heaven, not as a number but as a frail column of incense or as a slender flower.

The rosaries too which he said constantly—for he carried his beads loose in his trousers' pockets that he might tell them as he walked the streets—transformed themselves into coronals of flowers of such vague unearthly texture that they seemed to him as hueless and odourless as they were nameless. He offered up each of his three daily chaplets that his soul might grow strong in each of the three theological virtues, in faith in the Father Who had created him, in hope in the Son Who had redeemed him and in love of the Holy Ghost Who had sanctified him; and this thrice triple prayer he offered to the Three Persons through Mary in the name of her joyful and sorrowful and glorious mysteries.

On each of the seven days of the week he further prayed that one of the seven gifts of the Holy Ghost might descend upon his soul and drive out of it day by day the seven deadly sins which had defiled it in the past; and he prayed for each gift on its appointed day, confident that it would descend upon him, though it seemed strange to him at times that wisdom and understanding and knowledge were so distinct in their nature that each should be prayed for apart from the others. Yet he believed that at some future stage of his spiritual progress this difficulty would be removed when his sinful soul had been raised up from its weakness and enlightened by the Third Person of the Most Blessed Trinity. He believed this all the more, and with trepidation, because of the divine gloom and silence wherein dwelt the unseen Paraclete, Whose symbols were a dove and a mighty wind, to sin against Whom was a sin beyond forgiveness, the eternal mysterious secret Being to Whom, as God, the priests offered up mass once a year, robed in the scarlet of the tongues of fire.

The imagery through which the nature and kinship of the Three Persons of the Trinity were darkly shadowed forth in the books of devotion which he read—the Father contemplating from all eternity as in a mirror His Divine Perfections and thereby begetting eternally the Eternal Son and the Holy Spirit proceeding out of Father and Son from all eternity—were easier of acceptance by his mind by reason of their august incomprehensibility than was the simple fact that God had loved his soul from all eternity, for ages before he had been born into the world, for ages before the world itself had existed.

He had heard the names of the passions of love and hate pronounced solemnly on the stage and in the pulpit, had found them set forth solemnly in books, and had wondered why his soul was unable to harbour them for any time or to force his lips to utter their names with conviction. A brief anger had often invested him but he had never been able to make it an abiding passion and had always felt himself passing out of it as if his very body were being divested with ease of some outer skin or peel. He had felt a subtle, dark and murmurous presence penetrate his being and fire him with a brief iniquitous lust: it too had slipped beyond his grasp leaving his mind lucid and indifferent. This, it seemed, was the only love and that the only hate his soul would harbour.

But he could no longer disbelieve in the reality of love since God Himself had loved his individual soul with divine love from all eternity. Gradually, as his soul was enriched with spiritual knowledge, he saw the whole world forming one vast symmetrical expression of God's power and love. Life became a divine gift for every moment and sensation of which, were it even the sight of a single leaf hanging on the twig of a tree, his soul should praise and thank the Giver. The world for all its solid substance and complexity no longer existed for his soul save as a theorem of divine power and love and universality. So entire and unquestionable was this sense of the divine meaning in all nature granted to his soul that he could scarcely understand why it was in any way necessary that he should continue to live. Yet that was part of the divine purpose and he dared not question its use, he above all others who had sinned so deeply and so foully against the divine purpose. Meek and abased by this consciousness of the one eternal omnipresent perfect reality his soul took up again her burden of pieties, masses and prayers and sacraments and mortifications, and only then for the first time since he had brooded on the great mystery of love did he feel within him a warm movement like that of some newly born life or virtue of the soul itself. The attitude of rapture in sacred art, the raised and parted hands, the parted lips and eyes as of one about to swoon, became for him an image of the soul in prayer, humiliated and faint before her Creator.

But he had been forewarned of the dangers of spiritual exaltation and did not allow himself to desist from even the least or lowliest devotion, striving also by constant mortification to undo the sinful past rather than to achieve a saintliness fraught with peril. Each of his senses was brought under a rigorous discipline. In order to mortify the sense of sight he made it his rule to walk in the street with downcast eyes, glancing neither to right nor left and never behind him. His eyes shunned every encounter with the eyes of women. From time to time also he balked them by a sudden effort of the will, as by lifting them suddenly in the middle of an unfinished sentence and closing the book. To mortify his hearing he exerted no control over his voice which was then breaking, neither sang nor whistled and made no attempt to flee from noises which caused him painful nervous irritation such as the sharpening of knives on the knife-board, the gathering of cinders on the fireshovel and the twigging of the carpet. To mortify his smell was more difficult as he found in himself no instinctive repugnance to bad odours, whether they were the odours of the outdoor world such as those of dung and tar or the odours of his own person among which he had made many curious comparisons and experiments. He found in the end that the only odour against which his sense of smell revolted was a certain stale fishy stink like that of longstanding urine: and whenever it was possible he subjected himself to this unpleasant odour. To mortify the taste he practised strict habits at table, observed to the letter all the fasts of the church and sought by distraction to divert his mind from the savours of different foods. But it was to the mortification of touch that he brought the most assiduous ingenuity of inventiveness. He never consciously changed his position in bed, sat in the most uncomfortable positions, suffered patiently every itch and pain, kept away from the fire, remained on his knees all through the mass except at the gospels, left parts of his neck and face undried so that air might sting them and, whenever he was not saying his beads, carried his arms stiffly at his sides like a runner and never in his pockets or clasped behind him.

He had no temptations to sin mortally. It surprised him however to find that at the end of his course of intricate piety and selfrestraint he was so easily at the mercy of childish and unworthy imperfections. His prayers and fasts availed him little for the suppression of anger at hearing his mother sneeze or at being disturbed in his devotions. It needed an immense effort of his will to master the impulse which urged him to give outlet to such irritation. Images of the outbursts of trivial anger which he had often noted among his masters, their twitching mouths, closeshut lips and flushed cheeks, recurred to his memory, discouraging him, for all his practice of humility, by the comparison. To merge his life in the common tide of other lives was harder for him than any fasting or prayer and it was his constant failure to do this to his own satisfaction which caused in his soul at last a sensation of spiritual dryness together with a growth of doubts and scruples. His soul traversed a period of desolation in which the sacraments themselves seemed to have turned into dried up sources. His confession became a channel for the escape of scrupulous and unrepented imperfections. His actual reception of the eucharist did not bring him the same dissolving moments of virginal selfsurrender as did those spiritual communions made by him sometimes at the close of some visit to the Blessed Sacrament. The book which he used for these visits was an old neglected book written by saint Alphonsus Liguori, with fading characters and sere foxpapered leaves. A faded world of fervent love and virginal responses seemed to be evoked for his soul by the reading of its pages in which the imagery of the canticles was interwoven with the communicant's prayers. An inaudible voice seemed to caress the soul, telling her names and glories, bidding her arise as for espousal and come away, bidding her look forth, a spouse, from Amana and from the mountains of the leopards; and the soul seemed to answer with the same inaudible voice, surrendering herself: *Inter ubera mea commorabitur*.

This idea of surrender had a perilous attraction for his mind now that he felt his soul beset once again by the insistent voices of the flesh which began to murmur to him again during his prayers and meditations. It gave him an intense sense of power to know that he could by a single act of consent, in a moment of thought, undo all that he had done. He seemed to feel a flood slowly advancing towards his naked feet and to be waiting for the first faint timid noiseless wavelet to touch his fevered skin. Then, almost at the instant of that touch, almost at the verge of sinful consent, he found himself standing far away from the flood upon a dry shore, saved by a sudden act of the will or a sudden ejaculation: and, seeing the silver line of the flood far away and beginning again its slow advance towards his feet, a new thrill of power and satisfaction shook his soul to know that he had not yielded nor undone all.

When he had eluded the flood of temptation many times in this way he grew troubled and wondered whether the grace which he had refused to lose was not being filched from him little by little. The clear certitude of his own immunity grew dim and to it succeeded a vague fear that his soul had really fallen unawares. It was with difficulty that he won back his old consciousness of his state of grace by telling himself that he had prayed to God at every temptation and that the grace which he had prayed for must have been given to him inasmuch as God was obliged to give it. The very frequency and violence of temptations showed him at last the truth of what he had heard about the trials of the saints. Frequent and violent temptations were a proof that the citadel of the soul had not fallen and that the devil raged to make it fall.

Often when he had confessed his doubts and scruples, some momentary inattention at prayer, a movement of trivial anger in his soul or a subtle wilfulness in speech or act, he was bidden by his confessor to name some sin of his past life before absolution was given him. He named it with humility and shame and repented of it once more. It humiliated and shamed him to think that he would never be freed from it wholly, however holily he might live or whatever virtues or perfections he might attain. A restless feeling of guilt would always be present with him: he would confess and repent and be absolved, confess and repent again and be absolved again, fruitlessly. Perhaps that first hasty confession wrung from him by the fear of hell had not been good? Perhaps, concerned only for his imminent doom, he had not had sincere sorrow for his sin? But the surest sign that his confession had been good and that he had had sincere sorrow for his sin was, he knew, the amendment of his life.

—I have amended my life, have I not? he asked himself.

*   *   *

The director stood in the embrasure of the window, his back to the light, leaning an elbow on the brown crossblind and, as he spoke and smiled, slowly dangling and looping the cord of the other blind. Stephen stood before him, following for a moment with his eyes the waning of the long summer daylight above the roofs or the slow deft movements of the priestly fingers. The priest's face was in total shadow but the waning daylight from behind him touched the deeply grooved temples and the curves of the skull. Stephen followed also with his ears the accents and intervals of the priest's voice as he spoke gravely and cordially of indifferent themes, the vacation which had just ended, the colleges of the order abroad, the transference of masters. The grave and cordial voice went on easily with its tale, and in the pauses Stephen felt bound to set it on again with respectful questions. He knew that the tale was a prelude and his mind waited for the sequel. Ever since the message of summons had come for him from the director his mind had struggled to find the meaning of the message; and during the long restless time he had sat in the college parlour waiting for the director to come in his eyes had wandered from one sober picture to another around the walls and his mind wandered from one guess to another until the meaning of the summons had almost become clear. Then, just as he was wishing that some unforeseen cause might prevent the director from coming, he had heard the handle of the door turning and the swish of a soutane.

The director had begun to speak of the dominican and franciscan orders and of the friendship between saint Thomas and saint Bonaventure. The capuchin dress, he thought, was rather too . . .

Stephen's face gave back the priest's indulgent smile and, not being anxious to give an opinion, he made a slight dubitative movement with his lips.

—I believe, continued the director, that there is some talk now among the capuchins themselves of doing away with it and following the example of the other franciscans.

—I suppose they would retain it in the cloister, said Stephen.

—O, certainly, said the director. For the cloister it is all right but for the street I really think it would be better to do away with it, don't you?

—It must be troublesome, I imagine?

—Of course it is, of course. Just imagine when I was in Belgium I used to see them out cycling in all kinds of weather with this thing up about their knees! It was really ridiculous. *Les jupes*, they call them in Belgium.

The vowel was so modified as to be indistinct.

—What do they call them?

—*Les jupes*.

—O.

Stephen smiled again in answer to the smile which he could not see on the priest's shadowed face, its image or spectre only passing rapidly across his mind as the low discreet accent fell upon his ear. He gazed calmly before him at the waning sky, glad of the cool of the evening and of the faint yellow glow which hid the tiny flame kindling upon his cheek.

The names of articles of dress worn by women or of certain soft and delicate stuffs used in their making brought always to his mind a delicate and sinful perfume. As a boy he had imagined the reins by which horses are driven as slender silken bands and it shocked him to feel at Stradbrooke the greasy leather of harness. It had shocked him too when he had felt for the first time beneath his tremulous fingers the brittle texture of a woman's stocking for, retaining nothing of all he read save that which seemed to him an echo or a prophecy of his own state, it was only amid softworded phrases or within rosesoft stuffs that he dared to conceive of the soul or body of a woman moving with tender life.

But the phrase on the priest's lips was disingenuous for he knew that a priest should not speak lightly on that theme. The phrase had been spoken lightly with design and he felt that his face was being searched by the eyes in the shadow. Whatever he had heard or read of the craft of jesuits he had put aside frankly as not borne out by his own experience. His masters, even when they had not attracted him, had seemed to him always intelligent and serious priests, athletic and highspirited prefects. He thought of them as men who washed their bodies briskly with cold water and wore clean cold linen. During all the years he had lived among them in Clongowes and in Belvedere he had received only two pandies and, though these had been dealt him in the wrong, he knew that he had often escaped punishment. During all those years he had never heard from any of his masters a flippant word: it was they who had taught him christian doctrine and urged him to live a good life and, when he had fallen into grievous sin, it was they who had led him back to grace. Their presence had made him diffident of himself when he was a muff in Clongowes and it had made him diffident of himself also while he had held his equivocal position in Belvedere. A constant sense of this had remained with him up to the last year of his school life. He had never once disobeyed or allowed turbulent companions to seduce him from his habit of quiet obedience: and, even when he doubted some statement of a master, he had never presumed to doubt openly. Lately some of their judgments had sounded a little childish in his ears and had made him feel a regret and pity as though he were slowly passing out of an accustomed world and were hearing its language for the last time. One day when some boys had gathered round a priest under the shed near the chapel, he had heard the priest say:

—I believe that Lord Macaulay was a man who probably never committed a mortal sin in his life, that is to say, a deliberate mortal sin.

Some of the boys had then asked the priest if Victor Hugo were not the greatest French writer. The priest had answered that Victor Hugo had never written half so well when he had turned against the church as he had written when he was a catholic.

—But there are many eminent French critics, said the priest, who consider that even Victor Hugo, great as he certainly was, had not so pure a French style as Louis Veuillot.

The tiny flame which the priest's allusion had kindled upon Stephen's cheek had sunk down again and his eyes were still fixed calmly on the colourless sky. But an unresting doubt flew hither and thither before his mind. Masked memories passed quickly before him: he recognised scenes and persons yet he was conscious that he had failed to perceive some vital circumstance in them. He saw himself walking about the grounds watching the sports in Clongowes and eating slim jim out of his cricketcap. Some jesuits were walking round the cycletrack in the company of ladies. The echoes of certain expressions used in Clongowes sounded in remote caves of his mind.

His ears were listening to these distant echoes amid the silence of the parlour when he became aware that the priest was addressing him in a different voice.

—I sent for you today, Stephen, because I wished to speak to you on a very important subject.

—Yes, sir.

—Have you ever felt that you had a vocation?

Stephen parted his lips to answer yes and then withheld the word suddenly. The priest waited for the answer and added:

—I mean have you ever felt within yourself, in your soul, a desire to join the order. Think.

—I have sometimes thought of it, said Stephen.

The priest let the blindcord fall to one side and, uniting his hands, leaned his chin gravely upon them, communing with himself.

—In a college like this, he said at length, there is one boy or perhaps two or three boys whom God calls to the religious life. Such a boy is marked off from his companions by his piety, by the good example he shows to others. He is looked up to by them; he is chosen perhaps as prefect by his fellow sodalists. And you, Stephen, have been such a boy in this college, prefect of Our Blessed Lady's sodality. Perhaps you are the boy in this college whom God designs to call to Himself.

A strong note of pride reinforcing the gravity of the priest's voice made Stephen's heart quicken in response.

—To receive that call, Stephen, said the priest, is the greatest honour that the Almighty God can bestow upon a man. No king or emperor on this carth has the power of the priest of God. No angel or archangel in heaven, no saint, not even the Blessed Virgin herself has the power of a priest of God: the power of the keys, the power to bind and to loose from sin, the power of exorcism, the power to cast out from the creatures of God the evil spirits that have power over them, the power, the authority, to make the great God of Heaven come down upon the altar and take the form of bread and wine. What an awful power, Stephen!

A flame began to flutter again on Stephen's cheek as he heard in this proud address an echo of his own proud musings. How often had he seen himself as a priest wielding calmly and humbly the awful power of which angels and saints stood in reverence! His soul had loved to muse in secret on this desire. He had seen himself, a young and silentmannered priest, entering a confessional swiftly, ascending the altarsteps, incensing, genuflecting, accomplishing the vague acts of the priesthood which pleased him by reason of their semblance of reality and of their distance from it. In that dim life which he had lived through in his musings he had assumed the voices and gestures which he had noted with various priests. He had bent his knee sideways like such a one, he had shaken the thurible only slightly like such a one, his chasuble had swung open like that of such another as he had turned to the altar again after having blessed the people. And above all it had pleased him to fill the second place in those dim scenes of his imagining. He shrank from the dignity of celebrant because it displeased him to imagine that all the vague pomp should end in his own person or that the ritual should assign to him so clear and final an office. He longed for the minor sacred offices, to be vested with the tunicle of subdeacon at high mass, to stand aloof from the altar, forgotten by the people, his shoulders covered with a humeral veil, holding the paten within its folds, or, when the sacrifice had been accomplished, to stand as deacon in a dalmatic of cloth of gold on the step below the celebrant, his hands joined and his face towards the people, and sing the chant *Ite, missa est*. If ever he had seen himself celebrant it was as in the pictures of the mass in his child's massbook, in a church without worshippers, save for the angel of the sacrifice, at a bare altar and served by an acolyte scarcely more boyish than himself. In vague sacrificial or sacramental acts alone his will seemed drawn to go forth to encounter reality: and it was partly the absence of an appointed rite which had always constrained him to inaction whether he had allowed silence to cover his anger or pride or had suffered only an embrace he longed to give.

He listened in reverent silence now to the priest's appeal and through the words he heard even more distinctly a voice bidding him approach, offering him secret knowledge and secret power. He would know then what was the sin of Simon Magus and what the sin against the Holy Ghost for which there was no forgiveness. He would know obscure things, hidden from others, from those who were conceived and born children of wrath. He would know the sins, the sinful longings and sinful thoughts and sinful acts, of others, hearing them murmured into his ears in the confessional under the shame of a darkened chapel by the lips of women and of girls: but rendered immune mysteriously at his ordination by the imposition of hands his soul would pass again uncontaminated to the white peace of the altar. No touch of sin would linger upon the hands with which he would elevate and break the host; no touch of sin would linger on his lips in prayer to make him eat and drink damnation to himself, not discerning the body of the Lord. He would hold his secret knowledge and secret power, being as sinless as the innocent: and he would be a priest for ever according to the order of Melchisedec.

—I will offer up my mass tomorrow morning, said the director, that Almighty God may reveal to you His holy will. And let you, Stephen, make a novena to your holy patron saint, the first martyr, who is very powerful with God, that God may enlighten your mind. But you must be quite sure, Stephen, that you have a vocation because it would be terrible if you found afterwards that you had none. Once a priest ways a priest, remember. Your catechism tells you that the sacrament of Holy Orders is one of those which can be received only once because it imprints on the soul an indelible spiritual mark which can never be effaced. It is before you must weigh well, not after. It is a solemn question, Stephen, because on it may depend the salvation of your eternal soul. But we will pray to God together.

He held open the heavy halldoor and gave his hand as if already to a companion in the spiritual life. Stephen passed out on to the wide platform above the steps and was conscious of the caress of mild evening air. Towards Findlater's church a quartet of young men were striding along with linked arms, swaying their heads and stepping to the agile melody of their leader's concertina. The music passed in an instant, as the first bars of sudden music always did, over the fantastic fabrics of his mind, dissolving them painlessly and noiselessly as a sudden wave dissolves the sandbuilt turrets of children. Smiling at the trivial air he raised his eyes to the priest's face and, seeing in it a mirthless reflection of the sunken day, detached his hand slowly which had acquiesced faintly in that companionship.

As he descended the steps the impression which effaced his troubled selfcommunion was that of a mirthless mask reflecting a sunken day from the threshold of the college. The shadow, then, of the life of the college passed gravely over his consciousness. It was a grave and ordered and passionless life that awaited him, a life without material cares. He wondered how he would pass the first night in the novitiate and with what dismay he would wake the first morning in the dormitory. The troubling odour of the long corridors of Clongowes came back to him and he heard the discreet murmur of the burning gasflames. At once from every part of his being unrest began to irradiate. A feverish quickening of his pulses followed and a din of meaningless words drove his reasoned thoughts hither and thither confusedly. His lungs dilated and sank as if he were inhaling a warm moist unsustaining air and he smelt again the warm moist air which hung in the bath in Clongowes above the sluggish turf-coloured water.

Some instinct, waking at these memories, stronger than education or piety, quickened within him at every near approach to that life, an instinct subtle and hostile, and armed him against acquiescence. The chill and order of the life repelled him. He saw himself rising in the cold of the morning and filing down with the others to early mass and trying vainly to struggle with his prayers against the fainting sickness of his stomach. He saw himself sitting at dinner with the community of a college. What, then, had become of that deeprooted shyness of his which had made him loth to eat or drink under a strange roof? What had come of the pride of his spirit which had always made him conceive himself as a being apart in every order?

The Reverend Stephen Dedalus, S. J.

His name in that new life leaped into characters before his eyes and to it there followed a mental sensation of an undefined face or colour of a face. The colour faded and became strong like a changing glow of pallid brick red. Was it the raw reddish glow he had so often seen on wintry mornings on the shaven gills of the priests? The face was eyeless and sourfavoured and devout, shot with pink tinges of suffocated anger. Was it not a mental spectre of the face of one of the jesuits whom some of the boys called Lantern Jaws and others Foxy Campbell?

He was passing at that moment before the jesuit house in Gardiner Street, and wondered vaguely which window would be his if he ever joined the order. Then he wondered at the vagueness of his wonder, at the remoteness of his soul from what he had hitherto imagined her sanctuary, at the frail hold which so many years of order and obedience had of him when once a definite and irrevocable act of his threatened to end for ever, in time and in eternity, his freedom. The voice of the director urging upon him the proud claims of the church and the mystery and power of the priestly office repeated itself idly in his memory. His soul was not there to hear and greet it and he knew now that the exhortation he had listened to had already fallen into an idle formal tale. He would never swing the thurible before the tabernacle as priest. His destiny was to be elusive of social or religious orders. The wisdom of the priest's appeal did not touch him to the quick. He was destined to learn his own wisdom apart from others or to learn the wisdom of others himself wandering among the snares of the world.

The snares of the world were its ways of sin. He would fall. He had not yet fallen but he would fall silently, in an instant. Not to fall was too hard, too hard: and he felt the silent lapse of his soul, as it would be at some instant to come, falling, falling but not yet fallen, still unfallen but about to fall.

He crossed the bridge over the stream of the Tolka and turned his eyes coldly for an instant towards the faded blue shrine of the Blessed Virgin which stood fowlwise on a pole in the middle of a hamshaped encampment of poor cottages. Then, bending to the left, he followed the lane which led up to his house. The faint sour stink of rotted cabbages came towards him from the kitchengardens on the rising ground above the river. He smiled to think that it was this disorder, the misrule and confusion of his father's house and the stagnation of vegetable life, which was to win the day in his soul. Then a short laugh broke from his lips as he thought of that solitary farmhand in the kitchengardens behind their house whom they had nicknamed the man with the hat. A second laugh, taking rise from the first after a pause, broke from him involuntarily as he thought of how the man with the hat worked, considering in turn the four points of the sky and then regretfully plunging his spade in the earth.

He pushed open the latchless door of the porch and passed through the naked hallway into the kitchen. A group of his brothers and sisters was sitting round the table. Tea was nearly over and only the last of the second watered tea remained in the bottoms of the small glassjars and jampots which did service for teacups. Discarded crusts and lumps of sugared bread, turned brown by the tea which had been poured over them, lay scattered on the table. Little wells of tea lay here and there on the board and a knife with a broken ivory handle was stuck through the pith of a ravaged turnover.

The sad quiet greyblue glow of the dying day came through the window and the open door, covering over and allaying quietly a sudden instinct of remorse in Stephen's heart. All that had been denied them had been freely given to him, the eldest: but the quiet glow of evening showed him in their faces no sign of rancour.

He sat near them at the table and asked where his father and mother were. One answered:

—Goneboro toboro lookboro atboro aboro houseboro.

Still another removal! A boy named Fallon in Belvedere had often asked him with a silly laugh why they moved so often. A frown of scorn darkened quickly his forehead as he heard again the silly laugh of the questioner.

He asked:

—Why are we on the move again, if it's a fair question?

The same sister answered:

—Becauseboro theboro landboro lordboro willboro putboro usboro outboro.

The voice of his youngest brother from the farther side of the fireplace began to sing the air *Oft in the Stilly Night*. One by one the others took up the air until a full choir of voices was singing. They would sing so for hours, melody after melody, glee after glee, till the last pale light died down on the horizon, till the first dark night-clouds came forth and night fell.

He waited for some moments, listening, before he too took up the air with them. He was listening with pain of spirit to the overtone of weariness behind their frail fresh innocent voices. Even before they set out on life's journey they seemed weary already of the way.

He heard the choir of voices in the kitchen echoed and multiplied through an endless reverberation of the choirs of endless generations of children: and heard in all the echoes an echo also of the recurring note of weariness and pain. All seemed weary of life even before entering upon it. And he remembered that Newman had heard this note also in the broken lines of Virgil *giving utterance, like the voice of Nature herself, to that pain and weariness yet hope of better things which has been the experience of her children in every time.*

*   *   *

He could wait no longer.

From the door of Byron's publichouse to the gate of Clontarf Chapel, from the gate of Clontarf Chapel to the door of Byron's publichouse and then back again to the chapel and then back again to the publichouse he had paced slowly at first, planting his steps scrupulously in the spaces of the patchwork of the footpath, then timing their fall to the fall of verses. A full hour had passed since his father had gone in with Dan Crosby, the tutor, to find out for him something about the university. For a full hour he had paced up and down, waiting: but he could wait no longer.

He set off abruptly for the Bull, walking rapidly lest his father's shrill whistle might call him back; and in a few moments he had rounded the curve at the police barrack and was safe.

Yes, his mother was hostile to the idea, as he had read from her listless silence. Yet her mistrust pricked him more keenly than his father's pride and he thought coldly how he had watched the faith which was fading down in his soul aging and strengthening in her eyes. A dim antagonism gathered force within him and darkened his mind as a cloud against her disloyalty: and when it passed, cloudlike, leaving his mind serene and dutiful towards her again, he was made aware dimly and without regret of a first noiseless sundering of their lives.

The university! So he had passed beyond the challenge of the sentries who had stood as guardians of his boyhood and had sought to keep him among them that he might be subject to them and serve their ends. Pride after satisfaction uplifted him like long slow waves. The end he had been born to serve yet did not see had led him to escape by an unseen path: and now it beckoned to him once more and a new adventure was about to be opened to him. It seemed to him that he heard notes of fitful music leaping upwards a tone and downwards a diminished fourth, upwards a tone and downwards a major third, like triplebranching flames leaping fitfully, flame after flame, out of a midnight wood. It was an elfin prelude, endless and formless; and, as it grew wilder and faster, the flames leaping out of time, he seemed to hear from under the boughs and grasses wild creatures racing, their feet pattering like rain upon the leaves. Their feet passed in pattering tumult over his mind, the feet of hare and rabbits, the feet of harts and hinds and antelopes, until he heard them no more and remembered only a proud cadence from Newman: *Whose feet are as the feet of harts and underneath the everlasting arms.*

The pride of that dim image brought back to his mind the dignity of the office he had refused. All through his boyhood he had mused upon that which he had so often thought to be his destiny and when the moment had come for him to obey the call he had turned aside, obeying a wayward instinct. Now time lay between: the oils of ordination would never anoint his body. He had refused. Why?

He turned seaward from the road at Dollymount and as he passed on to the thin wooden bridge he felt the planks shaking with the tramp of heavily shod feet. A squad of christian brothers was on its way back from the Bull and had begun to pass, two by two, across the bridge. Soon the whole bridge was trembling and resounding. The uncouth faces passed him two by two, stained yellow or red or livid by the sea and, as he strove to look at them with ease and indifference, a faint stain of personal shame and commiseration rose to his own face. Angry with himself he tried to hide his face from their eyes by gazing down sideways into the shallow swirling water under the bridge but he still saw a reflection therein of their topheavy silk hats and humble tapelike collars and loosely hanging clerical clothes.

—Brother Hickey.

Brother Quaid.

Brother MacArdle.

Brother Keogh.

Their piety would be like their names, like their faces, like their clothes and it was idle for him to tell himself that their humble and contrite hearts, it might be, paid a far richer tribute of devotion than his had ever been, a gift tenfold more acceptable than his elaborate adoration. It was idle for him to move himself to be generous towards them, to tell himself that if he ever came to their gates, stripped of his pride, beaten and in beggar's weeds, that they would be generous towards him, loving him as themselves. Idle and embittering, finally, to argue, against his own dispassionate certitude, that the commandment of love bade us not to love our neighbour as ourselves with the same amount and intensity of love but to love him as ourselves with the same kind of love.

He drew forth a phrase from his treasure and spoke it softly to himself:

—A day of dappled seaborne clouds.

The phrase and the day and the scene harmonised in a chord. Words. Was it their colours? He allowed them to glow and fade, hue after hue: sunrise gold, the russet and green of apple orchards, azure of waves, the greyfringed fleece of clouds. No, it was not their colours: it was the poise and balance of the period itself. Did he then love the rhythmic rise and fall of words better than their associations of legend and colour? Or was it that, being as weak of sight as he was shy of mind, he drew less pleasure from the reflection of the glowing sensible world through the prism of language many coloured and richly storied than from the contemplation of an inner world of individual emotions mirrored perfectly in a lucid supple periodic prose?

He passed from the trembling bridge on to firm land again. At that instant, as it seemed to him, the air was chilled and looking askance towards the water he saw a flying squall darkening and crisping suddenly the tide. A faint click at his heart, a faint throb in his throat told him once more of how his flesh dreaded the cold infrahuman odour of the sea: yet he did not strike across the downs on his left but held straight on along the spine of rocks that pointed against the river's mouth.

A veiled sunlight lit up faintly the grey sheet of water where the river was embayed. In the distance along the course of the slow-flowing Liffey slender masts flecked the sky and, more distant still, the dim fabric of the city lay prone in haze. Like a scene on some vague arras, old as man's weariness, the image of the seventh city of christendom was visible to him across the timeless air, no older nor more weary nor less patient of subjection than in the days of the thingmote.

Disheartened, he raised his eyes towards the slowdrifting clouds, dappled and seaborne. They were voyaging across the deserts of the sky, a host of nomads on the march, voyaging high over Ireland, westward bound. The Europe they had come from lay out there beyond the Irish Sea, Europe of strange tongues and valleyed and woodbegirt and citadelled and of entrenched and marshalled races. He heard a confused music within him as of memories and names which he was almost conscious of but could not capture even for an instant; then the music seemed to recede, to recede, to recede: and from each receding trail of nebulous music there fell always one longdrawn calling note, piercing like a star the dusk of silence. Again! Again! Again! A voice from beyond the world was calling.

—Hello, Stephanos!

—Here comes The Dedalus!

—Ao! . . . Eh, give it over, Dwyer, I'm telling you or I'll give you a stuff in the kisser for yourself. . . . Ao!

—Good man, Towser! Duck him!

—Come along, Dedalus! Bous Stephanoumenos! Bous Stephaneforos!

—Duck him! Guzzle him now, Towser!

—Help! Help! . . . Ao!

He recognised their speech collectively before he distinguished their faces. The mere sight of that medley of wet nakedness chilled him to the bone. Their bodies, corpsewhite or suffused with a pallid golden light or rawly tanned by the suns, gleamed with the wet of the sea. Their divingstone, poised on its rude supports and rocking under their plunges, and the roughhewn stones of the sloping breakwater over which they scrambled in their horseplay gleamed with cold wet lustre. The towels with which they smacked their bodies were heavy with cold seawater: and drenched with cold brine was their matted hair.

He stood still in deference to their calls and parried their banter with easy words. How characterless they looked: Shuley without his deep unbuttoned collar, Ennis without his scarlet belt with the snaky clasp and Connolly without his Norfolk coat with the flapless side-pockets! It was a pain to see them and a swordlike pain to see the signs of adolescence that made repellent their pitiable nakedness. Perhaps they had taken refuge in number and noise from the secret dread in their souls. But he, apart from them and in silence, remembered in what dread he stood of the mystery of his own body.

—Stephanos Dedalos! Bous Stephanoumenos! Bous Stephane-foros!

Their banter was not new to him and now it flattered his mild proud sovereignty. Now, as never before, his strange name seemed to him a prophecy. So timeless seemed the grey warm air, so fluid and impersonal his own mood, that all ages were as one to him. A moment before the ghost of the ancient kingdom of the Danes had looked forth through the vesture of the hazewrapped city. Now, at the name of the fabulous artificer, he seemed to hear the noise of dim waves and to see a winged form flying above the waves and slowly climbing the air. What did it mean? Was it a quaint device opening a page of some medieval book of prophecies and symbols, a hawklike man flying sunward above the sea, a prophecy of the end he had been born to serve and had been following through the mists of childhood and boyhood, a symbol of the artist forging anew in his workshop out of the sluggish matter of the earth a new soaring impalpable imperishable being?

His heart trembled; his breath came faster and a wild spirit passed over his limbs as though he were soaring sunward. His heart trembled in an ecstasy of fear and his soul was in flight. His soul was soaring in an air beyond the world and the body he knew was purified in a breath and delivered of incertitude and made radiant and commingled with the element of the spirit. An ecstasy of flight made radiant his eyes and wild his breath and tremulous and wild and radiant his windswept limbs.

—One! Two! . . . Look out!

—O, Cripes, I'm drownded!

—One! Two! Three and away!

—Me next! Me next!

—One! . . . Uk!

—Stephaneforos!

His throat ached with a desire to cry aloud, the cry of a hawk or eagle on high, to cry piercingly of his deliverance to the winds. This was the call of life to his soul not the dull gross voice of the world of duties and despair, not the inhuman voice that had called him to the pale service of the altar. An instant of wild flight had delivered him and the cry of triumph which his lips withheld cleft his brain.

—Stephaneforos!

What were they now but cerements shaken from the body of death—the fear he had walked in night and day, the incertitude that had ringed him round, the shame that had abased him within and without—cerements, the linens of the grave?

His soul had arisen from the grave of boyhood, spurning her graveclothes. Yes! Yes! Yes! He would create proudly out of the freedom and power of his soul, as the great artificer whose name he bore, a living thing, new and soaring and beautiful, impalpable, imperishable.

He started up nervously from the stoneblock for he could no longer quench the flame in his blood. He felt his cheeks aflame and his throat throbbing with song. There was a lust of wandering in his feet that burned to set out for the ends of the earth. On! On! his heart seemed to cry. Evening would deepen above the sea, night fall upon the plains, dawn glimmer before the wanderer and show him strange fields and hills and faces. Where?

He looked northward towards Howth. The sea had fallen below the line of seawrack on the shallow side of the breakwater and already the tide was running out fast along the foreshore. Already one long oval bank of sand lay warm and dry amid the wavelets. Here and there warm isles of sand gleamed above the shallow tide, and about the isles and around the long bank and amid the shallow currents of the beach were lightclad gayclad figures, wading and delving.

In a few moments he was barefoot, his stockings folded in his pockets and his canvas shoes dangling by their knotted laces over his shoulders and, picking a pointed salteaten stick out of the jetsam among the rocks, he clambered down the slope of the breakwater.

There was a long rivulet in the strand and, as he waded slowly up its course, he wondered at the endless drift of seaweed. Emerald and black and russet and olive, it moved beneath the current, swaying and turning. The water of the rivulet was dark with endless drift and mirrored the highdrifting clouds. The clouds were drifting above him silently and silently the seatangle was drifting below him; and the grey warm air was still: and a new wild life was singing in his veins.

Where was his boyhood now? Where was the soul that had hung back from her destiny, to brood alone upon the shame of her wounds and in her house of squalor and subterfuge to queen it in faded cerements and in wreaths that withered at the touch? Or where was he?

He was alone. He was unheeded, happy and near to the wild heart of life. He was alone and young and wilful and wildhearted, alone amid a waste of wild air and brackish waters and the seaharvest of shells and tangle and veiled grey sunlight and gayclad lightclad figures of children and girls and voices childish and girlish in the air.

A girl stood before him in midstream, alone and still, gazing out to sea. She seemed like one whom magic had changed into the likeness of a strange and beautiful seabird. Her long slender bare legs were delicate as a crane's and pure save where an emerald trail of seaweed had fashioned itself as a sign upon the flesh. Her thighs, fuller and softhued as ivory, were bared almost to the hips where the white fringes of her drawers were like featherings of soft white down. Her slateblue skirts were kilted boldly about her waist and dovetailed behind her. Her bosom was as a bird's soft and slight, slight and soft as the breast of some darkplumaged dove. But her long fair hair was girlish: and girlish, and touched with the wonder of mortal beauty, her face.

She was alone and still, gazing out to sea: and when she felt his presence and the worship of his eyes her eyes turned to him in quiet sufferance of his gaze, without shame or wantonness. Long, long she suffered his gaze and then quietly withdrew her eyes from his and bent them towards the stream, gently stirring the water with her foot hither and thither. The first faint noise of gently moving water broke the silence, low and faint and whispering, faint as the bells of sleep; hither and thither, hither and thither: and a faint flame trembled on her cheek.

—Heavenly God! cried Stephen's soul, in an outburst of profane joy.

He turned away from her suddenly and set off across the strand. His cheeks were aflame; his body was aglow; his limbs were trembling. On and on and on and on he strode, far out over the sands, singing wildly to the sea, crying to greet the advent of the life that had cried to him.

Her image had passed into his soul for ever and no word had broken the holy silence of his ecstasy. Her eyes had called him and his soul had leaped at the call. To live, to err, to fall, to triumph, to recreate life out of life! A wild angel had appeared to him, the angel of mortal youth and beauty, an envoy from the fair courts of life, to throw open before him in an instant of ecstasy the gates of all the ways of error and glory. On and on and on and on!

He halted suddenly and heard his heart in the silence. How far had he walked? What hour was it?

There was no human figure near him nor any sound borne to him over the air. But the tide was near the turn and already the day was on the wane. He turned landward and ran towards the shore and, running up the sloping beach, reckless of the sharp shingle, found a sandy nook amid a ring of tufted sandknolls and lay down there that the peace and silence of the evening might still the riot of his blood.

He felt above him the vast indifferent dome and the calm processes of the heavenly bodies: and the earth beneath him, the earth that had borne him, had taken him to her breast.

He closed his eyes in the languor of sleep. His eyelids trembled as if they felt the vast cyclic movement of the earth and her watchers, trembled as if they felt the strange light of some new world. His soul was swooning into some new world, fantastic, dim, uncertain as under sea, traversed by cloudy shapes and beings. A world, a glimmer or a flower? Glimmering and trembling, trembling and unfolding, a breaking light, an opening flower, it spread in endless succession to itself, breaking in full crimson and unfolding and fading to palest rose, leaf by leaf and wave of light by wave of light, flooding all the heavens with its soft flushes, every flush deeper than other.

Evening had fallen when he woke and the sand and arid grasses of his bed glowed no longer. He rose slowly and, recalling the rapture of his sleep, sighed at its joy.

He climbed to the crest of the sandhill and gazed about him. Evening had fallen. A rim of the young moon cleft the pale waste of sky like the rim of a silver hoop embedded in grey sand; and the tide was flowing in fast to the land with a low whisper of her waves, islanding a few last figures in distant pools.

HE drained his third cup of watery tea to the dregs and set to chewing the crusts of fried bread that were scattered near him, staring into the dark pool of the jar. The yellow dripping had been scooped out like a boghole and the pool under it brought back to his memory the dark turfcoloured water of the bath in Clongowes. The box of pawn tickets at his elbow had just been rifled and he took up idly one after another in his greasy fingers the blue and white dockets, scrawled and sanded and creased and bearing the name of the pledger as Daly or MacEvoy.

1 Pair Buskins.

1 D. Coat.

3 Articles and White.

1 Man's Pants.

Then he put them aside and gazed thoughtfully at the lid of the box, speckled with lousemarks, and asked vaguely:

—How much is the clock fast now?

His mother straightened the battered alarmclock that was lying on its side in the middle of the kitchen mantelpiece until its dial showed a quarter to twelve and then laid it once more on its side.

—An hour and twentyfive minutes, she said. The right time now is twenty past ten. The dear knows you might try to be in time for your lectures.

—Fill out the place for me to wash, said Stephen.

—Katey, fill out the place for Stephen to wash.

—Boody, fill out the place for Stephen to wash.

—I can't, I'm going for blue. Fill it out, you, Maggie.

When the enamelled basin had been fitted into the well of the sink and the old washingglove flung on the side of it he allowed his mother to scrub his neck and root into the folds of his ears and into the interstices at the wings of his nose.

—Well, it's a poor case, she said, when a university student is so dirty that his mother has to wash him.

—But it gives you pleasure, said Stephen calmly.

An earsplitting whistle was heard from upstairs and his mother thrust a damp overall into his hands, saying:

—Dry yourself and hurry out for the love of goodness.

A second shrill whistle, prolonged angrily, brought one of the girls to the foot of the staircase.

—Yes, father?

—Is your lazy bitch of a brother gone out yet?

—Yes, father.

—Sure?

—Ycs, father.

—Hm!

The girl came back making signs to him to be quick and go out quietly by the back. Stephen laughed and said:

—He has a curious idea of genders if he thinks a bitch is masculine.

—Ah, it's a scandalous shame for you, Stephen, said his mother, and you'll live to rue the day you set your foot in that place. I know how it has changed you.

—Good morning, everybody, said Stephen, smiling and kissing the tips of his fingers in adieu.

The lane behind the terrace was waterlogged and as he went down it slowly, choosing his steps amid heaps of wet rubbish, he heard a mad nun screeching in the nuns' madhouse beyond the wall.

—Jesus! O Jesus! Jesus!

He shook the sound out of his ears by an angry toss of his head and hurried on, stumbling through the mouldering offal, his heart already bitten by an ache of loathing and bitterness. His father's whistle, his mother's mutterings, the screech of an unseen maniac were to him now so many voices offending and threatening to humble the pride of his youth. He drove their echoes even out of his heart with an execration: but, as he walked down the avenue and felt the grey morning light falling about him through the dripping trees and smelt the strange wild smell of the wet leaves and bark, his soul was loosed of her miseries.

The rainladen trees of the avenue evoked in him, as always, memories of the girls and women in the plays of Gerhart Hauptmann; and the memory of their pale sorrows and the fragrance falling from the wet branches mingled in a mood of quiet joy. His morning walk across the city had begun, and he foreknew that as he passed the sloblands of Fairview he would think of the cloistral silverveined prose of Newman, that as he walked along the North Strand Road, glancing idly at the windows of the provision shops, he would recall the dark humour of Guido Cavalcanti and smile, that as he went by Baird's stonecutting works in Talbot Place the spirit of Ibsen would blow through him like a keen wind, a spirit of wayward boyish beauty, and that passing a grimy marinedealer's shop beyond the Liffey he would repeat the song by Ben Jonson which begins:

I was not wearier where I lay.

His mind, when wearied of its search for the essence of beauty amid the spectral words of Aristotle or Aquinas, turned often for its pleasure to the dainty songs of the Elizabethans. His mind, in the vesture of a doubting monk, stood often in shadow under the windows of that age, to hear the grave and mocking music of the lutenists or the frank laughter of waistcoaters until a laugh too low, a phrase, tarnished by time, of chambering and false honour, stung his monkish pride and drove him on from his lurkingplace.

The lore which he was believed to pass his days brooding upon so that it had rapt him from the companionships of youth was only a garner of slender sentences from Aristotle's poetics and psychology and a *Synopsis Philosophiæ Scholasticæ ad mentem divi Thomæ*. His thinking was a dusk of doubt and selfmistrust lit up at moments by the lightnings of intuition, but lightnings of so clear a splendour that in those moments the world perished about his feet as if it had been fireconsumed: and thereafter his tongue grew heavy and he met the eyes of others with unanswering eyes for he felt that the spirit of beauty had folded him round like a mantle and that in revery at least he had been acquainted with nobility. But, when this brief pride of silence upheld him no longer, he was glad to find himself still in the midst of common lives, passing on his way amid the squalor and noise and sloth of the city fearlessly and with a light heart.

Near the hoardings on the canal he met the consumptive man with the doll's face and the brimless hat coming towards him down the slope of the bridge with little steps, tightly buttoned into his chocolate overcoat, and holding his furled umbrella a span or two from him like a diviningrod. It must be eleven, he thought, and peered into a dairy to see the time. The clock in the dairy told him that it was five minutes to five but, as he turned away, he heard a clock somewhere near him, but unseen, beating eleven strokes in swift precision. He laughed as he heard it for it made him think of Mac-Cann and he saw him a squat figure in a shooting jacket and breeches and with a fair goatee, standing in the wind at Hopkins' corner, and heard him say:

—Dedalus, you're an antisocial being, wrapped up in yourself. I'm not. I'm a democrat: and I'll work and act for social liberty and equality among all classes and sexes in the United States of the Europe of the future.

Eleven! Then he was late for that lecture too. What day of the week was it? He stopped at a newsagent's to read the headline of a placard. Thursday. Ten to eleven, English; eleven to twelve, French; twelve to one, physic. He fancied to himself the English lecture and felt, even at that distance, restless and helpless. He saw the heads of his classmates meekly bent as they wrote in their notebooks the points they were bidden to note, nominal definitions, essential definitions and examples or dates of birth or death, chief works, a favourable and an unfavourable criticism side by side. His own head was unbent for his thoughts wandered abroad and whether he looked around the little class of students or out of the window across the desolate gardens of the green an odour assailed him of cheerless cellardamp and decay. Another head than his, right before him in the first benches, was poised squarely above its bending fellows like the head of a priest appealing without humility to the tabernacle for the humble worshippers about him. Why was it that when he thought of Cranly he could never raise before his mind the entire image of his body but only the image of the head and face? Even now against the grey curtain of the morning he saw it before him like the phantom of a dream, the face of a severed head or deathmask, crowned on the brows by its stiff black upright hair as by an iron crown. It was a priestlike face, priestlike in its pallor, in the widewinged nose, in the shadowings below the eyes and along the jaws, priestlike in the lips that were long and bloodless and faintly smiling: and Stephen, remembering swiftly how he had told Cranly of all the tumults and unrest and longings in his soul, day after day and night by night, only to be answered by his friend's listening silence, would have told himself that it was the face of a guilty priest who heard confessions of those whom he had not power to absolve but that he felt again in memory the gaze of its dark womanish eyes.

Through this image he had a glimpse of a strange dark cavern of speculation but at once turned away from it, feeling that it was not yet the hour to enter it. But the nightshade of his friend's listlessness seemed to be diffusing in the air around him a tenuous and deadly exhalation and he found himself glancing from one casual word to another on his right or left in stolid wonder that they had been so silently emptied of instantaneous sense until every mean shop legend bound his mind like the words of a spell and his soul shrivelled up, sighing with age as he walked on in a lane among heaps of dead language. His own consciousness of language was ebbing from his brain and trickling into the very words themselves which set to band and disband themselves in wayward rhythms:

> The ivy whines upon the wall
> And whines and twines upon the wall
> The ivy whines upon the wall
> The yellow ivy on the wall
> Ivy, ivy up the wall.

Did any one ever hear such drivel? Lord Almighty! Who ever heard of ivy whining on a wall? Yellow ivy: that was all right. Yellow ivory also. And what about ivory ivy?

The word now shone in his brain, clearer and brighter than any ivory sawn from the mottled tusks of elephants. *Ivory, ivoire, avorio, ebur.* One of the first examples that he had learnt in Latin had run: *India mittit ebur;* and he recalled the shrewd northern face of the rector who had taught him to construe the Metamorphoses of Ovid in a courtly English, made whimsical by the mention of porkers and potsherds and chines of bacon. He had learnt what little he knew of the laws of Latin verse from a ragged book written by a Portuguese priest.

> *Contrahit orator, variant in carmine vates.*

The crises and victories and secessions in Roman history were handed on to him in the trite words *in tanto discrimine* and he had tried to peer into the social life of the city of cities through the words *implere ollam denariorum* which the rector had rendered sonorously as the filling of a pot with denaries. The pages of his timeworn Horace never felt cold to the touch even when his own fingers were cold: they were human pages: and fifty years before they had been turned by the human fingers of John Duncan Inverarity and by his brother, William Malcolm Inverarity. Yes, those were noble names on the dusky flyleaf and, even for so poor a Latinist as he, the dusky verses were as fragrant as though they had laid all those years in myrtle and lavender and vervain; but yet it wounded him to think that he would never be but a shy guest at the feast of the world's culture and that the monkish learning, in terms of which he was striving to forge out an esthetic philosophy, was held no higher by the age he lived in than the subtle and curious jargons of heraldry and falconry.

The grey block of Trinity on his left, set heavily in the city's ignorance like a great dull stone set in a cumbrous ring, pulled his mind downward; and while he was striving this way and that to free his feet from the fetters of the reformed conscience he came upon the droll statue of the national poet of Ireland.

He looked at it without anger for, though sloth of the body and of the soul crept over it like unseen vermin, over the shuffling feet and up the folds of the cloak and around the servile head, it seemed humbly conscious of its indignity. It was a Firbolg in the borrowed cloak of a Milesian; and he thought of his friend Davin, the peasant student. It was a jesting name between them but the young peasant bore with it lightly saying:

—Go on, Stevie, I have a hard head, you tell me. Call me what you will.

The homely version of his christian name on the lips of his friend had touched Stephen pleasantly when first heard for he was as formal in speech with others as they were with him. Often, as he sat in Davin's rooms in Grantham Street, wondering at his friend's well-made boots that flanked the wall pair by pair and repeating for his friend's simple ear the verses and cadences of others which were the veils of his own longing and dejection, the rude Firbolg mind of his listener had drawn his mind towards it and flung it back again, drawing it by a quiet inbred courtesy of attention or by a quaint turn of old English speech or by the force of its delight in rude bodily skill—for Davin had sat at the feet of Michael Cusack, the Gael—repelling swiftly and suddenly by a grossness of intelligence or by a bluntness of feeling or by a dull stare of terror in the eyes, the terror of soul of a starving Irish village in which the curfew was still a nightly fear.

Side by side with his memory of the deeds of prowess of his uncle Mat Davin, the athlete, the young peasant worshipped the sorrowful legend of Ireland. The gossip of his fellowstudents which strove to render the flat life of the college significant at any cost loved to think of him as a young fenian. His nurse had taught him Irish and shaped his rude imagination by the broken lights of Irish myth. He stood towards this myth upon which no individual mind had ever drawn out a line of beauty and to its unwieldy tales that divided themselves as they moved down the cycles in the same attitude as towards the Roman catholic religion, the attitude of a dullwitted loyal serf. Whatsoever of thought or of feeling came to him from England or by way of English culture his mind stood armed against in obedience to a password: and of the world that lay beyond England he knew only the foreign legion of France in which he spoke of serving.

Coupling this ambition with the young man's humour Stephen had often called him one of the tame geese: and there was even a point of irritation in the name pointed against that very reluctance of speech and deed in his friend which seemed so often to stand between Stephen's mind, eager of speculation, and the hidden ways of Irish life.

One night the young peasant, his spirit stung by the violent or luxurious language in which Stephen escaped from the cold silence of intellectual revolt, had called up before Stephen's mind a strange vision. The two were walking slowly towards Davin's rooms through the dark narrow streets of the poorer jews.

—A thing happened to myself, Stevie, last autumn, coming on winter, and I never told it to a living soul and you are the first person now I ever told it to. I disremember if it was October or November. It was October because it was before I came up here to join the matriculation class.

Stephen had turned his smiling eyes towards his friend's face, flattered by his confidence and won over to sympathy by the speaker's simple accent.

—I was away all that day from my own place over in Buttevant —I don't know if you know where that is—at a hurling match between the Croke's Own Boys and the Fearless Thurles and by God, Stevie, that was the hard fight. My first cousin, Fonsy Davin, was stripped to his buff that day minding cool for the Limericks but he was up with the forwards half the time and shouting like mad. I never will forget that day. One of the Crokes made a woeful wipe at him one time with his camann and I declare to God he was within an aim's ace of getting it at the side of the temple. Oh, honest to God, if the crook of it caught him that time he was done for.

—I am glad he escaped, Stephen had said with a laugh, but surely that's not the strange thing that happened you?

—Well, I suppose that doesn't interest you but leastways there was such noise after the match that I missed the train home and I couldn't get any kind of a yoke to give me a lift for, as luck would have it, there was a mass meeting that same day over in Castletown-roche and all the cars in the country were there. So there was nothing for it only to stay the night or to foot it out. Well, I started to walk and on I went and it was coming on night when I got into the Ballyhoura hills; that's better than ten miles from Kilmallock and there's a long lonely road after that. You wouldn't see the sign of a christian house along the road or hear a sound. It was pitch dark almost. Once or twice I stopped by the way under a bush to redden my pipe and only for the dew was thick I'd have stretched out there and slept. At last, after a bend of the road, I spied a little cottage with a light in the window. I went up and knocked at the door. A voice asked who was there and I answered I was over at the match in Buttevant and was walking back and that I'd be thankful for a glass of water. After a while a young woman opened the door and brought me out a big mug of milk. She was half undressed as if she was going to bed when I knocked and she had her hair hanging; and I thought by her figure and by something in the look of her eyes that she must be carrying a child. She kept me in talk a long while at the door and I thought it strange because her breast and her shoulders were bare. She asked me was I tired and would I like to stop the night there. She said she was all alone in the house and that her husband had gone that morning to Queenstown with her sister to see her off. And all the time she was talking, Stevie, she had her eyes fixed on my face and she stood so close to me I could hear her breathing. When I handed her back the mug at last she took my hand to draw me in over the threshold and said: *Come in and stay the night here. You've no call to be frightened. There's no one in it but ourselves.* . . . I didn't go in, Stevie. I thanked her and went on my way again, all in a fever. At the first bend of the road I looked back and she was standing at the door.

The last words of Davin's story sang in his memory and the figure of the woman in the story stood forth, reflected in other figures of the peasant women whom he had seen standing in the doorways at

Clane as the college cars drove by, as a type of her race and his own, a batlike soul waking to the consciousness of itself in darkness and secrecy and loneliness and, through the eyes and voice and gesture of a woman without guile, calling the stranger to her bed.

A hand was laid on his arm and a young voice cried:

—Ah, gentleman, your own girl, sir! The first handsel today, gentleman. Buy that lovely bunch. Will you, gentleman?

The blue flowers which she lifted towards him and her young blue eyes seemed to him at that instant images of guilelessness; and he halted till the image had vanished and he saw only her ragged dress and damp coarse hair and hoydenish face.

—Do, gentleman! Don't forget your own girl, sir!

—I have no money, said Stephen.

—Buy them lovely ones, will you, sir? Only a penny.

—Did you hear what I said? asked Stephen, bending towards her. I told you I had no money. I tell you again now.

—Well, sure, you will some day, sir, please God, the girl answered after an instant.

—Possibly, said Stephen, but I don't think it likely.

He left her quickly, fearing that her intimacy might turn to gibing and wishing to be out of the way before she offered her ware to another, a tourist from England or a student of Trinity. Grafton Street, along which he walked, prolonged that moment of discouraged poverty. In the roadway at the head of the street a slab was set to the memory of Wolfe Tone and he remembered having been present with his father at its laying. He remembered with bitterness that scene of tawdry tribute. There were four French delegates in a brake and one, a plump smiling young man, held, wedged on a stick, a card on which were printed the words: *Vive l'Irlande!*

But the trees in Stephen's Green were fragrant of rain and the rainsodden earth gave forth its mortal odour, a faint incense rising upward through the mould from many hearts. The soul of the gallant venal city which his elders had told him of had shrunk with time to a faint mortal odour rising from the earth and he knew that in a moment when he entered the sombre college he would be conscious of a corruption other than that of Buck Egan and Burnchapel Whaley.

It was too late to go upstairs to the French class. He crossed the hall and took the corridor to the left which led to the physics theatre.

The corridor was dark and silent but not unwatchful. Why did he feel that it was not unwatchful? Was it because he had heard that in Buck Whaley's time there was a secret staircase there? Or was the jesuit house extraterritorial and was he walking among aliens? The Ireland of Tone and of Parnell seemed to have receded in space.

He opened the door of the theatre and halted in the chilly grey light that struggled through the dusty windows. A figure was crouching before the large grate and by its leanness and greyness he knew that it was the dean of studies lighting the fire. Stephen closed the door quietly and approached the fireplace.

—Good morning, sir! Can I help you?

The priest looked up quickly and said:

—One moment now, Mr Dedalus, and you will see. There is an art in lighting a fire. We have the liberal arts and we have the useful arts. This is one of the useful arts.

—I will try to learn it, said Stephen.

—Not too much coal, said the dean, working briskly at his task, that is one of the secrets.

He produced four candle butts from the sidepockets of his soutane and placed them deftly among the coals and twisted papers. Stephen watched him in silence. Kneeling thus on the flagstone to kindle the fire and busied with the disposition of his wisps of paper and candle butts he seemed more than ever a humble server making ready the place of sacrifice in an empty temple, a levite of the Lord. Like a levite's robe of plain linen the faded worn soutane draped the kneeling figure of one whom the canonicals or the bellbordered ephod would irk and trouble. His very body had waxed old in lowly service of the Lord—in tending the fire upon the altar, in bearing tidings secretly, in waiting upon worldlings, in striking swiftly when bidden—and yet had remained ungraced by aught of saintly or of prelatic beauty. Nay, his very soul had waxed old in that service without growing towards light and beauty or spreading abroad a sweet odour of her sanctity—a mortified will no more responsive to the thrill of its obedience than was to the thrill of love or combat his aging body, spare and sinewy, greyed with a silverpointed down.

The dean rested back on his hunkers and watched the sticks catch. Stephen, to fill the silence, said:

—I am sure I could not light a fire.

—You are an artist, are you not, Mr Dedalus? said the dean,

glancing up and blinking his pale eyes. The object of the artist is the creation of the beautiful. What the beautiful is is another question.

He rubbed his hands slowly and drily over the difficulty.

—Can you solve that question now? he asked.

—Aquinas, answered Stephen, says *Pulcra sunt quæ visa placent*.

—This fire before us, said the dean, will be pleasing to the eye. Will it therefore be beautiful?

—In so far as it is apprehended by the sight, which I suppose means here esthetic intellection, it will be beautiful. But Aquinas also says *Bonum est in quod tendit appetitus*. In so far as it satisfies the animal craving for warmth fire is a good. In hell however it is an evil.

—Quite so, said the dean, you have certainly hit the nail on the head.

He rose nimbly and went towards the door, set it ajar and said:

—A draught is said to be a help in these matters.

As he came back to the hearth, limping slightly but with a brisk step, Stephen saw the silent soul of a jesuit look out at him from the pale loveless eyes. Like Ignatius he was lame but in his eyes burned no spark of Ignatius' enthusiasm. Even the legendary craft of the company, a craft subtler and more secret than its fabled books of secret subtle wisdom, had not fired his soul with the energy of apostleship. It seemed as if he used the shifts and lore and cunning of the world, as bidden to do, for the greater glory of God, without joy in their handling or hatred of that in them which was evil but turning them, with a firm gesture of obedience, back upon themselves: and for all this silent service it seemed as if he loved not at all the master and little, if at all, the ends he served. *Similiter atque senis baculus*, he was, as the founder would have had him, like a staff in an old man's hand, to be left in a corner, to be leaned on in the road at nightfall or in stress of weather, to lie with a lady's nosegay on a garden seat, to be raised in menace.

The dean returned to the hearth and began to stroke his chin.

—When may we expect to have something from you on the esthetic question? he asked.

—From me! said Stephen in astonishment. I stumble on an idea once a fortnight if I am lucky.

—These questions are very profound, Mr Dedalus, said the dean. It is like looking down from the cliffs of Moher into the depths.

Many go down into the depths and never come up. Only the trained diver can go down into those depths and explore them and come to the surface again.

—If you mean speculation, sir, said Stephen, I also am sure that there is no such thing as free thinking inasmuch as all thinking must be bound by its own laws.

—Ha!

—For my purpose I can work on at present by the light of one or two ideas of Aristotle and Aquinas.

—I sec. I quite sec your point.

—I need them only for my own use and guidance until I have done something for myself by their light. If the lamp smokes or smells I shall try to trim it. If it does not give light enough I shall sell it and buy another.

—Epictetus also had a lamp, said the dean, which was sold for a fancy price after his death. It was the lamp he wrote his philosophical dissertations by. You know Epictetus?

—An old gentleman, said Stephen coarsely, who said that the soul is very like a bucketful of water.

—He tells us in his homely way, the dean went on, that he put an iron lamp before a statue of one of the gods and that a thief stole the lamp. What did the philosopher do? He reflected that it was in the character of a thief to steal and determined to buy an earthen lamp next day instead of the iron lamp.

A smell of molten tallow came up from the dean's candle butts and fused itself in Stephen's consciousness with the jingle of the words, bucket and lamp and lamp and bucket. The priest's voice too had a hard jingling tone. Stephen's mind halted by instinct, checked by the strange tone and the imagery and by the priest's face which seemed like an unlit lamp or a reflector hung in a false focus. What lay behind it or within it? A dull torpor of the soul or the dullness of the thundercloud, charged with intellection and capable of the gloom of God?

—I meant a different kind of lamp, sir, said Stephen.

—Undoubtedly, said the dean.

—One difficulty, said Stephen, in esthetic discussion is to know whether words are being used according to the literary tradition or according to the tradition of the marketplace. I remember a sentence of Newman's in which he says of the Blessed Virgin that she was detained in the full company of the saints. The use of the word in the marketplace is quite different. *I hope I am not detaining you.*

—Not in the least, said the dean politely.

—No, no, said Stephen, smiling, I mean . . .

—Yes, yes: I see, said the dean quickly, I quite catch the point: *detain.*

He thrust forward his under jaw and uttered a dry short cough.

—To return to the lamp, he said, the feeding of it is also a nice problem. You must choose the pure oil and you must be careful when you pour it in not to overflow it, not to pour in more than the funnel can hold.

—What funnel? asked Stephen.

—The funnel through which you pour the oil into your lamp.

—That? said Stephen. Is that called a funnel? Is it not a tundish?

—What is a tundish?

—That. The . . . the funnel.

—Is that called a tundish in Ireland? asked the dean. I never heard the word in my life.

—It is called a tundish in Lower Drumcondra, said Stephen laughing, where they speak the best English.

—A tundish, said the dean reflectively. That is a most interesting word. I must look that word up. Upon my word I must.

His courtesy of manner rang a little false, and Stephen looked at the English convert with the same eyes as the elder brother in the parable may have turned on the prodigal. A humble follower in the wake of clamorous conversions, a poor Englishman in Ireland, he seemed to have entered on the stage of jesuit history when that strange play of intrigue and suffering and envy and struggle and indignity had been all but given through—a late comer, a tardy spirit. From what had he set out? Perhaps he had been born and bred among serious dissenters, seeing salvation in Jesus only and abhorring the vain pomps of the establishment. Had he felt the need of an implicit faith amid the welter of sectarianism and the jargon of its turbulent schisms, six principle men, peculiar people, seed and snake baptists, supralapsarian dogmatists? Had he found the true church all of a sudden in winding up to the end like a reel of cotton some finespun line of reasoning upon insufflation or the imposition of hands or the procession of the Holy Ghost? Or had Lord Christ touched him and bidden him follow, like that disciple who had sat at the receipt of custom, as he sat by the door of some zincroofed chapel, yawning and telling over his church pence?

The dean repeated the word yet again.

—Tundish! Well now, that is interesting!

—The question you asked me a moment ago seems to me more interesting. What is that beauty which the artist struggles to express from lumps of earth, said Stephen coldly.

The little word seemed to have turned a rapier point of his sensitiveness against this courteous and vigilant foe. He felt with a smart of dejection that the man to whom he was speaking was a countryman of Ben Jonson. He thought:

—The language in which we are speaking is his before it is mine. How different are the words *home, Christ, ale, master*, on his lips and on mine! I cannot speak or write these words without unrest of spirit. His language, so familiar and so foreign, will always be for me an acquired speech. I have not made or accepted its words. My voice holds them at bay. My soul frets in the shadow of his language.

—And to distinguish between the beautiful and the sublime, the dean added. To distinguish between moral beauty and material beauty. And to inquire what kind of beauty is proper to each of the various arts. These are some interesting points we might take up.

Stephen, disheartened suddenly by the dean's firm dry tone, was silent. The dean also was silent: and through the silence a distant noise of many boots and confused voices came up the staircase.

—In pursuing these speculations, said the dean conclusively, there is however the danger of perishing of inanition. First you must take your degree. Set that before you as your first aim. Then little by little, you will see your way. I mean in every sense, your way in life and in thinking. It may be uphill pedalling at first. Take Mr Moonan. He was a long time before he got to the top. But he got there.

—I may not have his talent, said Stephen quietly.

—You never know, said the dean brightly. We never can say what is in us. I most certainly should not be despondent. *Per aspera ad astra.*

He left the hearth quickly and went towards the landing to oversee the arrival of the first arts' class.

Leaning against the fireplace Stephen heard him greet briskly and impartially every student of the class and could almost see the frank smiles of the coarser students. A desolating pity began to fall like a dew upon his easily embittered heart for this faithful servingman of the knightly Loyola, for this halfbrother of the clergy, more venal than they in speech, more steadfast of soul than they, one whom he would never call his ghostly father: and he thought how this man and his companions had earned the name of worldlings at the hands not of the unworldly only but of the worldly also for having pleaded, during all their history, at the bar of God's justice for the souls of the lax and the lukewarm and the prudent.

The entry of the professor was signalled by a few rounds of Kentish fire from the heavy boots of those students who sat on the highest tier of the gloomy theatre under the grey cobwebbed windows. The calling of the roll began and the responses to the names were given out in all tones until the name of Peter Byrne was reached.

—Here!

A deep bass note in response came from the upper tier, followed by coughs of protest along the other benches.

The professor paused in his reading and called the next name:

—Cranly!

No answer.

—Mr Cranly!

A smile flew across Stephen's face as he thought of his friend's studies.

—Try Leopardstown! said a voice from the bench behind.

Stephen glanced up quickly but Moynihan's snoutish face, outlined on the grey light, was impassive. A formula was given out. Amid the rustling of the notebooks Stephen turned back again and said:

—Give me some paper for God's sake.

—Are you as bad as that? asked Moynihan with a broad grin.

He tore a sheet from his scribbler and passed it down, whispering:

—In case of necessity any layman or woman can do it.

The formula which he wrote obediently on the sheet of paper, the coiling and uncoiling calculations of the professor, the spectrelike symbols of force and velocity fascinated and jaded Stephen's mind, He had heard some say that the old professor was an atheist freemason. O the grey dull day! It seemed a limbo of painless patient consciousness through which souls of mathematicians might wander, projecting long slender fabrics from plane to plane of ever rarer and paler twilight, radiating swift eddies to the last verges of a universe ever vaster, farther and more impalpable.

—So we must distinguish between elliptical and ellipsoidal. Perhaps some of you gentlemen may be familiar with the works of Mr W. S. Gilbert. In one of his songs he speaks of the billiard sharp who is condemned to play:

> *On a cloth untrue*
> *With a twisted cue*
> *And elliptical billiard balls.*

—He means a ball having the form of the ellipsoid of the principal axes of which I spoke a moment ago.

Moynihan leaned down towards Stephen's ear and murmured:

—What price ellipsoidal balls! Chase me, ladies, I'm in the cavalry!

His fellowstudent's rude humour ran like a gust through the cloister of Stephen's mind, shaking into gay life limp priestly vestments that hung upon the walls, setting them to sway and caper in a sabbath of misrule. The forms of the community emerged from the gustblown vestments, the dean of studies, the portly florid bursar with his cap of grey hair, the president, the little priest with feathery hair who wrote devout verses, the squat peasant form of the professor of economics, the tall form of the young professor of mental science discussing on the landing a case of conscience with his class like a giraffe cropping high leafage among a herd of antelopes, the grave troubled prefect of the sodality, the plump roundheaded professor of Italian with his rogue's eyes. They came ambling and stumbling, tumbling and capering, kilting their gowns for leap frog, holding one another back, shaken with deep false laughter, smacking one another behind and laughing at their rude malice, calling to one another by familiar nicknames, protesting with sudden dignity at some rough usage, whispering two and two behind their hands.

The professor had gone to the glass cases on the sidewall from a shelf of which he took down a set of coils, blew away the dust from many points and, bearing it carefully to the table, held a finger on it while he proceeded with his lecture. He explained that the wires in modern coils were of compound called platinoid lately discovered by F. W. Martino.

He spoke clearly the initials and surname of the discoverer. Moynihan whispered from behind:

—Good old Fresh Water Martin!

—Ask him, Stephen whispered back with weary humour, if he wants a subject for electrocution. He can have me.

Moynihan, seeing the professor bend over the coils, rose in his bench and, clacking noiselessly the fingers of his right hand, began to call with the voice of a slobbering urchin:

—Please, teacher! Please, teacher! This boy is after saying a bad word, teacher.

—Platinoid, the professor said solemnly, is preferred to German silver because it has a lower coefficient of resistance variation by changes of temperature. The platinoid wire is insulated and the covering of silk that insulates it is wound on the ebonite bobbins just where my finger is. If it were wound single an extra current would be induced in the coils. The bobbins are saturated in hot paraffinwax . . .

A sharp Ulster voice said from the bench below Stephen:

—Are we likely to be asked questions on applied science?

The professor began to juggle gravely with the terms pure science and applied science. A heavybuilt student wearing gold spectacles stared with some wonder at the questioner. Moynihan murmured from behind in his natural voice:

—Isn't MacAlister a devil for his pound of flesh?

Stephen looked down coldly on the oblong skull beneath him overgrown with tangled twinecoloured hair. The voice, the accent, the mind of the questioner offended him and he allowed the offence to carry him towards wilful unkindness, bidding his mind think that the student's father would have done better had he sent his son to Belfast to study and have saved something on the train fare by so doing.

The oblong skull beneath did not turn to meet this shaft of thought and yet the shaft came back to its bowstring: for he saw in a moment the student's wheypale face.

—That thought is not mine, he said to himself quickly. It came from the comic Irishman in the bench behind. Patience. Can you say with certitude by whom the soul of your race was bartered and its elect betrayed—by the questioner or by the mocker? Patience. Remember Epictetus. It is probably in his character to ask such a question at such a moment in such a tone and to pronounce the word *science* as a monosyllable.

The droning voice of the professor continued to wind itself slowly round and round the coils it spoke of, doubling, trebling, quadrupling its somnolent energy as the coil multiplied its ohms of resistance.

Moynihan's voice called from behind in echo to a distant bell:

—Closing time, gents!

The entrance hall was crowded and loud with talk. On a table near the door were two photographs in frames and between them a long roll of paper bearing an irregular tail of signatures. MacCann went briskly to and fro among the students, talking rapidly, answering rebuffs and leading one after another to the table. In the inner hall the dean of studies stood talking to a young professor, stroking his chin gravely and nodding his head.

Stephen, checked by the crowd at the door, halted irresolutely. From under the wide falling leaf of a soft hat Cranly's dark eyes were watching him.

—Have you signed? Stephen asked.

Cranly closed his long thinlipped mouth, communed with himself an instant and answered:

—*Ego habeo.*

—What is it for?

—*Quod?*

—What is it for?

Cranly turned his pale face to Stephen and said blandly and bitterly:

—*Per pax universalis.*

Stephen pointed to the Czar's photograph and said:

—He has the face of a besotted Christ.

The scorn and anger in his voice brought Cranly's eyes back from a calm survey of the walls of the hall.

—Are you annoyed? he asked.

—No, answered Stephen.

—Are you in bad humour?

—No.

—*Credo ut vos sanguinarius mendax estis*, said Cranly, *quia facies vostra monstrat ut vos in damno malo humore estis.*

Moynihan, on his way to the table, said in Stephen's ear:

—MacCann is in tiptop form. Ready to shed the last drop. Brand new world. No stimulants and votes for the bitches.

Stephen smiled at the manner of this confidence and, when Moynihan had passed, turned again to meet Cranly's eyes.

—Perhaps you can tell me, he said, why he pours his soul so freely into my ear. Can you?

A dull scowl appeared on Cranly's forehead. He stared at the table where Moynihan had bent to write his name on the roll and then said flatly:

—A sugar!

—*Quis est in malo humore*, said Stephen, *ego aut vos?*

Cranly did not take up the taunt. He brooded sourly on his judgment and repeated with the same flat force:

—A flaming bloody sugar, that's what he is!

It was his epitaph for all dead friendships and Stephen wondered whether it would ever be spoken in the same tone over his memory. The heavy lumpish phrase sank slowly out of hearing like a stone through a quagmire. Stephen saw it sink as he had seen many another, feeling its heaviness depress his heart. Cranly's speech, unlike that of Davin, had neither rare phrases of Elizabethan English nor quaintly turned versions of Irish idioms. Its drawl was an echo of the quays of Dublin given back by a bleak decaying seaport, its energy an echo of the sacred eloquence of Dublin given back flatly by a Wicklow pulpit.

The heavy scowl faded from Cranly's face as MacCann marched briskly towards them from the other side of the hall.

—Here you are! said MacCann cheerily.

—Here I am! said Stephen.

—Late as usual. Can you not combine the progressive tendency with a respect for punctuality?

—That question is out of order, said Stephen. Next business.

His smiling eyes were fixed on a silverwrapped tablet of milk chocolate which peeped out of the propagandist's breastpocket. A little ring of listeners closed round to hear the war of wits. A lean student with olive skin and lank black hair thrust his face between the two, glancing from one to the other at each phrase and seeming to try to catch each flying phrase in his open moist mouth. Cranly took a small grey handball from his pocket and began to examine it closely, turning it over and over.

—Next business? said MacCann. Hom!

He gave a loud cough of laughter, smiled broadly and tugged twice at the strawcoloured goatee which hung from his blunt chin.

—The next business is to sign the testimonial.

—Will you pay me anything if I sign? asked Stephen.

—I thought you were an idealist, said MacCann.

The gipsylike student looked about him and addressed the onlookers in an indistinct bleating voice.

—By hell, that's a queer notion. I consider that notion to be a mercenary notion.

His voice faded into silence. No heed was paid to his words. He turned his olive face, equine in expression, towards Stephen, inviting him to speak again.

MacCann began to speak with fluent energy of the Czar's rescript, of Stead, of general disarmament, arbitration in cases of international disputes, of the signs of the times, of the new humanity and the new gospel of life which would make it the business of the community to secure as cheaply as possible the greatest possible happiness of the greatest possible number.

The gipsy student responded to the close of the period by crying:

—Three cheers for universal brotherhood!

—Go on, Temple, said a stout ruddy student near him. I'll stand you a pint after.

—I'm a believer in universal brotherhood, said Temple, glancing about him out of his dark oval eyes. Marx is only a bloody cod.

Cranly gripped his arm tightly to check his tongue, smiling uneasily, and repeated:

—Easy, easy, easy!

Temple struggled to free his arm but continued, his mouth flecked by a thin foam:

—Socialism was founded by an Irishman and the first man in Europe who preached the freedom of thought was Collins. Two hundred years ago. He denounced priestcraft, the philosopher of Middlesex. Three cheers for John Anthony Collins!

A thin voice from the verge of the ring replied:

—Pip! pip!

Moynihan murmured beside Stephen's ear:

—And what about John Anthony's poor little sister:

> *Lottie Collins lost her drawers;*
> *Won't you kindly lend her yours?*

Stephen laughed and Moynihan, pleased with the result, murmured again:

—We'll have five bob each way on John Anthony Collins.

—I am waiting for your answer, said MacCann briefly.

—The affair doesn't interest me in the least, said Stephen wearily. You know that well. Why do you make a scene about it?

—Good! said MacCann, smacking his lips. You are a reactionary then?

—Do you think you impress me, Stephen asked, when you flourish your wooden sword?

—Metaphors! said MacCann bluntly. Come to facts.

Stephen blushed and turned aside. MacCann stood his ground and said with hostile humour:

—Minor poets, I suppose, are above such trivial questions as the question of universal peace.

Cranly raised his head and held the handball between the two students by way of a peaceoffering, saying:

—*Pax super totum sanguinarium globum.*

Stephen, moving away the bystanders, jerked his shoulder angrily in the direction of the Czar's image, saying:

—Keep your icon. If we must have a Jesus let us have a legitimate Jesus.

—By hell, that's a good one! said the gipsy student to those about him. That's a fine expression. I like that expression immensely.

He gulped down the spittle in his throat as if he were gulping down the phrase and, fumbling at the peak of his tweed cap, turned to Stephen, saying:

—Excuse me, sir, what do you mean by that expression you uttered just now?

Feeling himself jostled by the students near him, he said to them:

—I am curious to know now what he meant by that expression.

He turned again to Stephen and said in a whisper:

—Do you believe in Jesus? I believe in man. Of course, I don't know if you believe in man. I admire you, sir. I admire the mind of man independent of all religions. Is that your opinion about the mind of Jesus?

—Go on, Temple, said the stout ruddy student, returning, as was his wont, to his first idea, that pint is waiting for you.

—He thinks I'm an imbecile, Temple explained to Stephen, because I'm a believer in the power of mind.

Cranly linked his arms into those of Stephen and his admirer and said:

—*Nos ad manum ballum jocabimus.*

Stephen, in the act of being led away, caught sight of MacCann's flushed bluntfeatured face.

—My signature is of no account, he said politely. You are right to go your way. Leave me to go mine.

—Dedalus, said MacCann crisply, I believe you're a good fellow but you have yet to learn the dignity of altruism and the responsibility of the human individual.

A voice said:

—Intellectual crankery is better out of this movement than in it.

Stephen, recognizing the harsh tone of MacAlister's voice, did not turn in the direction of the voice. Cranly pushed solemnly through the throng of students, linking Stephen and Temple like a celebrant attended by his ministers on his way to the altar.

Temple bent eagerly across Cranly's breast and said:

—Did you hear MacAlister what he said? That youth is jealous of you. Did you see that? I bet Cranly didn't see that. By hell, I saw that at once.

As they crossed the inner hall the dean of studies was in the act of escaping from the student with whom he had been conversing. He stood at the foot of the staircase, a foot on the lowest step, his threadbare soutane gathered about him for the ascent with womanish care, nodding his head often and repeating:

—Not a doubt of it, Mr Hackett! Very fine! Not a doubt of it!

In the middle of the hall the prefect of the college sodality was speaking earnestly, in a soft querulous voice, with a boarder. As he spoke he wrinkled a little his freckled brow and bit, between his phrases, at a tiny bone pencil.

—I hope the matric men will all come. The first arts men are pretty sure. Second arts too. We must make sure of the newcomers.

Temple bent again across Cranly, as they were passing through the doorway, and said in a swift whisper:

—Do you know that he is a married man? He was a married man before they converted him. He has a wife and children somewhere. By hell, I think that's the queerest notion I ever heard! Eh?

His whisper trailed off into sly cackling laughter. The moment they were through the doorway Cranly seized him rudely by the neck and shook him, saying:

—You flaming floundering fool! I'll take my dying bible there isn't a bigger bloody ape, do you know, than you in the whole flaming bloody world!

Temple wriggled in his grip, laughing still with sly content, while Cranly repeated flatly at every rude shake:

—A flaming flaring bloody idiot!

They crossed the weedy garden together. The president, wrapped in a heavy loose cloak, was coming towards them along one of the walks, reading his office. At the end of the walk he halted before turning and raised his eyes. The students saluted, Temple fumbling as before at the peak of his cap. They walked forward in silence. As they neared the alley Stephen could hear the thuds of the players' hands and the wet smacks of the ball and Davin's voice crying out excitedly at each stroke.

The three students halted round the box on which Davin sat to follow the game. Temple, after a few moments, sidled across to Stephen and said:

—Excuse me, I wanted to ask you do you believe that Jean Jacques Rousseau was a sincere man?

Stephen laughed outright. Cranly, picking up the broken stave of a cask from the grass at his foot, turned swiftly and said sternly:

—Temple, I declare to the living God if you say another word, do you know, to anybody on any subject I'll kill you *super spottum*.

—He was like you, I fancy, said Stephen, an emotional man.

—Blast him, curse him! said Cranly broadly. Don't talk to him at all. Sure, you might as well be talking, do you know, to a flaming chamberpot as talking to Temple. Go home, Temple. For God's sake, go home.

—I don't care a damn about you, Cranly, answered Temple, moving out of reach of the uplifted stave and pointing at Stephen. He's the only man I see in this institution that has an individual mind.

—Institution! Individual! cried Cranly. Go home, blast you, for you're a hopeless bloody man.

—I'm an emotional man, said Temple. That's quite rightly expressed. And I'm proud that I'm an emotionalist.

He sidled out of the alley, smiling slily. Cranly watched him with a blank expressionless face.

—Look at him! he said. Did you ever see such a go-by-the-wall?

His phrase was greeted by a strange laugh from a student who lounged against the wall, his peaked cap down on his eyes. The laugh, pitched in a high key and coming from a so muscular frame, seemed like the whinny of an elephant. The student's body shook all over and, to ease his mirth, he rubbed both his hands delightedly, over his groins.

—Lynch is awake, said Cranly.

Lynch, for answer, straightened himself and thrust forward his chest.

—Lynch puts out his chest, said Stephen, as a criticism of life.

Lynch smote himself sonorously on the chest and said:

—Who has anything to say about my girth?

Cranly took him at the word and the two began to tussle. When their faces had flushed with the struggle they drew apart, panting. Stephen bent down towards Davin who, intent on the game, had paid no heed to the talk of the others.

—And how is my little tame goose? he asked. Did he sign too?

Davin nodded and said:

—And you, Stevie?

Stephen shook his head.

—You're a terrible man, Stevie, said Davin, taking the short pipe from his mouth. Always alone.

—Now that you have signed the petition for universal peace, said Stephen, I suppose you will burn that little copybook I saw in your room.

As Davin did not answer Stephen began to quote:

—Long pace, fianna! Right incline, fianna! Fianna, by numbers, salute, one, two!

—That's a different question, said Davin. I'm an Irish nationalist, first and foremost. But that's you all out. You're a born sneerer, Stevie.

—When you make the next rebellion with hurleysticks, said Stephen, and want the indispensable informer, tell me. I can find you a few in this college.

—I can't understand you, said Davin. One time I hear you talk against English literature. Now you talk against the Irish informers. What with your name and your ideas . . . Are you Irish at all?

—Come with me now to the office of arms and I will show you the tree of my family, said Stephen.

—Then be one of us, said Davin. Why don't you learn Irish? Why did you drop out of the league class after the first lesson?

—You know one reason why, answered Stephen.

Davin tossed his head and laughed.

—O, come now, he said. Is it on account of that certain young lady and Father Moran? But that's all in your own mind, Stevie. They were only talking and laughing.

Stephen paused and laid a friendly hand upon Davin's shoulder.

—Do you remember, he said, when we knew each other first? The first morning we met you asked me to show you the way to the matriculation class, putting a very strong stress on the first syllable. You remember? Then you used to address the jesuits as father, you remember? I ask myself about you: *Is he as innocent as his speech?*

—I'm a simple person, said Davin. You know that. When you told me that night in Harcourt Street those things about your private life, honest to God, Stevie, I was not able to eat my dinner. I was quite bad. I was awake a long time that night. Why did you tell me those things?

—Thanks, said Stephen. You mean I am a monster.

—No, said Davin, but I wish you had not told me.

A tide began to surge beneath the calm surface of Stephen's friendliness.

—This race and this country and this life produced me, he said. I shall express myself as I am.

—Try to be one of us, repeated Davin. In your heart you are an Irishman but your pride is too powerful.

—My ancestors threw off their language and took another, Stephen said. They allowed a handful of foreigners to subject them. Do you fancy I am going to pay in my own life and person debts they made? What for?

—For our freedom, said Davin.

—No honourable and sincere man, said Stephen, has given up to you his life and his youth and his affections from the days of Tone to those of Parnell but you sold him to the enemy or failed him in need or reviled him and left him for another. And you invite me to be one of you. I'd see you damned first.

—They died for their ideals, Stevie, said Davin. Our day will come yet, believe me.

Stephen, following his own thought, was silent for an instant.

—The soul is born, he said vaguely, first in those moments I told you of. It has a slow and dark birth, more mysterious than the birth of the body. When the soul of a man is born in this country there are nets flung at it to hold it back from flight. You talk to me of nationality, language, religion. I shall try to fly by those nets.

Davin knocked the ashes from his pipe.

—Too deep for me, Stevie, he said. But a man's country comes first. Ireland first, Stevie. You can be a poet or a mystic after.

—Do you know what Ireland is? asked Stephen with cold violence. Ireland is the old sow that eats her farrow.

Davin rose from his box and went towards the players, shaking his head sadly. But in a moment his sadness left him and he was hotly disputing with Cranly and the two players who had finished their game. A match of four was arranged, Cranly insisting, however, that his ball should be used. He let it rebound twice or thrice to his hand and struck it strongly and swiftly towards the base of the alley, exclaiming in answer to its thud:

—Your soul!

Stephen stood with Lynch till the score began to rise. Then he plucked him by the sleeve to come away. Lynch obeyed, saying:

—Let us eke go, as Cranly has it.

Stephen smiled at this sidethrust. They passed back through the garden and out through the hall where the doddering porter was pinning up a notice in the frame. At the foot of the steps they halted and Stephen took a packet of cigarettes from his pocket and offered it to his companion.

—I know you are poor, he said.

—Damn your yellow insolence, answered Lynch.

This second proof of Lynch's culture made Stephen smile again.

—It was a great day for European culture, he said, when you made up your mind to swear in yellow.

They lit their cigarettes and turned to the right. After a pause Stephen began:

—Aristotle has not defined pity and terror. I have. I say . . .

Lynch halted and said bluntly:

—Stop! I won't listen! I am sick. I was out last night on a yellow drunk with Horan and Goggins.

Stephen went on:

—Pity is the feeling which arrests the mind in the presence of whatsoever is grave and constant in human sufferings and unites it with the human sufferer. Terror is the feeling which arrests the mind in the presence of whatsoever is grave and constant in human sufferings and unites it with the secret cause.

—Repeat, said Lynch.

Stephen repeated the definitions slowly.

—A girl got into a hansom a few days ago, he went on, in London. She was on her way to meet her mother whom she had not seen for many years. At the corner of a street the shaft of a lorry shivered the window of the hansom in the shape of a star. A long fine needle of the shivered glass pierced her heart. She died on the instant. The reporter called it a tragic death. It is not. It is remote from terror and pity according to the terms of my definitions.

—The tragic emotion, in fact, is a face looking two ways, towards terror and towards pity, both of which are phases of it. You see I use the word *arrest*. I mean that the tragic emotion is static. Or rather the dramatic emotion is. The feelings excited by improper art are kinetic, desire or loathing. Desire urges us to possess, to go to something; loathing urges us to abandon, to go from something. These are kinetic emotions. The arts which excite them, pornographical or didactic, are therefore improper arts. The esthetic emotion (I use the general term) is therefore static. The mind is arrested and raised above desire and loathing.

—You say that art must not excite desire, said Lynch. I told you that one day I wrote my name in pencil on the backside of the Venus of Praxiteles in the Museum. Was that not desire?

—I speak of normal natures, said Stephen. You also told me that when you were a boy in that charming carmelite school you ate pieces of dried cowdung.

Lynch broke again into a whinny of laughter and again rubbed both his hands over his groins but without taking them from his pockets.

—O I did! I did! he cried.

Stephen turned towards his companion and looked at him for a moment boldly in the eyes. Lynch, recovering from his laughter, answered his look from his humbled eyes. The long slender flattened skull beneath the long pointed cap brought before Stephen's mind the image of a hooded reptile. The eyes, too, were reptilelike in glint and gaze. Yet at that instant, humbled and alert in their look, they were lit by one tiny human point, the window of a shrivelled soul, poignant and selfembittered.

—As for that, Stephen said in polite parenthesis, we are all animals. I also am an animal.

—You are, said Lynch.

—But we are just now in a mental world, Stephen continued. The desire and loathing excited by improper esthetic means are really unesthetic emotions not only because they are kinetic in character but also because they are not more than physical. Our flesh shrinks from what it dreads and responds to the stimulus of what it desires by a purely reflex action of the nervous system. Our eyelid closes before we are aware that the fly is about to enter our eye.

—Not always, said Lynch critically.

—In the same way, said Stephen, your flesh responded to the stimulus of a naked statue but it was, I say, simply a reflex action of the nerves. Beauty expressed by the artist cannot awaken in us an emotion which is kinetic or a sensation which is purely physical. It awakens, or ought to awaken, or induces, or ought to induce, an esthetic stasis, an ideal pity or an ideal terror, a stasis called forth, prolonged and at last dissolved by what I call the rhythm of beauty.

—What is that exactly? asked Lynch.

—Rhythm, said Stephen, is the first formal esthetic relation of part to part in any esthetic whole or of an esthetic whole to its part or parts or of any part to the esthetic whole of which it is a part.

—If that is rhythm, said Lynch, let me hear what you call beauty: and, please remember, though I did eat a cake of cowdung once, that I admire only beauty.

Stephen raised his cap as if in greeting. Then, blushing slightly, he laid his hand on Lynch's thick tweed sleeve.

—We are right, he said, and the others are wrong. To speak of these things and to try to understand their nature and, having understood it, to try slowly and humbly and constantly to express, to press out again, from the gross earth or what it brings forth, from sound and shape and colour which are the prison gates of our soul, an image of the beauty we have come to understand—that is art.

They had reached the canal bridge and, turning from their course, went on by the trees. A crude grey light, mirrored in the sluggish water, and a smell of wet branches over their heads seemed to war against the course of Stephen's thought.

—But you have not answered my question, said Lynch. What is art? What is the beauty it expresses?

—That was the first definition I gave you, you sleepyheaded wretch, said Stephen, when I began to try to think out the matter for myself. Do you remember the night? Cranly lost his temper and began to talk about Wicklow bacon.

—I remember, said Lynch. He told us about them flaming fat devils of pigs.

—Art, said Stephen, is the human disposition of sensible or intelligible matter for an esthetic end. You remember the pigs and forget that. You are a distressing pair, you and Cranly.

Lynch made a grimace at the raw grey sky and said:

—If I am to listen to your esthetic philosophy give me at least another cigarette. I don't care about it. I don't even care about women. Damn you and damn everything. I want a job of five hundred a year. You can't get me one.

Stephen handed him the packet of cigarettes. Lynch took the last one that remained, saying simply:

—Proceed!

—Aquinas, said Stephen, says that is beautiful the apprehension of which pleases.

Lynch nodded.

—I remember that, he said. *Pulcra sunt quæ visa placent.*

—He uses the word *visa*, said Stephen, to cover esthetic apprehensions of all kinds, whether through sight or hearing or through any other avenue of apprehension. This word, though it is vague, is clear enough to keep away good and evil which excite desire and loathing. It means certainly a stasis and not a kinesis. How about the true? It produces also a stasis of the mind. You would not write your name in pencil across the hypothenuse of a rightangled triangle.

—No, said Lynch, give me the hypothenuse of the Venus of Praxiteles.

—Static therefore, said Stephen. Plato, I believe, said that beauty is the splendour of truth. I don't think that it has a meaning but the true and the beautiful are akin. Truth is beheld by the intellect which is appeased by the most satisfying relations of the intelligible: beauty is beheld by the imagination which is appeased by the most satisfying relations of the sensible. The first step in the direction of truth is to understand the frame and scope of the intellect itself, to comprehend the act itself of intellection. Aristotle's entire system of philosophy rests upon his book of psychology and that, I think, rests on his statement that the same attribute cannot at the same time and in the same connection belong to and not belong to the same subject. The first step in the direction of beauty is to understand the frame and scope of the imagination, to comprehend the act itself of esthetic apprehension. Is that clear?

—But what is beauty? asked Lynch impatiently. Out with another definition. Something we see and like! Is that the best you and Aquinas can do?

—Let us take woman, said Stephen.

—Let us take her! said Lynch fervently.

—The Greek, the Turk, the Chinese, the Copt, the Hottentot, said Stephen, all admire a different type of female beauty. That seems to be a maze out of which we cannot escape. I see however two ways out. One is this hypothesis: that every physical quality admired by men in women is in direct connection with the manifold functions of women for the propagation of the species. It may be so. The world, it seems, is drearier than even you, Lynch, imagined. For my part I dislike that way out. It leads to eugenics rather than to esthetic. It leads you out of the maze into a new gaudy lectureroom where MacCann, with one hand on *The Origin of Species* and the other hand on the new testament, tells you that you admired the great flanks of Venus because you felt that she would bear you burly offspring and admired her great breasts because you felt that she would give good milk to her children and yours.

—Then MacCann is a sulphuryellow liar, said Lynch energetically.

—There remains another way out, said Stephen, laughing.

—To wit? said Lynch.

—This hypothesis, Stephen began.

A long dray laden with old iron came round the corner of sir Patrick Dun's hospital covering the end of Stephen's speech with the harsh roar of jangled and rattling metal. Lynch closed his ears and gave out oath after oath till the dray had passed. Then he turned on his heel rudely. Stephen turned also and waited for a few moments till his companion's illhumour had had its vent.

—This hypothesis, Stephen repeated, is the other way out: that, though the same object may not seem beautiful to all people, all people who admire a beautiful object find in it certain relations which satisfy and coincide with the stages themselves of all esthetic apprehension. These relations of the sensible, visible to you through one form and to me through another, must be therefore the necessary qualities of beauty. Now, we can return to our old friend saint Thomas for another pennyworth of wisdom.

Lynch laughed.

—It amuses me vastly, he said, to hear you quoting him time after time like a jolly round friar. Are you laughing in your sleeve?

—MacAlister, answered Stephen, would call my esthetic theory applied Aquinas. So far as this side of esthetic philosophy extends Aquinas will carry me all along the line. When we come to the phenomena of artistic conception, artistic gestation and artistic reproduction I require a new terminology and a new personal experience.

—Of course, said Lynch. After all Aquinas, in spite of his intellect, was exactly a good round friar. But you will tell me about the new personal experience and new terminology some other day. Hurry up and finish the first part.

—Who knows? said Stephen, smiling. Perhaps Aquinas would understand me better than you. He was a poet himself. He wrote a hymn for Maundy Thursday. It begins with the words *Pange lingua gloriosi.* They say it is the highest glory of the hymnal. It is an intricate and soothing hymn. I like it: but there is no hymn that can be put beside that mournful and majestic processional song, the *Vexilla Regis* of Venantius Fortunatus.

Lynch began to sing softly and solemnly in a deep bass voice:

> *Impleta sunt quæ concinit*
> *David fideli carmine*
> *Dicendo nationibus*
> *Regnavit a ligno Deus.*

—That's great! he said, well pleased. Great music!

They turned into Lower Mount Street. A few steps from the

corner a fat young man, wearing a silk neckcloth, saluted them and stopped.

—Did you hear the results of the exams? he asked. Griffin was plucked. Halpin and O'Flynn are through the home civil. Moonan got fifth place in the Indian. O'Shaughnessy got fourteenth. The Irish fellows in Clarke's gave them a feed last night. They all ate curry.

His pallid bloated face expressed benevolent malice and as he had advanced through his tidings of success, his small fatencircled eyes vanished out of sight and his weak wheezing voice out of hearing.

In reply to a question of Stephen's his eyes and his voice came forth again from their lurkingplaces.

—Yes, MacCullagh and I, he said. He's taking pure mathematics and I'm taking constitutional history. There are twenty subjects. I'm taking botany too. You know I'm a member of the field club.

He drew back from the other two in a stately fashion and placed a plump woollengloved hand on his breast, from which muttered wheezing laughter at once broke forth.

—Bring us a few turnips and onions the next time you go out, said Stephen drily, to make a stew.

The fat student laughed indulgently and said:

—We are all highly respectable people in the field club. Last Saturday we went out to Glenmalure, seven of us.

—With women, Donovan? said Lynch.

Donovan again laid his hand on his chest and said:

—Our end is the acquisition of knowledge.

Then he said quickly:

—I hear you are writing some essay about esthetics.

Stephen made a vague gesture of denial.

—Goethe and Lessing, said Donovan, have written a lot on that subject, the classical school and the romantic school and all that. The *Laocoon* interested me very much when I read it. Of course it is idealistic, German, ultraprofound.

Neither of the others spoke. Donovan took leave of them urbanely.

—I must go, he said softly and benevolently. I have a strong suspicion, amounting almost to a conviction, that my sister intended to make pancakes today for the dinner of the Donovan family.

—Goodbye, Stephen said in his wake. Don't forget the turnips for me and my mate.

Lynch gazed after him, his lip curling in slow scorn till his face resembled a devil's mask:

—To think that that yellow pancakeeating excrement can get a good job, he said at length, and I have to smoke cheap cigarettes!

They turned their faces towards Merrion Square and went on for a little in silence.

—To finish what I was saying about beauty, said Stephen, the most satisfying relations of the sensible must therefore correspond to the necessary phases of artistic apprehension. Find these and you find the qualities of universal beauty. Aquinas says: *ad pulcritudinem tria requiruntur, integritas, consonantia, claritas.* I translate it so: *Three things are needed for beauty, wholeness, harmony and radiance.* Do these correspond to the phases of apprehension? Are you following?

Of course, I am, said Lynch. If you think I have an excrementitious intelligence run after Donovan and ask him to listen to you.

Stephen pointed to a basket which a butcher's boy had slung inverted on his head.

—Look at that basket, he said.

—I see it, said Lynch.

—In order to see that basket, said Stephen, your mind first of all separates the basket from the rest of the visible universe which is not the basket. The first phase of apprehension is a bounding line drawn about the object to be apprehended. An esthetic image is presented to us either in space or in time. What is audible is presented in time, what is visible is presented in space. But, temporal or spatial, the esthetic image is first luminously apprehended as selfbounded and selfcontained upon the immeasurable background of space or time which is not it. You apprehend it as *one* thing. You see it as one whole. You apprehend its wholeness. That is *integritas.*

—Bull's eye! said Lynch, laughing. Go on.

—Then, said Stephen, you pass from point to point, led by its formal lines; you apprehend it as balanced part against part within its limits; you feel the rhythm of its structure. In other words the synthesis of immediate perception is followed by the analysis of apprehension. Having first felt that it is *one* thing you feel now that it is a *thing.* You apprehend it as complex, multiple, divisible, separable, made up of its parts, the result of its parts and their sum, harmonious. That is *consonantia.*

—Bull's eye again! said Lynch wittily. Tell me now what is *claritas* and you win the cigar.

—The connotation of the word, Stephen said, is rather vague. Aquinas uses a term which seems to be inexact. It baffled me for a long time. It would lead you to believe that he had in mind symbolism or idealism, the supreme quality of beauty being a light from some other world, the idea of which the matter is but the shadow, the reality of which it is but the symbol. I thought he might mean that *claritas* is the artistic discovery and representation of the divine purpose in anything or a force of generalisation which would make the esthetic image a universal one, make it outshine its proper conditions. But that is literary talk. I understand it so. When you have apprehended that basket as one thing and have then analysed it according to its form and apprehended it as a thing you make the only synthesis which is logically and esthetically permissible. You see that it is that thing which it is and no other thing. The radiance of which he speaks is the scholastic *quidditas*, the *whatness* of a thing. This supreme quality is felt by the artist when the esthetic image is first conceived in his imagination. The mind in that mysterious instant Shelley likened beautifully to a fading coal. The instant wherein that supreme quality of beauty, the clear radiance of the esthetic image, is apprehended luminously by the mind which has been arrested by its wholeness and fascinated by its harmony is the luminous silent stasis of esthetic pleasure, a spiritual state very like to that cardiac condition which the Italian physiologist Luigi Galvani, using a phrase almost as beautiful as Shelley's, called the enchantment of the heart.

Stephen paused and, though his companion did not speak, felt that his words had called up around them a thoughtenchanted silence.

—What I have said, he began again, refers to beauty in the wider sense of the word, in the sense which the word has in the literary tradition. In the marketplace it has another sense. When we speak of beauty in the second sense of the term our judgment is influenced in the first place by the art itself and by the form of that art. The image, it is clear, must be set between the mind or senses of the artist himself and the mind or senses of others. If you bear this in memory you will see that art necessarily divides itself into three forms progressing from one to the next. These forms are: the lyrical form, the form wherein the artist presents his image in immediate relation to himself; the epical form, the form wherein he presents his image in mediate relation to himself and to others; the dramatic form, the form wherein he presents his image in immediate relation to others.

—That you told me a few nights ago, said Lynch, and we began the famous discussion.

—I have a book at home, said Stephen, in which I have written down questions which are more amusing than yours were. In finding the answers to them I found the theory of esthetic which I am trying to explain. Here are some questions I set myself: *Is a chair finely made tragic or comic? Is the portrait of Mona Lisa good if I desire to see it? Is the bust of Sir Philip Crampton lyrical, epical or dramatic? Can excrement or a child or a louse be a work of art? If not, why not?*

—Why not, indeed? said Lynch, laughing.

—*If a man hacking in fury at a blade of wood*, Stephen continued, *make there an image of a cow, is that image a work of art? If not, why not?*

—That's a lovely one, said Lynch, laughing again. That has the true scholastic stink.

—Lessing, said Stephen, should not have taken a group of statues to write of. The art, being inferior, does not present the forms I spoke of distinguished clearly one from another. Even in literature, the highest and most spiritual art, the forms are often confused. The lyrical form is in fact the simplest verbal vesture of an instant of emotion, a rhythmical cry as ages ago cheered on the man who pulled at the oar or dragged stones up a slope. He who utters it is more conscious of the instant of emotion than of himself as feeling emotion. The simplest epical form is seen emerging out of lyrical literature when the artist prolongs and broods upon himself as the centre of an epical event and this form progresses till the centre of emotional gravity is equidistant from the artist himself and from others. The narrative is no longer purely personal. The personality of the artist passes into the narration itself, flowing round and round the persons and the action like a vital sea. This progress you will see easily in that old English ballad *Turpin Hero* which begins in the first person and ends in the third person. The dramatic form is reached when the vitality which has flowed and eddied round each person fills every person with such vital force that he or she assumes a proper and intangible esthetic life. The personality of the artist, at first a cry or a cadence or a mood and then a fluid and lambent narrative, finally refines itself out of existence, impersonalises itself, so to speak. The esthetic image in the dramatic form is life purified in and reprojected from the human imagination. The mystery of esthetic like that of material creation is accomplished. The artist, like the God of the creation, remains within or behind or beyond or above his handiwork, invisible, refined out of existence, indifferent, paring his fingernails.

—Trying to refine them also out of existence, said Lynch.

A fine rain began to fall from the high veiled sky and they turned into the duke's lawn to reach the national library before the shower came.

—What do you mean, Lynch asked surlily, by prating about beauty and the imagination in this miserable Godforsaken island? No wonder the artist retired within or behind his handiwork after having perpetrated this country.

The rain fell faster. When they passed through the passage beside Kildare house they found many students sheltering under the arcade of the library. Cranly, leaning against a pillar, was picking his teeth with a sharpened match, listening to some companions. Some girls stood near the entrance door. Lynch whispered to Stephen:

—Your beloved is here.

Stephen took his place silently on the step below the group of students, heedless of the rain which fell fast, turning his eyes towards her from time to time. She too stood silently among her companions. She has no priest to flirt with, he thought with conscious bitterness, remembering how he had seen her last. Lynch was right. His mind, emptied of theory and courage, lapsed back into a listless peace.

He heard the students talking among themselves. They spoke of two friends who had passed the final medical examination, of the chances of getting places on ocean liners, of poor and rich practices.

—That's all a bubble. An Irish country practice is better.

—Hynes was two years in Liverpool and he says the same. A frightful hole he said it was. Nothing but midwifery cases. Half a crown cases.

—Do you mean to say it is better to have a job here in the country than in a rich city like that? I know a fellow . . .

—Hynes has no brains. He got through by stewing, pure stewing.

—Don't mind him. There's plenty of money to be made in a big commercial city.

—Depends on the practice.

—*Ego credo ut vita pauperum est simpliciter atrox, simpliciter sanguinarius atrox, in Liverpoolio.*

Their voices reached his ears as if from a distance in interrupted pulsation. She was preparing to go away with her companions.

The quick light shower had drawn off, tarrying in clusters of diamonds among the shrubs of the quadrangle where an exhalation was breathed forth by the blackened earth. Their trim boots prattled as they stood on the steps of the colonnade, talking quietly and gaily, glancing at the clouds, holding their umbrellas at cunning angles against the few last raindrops, closing them again, holding their skirts demurely.

And if he had judged her harshly? If her life were a simple rosary of hours, her life simple and strange as a bird's life, gay in the morning, restless all day, tired at sundown? Her heart simple and wilful as a bird's heart?

*   *   *

Towards dawn he awoke. O what sweet music! His soul was all dewy wet. Over his limbs in sleep pale cool waves of light had passed. He lay still, as if his soul lay amid cool waters, conscious of faint sweet music. His mind was waking slowly to a tremulous morning knowledge, a morning inspiration. A spirit filled him, pure as the purest water, sweet as dew, moving as music. But how faintly it was inbreathed, how passionlessly, as if the seraphim themselves were breathing upon him! His soul was waking slowly, fearing to awake wholly. It was that windless hour of dawn when madness wakes and strange plants open to the light and the moth flies forth silently.

An enchantment of the heart! The night had been enchanted. In a dream or vision he had known the ecstasy of seraphic life. Was it an instant of enchantment only or long hours and days and years and ages?

The instant of inspiration seemed now to be reflected from all sides at once from a multitude of cloudy circumstance of what had happened or of what might have happened. The instant flashed forth like a point of light and now from cloud on cloud of vague circumstance confused form was veiling softly its afterglow. O! In the virgin womb of the imagination the word was made flesh. Gabriel the seraph had come to the virgin's chamber. An afterglow deepened within his spirit, whence the white flame had passed, deepening to a rose and ardent light. That rose and ardent light was her strange wilful heart, strange that no man had known or would know, wilful from before the beginning of the world: and lured by that ardent roselike glow the choirs of the seraphim were falling from heaven.

> *Are you not weary of ardent ways,*
> *Lure of the fallen seraphim?*
> *Tell no more of enchanted days.*

The verses passed from his mind to his lips and, murmuring them over, he felt the rhythmic movement of a villanelle pass through them. The roselike glow sent forth its rays of rhyme; ways, days, blaze, praise, raise. Its rays burned up the world, consumed the hearts of men and angels: the rays from the rose that was her wilful heart.

> *Your eyes have set man's heart ablaze*
> *And you have had your will of him.*
> *Are you not weary of ardent ways?*

And then? The rhythm died away, ceased, began again to move and beat. And then? Smoke, incense ascending from the altar of the world.

> *Above the flame the smoke of praise*
> *Goes up from ocean rim to rim.*
> *Tell no more of enchanted days.*

Smoke went up from the whole earth, from the vapoury oceans, smoke of her praise. The earth was like a swinging smoking swaying censer, a ball of incense, an ellipsoidal ball. The rhythm died out at once; the cry of his heart was broken. His lips began to murmur the first verses over and over; then went on stumbling through half verses, stammering and baffled; then stopped. The heart's cry was broken.

The veiled windless hour had passed and behind the panes of the naked window the morning light was gathering. A bell beat faintly very far away. A bird twittered; two birds, three. The bell and the bird ceased: and the dull white light spread itself east and west, covering the world, covering the roselight in his heart.

Fearing to lose all, he raised himself suddenly on his elbow to look for paper and pencil. There was neither on the table; only the soup-plate he had eaten the rice from for supper and the candlestick with its tendrils of tallow and its paper socket, singed by the last flame. He stretched his arm wearily towards the foot of the bed, groping with his hand in the pockets of the coat that hung there. His fingers found a pencil and then a cigarette packet. He lay back and, tearing open the packet, placed the last cigarette on the windowledge and began to write out the stanzas of the villanelle in small neat letters on the rough cardboard surface.

Having written them out he lay back on the lumpy pillow, murmuring them again. The lumps of knotted flock under his head reminded him of the lumps of knotted horsehair in the sofa of her parlour on which he used to sit, smiling or serious, asking himself why he had come, displeased with her and with himself, confounded by the print of the Sacred Heart above the untenanted sideboard. He saw her approach him in a lull of the talk and beg him to sing one of his curious songs. Then he saw himself sitting at the old piano, striking chords softly from its speckled keys and singing, amid the talk which had risen again in the room, to her who leaned beside the mantelpiece a dainty song of the Elizabethans, a sad and sweet loth to depart, the victory chant of Agincourt, the happy air of Greensleeves. While he sang and she listened, or feigned to listen, his heart was at rest but when the quaint old songs had ended and he heard again the voices in the room he remembered his own sarcasm: the house where young men are called by their christian names a little too soon.

At certain instants her eyes seemed about to trust him but he had waited in vain. She passed now dancing lightly across his memory as she had been that night at the carnival ball, her white dress a little lifted, a white spray nodding in her hair. She danced lightly in the round. She was dancing towards him and, as she came, her eyes were a little averted and a faint glow was on her cheek. At the pause in the chain of hands her hand had lain in his an instant, a soft merchandise.

—You are a great stranger now.

—Yes. I was born to be a monk.

—I am afraid you are a heretic.

—Are you much afraid?

For answer she had danced away from him along the chain of hands, dancing lightly and discreetly, giving herself to none. The white spray nodded to her dancing and when she was in shadow the glow was deeper on her cheek.

A monk! His own image started forth a profaner of the cloister, a heretic franciscan, willing and willing not to serve, spinning like Gherardino da Borgo San Donnino, a lithe web of sophistry and whispering in her ear.

No, it was not his image. It was like the image of the young priest in whose company he had seen her last, looking at him out of dove's eyes, toying with the pages of her Irish phrasebook.

—Yes, yes, the ladies are coming round to us. I can see it every day. The ladies are with us. The best helpers the language has.

—And the church, Father Moran?

—The church too. Coming round too. The work is going ahead there too. Don't fret about the church.

Bah! he had done well to leave the room in disdain. He had done well not to salute her on the steps of the library. He had done well to leave her to flirt with her priest, to toy with a church which was the scullerymaid of christendom.

Rude brutal anger routed the last lingering instant of ecstasy from his soul. It broke up violently her fair image and flung the fragments on all sides. On all sides distorted reflections of her image started from his memory: the flowergirl in the ragged dress with damp coarse hair and a hoyden's face who had called herself his own girl and begged his handsel, the kitchengirl in the next house who sang over the clatter of her plates with the drawl of a country singer the first bars of *By Killarney's Lakes and Fells*, a girl who had laughed gaily to see him stumble when the iron grating in the footpath near Cork Hill had caught the broken sole of his shoe, a girl he had glanced at, attracted by her small ripe mouth, as she passed out of Jacob's biscuit factory, who had cried to him over her shoulder:

—Do you like what you seen of me, straight hair and curly eyebrows?

And yet he felt that, however he might revile and mock her image, his anger was also a form of homage. He had left the classroom in disdain that was not wholly sincere, feeling that perhaps the secret of her race lay behind those dark eyes upon which her long lashes flung a quick shadow. He had told himself bitterly as he walked through the streets that she was a figure of the womanhood of her country, a batlike soul waking to the consciousness of itself in darkness and secrecy and loneliness, tarrying awhile, loveless and sinless, with her mild lover and leaving him to whisper of innocent transgressions in the latticed ear of a priest. His anger against her found vent in coarse railing at her paramour, whose name and voice and features offended his baffled pride: a priested peasant, with a brother a policeman in Dublin and a brother a potboy in Moycullen. To him she would unveil her soul's shy nakedness, to one who was but schooled in the discharging of a formal rite rather than to him, a priest of the eternal imagination, transmuting the daily bread of experience into the radiant body of everliving life.

The radiant image of the eucharist united again in an instant his bitter and despairing thoughts, their cries arising unbroken in a hymn of thanksgiving.

> *Our broken cries and mournful lays*
> *Rise in one eucharistic hymn.*
> *Are you not weary of ardent ways?*
>
> *While sacrificing hands upraise*
> *The chalice flowing to the brim,*
> *Tell no more of enchanted days.*

He spoke the verses aloud from the first lines till the music and rhythm suffused his mind, turning it to quiet indulgence; then copied them painfully to feel them the better by seeing them; then lay back on his bolster.

The full morning light had come. No sound was to be heard: but he knew that all around him life was about to awaken in common noises, hoarse voices, sleepy prayers. Shrinking from that life he turned towards the wall, making a cowl of the blanket and staring at the great overblown scarlet flowers of the tattered wallpaper. He tried to warm his perishing joy in their scarlet glow, imagining a roseway from where he lay upwards to heaven all strewn with scarlet flowers. Weary! Weary! He too was weary of ardent ways.

A gradual warmth, a languorous weariness passed over him, descending along his spine from his closely cowled head. He felt it descend and, seeing himself as he lay, smiled. Soon he would sleep.

He had written verses for her again after ten years. Ten years before she had worn her shawl cowlwise about her head, sending sprays of her warm breath into the night air, tapping her foot upon the glassy road. It was the last tram; the lank brown horses knew it and shook their bells to the clear night in admonition. The conductor talked with the driver, both nodding often in the green light of the lamp. They stood on the steps of the tram, he on the upper, she on the lower. She came up to his step many times between their phrases and went down again and once or twice remained beside him forgetting to go down and then went down: Let be! Let be!

Ten years from that wisdom of children to his folly. If he sent her the verses? They would be read out at breakfast amid the tapping of eggshells. Folly indeed! The brothers would laugh and try to wrest the page from each other with their strong hard fingers. The suave priest, her uncle, seated in his armchair, would hold the page at arm's length, read it smiling and approve of the literary form.

No, no: that was folly. Even if he sent her the verses she would not show them to others. No, no: she could not.

He began to feel that he had wronged her. A sense of her innocence moved him almost to pity her, an innocence he had never understood till he had come to the knowledge of it through sin, an innocence which she too had not understood while she was innocent or before the strange humiliation of her nature had first come upon her. Then first her soul had begun to live as his soul had when he had first sinned: and a tender compassion filled his heart as he remembered her frail pallor and her eyes, humbled and saddened by the dark shame of womanhood.

While his soul had passed from ecstasy to languor where had she been? Might it be, in the mysterious ways of spiritual life, that her soul at those same moments had been conscious of his homage? It might be.

A glow of desire kindled again his soul and fired and fulfilled all his body. Conscious of his desire she was waking from odorous sleep, the temptress of his villanelle. Her eyes, dark and with a look of languor, were opening to his eyes. Her nakedness yielded to him, radiant, warm, odorous and lavishlimbed, enfolded him like a shining cloud, enfolded him like water with a liquid life: and like a cloud

of vapour or like waters circumfluent in space the liquid letters of
speech, symbols of the element of mystery, flowed forth over his
brain.

> *Are you not weary of ardent ways,*
> *Lure of the fallen seraphim?*
> *Tell no more of enchanted days.*
>
> *Your eyes have set man's heart ablaze*
> *And you have had your will of him.*
> *Are you not weary of ardent ways?*
>
> *Above the flame the smoke of praise*
> *Goes up from ocean rim to rim.*
> *Tell no more of enchanted days.*
>
> *Our broken cries and mournful lays*
> *Rise in one eucharistic hymn.*
> *Are you not weary of ardent ways?*
>
> *While sacrificing hands upraise*
> *The chalice flowing to the brim,*
> *Tell no more of enchanted days.*
>
> *And still you hold our longing gaze*
> *With languorous look and lavish limb!*
> *Are you not weary of ardent ways?*
> *Tell no more of enchanted days.*

*   *   *

What birds were they? He stood on the steps of the library to look
at them, leaning wearily on his ashplant. They flew round and round
the jutting shoulder of a house in Molesworth Street. The air of the
late March evening made clear their flight, their dark darting quivering bodies flying clearly against the sky as against a limphung cloth
of smoky tenuous blue.

He watched their flight; bird after bird: a dark flash, a swerve, a
flash again, a dart aside, a curve, a flutter of wings. He tried to count
them before all their darting quivering bodies passed: six, ten,
eleven: and wondered were they odd or even in number. Twelve,
thirteen: for two came wheeling down from the upper sky. They
were flying high and low but ever round and round in straight and

curving lines and ever flying from left to right, circling about a temple of air.

He listened to the cries: like the squeak of mice behind the wainscot: a shrill twofold note. But the notes were long and shrill and whirring, unlike the cry of vermin, falling a third or a fourth and trilled as the flying beaks clove the air. Their cry was shrill and clear and fine and falling like threads of silken light unwound from whirring spools.

The inhuman clamour soothed his ears in which his mother's sobs and reproaches murmured insistently and the dark frail quivering bodies wheeling and fluttering and swerving round an airy temple of the tenuous sky soothed his eyes which still saw the image of his mother's face.

Why was he gazing upwards from the steps of the porch, hearing their shrill twofold cry, watching their flight? For an augury of good or evil? A phrase of Cornelius Agrippa flew through his mind and then there flew hither and thither shapeless thoughts from Swedenborg on the correspondence of birds to things of the intellect and of how the creatures of the air have their knowledge and know their times and seasons because they, unlike man, are in the order of their life and have not perverted that order by reason.

And for ages men had gazed upward as he was gazing at birds in flight. The colonnade above him made him think vaguely of an ancient temple and the ashplant on which he leaned wearily of the curved stick of an augur. A sense of fear of the unknown moved in the heart of his weariness, a fear of symbols and portents, of the hawklike man whose name he bore soaring out of his captivity on osierwoven wings, of Thoth, the god of writers, writing with a reed upon a tablet and bearing on his narrow ibis head the cusped moon.

He smiled as he thought of the god's image for it made him think of a bottlenosed judge in a wig, putting commas into a document which he held at arm's length and he knew that he would not have remembered the god's name but that it was like an Irish oath. It was folly. But was it for this folly that he was about to leave for ever the house of prayer and prudence into which he had been born and the order of life out of which he had come?

They came back with shrill cries over the jutting shoulder of the house, flying darkly against the fading air. What birds were they? He thought that they must be swallows who had come back from the south. Then he was to go away for they were birds ever going and coming, building ever an unlasting home under the eaves of men's houses and ever leaving the homes they had built to wander.

> *Bend down your faces, Oona and Aleel.*
> *I gaze upon them as the swallow gazes*
> *Upon the nest under the eave before*
> *He wander the loud waters.*

A soft liquid joy like the noise of many waters flowed over his memory and he felt in his heart the soft peace of silent spaces of fading tenuous sky above the waters, of oceanic silence, of swallows flying through the seadusk over the flowing waters.

A soft liquid joy flowed through the words where the soft long vowels hurtled noiselessly and fell away, lapping and flowing back and ever shaking the white bells of their waves in mute chime and mute peal and soft low swooning cry; and he felt that the augury he had sought in the wheeling darting birds and in the pale space of sky above him had come forth from his heart like a bird from a turret quietly and swiftly.

Symbol of departure or of loneliness? The verses crooned in the ear of his memory composed slowly before his remembering eyes the scene of the hall on the night of the opening of the national theatre. He was alone at the side of the balcony, looking out of jaded eyes at the culture of Dublin in the stalls and at the tawdry scenecloths and human dolls framed by the garish lamps of the stage. A burly policeman sweated behind him and seemed at every moment about to act. The catcalls and hisses and mocking cries ran in rude gusts round the hall from his scattered fellowstudents.

—A libel on Ireland!
—Made in Germany!
—Blasphemy!
—We never sold our faith!
—No Irish woman ever did it!
—We want no amateur atheists.
—We want no budding buddhists.

A sudden swift hiss fell from the windows above him and he knew that the electric lamps had been switched on in the reader's room. He turned into the pillared hall, now calmly lit, went up the staircase and passed in through the clicking turnstile.

Cranly was sitting over near the dictionaries. A thick book, opened at the frontispiece, lay before him on the wooden rest. He leaned back in his chair, inclining his ear like that of a confessor to the face of the medical student who was reading to him a problem from the chess page of a journal. Stephen sat down at his right and the priest at the other side of the table closed his copy of *The Tablet* with an angry snap and stood up.

Cranly gazed after him blandly and vaguely. The medical student went on in a softer voice:

—Pawn to king's fourth.

—We had better go, Dixon, said Stephen in warning. He has gone to complain.

Dixon folded the journal and rose with dignity, saying:

—Our men retired in good order.

—With guns and cattle, added Stephen, pointing to the title-page of Cranly's book on which was printed *Diseases of the Ox*.

As they passed through a lane of the tables Stephen said:

—Cranly, I want to speak to you.

Cranly did not answer or turn. He laid his book on the counter and passed out, his wellshod feet sounding flatly on the floor. On the staircase he paused and gazing absently at Dixon repeated:

—Pawn to king's bloody fourth.

—Put it that way if you like, Dixon said.

He had a quiet toneless voice and urbane manners and on a finger of his plump clean hand he displayed at moments a signet ring.

As they crossed the hall a man of dwarfish stature came towards them. Under the dome of his tiny hat his unshaven face began to smile with pleasure and he was heard to murmur. The eyes were melancholy as those of a monkey.

—Good evening, captain, said Cranly, halting.

—Good evening, gentlemen, said the stubblegrown monkeyish face.

—Warm weather for March, said Cranly. They have the windows open upstairs.

Dixon smiled and turned his ring. The blackish monkeypuckered face pursed its human mouth with gentle pleasure: and its voice purred:

—Delightful weather for March. Simply delightful.

—There are two nice young ladies upstairs, captain, tired of waiting, Dixon said.

Cranly smiled and said kindly:

—The captain has only one love: sir Walter Scott. Isn't that so, captain?

—What are you reading now, captain? Dixon asked. *The Bride of Lammermoor?*

—I love old Scott, the flexible lips said. I think he writes something lovely. There is no writer can touch sir Walter Scott.

He moved a thin shrunken brown hand gently in the air in time to his praise and his thin quick eyelids beat often over his sad eyes.

Sadder to Stephen's ear was his speech: a genteel accent, low and moist, marred by errors: and listening to it he wondered was the story true and was the thin blood that flowed in his shrunken frame noble and come of an incestuous love?

The park trees were heavy with rain and rain fell still and ever in the lake, lying grey like a shield. A game of swans flew there and the water and the shore beneath were fouled with their greenwhite slime. They embraced softly, impelled by the grey rainy light, the wet silent trees, the shieldlike witnessing lake, the swans. They embraced without joy or passion, his arm about his sister's neck. A grey woollen cloak was wrapped athwart her from her shoulder to her waist: and her fair head was bent in willing shame. He had loose redbrown hair and tender shapely strong freckled hands. Face. There was no face seen. The brother's face was bent upon her fair rainfragrant hair. The hand freckled and strong and shapely and caressing was Davin's hand.

He frowned angrily upon his thought and on the shrivelled mannikin who had called it forth. His father's gibes at the Bantry gang leaped out of his memory. He held them at a distance and brooded uneasily on his own thought again. Why were they not Cranly's hands? Had Davin's simplicity and innocence stung him more secretly?

He walked on across the hall with Dixon, leaving Cranly to take leave elaborately of the dwarf.

Under the colonnade Temple was standing in the midst of a little group of students. One of them cried:

—Dixon, come over till you hear. Temple is in grand form.

Temple turned on him his dark gipsy eyes.

—You're a hypocrite, O'Keeffe, he said, and Dixon's a smiler. By hell, I think that's a good literary expression.

He laughed slily, looking in Stephen's face, repeating:

—By hell, I'm delighted with that name. A smiler.

A stout student who stood below them on the steps said:

—Come back to the mistress, Temple. We want to hear about that.

—He had, faith, Temple said. And he was a married man too. And all the priests used to be dining there. By hell, I think they all had a touch.

—We shall call it riding a hack to spare the hunter, said Dixon.

—Tell us, Temple, O'Keeffe said, how many quarts of porter have you in you?

—All your intellectual soul is in that phrase, O'Keeffe, said Temple with open scorn.

He moved with a shambling gait round the group and spoke to Stephen.

—Did you know that the Forsters are the kings of Belgium? he asked.

Cranly came out through the door of the entrance hall, his hat thrust back on the nape of his neck and picking his teeth with care.

—And here's the wiseacre, said Temple. Do you know that about the Forsters?

He paused for an answer. Cranly dislodged a figseed from his teeth on the point of his rude toothpick and gazed at it intently.

—The Forster family, Temple said, is descended from Baldwin the First, king of Flanders. He was called the Forester. Forester and Forster are the same name. A descendant of Baldwin the First, captain Francis Forster, settled in Ireland and married the daughter of the last chieftain of Clanbrassil. Then there are the Blake Forsters. That's a different branch.

—From Baldhead, king of Flanders, Cranly repeated, rooting again deliberately at his gleaming uncovered teeth.

—Where did you pick up all that history? O'Keeffe asked.

—I know all the history of your family too, Temple said, turning to Stephen. Do you know what Giraldus Cambrensis says about your family?

—Is he descended from Baldwin too? asked a tall consumptive student with dark eyes.

—Baldhead, Cranly repeated, sucking at a crevice in his teeth.

—*Pernobilis et pervetusta familia*, Temple said to Stephen.

The stout student who stood below them on the steps farted briefly. Dixon turned towards him saying in a soft voice:

—Did an angel speak?

Cranly turned also and said vehemently but without anger:

—Goggins, you're the flamingest dirty devil I ever met, do you know.

—I had it on my mind to say that, Goggins answered firmly. It did no one any harm, did it?

—We hope, Dixon said suavely, that it was not of the kind known to science as a *paulo post futurum*.

—Didn't I tell you he was a smiler? said Temple, turning right and left. Didn't I give him that name?

—You did. We're not deaf, said the tall consumptive.

Cranly still frowned at the stout student below him. Then, with a snort of disgust, he shoved him violently down the steps.

—Go away from here, he said rudely. Go away, you stinkpot. And you are a stinkpot.

Goggins skipped down on to the gravel and at once returned to his place with good humour. Temple turned back to Stephen and asked:

—Do you believe in the law of heredity?

—Are you drunk or what are you or what are you trying to say? asked Cranly, facing round on him with an expression of wonder.

—The most profound sentence ever written, Temple said with enthusiasm, is the sentence at the end of the zoology. Reproduction is the beginning of death.

He touched Stephen timidly at the elbow and said eagerly:

—Do you feel how profound that is because you are a poet?

Cranly pointed his long forefinger.

—Look at him! he said with scorn to the others. Look at Ireland's hope!

They laughed at his words and gesture. Temple turned on him bravely, saying:

—Cranly, you're always sneering at me. I can see that. But I am as good as you any day. Do you know what I think about you now as compared with myself?

—My dear man, said Cranly urbanely, you are incapable, do you know, absolutely incapable of thinking.

—But do you know, Temple went on, what I think of you and of myself compared together?

—Out with it, Temple! the stout student cried from the steps. Get it out in bits!

Temple turned right and left, making sudden feeble gestures as he spoke.

—I'm a ballocks, he said, shaking his head in despair. I am. And I know I am. And I admit it that I am.

Dixon patted him lightly on the shoulder and said mildly:

—And it does you every credit, Temple.

—But he, Temple said, pointing to Cranly. He is a ballocks too like me. Only he doesn't know it. And that's the only difference I see.

A burst of laughter covered his words. But he turned again to Stephen and said with a sudden eagerness:

—That word is a most interesting word. That's the only English dual number. Did you know?

—Is it? Stephen said vaguely.

He was watching Cranly's firmfeatured suffering face, lit up now by a smile of false patience. The gross name had passed over it like foul water poured over an old stone image, patient of injuries: and, as he watched him, he saw him raise his hat in salute and uncover the black hair that stood up stiffly from his forehead like an iron crown.

She passed out from the porch of the library and bowed across Stephen in reply to Cranly's greeting. He also? Was there not a slight flush on Cranly's cheek? Or had it come forth at Temple's words? The light had waned. He could not see.

Did that explain his friend's listless silence, his harsh comments, the sudden intrusions of rude speech with which he had shattered so often Stephen's ardent wayward confessions? Stephen had forgiven freely for he had found this rudeness also in himself towards himself. And he remembered an evening when he had dismounted from a borrowed creaking bicycle to pray to God in a wood near Malahide. He had lifted up his arms and spoken in ecstasy to the sombre nave of the trees, knowing that he stood on holy ground and in a holy hour. And when two constabularymen had come into sight round a bend in the gloomy road he had broken off his prayer to whistle loudly an air from the last pantomime.

He began to beat the frayed end of his ashplant against the base of a pillar. Had Cranly not heard him? Yet he could wait. The talk about him ceased for a moment: and a soft hiss fell again from a window above. But no other sound was in the air and the swallows whose flight he had followed with idle eyes were sleeping.

She had passed through the dusk. And therefore the air was silent save for one soft hiss that fell. And therefore the tongues about him had ceased their babble. Darkness was falling.

Darkness falls from the air.

A trembling joy, lambent as a faint light, played like a fairy host around him. But why? Her passage through the darkening air or the verse with its black vowels and its opening sound, rich and lutelike?

He walked away slowly towards the deeper shadows at the end of the colonnade, beating the stone softly with his stick to hide his revery from the students whom he had left: and allowed his mind to summon back to itself the age of Dowland and Byrd and Nash.

Eyes, opening from the darkness of desire, eyes that dimmed the breaking east. What was their languid grace but the softness of chambering? And what was their shimmer but the shimmer of the scum that mantled the cesspool of the court of a slobbering Stuart. And he tasted in the language of memory ambered wines, dying fallings of sweet airs, the proud pavan: and saw with the eyes of memory kind gentlewomen in Covent Garden wooing from their balconies with sucking mouths and the poxfouled wenches of the taverns and young wives that, gaily yielding to their ravishers, clipped and clipped again.

The images he had summoned gave him no pleasure. They were secret and enflaming but her image was not entangled by them. That was not the way to think of her. It was not even the way in which he thought of her. Could his mind then not trust itself? Old phrases, sweet only with a disinterred sweetness like the figseeds Cranly rooted out of his gleaming teeth.

It was not thought nor vision though he knew vaguely that her figure was passing homeward through the city. Vaguely first and then more sharply he smelt her body. A conscious unrest seethed in his blood. Yes, it was her body he smelt: a wild and languid smell: the tepid limbs over which his music had flowed desirously and the secret soft linen upon which her flesh distilled odour and a dew.

A louse crawled over the nape of his neck and, putting his thumb and forefinger deftly beneath his loose collar, he caught it. He rolled its body, tender yet brittle as a grain of rice, between thumb and finger for an instant before he let it fall from him and wondered would it live or die. There came to his mind a curious phrase from Cornelius a Lapide which said that the lice born of human sweat were not created by God with the other animals on the sixth day. But the tickling of the skin of his neck made his mind raw and red. The life of his body, illclad, illfed, louseeaten, made him close his eyelids in a sudden spasm of despair: and in the darkness he saw the brittle bright bodies of lice falling from the air and turning often as they fell. Yes; and it was not darkness that fell from the air. It was brightness.

Brightness falls from the air.

He had not even remembered rightly Nash's line. All the images it had awakened were false. His mind bred vermin. His thoughts were lice born of the sweat of sloth.

He came back quickly along the colonnade towards the group of students. Well then, let her go and be damned to her. She could love some clean athlete who washed himself every morning to the waist and had black hair on his chest. Let her.

Cranly had taken another dried fig from the supply in his pocket and was eating it slowly and noisily. Temple sat on the pediment of a pillar, leaning back, his cap pulled down on his sleepy eyes. A squat young man came out of the porch, a leather portfolio tucked under his armpit. He marched towards the group, striking the flags with the heels of his boots and with the ferrule of his heavy umbrella. Then, raising the umbrella in salute, he said to all:

—Good evening, sirs.

He struck the flags again and tittered while his head trembled with a slight nervous movement. The tall consumptive student and Dixon and O'Keeffe were speaking in Irish and did not answer him. Then, turning to Cranly, he said:

—Good evening, particularly to you.

He moved the umbrella in indication and tittered again. Cranly, who was still chewing the fig, answered with loud movements of his jaws.

—Good? Yes. It is a good evening.

The squat student looked at him seriously and shook his umbrella gently and reprovingly.

—I can see, he said, that you are about to make obvious remarks.

—Um, Cranly answered, holding out what remained of the halfchewed fig and jerking it towards the squat student's mouth in sign that he should eat.

The squat student did not eat it but, indulging his special humour, said gravely, still tittering and prodding his phrase with his umbrella:

—Do you intend that . . .

He broke off, pointed bluntly to the munched pulp of the fig and said loudly:

—I allude to that.

—Um, Cranly said as before.

—Do you intend that now, the squat student said, as *ipso facto* or, let us say, as so to speak?

Dixon turned aside from his group, saying:

—Goggins was waiting for you, Glynn. He has gone round to the Adelphi to look for you and Moynihan. What have you there? he asked, tapping the portfolio under Glynn's arm.

—Examination papers, Glynn answered. I give them monthly examinations to see that they are profiting by my tuition.

He also tapped the portfolio and coughed gently and smiled.

—Tuition! said Cranly rudely. I suppose you mean the barefooted children that are taught by a bloody ape like you. God help them!

He bit off the rest of the fig and flung away the butt.

—I suffer little children to come unto me, Glynn said amiably.

—A bloody ape, Cranly repeated with emphasis, and a blasphemous bloody ape!

Temple stood up and, pushing past Cranly, addressed Glynn:

—That phrase you said now, he said, is from the new testament about suffer the children to come to me.

—Go to sleep again, Temple, said O'Keeffe.

—Very well, then, Temple continued, still addressing Glynn, and if Jesus suffered the children to come why does the church send them all to hell if they die unbaptised? Why is that?

—Were you baptised yourself, Temple? the consumptive student asked.

—But why are they sent to hell if Jesus said they were all to come? Temple said, his eyes searching in Glynn's eyes.

Glynn coughed and said gently, holding back with difficulty the nervous titter in his voice and moving his umbrella at every word:

—And, as you remark, if it is thus I ask emphatically whence comes this thusness.

—Because the church is cruel like all old sinners, Temple said.

—Are you quite orthodox on that point, Temple? Dixon said suavely.

—Saint Augustine says that about unbaptised children going to hell, Temple answered, because he was a cruel old sinner too.

—I bow to you, Dixon said, but I had the impression that limbo existed for such cases.

—Don't argue with him, Dixon, Cranly said brutally. Don't talk to him or look at him. Lead him home with a sugan the way you'd lead a bleating goat.

—Limbo! Temple cried. That's a fine invention too. Like hell.

—But with the unpleasantness left out, Dixon said.

He turned smiling to the others and said:

—I think I am voicing the opinions of all present in saying so much.

—You are, Glynn said in a firm tone. On that point Ireland is united.

He struck the ferrule of his umbrella on the stone floor of the colonnade.

—Hell, Temple said. I can respect that invention of the grey spouse of Satan. Hell is Roman, like the walls of the Romans, strong and ugly. But what is limbo?

—Put him back into the perambulator, Cranly, O'Keeffe called out.

Cranly made a swift step towards Temple, halted, stamping his foot, crying as if to a fowl:

—Hoosh!

Temple moved away nimbly.

—Do you know what limbo is? he cried. Do you know what we call a notion like that in Roscommon?

—Hoosh! Blast you! Cranly cried, clapping his hands.

—Neither my arse nor my elbow! Temple cried out scornfully. And that's what I call limbo.

—Give us that stick here, Cranly said.

He snatched the ashplant roughly from Stephen's hand and sprang down the steps: but Temple, hearing him move in pursuit, fled through the dusk like a wild creature, nimble and fleetfooted.

Cranly's heavy boots were heard loudly charging across the quadrangle and then returning heavily, foiled and spurning the gravel at
each step.

His step was angry and with an angry abrupt gesture he thrust the
stick back into Stephen's hand. Stephen felt that his anger had
another cause but, feigning patience, touched his arm slightly and
said quietly:

—Cranly, I told you I wanted to speak to you. Come away.

Cranly looked at him for a few moments and asked:

—Now?

—Yes, now, Stephen said. We can't speak here. Come away.

They crossed the quadrangle together without speaking. The bird
call from *Siegfried* whistled softly followed them from the steps of
the porch. Cranly turned: and Dixon, who had whistled, called out:

—Where are you fellows off to? What about that game, Cranly?

They parleyed in shouts across the still air about a game of bil-
liards to be played in the Adelphi hotel. Stephen walked on alone
and out into the quiet of Kildare Street. Opposite Maple's hotel he
stood to wait, patient again. The name of the hotel, a colourless
polished wood, and its colourless quiet front stung him like a glance
of polite disdain. He stared angrily back at the softly lit drawing-
room of the hotel in which he imagined the sleek lives of the patricians of Ireland housed in calm. They thought of army commissions
and land agents: peasants greeted them along the roads in the country: they knew the names of certain French dishes and gave orders to
jarvies in highpitched provincial voices which pierced through their
skintight accents.

How could he hit their conscience or how cast his shadow over the
imaginations of their daughters, before their squires begat upon
them, that they might breed a race less ignoble than their own? And
under the deepened dusk he felt the thoughts and desires of the race
to which he belonged flitting like bats across the dark country lanes,
under trees by the edges of streams and near the poolmottled bogs. A
woman had waited in the doorway as Davin had passed by at night
and, offering him a cup of milk, had all but wooed him to her bed;
for Davin had the mild eyes of one who could be secret. But him no
woman's eyes had wooed.

His arm was taken in a strong grip and Cranly's voice said:

—Let us eke go.

They walked southward in silence. Then Cranly said:

—That blithering idiot Temple! I swear to Moses, do you know, that I'll be the death of that fellow one time.

But his voice was no longer angry and Stephen wondered was he thinking of her greeting to him under the porch.

They turned to the left and walked on as before. When they had gone on so for some time Stephen said.

—Cranly, I had an unpleasant quarrel this evening.

—With your people? Cranly asked.

—With my mother.

—About religion?

—Yes, Stephen answered.

After a pause Cranly asked:

—What age is your mother?

—Not old, Stephen said. She wishes me to make my easter duty.

—And will you?

—I will not, Stephen said.

—Why not? Cranly said.

—I will not serve, answered Stephen.

—That remark was made before, Cranly said calmly.

—It is made behind now, said Stephen hotly.

Cranly pressed Stephen's arm, saying:

—Go easy, my dear man. You're an excitable bloody man, do you know.

He laughed nervously as he spoke and, looking up into Stephen's face with moved and friendly eyes, said:

—Do you know that you are an excitable man?

—I daresay I am, said Stephen, laughing also.

Their minds, lately estranged, seemed suddenly to have been drawn closer, one to the other.

—Do you believe in the eucharist? Cranly asked.

—I do not, Stephen said.

—Do you disbelieve then?

—I neither believe in it nor disbelieve in it, Stephen answered.

—Many persons have doubts, even religious persons, yet they overcome them or put them aside, Cranly said. Are your doubts on that point too strong?

—I do not wish to overcome them, Stephen answered.

Cranly, embarrassed for a moment, took another fig from his pocket and was about to eat it when Stephen said:

—Don't, please. You cannot discuss this question with your mouth full of chewed fig.

Cranly examined the fig by the light of a lamp under which he halted. Then he smelt it with both nostrils, bit a tiny piece, spat it out and threw the fig rudely into the gutter. Addressing it as it lay, he said:

—Depart from me, ye cursed, into everlasting fire!

Taking Stephen's arm, he went on again and said:

—Do you not fear that those words may be spoken to you on the day of judgment?

—What is offered me on the other hand? Stephen asked. An eternity of bliss in the company of the dean of studies?

—Remember, Cranly said, that he would be glorified.

—Ay, Stephen said somewhat bitterly, bright, agile, impassible and, above all, subtle.

—It is a curious thing, do you know, Cranly said dispassionately, how your mind is supersaturated with the religion in which you say you disbelieve. Did you believe in it when you were at school? I bet you did.

—I did, Stephen answered.

—And were you happier then? Cranly asked softly. Happier than you are now, for instance?

—Often happy, Stephen said, and often unhappy. I was someone else then.

—How someone else? What do you mean by that statement?

—I mean, said Stephen, that I was not myself as I am now, as I had to become.

—Not as you are now, not as you had to become, Cranly repeated. Let me ask you a question. Do you love your mother?

Stephen shook his head slowly.

—I don't know what your words mean, he said simply.

—Have you never loved anyone? Cranly asked.

—Do you mean women?

—I am not speaking of that, Cranly said in a colder tone. I ask you if you ever felt love towards anyone or anything.

Stephen walked on beside his friend, staring gloomily at the footpath.

—I tried to love God, he said at length. It seems now I failed. It is very difficult. I tried to unite my will with the will of God instant by instant. In that I did not always fail. I could perhaps do that still . . .

Cranly cut him short by asking:

—Has your mother had a happy life?

—How do I know? Stephen said.

—How many children had she?

—Nine or ten, Stephen answered. Some died.

—Was your father. . . . Cranly interrupted himself for an instant: and then said: I don't want to pry into your family affairs. But was your father what is called well-to-do? I mean when you were growing up?

—Yes, Stephen said.

—What was he? Cranly asked after a pause.

Stephen began to enumerate glibly his father's attributes.

—A medical student, an oarsman, a tenor, an amateur actor, a shouting politician, a small landlord, a small investor, a drinker, a good fellow, a storyteller, somebody's secretary, something in a distillery, a taxgatherer, a bankrupt and at present a praiser of his own past.

Cranly laughed, tightening his grip on Stephen's arm, and said:

—The distillery is damn good.

—Is there anything else you want to know? Stephen asked.

—Are you in good circumstances at present?

—Do I look it? Stephen asked bluntly.

—So then, Cranly went on musingly, you were born in the lap of luxury.

He used the phrase broadly and loudly as he often used technical expressions as if he wished his hearer to understand that they were used by him without conviction.

—Your mother must have gone through a good deal of suffering, he said then. Would you not try to save her from suffering more even if . . . or would you?

—If I could, Stephen said. That would cost me very little.

—Then do so, Cranly said. Do as she wishes you to do. What is it for you? You disbelieve in it. It is a form: nothing else. And you will set her mind at rest.

He ceased and, as Stephen did not reply, remained silent. Then, as if giving utterance to the process of his own thought, he said:

—Whatever else is unsure in this stinking dunghill of a world a mother's love is not. Your mother brings you into the world, carries you first in her body. What do we know about what she feels? But whatever she feels, it, at least, must be real. It must be. What are our ideas or ambitions? Play. Ideas! Why, that bloody bleating goat Temple has ideas. MacCann has ideas too. Every jackass going the roads thinks he has ideas.

Stephen, who had been listening to the unspoken speech behind the words, said with assumed carelessness:

—Pascal, if I remember rightly, would not suffer his mother to kiss him as he feared the contact of her sex.

—Pascal was a pig, said Cranly.

—Aloysius Gonzaga, I think, was of the same mind, Stephen said.

—And he was another pig then, said Cranly.

—The church calls him a saint, Stephen objected.

—I don't care a flaming damn what anyone calls him, Cranly said rudely and flatly. I call him a pig.

Stephen, preparing the words neatly in his mind, continued:

—Jesus, too, seems to have treated his mother with scant courtesy in public but Suarez, a jesuit theologian and Spanish gentleman, has apologised for him.

—Did the idea ever occur to you, Cranly asked, that Jesus was not what he pretended to be?

—The first person to whom that idea occurred, Stephen answered, was Jesus himself.

—I mean, Cranly said, hardening in his speech, did the idea ever occur to you that he was himself a conscious hypocrite, what he called the jews of his time, a whited sepulchre? Or, to put it more plainly, that he was a blackguard?

—That idea never occurred to me, Stephen answered. But I am curious to know are you trying to make a convert of me or a pervert of yourself?

He turned towards his friend's face and saw there a raw smile which some force of will strove to make finely significant.

Cranly asked suddenly in a plain sensible tone:

—Tell me the truth. Were you at all shocked by what I said?

—Somewhat, Stephen said.

—And why were you shocked, Cranly pressed on in the same tone, if you feel sure that our religion is false and that Jesus was not the son of God?

—I am not at all sure of it, Stephen said. He is more like a son of God than a son of Mary.

—And is that why you will not communicate, Cranly asked, because you are not sure of that too, because you feel that the host too may be the body and blood of the son of God and not a wafer of bread? And because you fear that it may be?

—Yes, Stephen said quietly. I feel that and I also fear it.

—I see, Cranly said.

Stephen, struck by his tone of closure, reopened the discussion at once by saying:

—I fear many things: dogs, horses, firearms, the sea, thunderstorms, machinery, the country roads at night.

—But why do you fear a bit of bread?

—I imagine, Stephen said, that there is a malevolent reality behind those things I say I fear.

—Do you fear then, Cranly asked, that the God of the Roman catholics would strike you dead and damn you if you made a sacrilegious communion?

—The God of the Roman catholics could do that now, Stephen said. I fear more than that the chemical action which would be set up in my soul by a false homage to a symbol behind which are massed twenty centuries of authority and veneration.

—Would you, Cranly asked, in extreme danger commit that particular sacrilege? For instance, if you lived in the penal days?

—I cannot answer for the past, Stephen replied. Possibly not.

—Then, said Cranly, you do not intend to become a protestant?

—I said that I had lost the faith, Stephen answered, but not that I had lost selfrespect. What kind of liberation would that be to forsake an absurdity which is logical and coherent and to embrace one which is illogical and incoherent?

They had walked on towards the township of Pembroke and now, as they went on slowly along the avenues, the trees and the scattered lights in the villas soothed their minds. The air of wealth and repose diffused about them seemed to comfort their neediness. Behind a hedge of laurel a light glimmered in the window of a kitchen and the voice of a servant was heard singing as she sharpened knives. She sang, in short broken bars, *Rosie O'Grady*.

Cranly stopped to listen, saying:

—*Mulier cantat.*

The soft beauty of the Latin word touched with an enchanting touch the dark of the evening, with a touch fainter and more persuading than the touch of music or of a woman's hand. The strife of their minds was quelled. The figure of woman as she appears in the liturgy of the church passed silently through the darkness: a white-robed figure, small and slender as a boy and with a falling girdle. Her voice, frail and high as a boy's, was heard intoning from a distant choir the first words of a woman which pierce the gloom and clamour of the first chanting of the passion:

— *Et tu cum Jesu Galilæo eras.*

And all hearts were touched and turned to her voice, shining like a young star, shining clearer as the voice intoned the proparoxyton and more faintly as the cadence died.

The singing ceased. They went on together, Cranly repeating in strongly stressed rhythm the end of the refrain:

> *And when we are married.*
> *O, how happy we'll be*
> *For I love sweet Rosie O'Grady*
> *And Rosie O'Grady loves me.*

—There's real poetry for you, he said. There's real love.

He glanced sideways at Stephen with a strange smile and said:

—Do you consider that poetry? Or do you know what the words mean?

—I want to see Rosie first, said Stephen.

—She's easy to find, Cranly said.

His hat had come down on his forehead. He shoved it back: and in the shadow of the trees Stephen saw his pale face, framed by the dark, and his large dark eyes. Yes. His face was handsome: and his body was strong and hard. He had spoken of a mother's love. He felt then the sufferings of women, the weaknesses of their bodies and souls: and would shield them with strong and resolute arm and bow his mind to them.

Away then: it is time to go. A voice spoke softly to Stephen's lonely heart, bidding him go and telling him that his friendship was coming to an end. Yes; he would go. He could not strive against another. He knew his part.

—Probably I shall go away, he said.

—Where? Cranly asked.

—Where I can, Stephen said.

—Yes, Cranly said. It might be difficult for you to live here now. But is it that that makes you go?

—I have to go, Stephen answered.

—Because, Cranly continued, you need not look upon yourself as driven away if you do not wish to go or as a heretic or an outlaw. There are many good believers who think as you do. Would that surprise you? The church is not the stone building nor even the clergy and their dogmas. It is the whole mass of those born into it. I don't know what you wish to do in life. Is it what you told me the night we were standing outside Harcourt Street station?

—Yes, Stephen said, smiling in spite of himself at Cranly's way of remembering thoughts in connection with places. The night you spent half an hour wrangling with Doherty about the shortest way from Sallygap to Larras.

—Pothead! Cranly said with calm contempt. What does he know about the way from Sallygap to Larras? Or what does he know about anything for that matter? And the big slobbering washingpot head of him!

He broke out into a loud long laugh.

—Well? Stephen said. Do you remember the rest?

—What you said, is it? Cranly asked. Yes, I remember it. To discover the mode of life or of art whereby your spirit could express itself in unfettered freedom.

Stephen raised his hat in acknowledgment.

—Freedom! Cranly repeated. But you are not free enough yet to commit a sacrilege. Tell me, would you rob?

—I would beg first, Stephen said.

—And if you got nothing, would you rob?

—You wish me to say, Stephen answered, that the rights of property are provisional and that in certain circumstances it is not unlawful to rob. Everyone would act in that belief. So I will not make you that answer. Apply to the jesuit theologian Juan Mariana de Talavera who will also explain to you in what circumstances you may lawfully kill your king and whether you had better hand him his poison in a goblet or smear it for him upon his robe or his saddlebow. Ask me rather would I suffer others to rob me or, if they did, would I call down upon them what I believe is called the chastisement of the secular arm?

—And would you?

—I think, Stephen said, it would pain me as much to do so as to be robbed.

—I see, Cranly said.

He produced his match and began to clean the crevice between two teeth. Then he said carelessly:

—Tell me, for example, would you deflower a virgin?

—Excuse me, Stephen said politely, is that not the ambition of most young gentlemen?

—What then is your point of view? Cranly asked.

His last phrase, soursmelling as the smoke of charcoal and disheartening, excited Stephen's brain, over which its fumes seemed to brood.

—Look here, Cranly, he said. You have asked me what I would do and what I would not do. I will tell you what I will do and what I will not do. I will not serve that in which I no longer believe whether it call itself my home, my fatherland or my church: and I will try to express myself in some mode of life or art as freely as I can and as wholly as I can, using for my defence the only arms I allow myself to use—silence, exile, and cunning.

Cranly seized his arm and steered him round so as to lead him back towards Leeson Park. He laughed almost slily and pressed Stephen's arm with an elder's affection.

—Cunning indeed! he said. Is it you? You poor poet, you!

—And you made me confess to you, Stephen said, thrilled by his touch, as I have confessed to you so many other things, have I not?

—Yes, my child, Cranly said, still gaily.

—You made me confess the fears that I have. But I will tell you also what I do not fear. I do not fear to be alone or to be spurned for another or to leave whatever I have to leave. And I am not afraid to make a mistake, even a great mistake, a lifelong mistake and perhaps as long as eternity too.

Cranly, now grave again, slowed his pace and said:

—Alone, quite alone. You have no fear of that. And you know what that word means? Not only to be separate from all others but to have not even one friend.

—I will take the risk, said Stephen.

—And not to have any one person, Cranly said, who would be

more than a friend, more even than the noblest and truest friend a man ever had.

His words seemed to have struck some deep chord in his own nature. Had he spoken of himself, of himself as he was or wished to be? Stephen watched his face for some moments in silence. A cold sadness was there. He had spoken of himself, of his own loneliness which he feared.

—Of whom are you speaking? Stephen asked at length.

Cranly did not answer.

* * *

20 *March:* Long talk with Cranly on the subject of my revolt. He had his grand manner on. I supple and suave. Attacked me on the score of love for one's mother. Tried to imagine his mother: cannot. Told me once, in a moment of thoughtlessness, his father was sixty-one when he was born. Can see him. Strong farmer type. Pepper and salt suit. Square feet. Unkempt grizzled beard. Probably attends coursingmatches. Pays his dues regularly but not plentifully to Father Dwyer of Larras. Sometimes talks to girls after nightfall. But his mother? Very young or very old? Hardly the first. If so, Cranly would not have spoken as he did. Old then. Probably, and neglected. Hence Cranly's despair of soul: the child of exhausted loins.

21 *March, morning:* Thought this in bed last night but was too lazy and free to add it. Free, yes. The exhausted loins are those of Elisabeth and Zachary. Then he is the precursor. Item: he eats chiefly belly bacon and dried figs. Read locusts and wild honey. Also, when thinking of him, saw always a stern severed head or deathmask as if outlined on a grey curtain or veronica. Decollation they call it in the fold. Puzzled for the moment by saint John at the Latin gate. What do I see? A decollated precursor trying to pick the lock.

21 *March, night:* Free. Soulfree and fancyfree. Let the dead bury the dead. Ay. And let the dead marry the dead.

22 *March:* In company with Lynch followed a sizable hospital nurse. Lynch's idea. Dislike it. Two lean hungry greyhounds walking after a heifer.

23 *March:* Have not seen her since that night. Unwell? Sits at the fire perhaps with mamma's shawl on her shoulders. But not peevish. A nice bowl of gruel? Won't you now?

24 *March:* Began with a discussion with my mother. Subject:

B.V.M. Handicapped by my sex and youth. To escape held up relations between Jesus and Papa against those between Mary and her son. Said religion was not a lying-in hospital. Mother indulgent. Said I have a queer mind and have read too much. Not true. Have read little and understood less. Then she said I would come back to faith because I had a restless mind. This means to leave church by backdoor of sin and reenter through the skylight of repentance. Cannot repent. Told her so and asked for sixpence. Got threepence.

Then went to college. Other wrangle with little roundhead rogue's-eye Ghezzi. This time about Bruno the Nolan. Began in Italian and ended in pidgin English. He said Bruno was a terrible heretic. I said he was terribly burned. He agreed to this with some sorrow. Then gave me recipe for what he calls *risotto alla bergamasca*. When he pronounces a soft *o* he protrudes his full carnal lips as if he kissed the vowel. Has he? And could he repent? Yes, he could: and cry two round rogue's tears, one from each eye.

Crossing Stephen's, that is, my green, remembered that his countrymen and not mine had invented what Cranly the other night called our religion. A quartet of them, soldiers of the ninety-seventh infantry regiment, sat at the foot of the cross and tossed up dice for the overcoat of the crucified.

Went to library. Tried to read three reviews. Useless. She is not out yet. Am I alarmed? About what? That she will never be out again.

Blake wrote:

> *I wonder if William Bond will die*
> *For assuredly he is very ill.*

Alas, poor William!

I was once at a diorama in Rotunda. At the end were pictures of big nobs. Among them William Ewart Gladstone, just then dead. Orchestra played *O, Willie, we have missed you*.

A race of clodhoppers!

25 *March, morning:* A troubled night of dreams. Want to get them off my chest.

A long curving gallery. From the floor ascend pillars of dark vapours. It is peopled by the images of fabulous kings, set in stone. Their hands are folded upon their knees in token of weariness and their eyes are darkened for the errors of men go up before them for ever as dark vapours.

Strange figures advance from a cave. They are not as tall as men. One does not seem to stand quite apart from another. Their faces are phosphorescent, with darker streaks. They peer at me and their eyes seem to ask me something. They do not speak.

30 *March:* This evening Cranly was in the porch of the library, proposing a problem to Dixon and her brother. A mother let her child fall into the Nile. Still harping on the mother. A crocodile seized the child. Mother asked it back. Crocodile said all right if she told him what he was going to do with the child, eat it or not eat it.

This mentality, Lepidus would say, is indeed bred out of your mud by the operation of your sun.

And mine? Is it not too? Then into Nilemud with it!

1 *April:* Disapprove of this last phrase.

2 *April:* Saw her drinking tea and eating cakes in Johnston, Mooney and O'Brien's. Rather, lynxeyed Lynch saw her as we passed. He tells me Cranly was invited there by brother. Did he bring his crocodile? Is he the shining light now? Well, I discovered him. I protest I did. Shining quietly behind a bushel of Wicklow bran.

3 *April:* Met Davin at the cigar shop opposite Findlater's church. He was in a black sweater and had a hurleystick. Asked me was it true I was going away and why. Told him the shortest way to Tara was *via* Holyhead. Just then my father came up. Introduction. Father polite and observant. Asked Davin if he might offer him some refreshment. Davin could not, was going to a meeting. When we came away father told me he had a good honest eye. Asked me why I did not join a rowingclub. I pretended to think it over. Told me then how he broke Pennyfeather's heart. Wants me to read law. Says I was cut out for that. More mud, more crocodiles.

5 *April:* Wild spring. Scudding clouds. O life! Dark stream of swirling bogwater on which appletrees have cast down their delicate flowers. Eyes of girls among the leaves. Girls demure and romping. All fair or auburn: no dark ones. They blush better. Houp-la!

6 *April:* Certainly she remembers the past. Lynch says all women do. Then she remembers the time of her childhood—and mine if I was ever a child. The past is consumed in the present and the present is living only because it brings forth the future. Statues of

women, if Lynch be right, should always be fully draped, one hand of the woman feeling regretfully her own hinder parts.

6 *April, later:* Michael Robartes remembers forgotten beauty and, when his arms wrap her round, he presses in his arms the loveliness which has long faded from the world. Not this. Not at all. I desire to press in my arms the loveliness which has not yet come into the world.

10 *April:* Faintly, under the heavy night, through the silence of the city which has turned from dreams to dreamless sleep as a weary lover whom no caresses move, the sound of hoofs upon the road. Not so faintly now as they come near the bridge: and in a moment as they pass the darkened windows the silence is cloven by alarm as by an arrow. They are heard now far away, hoofs that shine amid the heavy night as gems, hurrying beyond the sleeping fields to what journey's end—what heart?—bearing what tidings?

11 *April:* Read what I wrote last night. Vague words for a vague emotion. Would she like it? I think so. Then I should have to like it also.

13 *April:* That tundish has been on my mind for a long time. I looked it up and find it English and good old blunt English too. Damn the dean of studies and his funnel! What did he come here for to teach us his own language or to learn it from us? Damn him one way or the other!

14 *April:* John Alphonsus Mulrennan has just returned from the west of Ireland. (European and Asiatic papers please copy.) He told us he met an old man there in a mountain cabin. Old man had red eyes and short pipe. Old man spoke Irish. Mulrennan spoke Irish. Then old man and Mulrennan spoke English. Mulrennan spoke to him about universe and stars. Old man sat, listened, smoked, spat. Then said:

—Ah, there must be terrible queer creatures at the latter end of the world.

I fear him. I fear his redrimmed horny eyes. It is with him I must struggle all through this night till day come, till he or I lie dead, gripping him by the sinewy throat till . . . Till what? Till he yield to me? No. I mean him no harm.

15 *April:* Met her today pointblank in Grafton Street. The crowd brought us together. We both stopped. She asked me why I never came, said she had heard all sorts of stories about me. This was only

to gain time. Asked me was I writing poems? About whom? I asked her. This confused her more and I felt sorry and mean. Turned off that valve at once and opened the spiritual-heroic refrigerating apparatus, invented and patented in all countries by Dante Alighieri. Talked rapidly of myself and my plans. In the midst of it unluckily I made a sudden gesture of a revolutionary nature. I must have looked like a fellow throwing a handful of peas into the air. People began to look at us. She shook hands a moment after and, in going away, said she hoped I would do what I said.

Now I call that friendly, don't you?

Yes, I liked her today. A little or much? Don't know. I liked her and it seems a new feeling to me. Then, in that case, all the rest, all that I thought I thought and all that I felt I felt, all the rest before now, in fact . . . O, give it up, old chap! Sleep it off!

16 *April:* Away! Away!

The spell of arms and voices: the white arms of roads, their promise of close embraces and the black arms of tall ships that stand against the moon, their tale of distant nations. They are held out to say: We are alone. Come. And the voices say with them: We are your kinsmen. And the air is thick with their company as they call to me, their kinsman, making ready to go, shaking the wings of their exultant and terrible youth.

26 *April:* Mother is putting my new secondhand clothes in order. She prays now, she says, that I may learn in my own life and away from home and friends what the heart is and what it feels. Amen. So be it. Welcome, O life! I go to encounter for the millionth time the reality of experience and to forge in the smithy of my soul the uncreated conscience of my race.

27 *April:* Old father, old artificer, stand me now and ever in good stead.

Dublin 1904
Trieste 1914

APPENDIX

LIST OF SELECTED VARIANTS

Key

MS	fair copy in the National Library of Ireland (MS 920 and MS 921); photoreproduced in *The James Joyce Archive*, ed. Michael Groden (New York and London: Garland, 1978), 9. 1–476 and 10. 477–1215.
TS	(for most of Chapter I and part of Chapter II) private collection; photoreproduced in *Archive*, 7. 158–229.
Eg	*Egoist* printing; 2 Feb. 1914–1 Sept. 1915.
a*Eg*C	Joyce's autograph errata lists (for Chs. III and IV) laid into composite copy of *Portrait* compiled by Joyce and Harriet Weaver from *Egoist* tearsheets and (for Ch. IV) galleys; in British Library (BL C.116.h.6); partially photoreproduced in *Archive* 7. 274–90 and 7. 230–73.
a*Eg*	Autograph corrections marked by Joyce (Chs. I, II, and V) and by Harriet Weaver from Joyce's autograph errata lists (for Chs. III and IV) on *Egoist* tearsheets; used as printer's copy for 16 (below); at Yale; photoreproduced in *Archive* 7. 292–453.
16	First edition; published by B. W. Huebsch in New York [English printing [1917]: used the American sheets from this edition with title-page laid in: 'THE EGOIST LTD.']
a16	Joyce's (and Harriet Weaver's) list of corrections to 16 (above); in British Library (BL C.116.c.6); photoreproduced in *Archive* 7. 475–490.
HSW	Corrections to 16 (above) marked by Harriet Weaver into copy of English issue of 16; served as printer's copy for 18 (below); in Bodleian Library, Oxford.
18	Second edition (England 1918); printed in Southport; published by The Egoist Press.
24	Third edition (England 1924), reset; published by Jonathan Cape.
64	Viking Edition, edited by Chester G. Anderson with Richard Ellmann: 'The definitive text corrected from the Dublin holograph'; in its 1968 Viking Critical Library printing.
68	Jonathan Cape printing of the 1964 'definitive text'.

5.0	I] *MS*, 18; CHAPTER I. *Eg*; CHAPTER I 16; § 1 24
5.11	green] geen *MS*
5.28	He] NEW PARAGRAPH *MS*, *Eg*
7.1	pocket] jacket *MS*
8.13	jump into] jump plop into *MS*
8.13	scum. Mother] scum. He shivered and longed to cry. It would be so nice to be at home. Mother *MS*
11.6	mother before] mother every night before *MS*
18.33	of the] of *MS*, *TS*
20.8	playgrounds. And] playgrounds. It was after lunchtime. And *MS*
23.16	poured a] poured out a *MS*, *TS*
24.23	turkey? But] turkey? It was not like a turkey. But *MS*
26.32	*depths*] *MS*–24; *depth* 64, 68
28.13	in] of *MS*
28.24	hoarse] harsh *MS*
29.19	brother] brothers *MS*
29.20	and the] and *MS*
32.1–2	Marquess] marquess *MS*, *TS*
32.3	their] this *MS*
34.15	in it] in *MS*–*16*
36.7	of] about *MS*
36.15	fellows] fellow *MS*, 24
36.18	*Cæsar*] Caesar *MS*, *TS*
36.30	ferulæ] ferulae *MS*, *TS*
38.16	playground] playgrounds *MS*, *TS*
38.24	of] in *MS*
38.35	there quietly] quietly there *MS*
42.9	say he] say that he *MS*
43.1	felt sorry] felt so sorry *MS*, *TS*
43.27	thought he] thought that he *MS*
44.16	go straight up] go up straight up *MS*, *TS*
44.33	lent] a16, 18–24; Lent *MS*–*16*, 64–68
44.39	men] man *MS*
46.22	quickly up to] quickly to *MS, TS*
50.0	II] *MS*, 18; II.*TS*, *Eg*; CHAPTER II 16; §2 24; 2 68
50.1	his nephew] his outspoken nephew *MS*
51.19	blue] bluer *MS*
52.2	nearer] nearest *MS*
52.7	take part] take his part *MS*, *TS*
53.5	Stradbrooke] Stradbrook *MS*, *Eg*–68; Shadbrook *TS*
53.14	he was] he knew he was *MS*

53.29   legs] limbs *MS, TS*
55.27   stocked] stacked *MS*
56.6   testing] tasting *MS–Eg*
56.35   changes she had seen] changes that she had seen *MS*;
             changes that she seen *Eg*; changes they had seen 16–24
57.8   break over] break out over *MS*
57.27   glance] glances *MS*
61.1–2   —I [. . .] Ha!] 24; —I [. . .] Ha!—*MS*;—I [. . .] Ha! *Eg*–18
61.2   *we all had*] 24; we all had *MS, Eg*–18; *we had* 64–68
61.18   on the] on to the *MS*
61.19   on the] on to the *MS*–24
61.23   had had] had *MS*
62.5   circling] arching *MS*
62.22   passed] pressed *MS*
62.31   among] amid *MS*
63.7–8   a doorway] the doorway *MS*
65.1   breast] heart *MS*
65.15   movement] moment 24
66.1   allured] allured him *MS, TS*
66.3   which] that *MS*
67.29   many say] many people say *MS*
67.30   explanation. Of] 64–68; explanation—Of *MS*; explana-
             tion—of *TS*; explanation; of 16; explanation, of a16,
             18–24
69.9–10   he, torn and flushed and panting, stumbled after them
             half blinded with tears,] he, torn and flushed and panting,
             stumbled after them, half blinded with tears, *MS*; he, half
             blinded with tears, *TS, Eg*; he, half blinded with tears,
             stumbled on, a*Eg*, 16–24
69.20   its] her *MS*
73.3   at] in *MS*
74.13   *bonny*] boney *MS, Eg*; bony a*Eg*, 16–24
74.31   boy who] boy *MS*
74.36   the] its *MS*
75.20   *Fœtus*] Foetus *MS*
78.29   Pickackafax] Pickackafox *MS*
80.4   it's time] it's about time *MS*
80.34   ineffectualness] ineffectiveness 18–24
81.13   to say he was] to say that he was *MS*
81.29   windows] window *MS*
82.30   water] waters *MS*, 24
82.35   from mother] from father and mother *MS*

83.2	subterfuge] subterfuges *MS*
86.0	III] *MS*, 18; CHAPTER III. *Eg*; CHAPTER III 16; §3 24; 3 68
88.37	thoughts] thought *MS*
89.3	*My excellent friend Bombados.*] *My excellent friend Pompados My dearest and best Patake MS*; *My excellent friend Pompados. Eg*; *My excellent friend Bombados.* a*EgC*, a*Eg*, 16–64
90.18	Friday confession] Fridays confessions *MS*
92.10	few years] few short years *MS*
93.19	who] which *MS*
93.22	its] His *Eg*–24
94.9–10	that through] that way through *MS*
94.26	poor breath] poor timid breath *MS*
96.9	children are torn] children *MS*
96.11	dear] dear and near *MS*
96.30	parent] parents *MS*
98.6	the] a *MS*
99.15	in the plain of Damascus, that lovely garden] that lovely garden in the plain of Damascus *MS*
99.24	came in] came to them in *MS*
100.2	degraded parents] degraded first parents *MS*
101.35	carcasses] carcases *MS*
102.10-11	sulphurous] sulphureous *MS*
103.13-14	of ties, of relationships] of ties or relationship *MS*; of ties of relationship *Eg*
108.18	*pœna*] *poena MS*
109.21	Ruler] ruler MS
110.14	of evils] of all evils *MS*
110.26	habit for] *MS*, a16, 18; habit, for *Eg*–16, 24; habit. For 64–68
110.31	soul is] soul in hell is *MS*
113.12	sake] sakes *MS*
115.1	though] a16, 18–24 although *MS*–16, 64–68
115.37	his soul] the soul *MS*
117.1	fragrance] fragrances *MS*
120.9	shame. Had] shame. O what shame! His face was burning with shame. Had *MS*
124.0	IV] *MS*, 18; CHAPTER IV. *Eg*; CHAPTER IV 16; §4; 4 68
125.9	in faith in the Father Who] in faith in the Father, in hope in the Son, in charity in the Holy Ghost, and as daily offerings of thanksgiving to the Father Who *MS*
125.18-19	seemed strange to him] seemed to him strange *MS*
126.1	He] NO NEW PARAGRAPH *MS*

126.24-25   Yet that was] Yet that also was *MS*
127.27-28   that air] that the air *MS*
130.8-9   mind wandered] mind had wandered *MS*
130.25   do away with it,] *MS*, a16, 18–24; do away with, *Eg*–16,
            64–68
131.1   and of the faint] a16, 18–24; and the faint *Eg*–16, 64–68
131.6   it shocked him] it had shocked him *MS*
131.7   Stradbrooke] *MS*–24; Stradbrook 64–68
132.20   slim jim] a16, 18–24, 64–68; chocolate *MS*–16
134.20   ears] ear *MS*
134.29   Melchisedec] Melchisedeck *MS*
134.32   your holy patron] your patron *MS*
135.39   had become] had come *MS*
136.17   his soul] his own soul *MS*
138.20   Chapel,] chapel, *MS*
138.20   Chapel] chapel *MS*
138.25   for him] from him *MS*
141.20   Again! Again! Again!] Again! Again! Again! Again! *MS*
141.33   suns] sun 18–24
142.12   now it] now, as always, it *MS*
142.36   Cripes] *MS*–24; cripes 64–68
146.0   V] *MS*, 18; CHAPTER V *Eg*–16; §5 24; 5 68
148.20   *Synopsis Philosophiæ Scholasticæ ad mentem divi Thomæ*]
            Synopsis Philosophiae Scholasticae ad mentem divi Thomae
            MS
149.16   or death] and death *MS*
152.4   his] the *MS*
152.6   divided themselves] divided against themselves *MS*, 24
152.13   man's humour] man's diffident humour *MS*
152.22   rooms] *MS*–24; room 64–68
152.38   woeful] woful *MS*
153.1   Oh] O *MS*
153.12   hills;] 64–68; Hills, *MS*–16; hills: a16; hills, HSW, 18–24
153.36   at] in *MS*
156.5   *quæ*] quae *MS*
157.14   buy another] buy or borrow another *MS*
161.26   false] *MS*–24, 68; fast 64
162.11   wound on] wound double on *MS*
163.25   Czar's] *MS*; Tsar's *Eg*–24; Csar's 64–68
164.15   another] an other *MS*
165.10   Czar's] *MS*; Tsar's *Eg*–24; Csar's 64–68
166.4   know] knew *MS*

166.18   Czar's] *MS*; Tsar's *Eg*–24; Csar's 64–68

167.27   fine] true *MS*

170.30   took another] took on another *MS*

171.11   or a mystic] a16, 18–24; or mystic *MS*–16, 64–68

171.19   and struck] and then struck *MS*

173.12   unesthetic] *MS*; not esthetic a*Eg*, 16–24; not æsthetic *Eg*

174.27   *quæ*] *quae MS*

174.29   apprehensions] apprehension *MS*

176.17   phenomena] phenomenon *MS*

176.32   *quæ*] *quae MS*

177.5   O'Shaughnessy] O'Shaughenessy *MS*

180.12   *Sir*] *sir MS*, 24

181.18   Kildare house] Joyce to Harriet Weaver, letter (16 xi 1917) in British Library Add. MS 57345; 18–24; the Royal Irish Academy *MS-Eg*; the royal Irish academy a*Eg*, 16, 64–68

182.29-30   In a dream] In dream *MS–Eg*

183.27   smoking swaying] swaying smoking *MS*; swaying *Eg*–24

184.1   bird] birds *MS*

185.11   was like the] was the *MS*

186.5   awhile] a while *MS*

186.12-13   of the eternal imagination] *MS*–24; of eternal imagination 64–68

188.23   He] NEW PARAGRAPH *MS*

189.3   the] their *MS*

190.35   swift] brief *MS*

192.22   athwart her] athwart *MS*

194.36   as you any] as you are any *MS*

196.22   wenches] wenchers *MS*

196.34   body he]body that he *MS*

197.25   ferrule] *Eg*–24; ferule *MS*, 64–68

199.20   ferrule] *Eg*–24; ferule *MS*, 64–68

199.28   foot, crying] foot and crying *MS*

200.29   imaginations] imagination *MS*, *Eg*

200.36   who] that *MS*

206.10   *Galilæo*] *Galilāeo MS*

208.21-22   to lead him back] a16, 18–24; to lead back *Eg*–16; to head back *MS*, 64–68

209.10   20 *March*] *March* 20 *Eg*–24

209.21   21 *March*] *March* 21 *Eg*–24

209.22-23   Elisabeth] *MS*, 64–68; Elizabeth *Eg*–24

209.23   he is] is he *MS*

209.29   21 *March*] *March* 21 *Eg*–24

209.31	22 *March*] March 22 *Eg–24*
209.34	23 *March*] March 23 *Eg–24*
209.37	24 *March*] March 24 *Eg–24*
210.3	was] is *MS*
210.26	Blake] NO NEW PARAGRAPH *MS*
210.34	25 *March*] March 25 *Eg–24*
211.7	30 *March*] March 30 *Eg–24*
211.16	1 *April*] April 1 *Eg–24*
211.17	2 *April*] April 2 *Eg–24*
211.22	3 *April*] April 3 *Eg–24*
211.32	5 *April*] April 5 *Eg–24*
211.36	6 *April*] April 6 *Eg–24*
212.3	6 *April*] April 6 *Eg–24*
212.8	10 *April*] April 10 *Eg–24*
212.16	11 *April*] April 11 *Eg–24*
212.19	13 *April*] April 13 *Eg–24*
212.20	find it English] find it is English *MS*
212.24	14 *April*] April 14 *Eg–24*
212.37	15 *April*] April 15 *Eg–24*
213.7	peas into] peas up into *MS–16*
213.15	16 *April*] April 16 *Eg–24*
213.23	26 *April*] April 26 *Eg–24*
213.29	27 *April*] April 27 *Eg–24*

EXPLANATORY NOTES

Loving attention of generations of scholars has already been given to tracing and documenting the sources of the astonishingly varied, wide range of allusions in Joyce's writings. In the case of *A Portrait of the Artist as a Young Man*, the careful and exhaustive work done by Chester Anderson and Don Gifford (full details of whose books are given below) stands out. Any subsequent annotator invariably owes them a great debt. I recommend them wholeheartedly to any reader who seeks more information.

Of course, any annotator reveals her own critical bias through what she chooses to draw to the reader's attention and this annotator is no exception. For example, the apparent resemblance between Stephen Dedalus and the young James Joyce has been the source of much speculative comment and the stimulus for much critical debate. The timing of the opening of *Portrait* follows only very loosely the actual autobiographical dates of Joyce's own life, and this fact has meant that some commentators have tied themselves in knots trying to bring the two into accord. A 'Chronology' of the events of Joyce's life is given elsewhere. Here, dates are given to historical events; no effort is made to wrench the chronology of *Portrait* to fit the details of Joyce's personal history. Further, those interested in the correspondences between the characters in *Portrait* and actual persons, correspondences which are *not*, with a single exception, spelled out below, should see, especially, *A, E, G, WD* (especially Part II: 'The Artist as a Young Man') (full bibliographical details below), as well as *The Complete Dublin Diary of Stanislaus Joyce*, ed. George H. Healey (Ithaca: Cornell University Press, 1971) and Stanislaus Joyce, *My Brother's Keeper: James Joyce's Early Years*, ed. Richard Ellmann (1958; repr. New York: Viking, 1969) and the works listed in the 'Introduction', n. 25.

As a writer Joyce practised what we might call, borrowing his own phrase, a 'scrupulous meanness' (letter to Grant Richards (*LII* 134; 5 May 1906)). That is, he kept what he had written early (in notes, drafts, fragments) until he could find a proper place for it in his finished work. This is especially true of *Portrait*, the novel for which he plundered the raw materials of his own early life with all the ruthlessness of a great writer. Of particular usefulness to him were his 1904 essay 'A Portrait of the Artist', his 1903 Paris, 1904 Pola, and 1907–9 Trieste notebooks, and *Stephen Hero*. Except in the case of this last, these 're-usings' are noted below.

Stephen Hero and *Portrait* are both like and utterly unlike one another, the relationship that obtains between them so complex that noting here the similarities and differences would double the length of these notes. The former, which Joyce described to Harriet Weaver as 'rubbish' (*c.*7 April 1934),[1] is the

---

[1] Joyce to Weaver, quoted in John J. Slocum and Herbert Cahoon, *A Bibliography of James Joyce [1882–1941]* (1953; repr. Westport, Conn.: Greenwood, 1971), 136.

kind of (unfinished) novel that Stephen Dedalus might have written. When Joyce rejected it, began again, and wrote *Portrait* he entered the world stage as 'a man of genius' whose early 'errors' became 'the portals of discovery' (*U* 182). I do not mean to imply that I agree with Joyce's assessment, however, merely that the two works are so different as to make the fact that one is the precursor of the other seem at times implausible. Anyone seriously interested in Joyce should read both. The former has been published: *Stephen Hero*, ed. Theodore Spencer, rev. edn. John J. Slocum and Herbert Cahoon (1963; repr. St Albans: Triad, 1977).

The following works are repeatedly referred to in the notes that follow by the abbreviations listed below, indicating either a source for the gloss or that readers may find therein fuller, more detailed information. Biblical references are to the King James version unless otherwise noted.

A	Chester G. Anderson (ed.), James Joyce, *A Portrait of the Artist as a Young Man*, Viking Critical Edition (New York: Viking, 1968).
Aubert	Jacques Aubert, *The Aesthetics of James Joyce* (1973; rev. edn. Baltimore: Johns Hopkins University Press, 1992).
CW	*The Critical Writings of James Joyce*, ed. Ellsworth Mason and Richard Ellmann (1959; repr. New York: Viking, 1973).
E	Richard Ellmann, *James Joyce* (1959; rev. edn. 1982; corr. New York: Oxford University Press, 1983).
F	R. F. Foster, *Modern Ireland 1600–1972* (1988; repr. London: Penguin, 1989).
G	Don Gifford, *Joyce Annotated: Notes for 'Dubliners' and 'A Portrait of the Artist as a Young Man'*, 2nd edn. (Berkeley: University of California Press, 1982).
JJA	*The James Joyce Archive*, ed. Michael Groden, 63 vols. (New York: Garland, 1977–80).
JSA	J. S. Atherton (ed.), James Joyce, *A Portrait of the Artist as a Young Man*, 2nd edn. (London: Heinemann Educational Books, 1973).
KB	James Joyce, *Occasional, Critical, and Political Writing*, ed. Kevin Barry (Oxford: Oxford University Press, 2000).
L	*Letters of James Joyce*, 3 vols.: vol. i ed. Stuart Gilbert; vols. ii and iii ed. Richard Ellmann (New York: Viking, 1957, 1966). Cited by volume and page number as follows: *LI* 33 (volume i, page 33).
O	Brendan O Hehir, *A Gaelic Lexicon for Finnegans Wake and Glossary for Joyce's Other Works* (Berkeley: University of California Press, 1967).
OERD	*Oxford English Reference Dictionary*, ed. Judy Pearsall and Bill Trumble (Oxford: Oxford University Press, 1995).
'Portrait'	James Joyce, 'A Portrait of the Artist' (1904; repr. in *PSW*, 211–18).
PSW	James Joyce, *Poems and Shorter Writings*, ed. Richard Ellmann,

A. Walton Litz, and John Whittier-Ferguson (London: Faber & Faber, 1991).

PWJ   P. W. Joyce, *English as We Speak it in Ireland* (1910); repr. with an introduction by Terence Dolan (Dublin: Wolfhound Press, 1979).

SL   *Selected Letters of James Joyce*, ed. Richard Ellmann (New York: Viking, 1975).

SOED   *Shorter Oxford English Dictionary on Historical Principles*, William Little *et al.*, 3rd edn. corrected (Oxford: Clarendon Press, 1975).

Sullivan   Kevin Sullivan, *Joyce Among the Jesuits* (New York: Columbia University Press, 1958).

T   James R. Thrane, 'Joyce's Sermon on Hell: Its Source and Its Backgrounds', *Modern Philology*, 57 (Feb. 1960), 172–98.

U   James Joyce, *Ulysses: The 1922 Text*, ed. Jeri Johnson, Oxford World's Classics (Oxford: Oxford University Press, 1993).

WD   *The Workshop of Daedalus: James Joyce and the Raw Materials for 'A Portrait of the Artist as a Young Man'*, ed. Robert Scholes and Richard M. Kain (Evanston, Ill.: Northwestern University Press, 1965).

[epigraph] *Et ignotas . . . Ovid, Metamorphoses, viii. 188*: Latin: 'So then to unimagined arts he set his mind' (the line continues 'and altered nature's laws'), of Daedalus in Ovid's *Metamorphoses*, viii. 188–9 (trans. A. D. Melville, Oxford World's Classics (Oxford: Oxford University Press, 1986), 177); Ovid (Publius Ovidius Naso, 43 BC–AD 17 or 18), Roman poet, author of *Heroides* and *Metamorphoses*, a loosely linked series of tales from ancient mythology all of which concern changes of shape. In this tale, Daedalus (whose name means 'cunning artificer') creates three devices, each of which leads to difficulty. In the first, he fashions for Queen Pasiphae a wooden bull into which she might get so that she might mate with a bull for which she has developed a passion. Of this union is born the Minotaur, a creature half man, half bull. Pasiphae's husband, King Minos of Crete, enraged at Daedalus's collusion with Pasiphae's plot, demands that he now build a labyrinth in which the Minotaur may be kept. Daedalus creates the labyrinth so cleverly that he finds he and his son Icarus are now trapped within it. To escape, he fashions wings of wax and feathers so that he and Icarus may fly away. This they do, though Icarus, overcome by euphoria (and no little pride in his own newfound ability) flies too near the sun. The wax in his wings melts; he falls into the sea and drowns. Daedalus flies safely, landing in Sicily where he finally dies, having continued his creative life. The line quoted comes as Daedalus sets about making the wings.

CHAPTER I

5.1–3 *moocow . . . tuckoo*: see John Joyce to his son James, 31 January 1931: 'I wonder do you recollect the old days in Brighton Square, when you were Babie Tuckoo and I used to take you out in the Square and tell you all about the moo-cow that used to come down from the mountain and take little boys across?' (*LIII* 212)—a version of the tale of the mythical cow (itself a version of 'silk of the kine', one of the names of Ireland) that took children away from ordinary life to an island fairy world whence they were eventually safely returned.

5.5 *glass*: monocle.

5.7 *lemon platt*: braided lemon candy.

5.8–9 *O, the wild . . . green place*: after H. S. Thompson, 'Lily Dale', the chorus of which is: 'Oh, sweet Lily, sweet Lily, dear Lily Dale, | Now the wild rose blossoms | O'er her little green grave, | 'Neath the trees in the flow'ry vale.' Note the change of 'grave' to 'place'.

5.20 *Dante*: not the Italian poet, but a childish mispronunciation of 'Auntie' (from the elision of 'and Auntie'?); the young James Joyce's name for Mrs Conway, on whom Dante Riordan is modelled (Stanislaus Joyce, *My Brother's Keeper: James Joyce's Early Years*, ed. Richard Ellmann (1958; New York: Viking, 1969), 7).

5.22 *press*: a wardrobe.

5.23–4 *Michael Davitt . . . Parnell*: Michael Davitt (1846–1906), Irish nationalist (organizing secretary of the Irish Republican Brotherhood in 1868), founded the Land League of Mayo (1878) and with Parnell the National Land League (1879) to agitate for reform of the practice of (often absentee) landlord ownership of land farmed by local farmers from whom rents were extracted. Davitt came to advocate national ownership of land, but in this he was virtually alone (*F* 415). Charles Stewart Parnell (1846–91) as Leader of the Irish Parliamentary Party at Westminster (to which Ireland had sent MPs since the 1800 Act of Union which dissolved the Irish Parliament and merged it with the British) parlayed his Party into a position of power which he used to try to secure Home Rule for Ireland: in exchange for securing Gladstone's commitment to Irish Home Rule, he agreed to support the Liberal Government (which needed Irish Party support to form a government in 1885). For Gladstone, see 210.31 n.

5.24 *cachou*: 'a sweetmeat, made of cashew-nut, etc., used by smokers to sweeten the breath' (*SOED*).

6.1–9 *eagles . . . Apologise*: cf. Joyce's first 'epiphany' (*PSW* 161).

6.11 *prefects*: boys or masters put in positions of particular authority or leadership.

6.13 *footballers*: probably rugby rather than Gaelic football, the latter being revived in 1884 with the Gaelic Athletic Association's endorsement of traditional Irish sports, but the former ('rugby union') much more likely to have been played at this date in an élite Jesuit school like Clongowes Wood College (see 46.34 and 12.21 nn. below). Both have fifteen players (see 35.26–7). The question remains, though, why the ball is described as an 'orb', for a rugby ball is oval, a Gaelic football round.

6.18 *third line*: the schoolboys were divided into three major groups by age. In descending order they were the higher (aged 15–18), lower (aged 13–15), and third (under 13) lines; each 'line' was further divided: the higher into poetry and rhetoric, the lower into second and first grammar, the third into elements and third grammar (*G*).

6.21 *greaves in his number*: 'shin guards in his locker'.

6.26 *Stephen Dedalus*: after St Stephen, the first Christian martyr (a Jew educated in Greek), who was stoned to death for blasphemy (*c.* AD 34) (Acts 7: 57–9,), and Daedalus, Ovid's 'cunning artificer' (see note to epigraph).

6.33 *magistrate*: one of 64 'resident magistrates' who acted as Ireland's judiciary throughout Ireland (excepting Dublin); though by the late nineteenth century open to Catholics, more usually occupied by Protestants.

7.9 *the castle*: the central buildings of Clongowes Wood School (see 12.21 n.); site of a medieval castle destroyed (1642) ostensibly because it was the site of Catholic resistance, rebuilt by the Browne family who bought Clongowes in 1667 (see 15.17–32 n.).

7.15 *peach*: to inform on.

7.16 *the rector*: an ecclesiastic and head of the whole college, which was divided into an academic and a domestic/disciplinary division, the former presided over by the prefect of studies (see below) and comprising the school masters, the latter by the minister and prefect of discipline. See Sullivan and *G*.

7.17 *soutane*: long black gown with sleeves, buttoned at the front, usual uniform of the Jesuits (see 46.34 n.).

7.22 *scrimmage*: (usually abbreviated 'scrum') in rugby football, 'an ordered formation in which the two sets of forwards pack themselves together with their heads down and endeavour by pushing to work their opponents off the ball and break away with it or heel it out (1857)' (*SOED*).

7.30 *seventyseven to seventysix*: days until the Christmas break, hence it is October.

7.33 *Hamilton Rowan*: Archibald Hamilton Rowan (1751–1834), member of the United Irishmen (which wanted Irish independence from England as well as Catholic emancipation); he was tried and sentenced for sedition in 1794 but escaped when being transported to prison, taking refuge at Clongowes Wood Castle. Local lore has it that the troops arrived just as he entered the castle, that to trick them into thinking he had leapt from a window and fled, he tossed his hat onto the 'haha' (see 7.34 n.) but actually hid inside. He did escape to France. (See *E* 29.)

7.34 *haha*: a ditch with a wall on its inner side below ground level; it forms a border without breaking into the view.

7.37 *the community*: the priests who comprise the faculty of the college.

7.39 *Leicester Abbey*: the Anglican abbey of Saint Mary Pré in Leicester in central England; Stephen thinks of it, of course, because of the 'spelling rhyme' recalled below.

8.1 *Doctor Cornwell's Spelling Book*: probably *A Grammar for Beginners* (1838) by James Cornwell (1812–1902) and Alexander Allen (1814–42), a spelling primer, used in Ireland as well as England (*G*). Education at the time was supervised by the Intermediate Education Board (founded by an

Act of 1878) which set up a system of education very like the English system of public examinations with funding tied to results. Memorization of set texts typically followed.

8.3 *Wolsey died in Leicester Abbey*: Thomas, Cardinal Wolsey (*c.*1474–1530), both cardinal (1515–30) and Lord Chancellor (1515–29) during the reign of Henry VIII (1491–1547; r. 1509–47); ultimately accused of treason due to his failure to secure the papal dispensation necessary to allow Henry to divorce Catherine of Aragon and marry Anne Boleyn; died at Leicester Abbey on his way to trial.

8.10 *square ditch*: 'square' refers not to the shape of the ditch, but to its location. The 'square' was the boys' nickname for the outside lavatory behind the dormitory; the 'ditch' either the slate trough running across it or the cesspool for it (see *A*).

8.11 *hacking chestnut*: as in the childhood game of 'conkers', a horse chestnut with a hole drilled in it through which a string is passed; held by the string, one chestnut is hit against another in an attempt to best the opponent by breaking his chestnut. This one has beaten forty others (either directly or by beating others which had themselves beaten others, so totalling forty).

8.17–18 *Mozambique . . . moon*: Anderson argues that each of these 'discoveries' can be tied to Catholic ingenuity, Mrs Riordan's reason for both knowing about them and passing them on to Stephen. See *A* and *G*.

8.25 *lower and third lines*: see 6.18 n.

8.32 *suck*: slang for a sycophant, as in one who 'sucks up' to another.

8.34 *the prefect's false sleeves*: the soutane has two strips of cloth with no functional use hanging down from the shoulders, as in some academic gowns.

9.13 *York . . . Lancaster*: the two sides in the Wars of the Roses (1455–85), the dynastic struggle in England which ended with the defeat of the Yorkist Richard III and the accession of the Lancastrian Henry Tudor (Henry VII), who then united the two houses by marrying the Yorkist Edward IV's daughter. The emblem of the House of York was the white rose, that of the House of Lancaster the red rose. Ireland supported York; Lancaster remembered.

9.18 *wax*: a fit of anger.

9.21 *red rose wins*: as it did historically. See 9.13 n. above.

9.26 *elements*: see 6.18 n.

9.38 *green rose*: we have already had one: see 5.11.

10.27 *Dalkey*: village on the east coast between Dublin and Bray (where the Dedalus family lives).

10.32 *higher line*: see 6.18 n.

11.3 *Tullabeg*: town west of Dublin where Peter Kenny (founder of Clongowes: see 12.21 n.) also founded St Stanislaus College, which in 1885–6 merged with Clongowes. Later the site of the Jesuit Novitiate in Ireland. (Cf. *G* and *A*.)

11.6 *kiss your mother*: a joke (to which Stephen is clearly not privy): Aloysius Gonzaga, one of the patron saints of youth (see 46.38–9 n.) (and of James

Augustine Aloysius Joyce) was reputed to be so intent on maintaining bodily purity that he would not even kiss (or in some accounts even look at) his own mother. Stephen's anxiety, though, has a double source: both his outsider status (the other boys understand something he doesn't) and the fraught question of a boy's relationship with his mother. Both will recur in the book. The latter returns at 204.12 (and in *U* 28, 199, 540).

11.21 *third of grammar*: see 6.18 n.

12.21 *Clongowes Wood College*: an extremely fashionable Jesuit school for boys, near Sallins, County Kildare, some miles west-south-west of Dublin; the school was founded by the Revd. Peter Kenny, SJ in 1814 and dedicated to St Aloysius Gonzaga. (See, too, 7.9 and 46.38–9 nn.)

12.28 *a cod*: a joke.

13.18 *Parnell was a bad man*: Parnell was so labelled, explicitly or implic- itly, by English nonconformists, the Irish Catholic leadership, the English Liberal Party, and the Irish Parliamentary Party, after he was named as co-respondent in the divorce petition (2 Dec. 1889) of Captain O'Shea (one of Parnell's political associates) against his wife Katherine ('Kitty') O'Shea. When the divorce was granted (Nov. 1890), a furore ensued (*F* 359).

13.22–3 *something in the paper about it*: the 1890–1 political reper- cussions of the O'Shea divorce scandal as Parnell continued to assert his leadership of the Irish Parliamentary Party against considerable opposition (see 26.18 n.) were extensively reported in the press.

13.26 *poetry and rhetoric*: see 6.17 n.

13.34 *prayers in the chapel*: 'The day [at Clongowes] . . . began around six in the morning with a visit to the Blessed Sacrament, followed later by the celebration of Mass, and ended around nine in the evening with the school assembled in chapel for night prayers' (Sullivan, 55).

14.8 *marbles*: the columns in the chapel, made of wood but painted to look like marble (*A*).

14.13 *the responses*: the ritual responses of the server, minister, choir, or congregation to the words spoken by the priest who is celebrating mass.

14.14–17 *O Lord . . . help us!*: the opening lines of the Matins in the Divine Office: 'Matins': one of the canonical hours at which the Divine Office was by obligation recited by all holy orders (properly a night office); 'Divine Office': the daily service of the Catholic breviary (book containing the service to be read for each day) (*OERD*); the second and fourth lines here are the 'responses'.

14.22 *Clane*: village a mile and a half from Clongowes; the college chapel was the parish church for Clane.

14.25 *Sallins*: see 12.21 n.

14.33–6 *Visit, we beseech . . . Amen*: the last prayer in Compline, the last of the canonical hours.

15.17–32 *Was it true . . . cloak of a marshal*: a very local ghost story: Maximilian Ulysses, Count von Browne (1705–57), Austrian-born son of an Irish expatriate member of the Browne family who owned Clongowes Wood Castle, and a marshal in the Austrian army, was killed at the Battle of

Prague; his ghost is said to have appeared in bloodstained clothing to the servants at Clongowes on the night of his death (see *E* 29).

16.4 *the cars*: horse-drawn form of public transport, supplementing train services.

16.10 *Bodenstown*: parish that includes Sallins, site of the grave of Wolfe Tone (see 154.24–5 n.).

16.21–2 *Hill of Allen*: a 219m. high hill some 8 miles west of Sallins; not on the train route Stephen would take to go home.

16.25 *pierglass*: a large mirror, originally used to fill the space between two windows.

16.30–1 *marshal . . . magistrate*: Stephen confuses the army office of Count von Browne ('marshal') with the judicial office ('magistrate') (see 6.33 n.).

17.20 *don't spy on us*: 'don't tell on me'.

17.34 *foxing*: now dialect or slang, 'to fox' means to sham (*SOED*).

18.5 *Father Minister*: the vice-rector in charge of all non-academic activities.

18.8 *Brother Michael*: called 'brother' because in the second grade (of six) of Jesuit membership: a temporal coadjutor; as such his duties would be more domestic than ecclesiastical or tutelary.

18.15 *Hayfoot! Strawfoot!*: after the supposed practice of putting a piece of hay on the left foot, a piece of straw on the right foot, of an Irish recruit to teach him one from the other and how to march (*G*).

19.5 *third of grammar*: see 6.18 n.

19.20 *a dead mass*: a requiem mass, i.e. one specifically for someone who has died.

19.21 *when Little had died*: Peter Stanislaus Little, died while a schoolboy at Clongowes, 10 December 1890, and is buried in the cemetery there (*A*).

19.23–4 *cope of black and gold*: the long cloaklike vestments worn by the priest at a requiem mass are black and gold.

19.25 *catafalque*: the decorated wooden framework used to support a coffin during the funeral, usually of a distinguished person (*OERD*).

19.31–8 *Dingdong! . . . soul away*: anonymous nursery rhyme (Iona and Peter Opie, *The Lore and Language of Schoolchildren* (Oxford: Oxford University Press, 1959), 34).

20.25 *Athy*: town in County Kildare some 40 miles south-west of Dublin.

21.18 *the liberator*: Daniel O'Connell (1775–1847), known as 'the Liberator', Irish nationalist leader and champion of Catholic Emancipation—the lifting of restrictions on the rights of Catholics that had been in place since the seventeenth century (see 28.22 and 38.36–7 nn.). Catholics were not admitted to Parliament, for example, which meant that from the time of the Act of Union (5.23–4 n.), no Irish Catholic could represent Ireland at Westminster. His election as MP for Clare (1828) forced the hand of the British government; Catholic Emancipation was granted in 1829. He went on to establish the Repeal Association, the aim of which was to repeal the Act of

Union, was tried and convicted of sedition (1844; sentence quashed) and finally died on his way to Rome on a pilgrimage (*F* 291).

21.21–2 *blue coats . . . rabbitskin*: the earliest uniform for Clongowes boys.

21.28 *legend*: the story of a saint's life.

22.1–5 *He saw the sea of waves . . . their harbour*: cf. Joyce's 'epiphany', no. 28 (*PSW* 188).

22.12 *Parnell! Parnell! He is dead!*: 6 October 1891; he lay in state in Dublin City Hall, 11 October, and was buried that afternoon in Glasnevin Cemetery in north-west Dublin.

22.26 *toasted boss*: 'a kind of foot-stool with two ears, stuffed without a wooden frame. The term is childish and popular. Compare the word "hassock"' (Joyce to Spanish translator of *Portrait* (31 Oct. 1925), *LIII* 129).

23.1–2 *birthday present for Queen Victoria*: imprisoned as an Irish revolutionary, he has 'picked oakum' at Her Majesty's leisure, that is in an English prison: i.e. picked old rope to obtain the loose fibres which are then used for other things.

23.7–8 *the Head*: Bray Head, a promontory just south of the village of Bray, itself on the coast south of Dublin.

23.25 *champagne*: explosives?

23.28 *jack foxes*: male foxes.

24.12–13 *Bless us . . . Amen*: standard Catholic grace.

24.19 *guinea*: one pound, one shilling; used for pricing expensive goods.

24.19 *Dunn's of D'Olier Street*: posh meat, fish, and game merchant in central Dublin.

24.22 *Ally Daly*: Dublin slang: 'the sine qua non' (after Alice Daly, whose butter was) (Bernard Share, *Slanguage: A Dictionary of Irish Slang* (Dublin: Gill and Macmillan, 1997)).

24.23 *Why . . . pandybat a turkey*: 'pandybat', from Latin *pande*, 'stretch out!' (*Oxford English Dictionary*): a leather strap, reinforced with whalebone, used to strike the palms of one being punished; Mr Barrett calls it a 'turkey' because it turns hands red, 'Turkey red' being the name of a brilliant and permanent red colour (*SOED*).

25.23–4 *I'll pay . . . pollingbooth*: the speaker suggests that the Catholic Church ought to stay out of political affairs, something the history of Ireland shows it seldom to have done. In particular, once O'Shea was granted his divorce (having implicated Parnell), various priests denounced Parnell from the pulpit ('You cannot remain Parnellite and remain Catholic', to quote one such). In the 1892 election 9 Parnellite and 71 anti-Parnellite candidates were elected (*F* 424).

26.18 *The bishops . . . have spoken*: they had, but most vociferously only once the Irish Parliamentary Party ('IPP') had acted. When the O'Shea divorce was granted (17 Nov. 1890) scandal erupted; Gladstone (whose Liberal Party had formed a coalition with the IPP) published an open letter declaring that his party would not continue this alliance if Parnell remained the IPP leader. Parnell refused to resign. In December 1890 in

Committee Room 15 of the Houses of Parliament, the IPP split: 44 against, 27 for Parnell. In the subsequent elections, Church leaders typically (if not unanimously) spoke against the Parnellites. (See preceding note and 13.18, 13.22–3 and 210.31 nn.)

26.25–6 *Were we . . . bidding of the English people*: see preceding note.

26.30–3 *Woe be . . . little ones*: Luke 17: 1–2; Jesus to his disciples, though he continues, 'Take heed to yourselves: If thy brother trespass against thee, rebuke him; and if he repent, forgive him' (Luke 17: 3).

27.8 *pope's nose*: the turkey's tail.

27.27 *Billy with the lip*: the Most Reverend William J. Walsh, DD (1841–1921), archbishop of Dublin (1885–1921), a strong nationalist and supporter of land reform who initially held back from denouncing Parnell and urged other clergy to do the same; nevertheless, he too finally spoke.

27.27–8 *tub of guts up in Armagh*: the Reverend Michael Logue (1840–1924), archbishop of Armagh (1887–1924), became a cardinal in 1893; after the divorce, Logue opposed the retention of Parnell as leader of the IPP.

27.30 *Lord Leitrim's coachman*: William Sydney Clements, Earl of Leitrim (1806–78), English, notorious absentee landlord of vast areas of Leitrim and Donegal, was murdered in 1877, his (Irish) coachmen supposedly attempting to save him from attack; the phrase is meant to indict those who would aid their oppressors.

28.22 *renegade catholics*: those who changed religion from Catholic to Protestant to escape the draconian effects of the Penal Laws against Catholics in Ireland (enacted in the late seventeenth and early eighteenth centuries); these included restricted rights to education, to the ownership of property (and livestock: famously, Catholics could not lawfully possess any horse worth more than £5), to the holding of public office, to the bearing of arms; the banishing of the Catholic clergy and ultimately the complete removal of the right to vote (see *F* 154, 205–7, 244–5, 602–4); see too 21.18 and 38.36–7 nn.

28.29 *county Wicklow*: county on the east coast south of Dublin. Parnell was a Wicklow man.

28.39–29.1 *blackest protestant*: i.e. the most anti-Catholic.

29.8–9 *O, come . . . mass*: parody of opening of traditional Irish ballads: 'Come all you . . . '. See 74.25 and n.

29.18 *spoiled nun*: one who has either left the convent or never quite got there in the first place. See *E* 25 for an account of what may have led to the 'spoiling' of the real-life counterpart of Dante.

29.19 *Alleghanies*: a mountain range in the eastern United States.

29.20 *chainies*: damaged china.

29.25 *Tower of Ivory . . . House of Gold*: lines from the 'Litany of Our Lady [of Loreto] To [and as elaborated epithetic description of] the Blessed Virgin Mary', seeking her intercession on behalf of the supplicant; sung or chanted by the priest, responses by the congregation; so: 'Tower of Ivory, pray for us. // House of Gold, pray for us'.

29.35 *Arklow*: town in County Wicklow, on the east coast of Ireland, *c.*40 miles south of Dublin.

29.35 *the chief*: Parnell.

30.9 *Priesthunter*: Parnell, in part, who was Protestant and suspected of anti-Catholicism, especially after the clergy's attack on him, but also those who in supporting him were seen to be opposing the clergy. The phrase dates back to the the time of the Penal Laws when the Catholic clergy had been officially banished and bounty hunters not infrequently actually hunted priests down (though see *F* 205).

30.9–10 *The Paris Funds*: the IPP kept funds in Paris (and so away from British hands); with the split, Parnell was still technically in control of the funds and so could use them for the advantage of the minority Parnellite MPs in his last campaign; it did not take long for rumours of his improper use of the money to circulate.

30.10 *Mr Fox*: pseudonym used by Parnell in his affair with Katherine O'Shea.

30.10 *Kitty O'Shea*: nickname of Katherine O'Shea which carried an insulting sexual innuendo (not unlike a similarly feline epithet in current use).

30.13–14 *a quid of Tullamore*: 'quid': 'a piece of something (usually tobacco) suitable to be held in the mouth and chewed' (from 'cud') (*SOED*); 'Tullamore': a chewing tobacco made in Tullamore, west of Dublin.

31.7 *Cabinteely road*: i.e. he travelled to Dublin by a little-used backroad.

31.14 *priestridden race*: the Catholic clergy were both numerous and often involved in the political affairs of Ireland, though not always against the nationalist cause Mr Casey espouses.

31.24 *whiteboy*: the 'Whiteboys' were a secret society organized loosely around demand for agrarian reform which flourished first in the 1760s and again in the 1820s; they made midnight raids, wore white shirts over their clothing (ostensibly so they could see one another at night), did considerable damage, and committed no little violence against both people and animals in protest against, among other things, the exaction of exorbitant rents; the Catholic Church spoke against them. (See *F* 223, 292–3.)

31.29–30 *Touch them not . . . apple of My eye*: not quite Jesus; this echoes verses from Zech. 2: 8–9 (read as a prophecy of Christ's Church): 'For thus saith the Lord of hosts: After the glory he hath sent me to the nations that have robbed you: for he that toucheth you, toucheth the apple of my eye: for behold I lift up my hand upon them, and they shall be a prey to those that served them' (Douay).

31.39–32.2 *Didn't the bishops . . . Marquess Cornwallis?*: During the rebellion of 1798, Charles, Marquess Cornwallis (1738–1805), was made Viceroy and Commander-in-Chief in Ireland; once the rebellion was suppressed, his task became the securing of the Act of Union (1800) (5.23–4 n.). This was managed through 'the favour and patronage of the Crown' (read 'virtual bribery'), though many Catholics were persuaded to support the Union in exchange for Catholic Emancipation. James Lanigan (d. 1812), Bishop of

Ossory, was one such who did deliver at least a complimentary address if not strictly one of 'loyalty'. Cornwallis resigned when it became clear that Catholic Emancipation would not be forthcoming (it finally came 29 years later: see 21.18 n. above) (*F* 280).

32.2–3 *Didn't the bishops . . . catholic emancipation?*: see preceding note. It is unclear exactly what 'aspirations' the Catholic bishops are meant to have so exchanged; they were less keen on independence than might have been wished, and were less supportive of O'Connell's moves to secure abolition of the Act of Union than they had been of Emancipation (*F* 316).

32.4 *fenian movement*: 'Fenian' became the generally used name of the fraternal Fenian and Irish Republican Brotherhoods (founded 1858), the former technically the American support branch of the latter, the Irish secret society aimed at securing an independent Irish republic by military means if necessary. The name echoes that of the 'Fianna', the army of the ancient Irish hero Fionn Mac Cumhail. The Catholic Church denounced the entire movement.

32.5–6 *Terence Bellew MacManus*: MacManus (1823–60) was a successful shipping agent in Liverpool who joined the Young Irelanders (1844), a group committed to repeal of the Union and dedicated to the promotion of an Irish cultural nationalism; arrested attempting to flee the country after an abortive rising in Tipperary; sentenced to death; commuted to transportation to Australia whence he escaped to die in poverty in San Francisco. His body was brought back to Ireland, where Cardinal Cullen (see 32.10 n.) rejected a request that it lie in state and banned participation by Catholic clergy in the funeral. It proceeded nevertheless and occasioned the Fenians' first great public demonstration in Ireland, 10 November 1861 (*F* 366). Cf. 'Portrait', the essay in which Joyce first treats the 'growth of the artist' (*PSW* 213).

32.10 *Paul Cullen*: (1803–78), archbishop of Ireland, first Irishman to be made a cardinal (1866); undertook the reorganization of the Catholic Church in Ireland, called the first synod of Irish Catholic clergy since the twelfth century; opposed Fenianism and any movement that was not first devoted to the promotion of Catholicism (see *F* 338–40). Cf. 'Portrait' (*PSW* 213).

33.8 *My dead king!*: Parnell, of course. Parnell died 6 October 1891, having married Katherine O'Shea fourteen weeks earlier. See Joyce's essay 'The Shade of Parnell' (1912) (*CW* 223–8 and *KB* 191–6) for his analysis of the lasting impact of Parnell on Ireland; he uses the phrase 'uncrowned king' here (228) (the phrase itself apparently having been coined by Timothy Healy (see 192.29 n.))

33.14 *Hill of Lyons*: hill about a third of the way between Clongowes and Dublin.

33.16 *the minister*: see 18.5 n.

33.21 *fecked*: 'stolen'; 'nicked'.

33.27 *scut*: 'ran away', from 'A short erect tail, esp. that of a hare, rabbit or deer' (*SOED*).

33.33 *sacristy*: room in a church or chapel where vestments, sacred vessels, etc. are kept and where the celebrant prepares for the service.

34.5 *surplices*: loose white linen vestments worn over cassocks by clergy and choristers at a service.

34.8 *boatbearer*: 'boat': the boat-shaped vessel in which the incense is carried; 'boatbearer': the one who carries the boat during the celebration of the mass; another carries the 'thurible' or 'censer' in which the incense is burned.

34.9 *altar in the wood*: in the park adjoining Clongowes; Benediction was held there as part of the regular calendar of college events. (See 38.37 n.)

34.19 *sprinter*: a cyclist, not a runner.

34.20 *second of grammar*: see 6.18 n.

34.26–7 *cricket . . . prof*: unclear; either the captain of the team, or the coach. 'So important was cricket to the school that every season a professional was imported from England to coach the boys' (Herbert Gorman, *James Joyce* (London: John Lane, 1941), 31).

34.29 *rounders*: ball game not unlike American baseball.

35.18 *Smugging*: 'to smug': 'To toy amourously in secret' (Joseph Wright, *English Dialect Dictionary* (London: Henry Frowde, 1898–1905)); here, clearly, 'homosexual amorous toying'.

35.26–7 *football fifteen*: see 6.13 n.

36.8–9 *wanted to do something*: Stephen has already internalized the social requirement to refer to bodily functions only euphemistically.

36.14 *Balbus was building a wall*: derived from the boys' Latin lessons; here, from Cicero (106–43 BC) in his *Letters to Atticus*, xii. 2: '[Balbus] is building [new mansions for himself]: for what cares he?' (See *A*.)

36.18 *Julius Caesar wrote The Calico Belly*: similar to the above, this time a pun on the title of the most famous work of [Gaius] Julius Caesar (100–44 BC), *Commentarii de Bello Gallico* ('Commentaries on the Gallic War').

36.27 *six and eight*: shorthand for a particular punishment: number of strokes that the palms of the hands are struck: three on each followed by four on each.

36.29–30 *twisting the note . . . open it*: the boy being punished would have to carry a note which bore the kind and degree of punishment to be administered from the teacher to the person who would then execute the sentence; 'old Barrett' has made it impossible for the boy to discover in advance his punishment without being detected.

36.30 *ferulæ*: Latin: plural of 'ferula': 'A rod, cane or other instrument of punishment [here, a pandybat]; *figuratively*, school punishment' (*SOED*); so, the strokes to be received.

36.32 *prefect of studies*: schoolmaster in charge of academic matters (and, here, of ensuring through punishment exacted or threatened that studies are properly attended to).

36.39 *flogged*: beaten with a cane or rod.

37.16 *twice nine*: see 36.27 n.; this time, nine on each hand.

37.17 *vital spot*: i.e. the boys will not get 'ferulæ' on their hands, they will be flogged on their buttocks.

38.34 *monstrance*: 'an open or transparent receptacle in which the consecrated Host is exposed for veneration' (*OERD*).

38.36–7 *flashing gold thing . . . God was put*: the upper part of the monstrance is made to represent rays of sun, as though issuing from the Host. In Catholicism, the consecrated Host is meant literally to have 'become God' through transubstantiation, rather than as in Protestantism where it metaphorically represents God and his sacrifice as Christ. (The 1673 Test Act in England required that anyone holding public office forswear belief in transubstantiation and take communion in the Church of England. It was not repealed until 1828.)

38.37 *benediction*: strictly, 'Benediction of the Most Blessed Sacrament': the ritual ceremony during which the celebrant exposes the Host in the monstrance to the congregation for veneration.

38.39 *censer*: see 34.8 n.

39.8 *first holy communion*: typically, children in the Catholic Church went through religious instruction and took their first communion at the age of 7 or 8.

39.20–1 *Gentlemen . . . holy communion*: wholly apocryphal and given his lack of piety undoubtedly untrue.

39.29–31 *decline the noun mare . . . plural*: nouns are 'declined' by stating their grammatical cases (there are six), number, and gender. *Mare*: Latin: 'the sea'; 'ablative': case of noun (sometimes called the 'adverbial case') which indicates means (by what), agent (by whom), accompaniment (with whom), manner (how), location (where), or time (when).

40.13–15 *minister . . . general of the jesuits*: hierarchy (from lowest to highest) of 'officers' in the Society of Jesus (the Jesuits: see 46.34 n.), the 'provincial' being head of the Jesuits in a 'province' (here, Ireland), and the 'general' overall head; there is no requirement that confession be to one higher in rank.

40.25 *prefect of studies*: see 36.32 n.

41.22 *Tomorrow and tomorrow and tomorrow*: *Macbeth*, v. v. 19, Macbeth on hearing of the death of Lady Macbeth, used here as tired cliché.

44.24 *The senate and the Roman people declared*: after the opening of a Roman senatorial decree (Latin: *Senatus populusque Romanus*).

44.33 *lent*: forty-day period preceding Easter during which various kinds of fasting and abstention may be practised; here, fish appears to have replaced meat.

45.1–2 *Richmal Magnall's Questions*: not Magnall, but Mangnall; Richmal Mangnall, *Historical and Miscellaneous Questions for the Use of Young People* (Stockport, 1800), used to teach elementary history and geography.

45.3–4 *Peter Parley's Tales about Greece and Rome*: Stephen has conflated two titles by 'Peter Parley' (pseudonym of the American Samuel Griswold

Goodrich (1793–1860), who produced numerous such books for children's education (Sullivan).

46.34 *saint Ignatius Loyola*: St Ignatius of Loyola (1491–1556), a Spanish soldier who fought for Ferdinand and Isabella, who was wounded and left lame, though through what he considered his miraculous recovery he became devout and pious and founded in 1540 the Society of Jesus ('the Jesuits'); the painting is symbolic: the book signifying his learning (he drew up the constitution for the Jesuits, and wrote *Spiritual Exercises*), the finger pointing to the motto, his founding of the society so dedicated (see below).

46.35–6 *Ad Majorem Dei Gloriam*: Latin: 'To the greater glory of God', the motto of the Jesuits.

46.36 *saint Francis Xavier*: (1506–52), the first and most famous of Loyola's disciples, went as missionary to India and Japan; points to (the cross on) his chest because of his emphasis in his mission on the cross.

46.36–7 *Lorenzo Ricci*: (1703–75), general of the Jesuits (1758), the biretta being a symbol of his office (and the mark of a cardinal).

46.37–8 *prefects of the lines*: masters responsible for specific class groups at the school; clearly they too wore birettas.

46.38–9 *three patrons ... John Berchmans*: all young Jesuit saints (so patrons of youth and of Jesuit boys' schools): Kostka (1550–68) walked from Vienna to Rome to join the order; Gonzaga (1568–91) died at 23 as a result of having attended plague victims; Berchmans (1599–1621) is called 'Blessed' by Stephen but he has recently been sanctified (1888). (See, too, 11.6 and 12.21 nn.)

47.1 *Father Peter Kenny*: founder of Clongowes Wood College (see 11.3 and 12.21 nn.).

47.16–17 *skull on the desk*: a *memento mori*, or reminder of one's mortality.

49.22 *Conmee*: rector of Clongowes and the name of the actual rector during Joyce's time there: Father John Conmee, SJ (1847–1910), who was later prefect of studies at Belvedere College, Dublin, and became in 1905 Rome provincial of the Irish Jesuits; this Conmee reappears in 'Wandering Rocks' (*U* 210–44).

49.26 *obedient*: like all good Jesuits; cf. Loyola's remarks: 'Above all, I desire that you be most outstanding in the virtue of obedience ... in true and perfect obedience, and in the abdication of your own will and judgment, I especially desire that you who serve God Our Lord in this Society, be outstanding' ('Epistola S. Ignatii de virtute obedientiaie', quoted in Sullivan, 119).

49.31 *Major Barton*: magistrate, high sheriff, and owner of the estate a couple of miles from Clongowes.

49.32 *gallnuts*: growths produced by insects or fungus on, especially, oak trees.

CHAPTER II

50.1 *black twist*: roll of tobacco in the form of a twist.

50.18 *O, twine me a bower*: ballad by Thomas Crofton Croker (1798–1854): 'O twine me a bow'r all of woodbine and roses', etc.; music by Alexander Roche.

50.18 *Blue eyes and golden hair*: Matthew C. Hodgart and Mabel P. Worthington suggest 'Blue Eyes' by the Irish composer James L. Molloy (1837–1909) (*Song in the Works of James Joyce*, New York: Columbia University Press, 1959); Seamus Deane suggests the more likely 'I Would Not Give My Irish Wife' by the Young Irelander Thomas D'Arcy McGee (1825–68) (ed., *A Portrait of the Artist as a Young Man* (London: Penguin, 1993), 291).

50.19 *The Groves of Blarney*: song by Richard Alfred Milliken (1767–1815): 'the groves of Blarney, they look so charming | down by the purlings of sweet silent brooks', etc.

50.21 *Blackrock*: the family has moved from Bray (12 miles south of Dublin on the coast) to Blackrock (5 miles south of Dublin on Dublin Bay), the first move in a downward direction, though Blackrock is still a respectable address.

50.24–5 *Carysfort Avenue*: in Blackrock.

51.13 *athletics and politics*: a pair that had been yoked together with the founding of the Gaelic Athletic Association in 1884 and the Gaelic League in 1893, the aims of which were the re-establishment of Irish pastimes (especially sports), the Irish language, and particularly Irish (as against English) culture (see *F* 446–56).

51.27 *prayerbook*: book containing the forms of prayer in regular use, as well as hymns and parts of the different masses performed.

51.30–1 *prayed for . . . happy death*: in Catholicism, those who died with venial (as opposed to mortal) sins still to expiate would go to purgatory (rather than to hell); their time there could be alleviated by the prayers of the living. To pray for God's grace (the unmerited favour of God through which alone individuals could be saved), which would bring a 'happy death', would be standard practice.

51.33 *Cork*: county on the south coast of Ireland, the principal city of which is also called Cork.

51.37–9 *Stillorgan . . . Dundrum . . . Sandyford*: all villages within a few miles of Blackrock.

52.3 *Munster*: one of the traditional four 'provinces' of Ireland: Ulster (north), Connacht (west), Leinster (east), and Munster (south); Cork lies in, and was the capital of, Munster whence Simon Dedalus comes.

52.12 *The Count of Monte Cristo*: romantic adventure novel (1844) by Alexandre Dumas *père* (1802–70) with the typically convoluted plot of such novels: Edmon Dantes falls victim to the machinations of his enemies, is wrongfully arrested (on the eve of his wedding to Mercedes), imprisoned for fourteen years during which time Mercedes is led to believe he is dead and so marries another, escapes (having been told by a dying prisoner of the location of a vast hidden treasure on the island of Monte Cristo), gains the treasure, returns to avenge his enemies, which includes revealing the treachery of Mercedes's husband; her son challenges Dantes to a duel but after her intervention Dantes spares him; her husband commits suicide but, rather than marrying her, Dantes provides her with a cottage in Marseilles and sails off with a Greek princess whom he has previously purchased in a Constantinople slave market.

52.12 *dark avenger*: Edmon Dantes.

52.15 *wonderful island cave*: where the treasure lay and which Dantes used as a hideout.

52.19 *Marseilles*: town on the south coast of France; see 52.12 n.

52.20–1 *small whitewashed house*: Mercedes's cottage in Marseilles.

52.30 *Madam, I never eat muscatel grapes*: Dantes on being offered the same by Mercedes in her house in Paris; her son explains that this is a sign that Dantes is bent on revenge, for such men never eat or drink in the house of their enemy.

52.35 *Napoleon's plain style of dress*: at the beginning of his career Napoleon did so dress.

52.39 *the castle*: one of the Martello towers on the east coast of Ireland, built during the Napoleonic wars (1803–6) to defend against possible invasion; Stephen lives in one at the opening of *Ulysses*.

53.5–9 *Carrickmines . . . Stradbrooke*: inland village and area south of Blackrock.

54.1 *Rock Road*: one of the connected roads that runs along the coast all the way from Bray to Dublin, this part in Blackrock.

54.22 *caravans*: covered horse-drawn carriages; here clearly used as removal vans.

54.29 *Merrion Road*: continues Rock Road in the direction of Dublin (see 54.1 n.).

55.19 *neighbouring square*: Mountjoy Square in the north of Dublin off which runs the large Gardiner Street.

55.22 *customhouse*: at the end of Gardiner Street, on the north bank of the River Liffey which runs west to east through the centre of Dublin; completed in 1791, the impressive Custom House held the custom and excise tax offices, the Board of Public Works, and the Poor Law Commission.

56.9 *japanned*: covered with hard black varnish (originally from Japan).

56.13 *Mabel Hunter*: may have been a real music-hall performer (see *G*).

56.25 *stone of coal*: a stone's weight (14 lbs.) of coal.

56.30–57.13 *He was sitting . . . Josephine . . . Stephen*: cf. Joyce's 'epiphany', no. 5 (*PSW* 165).

57.15 *Harold's Cross*: suburb in the south-south-west part of Dublin.

57.33–58.22 *the last tram . . . he did neither*: cf. Joyce's third 'epiphany' (*PSW* 163) and 187.4–11

58.27 *emerald exercise*: an emerald-green exercise book.

58.28 *A.M.D.G.* abbreviation of the Latin phrase *Ad Majorem Dei Gloriam*: 'For the greater glory of God': Jesuit motto, often put by students at the opening of essays.

58.31 *Lord Byron*: George Gordon, Lord Byron (1788–1824), poet, wrote such love poems in his early career; he was considered by Victorians as scandalous because of his notorious private life and his irreverent irony, particularly that directed at Church and State.

58.34 *Bray*: see 23.7–8 n.

58.36–7 *second moiety notices*: 'moiety': half; so notices for tax owed for the second half of the year.

59.15 *L.D.S.*: abbreviation of the Latin phrase *Laus Deo Semper*: 'Praise to God Always', Jesuit motto, often put at the end of essays; see 58.28 n. and e.g. James Joyce, 'Trust Not Appearances' (?1896) (*CW* 15, 16 and *KB* 3).

59.26 *him*: see 49.22 n.

59.29 *Belvedere*: Belvedere College, Jesuit boys' day school (founded 1841) in north-east Dublin, not quite as fashionable as Clongowes Wood College.

59.30–1 *provincial of the order*: see 40.13–15 and 49.22 nn; again, real historical time does not match fictional time; the 'real' Conmee did not become 'provincial' until 1905.

59.32 *christian brothers*: a lay teaching order of the Catholic Church, its members being bound only by temporary vows; here the Irish Christian Brothers (founded 1802), who provided education for those who could not pay; so, such an education was less fashionable than one provided by the Jesuits.

60.8 *Maurice*: Mr Dedalus is not the only one to 'forget about Maurice'; he plays a much larger part in Joyce's earlier *Stephen Hero*; this is his only appearance in *Portrait*.

60.16 *mumbled*: 'mumble': 'to chew or bite softly as with toothless gums' and/or 'to maul' (*SOED*).

60.25 *the corporation*: Dublin Corporation: the organization responsible for civic government in Dublin comprising the lord mayor, sheriffs, aldermen, and councilmen, and their various committees and attendant bureaucracy.

60.34 *twice nine*: see 37.16 n.

61.3 *Whitsuntide*: the week including Whit Sunday, the seventh Sunday after Easter which commemorates the descent of the Holy Spirit on the Apostles at Pentecost (Acts 2).

61.11 *Blessed Sacrament . . . tabernacle*: 'tabernacle': an ornamental receptacle for the already consecrated elements of the Eucharist (see 38.36–7 n.); the play is being held in the chapel on the altar of which the tabernacle would sit; the 'Blessed Sacrament' has been removed lest the boys upset the tabernacle during the performance.

61.25 *chief part, that of a farcical pedagogue*: Stephen's playing of the 'chief part' means it cannot be the same play that Joyce himself acted in—F. Anstey (pseudonym of Thomas Anstey Guthrie (1856–1934)), *Vice Versa*, adapted from his novel of 1882, *Vice Versa: Or a Lesson to Fathers*—for the pedagogue there is a minor part.

61.27–8 *number two*: room number of Stephen's class at Belvedere where room numbers indicated the number of years until school leaving (*G*).

62.7 *gospel side of the altar*: the two sides of the altar: gospel (on the left as the congregation faces it, where the gospels are read) and epistle (on the right, where the epistles are read).

63.27–9 *He that will not hear . . . the publicana*: after Matt. 18: 17, Jesus to his disciples: 'If he will not hear the church, let him be to thee as the heathen and publican' (Douay). (For Joyce's actual performance, see *E* 56 and Eugene Sheehy, *May it Please the Court* (Dublin: Fallon, 1951), 8–10.)

64.8 *after beads*: after the recitation of the rosary (a devotion in which the prayer to the Virgin Mary (the 'Hail Mary') is recited (in lots of ten or 'decades') preceded by an 'Our Father' and succeeded by a 'Glory Be'; count is kept using rosary beads); a regular feature in the school day.

64.9 *number one*: the oldest students; see 61.27–8 n.

64.21 *butter wouldn't melt in your mouth*: *PWJ* claims an Irish origin for this phrase (198).

65.11 *sure five*: a sure thing, after an arrangement of billiard balls which virtually guarantees the player the top score of five (*G*).

65.25 *Confiteor*: the prayer used at the beginning of confession (which, in Latin, begins '*Confiteor Deo omnipotenti*': 'I confess to almighty God'); so a parody admission on Stephen's part. *G* quotes in full.

65.35 *number six*: six years from completion; see 61.27–8 n.

66.15 *Mr Tate*: by his title, a lay teacher, not a member of the order.

66.30–3 *without a possibility . . . ever reaching*: doctrine allows that the soul yearns for communion with its creator, is granted grace to approach, but never reach, such communion; Stephen has not allowed for any approach, a heresy, which he corrects under questioning.

67.2 *Drumcondra Road*: main road through Drumcondra (a northern suburb of Dublin).

67.11 *Clonliffe Road*: thoroughfare running east off Drumcondra Road.

67.16 *Captain Marryat*: Captain Frederick Marryat (1792–1848), English naval officer and author of adventure tales, especially for boys. See *U* 18.

67.24 *Newman*: John Henry, Cardinal Newman (1801–90), English, founder (1833) of the Oxford Movement (to bring the Anglican Church closer to the Roman Catholic); converted to Catholicism (1845); became rector of the Catholic University in Ireland (1854; see 138.26 n.); made a cardinal (1879); wrote what are considered eloquent expositions in defence of his principles; Stephen's choice of prose writer is therefore orthodox.

67.32 *Lord Tennyson*: Alfred, Lord Tennyson (1809–1902), poet laureate of England and immensely popular; another safe choice.

68.3 *Byron*: definitely a heretical choice; see 58.31 n.

68.10–11 *on the slates in the yard*: according to *A*: 'the slates which made up the urinal trough in the "square" or "yard" ' (506).

68.11 *sent to the loft*: see *A*: 'at Clongowes it meant simply "sent to the prefect for punishment" ' (506).

68.15–16 *As Tyson . . . Kafoozelum*: after the anonymous ballad, 'The Daughter of Jerusalem' (vulgar version: 'The Harlot of Jerusalem'); *G* gives one version.

68.22 *trans*: Joyce to his translator; 'An abbreviation of the word, made by schoolboys, "translation" ' (*LIII* 129); could also mean a crib.

69.8 *Jones's Road*: leads back from Clonliffe Road towards the centre of Dublin.

69.35 *a great bake*: in a state of being cross and anxious.

70.19–20 *When the gymnasium had been opened*: in response to the Gaelic Athletic Association's call for a turn to Irish sports? See 51.13 n.

70.21 *movement towards national revival*: the Gaelic League, see 51.13 n.

70.23–4 *fallen language and tradition*: see 51.13 n.

71.16 *The Lily of Killarney*: the overture to the opera *The Lily of Killarney* (1862) by the English Julius Benedict (1804–85); based on the popular melodrama *The Colleen Bawn* (1861) written by the Irish Dion Boucicault (1820–90).

71.39 *mummery*: play-acting; see *PWJ* for a particularly Irish twist on the word (171–2).

72.16 *George's Street*: runs south-east from Belvedere College.

72.31 *Lotts*: small lane, parallel to and just north of the Liffey.

72.37 *Kingsbridge*: railway station serving south and west (now Heuston station).

73.1 *night mail to Cork*: the night mail train to Cork city from Dublin.

73.4–5 *telegraphpoles . . . four seconds*: the length of the journey time can be calculated from Stephen's close observation (see *G*) but note that the effects of trains passing telegraph poles have been noted by Stephen earlier (16.22).

73.17–18 *dispossession . . . phantasy*: cf. 'Portrait': 'he was at the difficult age, dispossessed and necessitous' (*PSW* 213).

73.19 *Maryborough*: town about one-third the 164-mile distance from Dublin to Cork.

73.20 *Mallow*: town *c*.20 miles from Cork.

73.35 *jingle*: covered, horse-drawn, two-wheeled carriage.

73.36 *Victoria Hotel*: fashionable hotel in Cork.

74.4–19 *'Tis youth and folly . . . The mountain dew*: perhaps from anonymous ballad, 'Love is Pleasin', Love is Teasin'' (see Deane (ed.), *Portrait of the Artist*).

74.25 *come-all-yous*: generic name for the typical Irish street ballads beginning 'Come all you . . . ' (see 29.8–9 n.).

74.33 *drisheens*: Gaelic: *drisín*: 'stuffed sheep's intestine cooked as pudding' (*O* 336).

75.1 *Queen's College*: Queen's College, Cork (opened 1849), was one of three 'Queen's Colleges' (with Belfast and Galway) established in 1845 as non-sectarian higher educational institutions (as against Trinity College, Dublin, founded by Elizabeth I in 1591 with the express purpose of furthering the reformation in Ireland, and which had remained Anglo-Irish and Protestant: until 1873 admission required submission to religious tests; after this date the Catholic hierarchy refused to sanction any Catholic going there).

75.3 *Mardyke*: then fashionable promenade in Cork city.

76.5 *Groceries*: a pub which also sold groceries.

76.7–8 *our names had been marked*: i.e. once roll had been called and they had been marked down as present.

76.11 *Tantiles*: area in the western part of County Cork.

76.17 *street arabs*: children from the slums.

76.25 *free boy*: one who did not pay tuition fees.

77.11 *South Terrace*: a then fashionable residential street in Cork.

77.12 *maneens*: *PWJ*: 'A boy who apes to be a man—puts on airs like a man—is called a *manneen* in contempt' (90).

77.20 *Queenstown*: the port city (now Cobh) for County Cork.

78.8 *first communion*: see 39.8 n.

78.8 *slim Jim*: Joyce to his translator: 'This is a kind of sweet meat made of a soft marshmellow [*sic*] jelly which is coated first with pink sugar and then powdered, so far as I remember with cocoanut chips. It is called "Slim Jim" because it is sold in strips about a foot or a foot and a half in length and an inch in breadth. It is very elastic and can be eaten by two people at the same time' (*LIII* 129).

78.26 *lob*: *PWJ*: 'A quantity, especially of money or of any valuable commodity' (287)

78.30 *jackeen*: *PWJ*: 'nickname for a conceited Dublin citizen of the lower class' (278).

78.31–2 *Newcombe's coffeehouse*: once fashionable Cork coffee-house.

78.36 *curvettings*: frisking about.

79.2–3 *Lee . . . Liffey*: rivers which run through the centres of, respectively, Cork city and Dublin.

79.4 *Dilectus*: properly '*Delectus*', an anthology (1816) of Latin sentences by Richard Valpy (1754–1836) gathered together to teach Latin in school (it was used at Clongowes in the 1880s). See *JSA*.

79.5–6 *Tempora mutantur . . . mutamur in illis*: Latin: both mean 'Times are changed and we are changed in them'; they differ metrically; the second is the title of a poem by Robert Greene (1560–92), the second line of which is 'Proud Icarus did fall he soared so high'. See *G* for full poem and *JSA*.

79.21 *Yerra*: from the Gaelic: '*A Dhia ara*: O God well!' (*O* 336), a deprecatory exclamation.

79.26 *Sunday's Well*: fashionable suburb west of Cork city.

80.9 *Kerry Boy*: Kerry is a county at the south-western tip of Ireland.

80.30–2 *Art thou pale for weariness . . . companionless*: opening lines of fragmentary poem, 'To the Moon' (1820), from *Poems Written in 1820* (1824) by Shelley (see following note).

80.33 *Shelley*: Percy Bysshe Shelley (1792–1822), English Romantic poet and, in his 'A Defence of Poetry' (1821; 1840), an aesthetic philosopher.

80.34–6 *ineffectualness . . . ineffectual*: the language of the prose as Stephen thinks about Shelley echoes that of Matthew Arnold in his description of Shelley as a 'beautiful and ineffectual angel, beating in the void his luminous wings in vain' (first in his essay on Byron and then quoting himself in his next essay, on Shelley (*Essays in Criticism*, Second Series (1888; repr. London: Macmillan, 1921), 204, 252)).

81.2 *Foster Place*: dead-end street off College Green in the centre of Dublin.

81.5 *bank of Ireland*: housed in the Irish parliament buildings, which were no longer needed with the Act of Union (see 5.23–4 and 31.39–32.2 nn.) and which the bank bought in 1802; on College Green.

81.6 *thirty and three pounds*: an extremely handsome sum for the time.

81.7 *exhibition*: a scholarship.

81.17 *house of commons of the old Irish parliament*: see 81.5 n.

81.19 *Hely Hutchinson*: John Hely-Hutchinson (1724–94), Irish statesman and economist and renowned orator; favoured Catholic emancipation (*F* 171).

81.19 *Flood*: Henry Flood (1732–91), Irish statesman and orator; opposed Catholic relief but supported parliamentary reform (*F* 171).

81.19 *Henry Grattan*: (1746–1820), Irish statesman and orator; championed Catholic relief, opposed the Union (*F* 171).

81.20 *Charles Kendal Bushe*: (1767–1843), Irish judge and renowned orator; ally of Grattan, opposed Union.

81.23–4 *as I roved out ... sweet July*: opening line of anonymous Irish street ballad, 'The Bonny Labouring Boy'; but see *PWJ*: ' "O that's all *as I roved out*": to express unbelief in what someone says as quite unworthy of credit. In allusion to songs beginning "As I roved out," which are generally fictitious' (113).

81.29 *Barnardo's*: J. M. Barnardo & Son, Grafton Street, Dublin; fashionable furriers.

82.7 *Ingomar*: *Ingomar the Barbarian* (1851), adaptation by Maria Anne Lovell of the German *Der Sohn der Wildnis* (1843) of E. F. J. Baron von Münch-Bellinghausen (1806–71), in which Ingomar finally wins the love of the noble lady who had first scorned him (*G*).

82.7 *The Lady of Lyons*: *The Lady of Lyons, or Love and Pride* (1838), a romantic comedy by Edward Bulwer-Lytton (1803–73), in which Claude Melnotte, poor boy, falls for Pauline, rich girl, and after various reverses of plot finally wins her.

82.32 *mole*: 'a massive structure, especially of stone, serving as a pier or breakwater, or joining two places separated by water' (*SOED*).

83.2 *mortal sin*: in Catholicism, a grave sin which deprives the soul of divine grace; here, the sin of sexual impurity, or lust.

83.18–19 *Mercedes*: see 52.12 n.

83.24 *Claude Melnotte*: see 82.7 n.

83.37–84.9 *He felt some dark presence ... iniquitous abandonment*: cf. Joyce's 'epiphany', no. 31 (*PSW* 191).

84.14 *quarter of the jews*: Stephen has wandered into Dublin's 'red light' district which at the time was in *east* central Dublin (see *Ulysses*'s 'Nighttown' in 'Circe', *U* 408–66). Oddly, as *G* notes, the only Jewish area at that time (such as it was) was in *south* central Dublin.

84.21 *slumber of centuries*: compare Joyce's use of the phrase in 'Portrait' and the 'iniquity' there with that here (*PSW* 216).

CHAPTER III

86.26 *widening tail . . . a peacock's*: emblematic of the sin of pride; note that earlier, Stephen's belly has gluttonously advised him to 'Stuff it into you' (86.6), gluttony being another of the seven deadly sins; Stephen, being guilty of the particular mortal sin of lust, is in Catholic doctrine guilty of all (see 89.17–18 n.).

86.33–87.1 *Shelley's fragment . . . pale for weariness*: see 80.30–2 and n.

87.6 *balefire*: in Old English, a funeral pyre; in Scots and lately in English, a great fire in the open air (*SOED*).

87.11 *his body . . . maimed by the excess*: Stephen's physical body bears the signs of his sinning.

87.20–3 *sanctifying grace . . . actual grace*: 'grace': the free and unmerited favour of God; it is, according to Catholic doctrine, present in individuals in two forms: 'sanctifying' or 'habitual' grace inheres in the soul, is marked by a state of habitual holiness, and can be lost only through the commission of mortal sin; 'actual grace' is the transient help (or impulse) to act morally.

87.32 *surd*: in mathematics, a number or quantity that cannot be expressed in finite terms of ordinary numbers, also known as an 'irrational' number (*SOED*).

87.37 *morally present*: though standing outside the church, individuals were deemed to be 'morally present' if they were so proximate during mass; a not uncommon practice of Irish men.

88.4 *prefecture*: the office of prefect, see 6.11 n.

88.4–5 *sodality of the Blessed Virgin Mary*: 'sodality': a confraternity of lay individuals who meet regularly for particular religious exercises (laid down in specific rules); this one is dedicated to the Virgin Mary; to hold such a position was a considerable honour.

88.6 *little office*: 'a collection of psalms and other readings, mainly from the Old Testament, which was compiled about the eighth century for daily recital in honour of the Blessed Virgin' (*JSA* 245), included in *The Sodality Manual . . . of the Sodality of the Blessed Virgin Mary* (see 124.1–5 n.).

88.8 *falsehood of his position*: obviously, Stephen's position is hypocritical as he is in mortal sin; he adds the sin of sacrilege to that of impurity.

88.11–12 *psalms of prophecy*: in the Vulgate Bible they are: Psalms 8, 18, 23, 44, 45, 86, 95–7 (and in the King James: 8, 19, 24, 45, 46, 87, 96–8); the most relevant here is Ps. 44: 9–10 (Vulgate; 45: 8–9 KJV).

88.12 *glories of Mary*: title of a book by St Alphonsus Liguori (see 128.13–14 n.) and, in part, of two sermons by Newman ('The Glories of Mary for the Sake of Her Son' and 'On the Fitness of the Glories of Mary', XVII and XVIII, *Discourses to Mixed Congregations* (1849; repr. London: Burns and Oates, 1886); Stephen alludes several times to phrases from the first of these).

88.14 *God's gifts to her soul*: in Catholic doctrine, her great gift from God is that she is preserved from all sin, for though she gives birth, she retains her virginity.

88.15 *royal lineage*: she is traditionally said to descend from King David.

88.15–16 *her emblems . . . lateblossoming tree*: symbols of her patience.

88.20–4 *Quasi cedrus . . . suavitatem odoris*: Latin: Ecclus. 24: 17–20 (Vulgate): 'I was exalted like a cedar in Libanus and as a cypress tree on mount Sion. I was exalted like a palm tree in Cades, and as a rose plant in Jericho. As a fair olive tree in the plains, and as a plane tree by the water in the streets, was I exalted. I gave a sweet smell like cinnamon and aromatical balm: I yielded a sweet odour like the best myrrh' (Douay). (The Latin is wrong four times: 'Libanon' should read 'Libano'; 'Gades' should read 'Cades'; 'uliva' should read 'oliva'; there should be no 'et' before 'quasi myrrha' (Sullivan, 138 n. 37). All are mistakes in the MS (*JJA* 10: 493).

88.26 *refuge of sinners*: from 'The Litany of Our Lady' (see 29.25 n.).

88.32–3 *emblem . . . infusing peace*: she is called 'the morning star' (in 'The Litany of Our Lady'), her appearance signalling the day of Redemption. The line comes from Newman, 'The Glories of Mary' (*Mixed Congregations*, 359) (see 88.12 n.).

88.38 *sums and cuts*: Joyce to his translator: 'Schoolboy's abbreviation for problems set by a master to his class on the model of some theorum [*sic*] or problem in whatever book of Euclid's Geometry they are reading' (*LIII* 129).

89.3 *My excellent friend Bombados*: Joyce to Michael Healy (Nora Joyce's uncle), 2 November 1915: 'I forget whether I thanked you for having verified the quotation about our excellent friend Bombados. If I did not I shall do so now. I shall correct it on the proof—if I ever see one' (*LI* 86). The *Egoist* (pub. 1 Aug. 1914) had '*Pompados*'; the first edition '*Bombados*'. (The MS has *Pompados* and an extra line: '*My dearest and best Patake*' (*JJA* 10: 495).) All of this seems to indicate that the line comes from a real panto-mime, but it remains elusive.

89.7 *game ball*: final, deciding ball; so, it's all over.

89.7 *scut*: see 33.27 n.

89.14–16 *following up . . . obscure silences*: Stephen's interest in the mysteries of obscure doctrine would be seen to be as likely to lead him from the Church as would sin (see *G*); but in one sense his interest has itself been cultivated by the scholastic practice of the Jesuits (see 131.18 n.), it's just that, as Buck Mulligan tells him in *Ulysses*, 'you have the cursed jesuit strain in you, only it's injected the wrong way' (*U* 8).

89.17–18 *saint James . . . guilty of all*: James 2: 10: 'For whosoever shall keep the whole law, and yet offend in one point, he is guilty of all.'

89.20–1 *deadly sins*: all seven are accounted for here: lust, pride, covetousness, envy, gluttony, anger, sloth.

89.29 *curious questions*: most of these have answers in the Catechism even if Stephen is (especially on the second and third) perilously close to being guilty of over scrupulousness: to the first, the money and all that it has produced; to the second, it is the intention that matters; to the third, in such a 'case of necessity' yes; to the fifth, because it is not only a Sacrament but an emblem of the Sacrifice; to the sixth, in entirety in each part; to the seventh, no. The fourth draws attention to a seeming contradiction. In the Sermon on the Mount, Jesus said, 'Blessed are the poor in spirit: for theirs is the kingdom of heaven. Blessed are the meek: for they shall possess the land' (Matt. 5: 3–4 (Douay)). Why give one heaven and the other earth, especially since elsewhere Jesus is said to have remarked, 'My kingdom is not of this world' (John 18: 36)?

90.16 *retreat*: a period of seclusion for prayer and religious meditation.

90.17 *saint Francis . . . feast day*: for 'saint Francis', see 46.36 n.; his feast day is 3 December which, since it falls here on a Saturday, makes this 1898.

90.19 *beads*: see 64.8 n.

90.31 *story of the life of saint Francis*: the account that follows is faithful in most respects (he did not go to the Indians 'at his own desire' but was asked by Loyola to replace his first choice who had fallen ill). See *G* for full details.

91.6 *Sancian*: island off the coast of China.

91.10 *faith . . . moves mountains*: 1 Cor. 13: 2: 'Though I have all faith, so that I could remove mountains, and have not charity, I am nothing.'

91.12 *ad majorem Dei gloriam*: see 46.35–6 n.

91.13 *power to intercede for us*: in Catholic doctrine, the saint could supplicate for God's favour on behalf of the one who prays in his name.

91.16 *fisher of souls*: after Jesus's call to Peter and Andrew: 'Come ye after me, and I will make you to be fishers of men' (Matt. 4: 19 (Douay)).

91.22 *simoom*: 'a hot dry dust-laden wind blowing at intervals especially in the Arabian desert' (*OERD*).

91.23–5 *Remember only . . . Ecclesiastes . . . fortieth verse*: actually Ecclesiasticus, the book included by Protestants in the Apocrypha, not Ecclesiastes, the book in the Old Testament 'proper'; Ecclus. 7: 40: 'In all thy works remember thy last end, and thou shalt never sin' (Douay). Father Arnall bases his sermons on precedent Jesuit texts. As *T* has exhaustively demonstrated, the main source (especially pp. 98 ff.) is Giovanni Pietro Pinamonti, SJ (1632–1703), *Hell Opened to Christians, to Caution them from Entering into It* (1688; in an 1868 English translation published in Dublin and excerpted in *T*; this text will be cited below as '*Hell* in T'). William T. Noon remarks that 'the purely negative and harrowing sermon of the *Portrait* is neither Catholic nor Ignatian' but rather takes a very conservatively dogmatic line ('Joyce and Catholicism', *James Joyce Review*, 1/4 (Dec. 1957), 13), but *T* convincingly shows that Arnall's sermon flows from a rich vein of Jesuit sermonizing. More broadly, as *G* argues, in its narrative form the chapter follows the outline of the programme for meditation proposed by Loyola in his *Spiritual Exercises* (1548): sin and its consequences, Jesus's life on earth, his passion, his risen life.

92.28 *four last things*: in Catholic doctrine, the four last things are (as Father Arnall says) death, judgement, heaven, and hell.

92.35–6 *What doth it profit . . . immortal soul*: cf. Matt. 16: 26: 'For what doth it profit a man, if he gain the whole world, and suffer the loss of his own soul?' (Douay).

93.31 *Ecclesiastes*: see 91.23–5 n.

94.17 *death and judgment*: the first two of the 'four last things'.

95.15 *particular judgment*: the individual judgement that each soul faces upon death and as a result of which it finds its immediate place (hell, purgatory, heaven).

95.16 *abode of bliss*: synonym for heaven; where those who have repented and whose penance on earth has been completed go; cf. *Ulysses* where the phrase is put to very different use (*U* 72, 163, 636).

95.16 *prison of purgatory*: where those who have sinned and repented but still have penance to do for their sins go after death.

95.17 *hell*: where those who have sinned and not repented, who die in mortal sin, go.

95.19 *general judgment*: the Final or Last Judgement (as opposed to the 'particular judgement' of each individual soul (see 95.15 n.) when all mankind is judged and all sins revealed.

95.20 *Doomsday*: the Last Judgement.

95.20–9 *The stars of heaven . . . shall be no more*: these phrases echo sections of the book of Revelation (6: 12–14; 10: 1–2, 5–6) in the New Testament (or Apocalypse (Douay)); the young Joyce copied the whole of the King James Revelation into a notebook (Cornell MS 9 (Robert Scholes (comp.), *The Cornell Joyce Collection* (Ithaca: Cornell University Press, 1961), 6)).

95.24 *Michael*: the Archangel Michael, otherwise known as the angel of the Church Militant, who announces the death of time in announcing the Last Judgement.

95.28–9 *Time is . . . be no more*: what is uttered by the Brazen Head; according to Brewer 'the legend of the wonderful head of brass that could speak and was omniscient, found in early romances, is of Eastern origin. . . . [T]he most famous [example] in English legend is that fabled to have been made by the great Roger Bacon. It was said if Bacon heard it speak he would succeed in his projects; if not, he would fail. His familiar, Miles, was set to watch, and while Bacon slept the Head spoke thrice: "Time is"; half an hour later it said, "Time was". In another half-hour it said, "Time's past", fell down and was broken to atoms. Byron refers to this legend. "Like Friar Bacon's head, I've spoken, | 'Time is', 'Time was', 'Time's past'" (*Don Juan*, i. 217) References to Bacon's brazen head are frequent in literature. Most notable is Robert Greene's *Honourable History of Friar Bacon and Friar Bungay*, 1594' (*Brewer's Dictionary of Phrase and Fable*, 14th edn., ed. Ivor H. Evans (1989; repr. London: Cassell, 1992), 152–3).

95.30 *Jehoshaphat*: valley east of Jerusalem which, according to Joel 3: 2, 12, is where 'all nations' will be gathered for the Lord's judgement.

95.34–6 *supreme judge . . . Lamb of God . . . Jesus of Nazareth . . . Man of Sorrows . . . Good Shepherd*: names for Jesus, drawing the contrast between his various roles: bearer of both judgement and mercy, God as man, God who suffers with man.

95.36–9 *He is seen . . . seraphim*: cf. Matt. 25: 31: 'when the Son of man shall come in his glory, and all the holy angels with him, then shall he sit upon the throne of his glory'; the ranks of angels listed by Father Arnall follow roughly the traditional hierarchy (after Dante Alighieri (1265–1321), *Il Paradiso* [third part of his *Divina Commedia*], xxviii. 90–114).

96.6–8 *Depart from me . . . his angels*: Jesus, in his account of the Last Judgement, says the good (sheep) will be separated from the bad (goats) and to the latter will be said (Matt. 25: 41): 'Depart from me, ye cursed, into everlasting fire, prepared for the devil and his angels' (and see 105.3–4 and 202.9 nn.)

96.16–17 *O you hypocrites . . . whited sepulchres*: Jesus, again, this time to the 'scribes and Pharisees' who, he says, 'say, and do not' (Matt. 23: 3): 'Woe unto you, scribes and Pharisees, hypocrites! for ye are like unto whited sepulchres, which indeed appear beautiful outward, but are within full of dead men's bones, and of all uncleanness' (Matt. 23: 27).

96.24 *Son of God . . . expect Him*: after Matt. 24: 36: 'But of that day and hour knoweth no man, no, not the angels of heaven, but my Father only.'

96.26–7 *Death and judgment . . . first parents*: in Catholic doctrine, Adam and Eve brought sin into the world, the consequence of which is that all are born in (original) sin and death and judgement result.

96.38–97.1 *Addison . . . meet his end*: story recounted by, among others, Samuel Johnson (1709–84), in his *Lives of the English Poets* (1779–81) of Joseph Addison (1672–1719) to the Lord Warwick, who was his stepson; his words were reportedly 'I have sent for you that you may see how a Christian can die' (ed. George Birkbeck Hill, 3 vols. (Oxford: Clarendon Press, 1905), ii. 117). An irony: Addison was a Tory and supporter of the anti-Irish, anti-Catholic policies of the Protestant William of Orange (1650–1702; r. 1689–1702 as William III) who defeated Catholic James II (1633–1701) and his Irish 'Jacobites' (supporters) at the Battle of the Boyne (1690).

97.3–4 *O grave . . . thy sting?*: Alexander Pope (1688–1744), 'The Dying Christian to His Soul', ll. 17–18; after 1 Cor. 15: 55: 'O death, where is thy sting? O grave, where is thy victory?'

97.17 *the square*: Mountjoy Square.

97.22–3 *The image of Emma . . . his heart*: cf. Dante on first seeing Beatrice: 'Mine eyes drooped down to the clear fount; but beholding me therein, I drew them back to the grass, so great a shame weighed down my brow' (*Purgatorio*, xxx. 76–8; Dent dual-language edn., ed. Hermann Oelsner, trans. Thomas Okey (1900; repr. London: Temple Classics, 1926), 383).

98.3 *he imagined . . . near Emma*: cf. Stephen's thoughts about Emma with Dante's treatment of Beatrice at the end of the *Purgatorio* and throughout the *Paradiso* where she acts as his guide.

98.9–11 *her whose beauty . . . bright and musical*: Newman, on the Blessed Virgin, 'The Glories of Mary' (*Mixed Congregations*, 359).

98.29–31 *Forty days . . . face of the earth*: cf. God to Noah in Gen. 7: 4: 'I will cause it to rain upon the earth forty days and forty nights; and every living substance that I have made will I destroy from off the face of the earth.'

98.33–5 *Hell has enlarged . . . fourteenth verse*: Father Arnall's citation of chapter and verse is correct (Douay). As *T* points out, this particular text and much of the ensuing sermon follows Pinamonti's *Hell Opened to Christians* (see 91.23–5 n.; *T* 175), itself following 'a traditional pattern in devotional literature consisting of seven daily "Considerations" or meditations . . . (1) The Prison of Hell . . . [100.32–101.28] (2) The Fire . . . [101.38–103.8] (3) The Company of the Damned . . . [103.9–105.4] (4) The Pain of Loss . . . [107.8–108.18] (5) The Sting of Conscience . . . [108.19–109.35] (6) The Pain of Extension . . . [109.36–110.38] (7) Eternity [110.39–113.6]' (*T* 173–4).

99.2–5 *Adam and Eve . . . filled again*: As *G* argues, Father Arnall's reasoning here is more St Anselm of Canterbury (see 101.5 n.) in his *Cur Deus Homo* (*c*.1094–*c*.1098) or even John Milton (1608–74) in *Paradise Lost* (1667) than orthodox Catholic doctrine.

99.5–6 *son of the morning*: Isa. 14: 12: 'How art thou fallen from heaven, O Lucifer, son of the morning!'; Lucifer's name strictly means 'light-bringing' or 'morning star'.

99.7 *a third part of the host of heaven*: the traditional tale of Lucifer/Satan taking 'a third part of the host of heaven' with him derives from Rev. 12: 3–4 and 7–9: the former gives an account of the 'red dragon' drawing 'the third part of the stars of heaven' and 'cast[ing] them to earth'; the latter recounts that 'there was a war in heaven: Michael and his angels fought against the dragon; and the dragon . . . prevailed not . . . and . . . was cast out'. Milton promotes the tale: 'art thou he, | Who first broke peace in Heaven and faith, till then | Unbroken, and in proud rebellious arms | Drew after him the third part of Heaven's sons | Conjured against the Highest?' (*Paradise Lost*, ii. 689–93).

99.10 *non serviam: I will not serve*: '*non serviam*': Latin: 'I shall not serve'; what, traditionally, Lucifer says on falling (cf. Jer. 2: 20 (Douay); *Hell* in *T* 175–6).

99.14–15 *Eden, in the plain of Damascus*: a very odd location for the Garden of Eden; see *G*.

99.18 *ills our flesh is heir to*: misquotation of lines from Hamlet's soliloquy: 'To die: to sleep; | No more; and, by a sleep to say we end | The heart-ache and the thousand natural shocks | That flesh is heir to, 'tis a consummation | Devoutly to be wish'd' (*Hamlet*, III. i. 60–4).

99.21–2 *not to eat . . . forbidden tree*: Gen. 2: 16–17: 'And the Lord God commanded the man, saying, Of every tree of the garden thou mayest freely eat: But of the tree of the knowledge of good and evil, thou shall not eat of it: for in the day that thou eatest thereof thou shalt surely die.'

99.25 *serpent . . . beasts of the field*: Gen. 3: 1: 'Now the serpent was more subtil than any beast of the field which the Lord God had made.'

99.28 *woman, the weaker vessel*: cf. 1 Pet. 3: 7: 'Likewise, ye husbands, dwell with them according to knowledge, giving honour unto the wife, as unto the weaker vessel.'

99.28–9 *poured the poison . . . her ear*: cf. *Hamlet*, I. v. 63–4 where the Ghost claims to have been poisoned by Claudius: '[He] in the porches of mine ears did pour | The leprous distilment.'

99.31 *become as gods, nay as God Himself*: Gen. 3: 4–5: 'The serpent said unto the woman, Ye shall not surely die: For God doth know that in the day ye eat thereof, then your eyes shall be opened, and ye shall be as gods, knowing good and evil.'

99.33 *Adam . . . to resist her*: not doctrine.

99.35–6 *voice of God . . . to account*: Gen. 3: 8–9, 11, 13: 'And they heard the voice of the Lord God walking in the garden . . . And the Lord God called unto Adam, and said unto him, Where art thou? . . . And he said, Who told thee that thou wast naked? Hast thou eaten of the tree, whereof I commanded thee that thou shouldest not eat? . . . And the Lord God said unto the woman, What is this that thou hast done?'

99.36–8 *Michael . . . forth from Eden*: Gen. 3: 24: 'So [the Lord God] drove out the man; and he placed at the east of the garden of Eden Cherubims, and a flaming sword which turned every way, to keep the way of the tree of life.' The Bible does not identify Michael as the one holding the flaming sword; that's Catholic interpretation.

100.1 *earn their bread . . . their brow*: Gen. 3: 19: 'In the sweat of thy face shalt thou eat bread, till thou return unto the ground.'

100.7 *the Eternal Word*: John 1: 1, 14: 'In the beginning was the Word, and the Word was with God, and the Word was God'; 'And the Word was made flesh, and dwelt among us, (and we beheld his glory, the glory as of the only begotten of the Father,) full of grace and truth.'

100.8–12 *He came . . . the new gospel*: this passage mixes material from the New Testament with material more traditional than canonical; for the 'cowshed', see Luke 2: 7; for 'the new gospel', John 1: 17: 'For the law was given by Moses, but grace and truth came by Jesus Christ.'

100.14–20 *seized and bound . . . issued continually*: each of the Gospels gives a slightly different account of Jesus's last days and his treatment; see, most relevantly, John 18: 40; Matt. 27, John 19, Mark 15. The 5,000 lashes is an embellishment. He was, of course, crucified on a cross, not 'hanged on a gibbet' (this latter being an upright post with a projecting arm on which the bodies of executed criminals were hung up (*OERD*)).

100.21–2 *Our Merciful . . . mankind*: see Luke 23: 34: 'Then said Jesus, Father, forgive them; for they know not what they do.'

100.23–5 *He founded . . . rock of ages*: see Matt. 16: 18–19: 'And I say also unto thee, That thou art Peter, and upon this rock I will build my church; and the gates of hell shall not prevail against it. And I will give unto thee the keys of the kingdom of heaven: and whatsoever thou shalt bind on earth shall be bound in heaven: and whatsoever thou shalt loose on earth shall be loosed in heaven.' (Herein a pun that Joyce approved: Peter's name in Latin, *Petrus*, means 'rock'.) The 'rock of ages' is not a Catholic rock, but the title of a Protestant hymn (1776) by Augustus Toplady (1740–78).

100.25 *sacraments*: religious ceremonies or acts regarded as outward and visible signs of inward and spiritual grace; in Catholicism there are seven sacraments: baptism, confirmation, the Eucharist, penance, extreme unction, ordination, and matrimony.

100.26–9 *promised . . . torment: hell*: see Matt. 25: 31–46 and 96.6–8 n.

100.32 *Now let us try for a moment to realise . . .*: in his *Spiritual Exercises* (1548), Loyola recommends that the First Week 'Fifth Exercise', 'a meditation on Hell', begin with 'a composition of place, which is here to see with the eyes of the imagination the length, breadth and depth of hell' (*The Spiritual Exercises of Saint Ignatius of Loyola*, trans. W. H. Longridge, rev. edn. (London: Robert Scott, 1930), 66). Father Arnall follows Loyola's recommendation.

101.4 *four thousand miles thick*: because hell was imagined to be within the earth, and the diameter of the earth is approximately 8,000 miles. (See *Hell* in *T* 176.)

101.5 *saint Anselm*: St Anselm of Canterbury (*c.*1033–1109), Benedictine monk, archbishop of Canterbury from 1093 until his death, philosophical theologian; author of *On the Grammarian, On Truth, On Free Will*, and *The Sin of the Devil*.

101.5–6 *book on similitudes*: *De Similitudinibus*, not by Anselm, though in his spirit.

101.6–7 *worm that gnaws it*: cf. Pinamonti: 'If a blessed saint, as St Anselm says, in his book of Similitudes, will be strong enough . . . to move the whole earth: a damned soul will be so weak, as not to be able even to remove from the eye a worm that is gnawing it' (*Hell* in *T* 176.)

101.9–10 *at the command of God . . . not its light*: see Dan. 3: 49–50 (Douay) and *Hell* in *T* 176.

101.12 *neverending storm of darkness*: after Jude 4 and 13 of 'ungodly men [who turn] the grace of our God into lasciviousness', 'to whom is reserved the blackness of darkness for ever' (see *Hell* in *T* 176).

101.15 *the plagues . . . Pharaohs was smitten*: when the Pharaoh of Egypt not only refused to grant Moses's request to release the children of Israel but increased their hardship, God instructed Moses to call down various plagues: of frogs, lice, flies, boils, blains, hail, locusts, and finally darkness: 'And Moses stretched forth his hand toward heaven; and there was a thick darkness in all the land of Egypt three days: They saw not one another, neither rose any from his place for three days . . . And Pharaoh called unto Moses, and said, Go ye, serve the Lord' (Exod. 10: 22–4) (*Hell* in *T* 176).

101.20–2 *All the filth of the world . . . purged the world*: adaptation of Pinamonti, whose source may be in part Aquinas (*Summa Theologiae*, Part III, Query 97, Article 1, 'Whether in Hell the Damned are Tormented by the Sole Punishment of Fire'), who admits that there may be other punishments than fire, as long as this brings no alleviation of pain (trans. Fr. Laurence Shapcote, rev. Daniel J. Sullivan, 2 vols., 2nd edn. (Chicago: Encyclopaedia Britannica, Inc., 1990), ii. 1066) (*Hell* in *T* 176–7). For Aquinas, see 107.30–1 n.

101.24–6 *bodies of the damned . . . whole world*: adaptation of Pinamonti, who cites St Bonaventure (1221–74), Franciscan monk, Professor of Theology at Paris, minister-general of the Franciscans (1257), cardinal (1273) (*Hell* in *T* 177).

101.39–102.16 *torment of fire . . . it rages for ever*: Pinamonti, after Aquinas

(*Summa Theologiae*, Part III, Query 97, Articles 5 and 6 (trans. Shapcote, ii. 1068–71) (*Hell* in *T* 177).

102.19–22 *the devil himself . . . piece of wax*: Pinamonti, perhaps from St Caesarius of Arles (470–542) (*G*) (*Hell* in *T* 177).

103.21–4 *parricide. . . a serpent*: a Pinamonti example (*Hell* in *T* 179); the punishment for parricide (murder of grandfather, father, *or* son) in Roman law was to be sewn into a leather sack with a live dog, a viper, a cock, and an ape and to be cast into the sea (*G*).

104.1–4 *Saint Catherine of Siena . . . red coals*: Catherine of Siena (1347–80), whom Pinamonti cites (*Hell* in *T* 179).

104.17 *Time is . . . no more!*: see 95.28–9 n.

104.31 *rebellion of the intellect*: Lucifer's sin; see 99.10 n.

104.34–5 *temple of the Holy Ghost*: the body; 1 Cor. 6: 19: 'What? know ye not that your body is the temple of the Holy Ghost which is in you, which ye have of God, and ye are not your own?'

104.37–8 *last day of terrible reckoning*: the Last (or 'general') Judgement; see 95.19 n.

105.3–4 *Depart from me . . . his angels!*: Matt. 25: 41 (see 96.6–8 and 202.9 nn.); *T* says *Hell* uses it twice (in unexcerpted passages) (*T* 179).

105.11–12 *plunging headlong through space*: in the manner of Lucifer being thrown out of heaven in, especially, Milton's *Paradise Lost*, i. 44–7: 'Him the Almighty Power | Hurled headlong flaming from the ethereal sky | With hideous ruin and combustion, down | To bottomless perdition.'

105.29 *blue funk*: 'cowering fear; a state of panic; extreme nervousness' (*SOED*).

105.37 *Malahide*: fishing village on coast north of Dublin.

106.5–6 *O Mary . . . gulf of death!*: from 'The Litany of Our Lady' (see 29.25 n.).

106.9–10 *What did it profit . . . lost his soul?*: see 92.35–6 n.

106.33 *Father, I . . .*: after the opening words of one who confesses: 'Bless me, father, for I have sinned.'

107.8–10 *I am cast away . . . twentythird verse*: the citation of chapter and verse is correct (Douay; 31:22 in KJV); in *Hell* in *T* 179.

107.16–17 *what our holy founder . . . composition of place*: see 46.34 and 100.32 nn.; Loyola stresses the effectiveness in meditation of seeing 'with the eyes of imagination' the 'corporeal place' or 'visible object' which is to be contemplated (*Spiritual Exercises*, First Week, 'First Exercise', 'The First Prelude', trans. Longridge, 53).

107.22–7 *Sin . . . spiritual*: after Pinamonti (*Hell* in *T* 180). In Catholic doctrine, sin comprises two kinds or degrees, each with its particular punishment: the first is the sinful action itself and is punished by *poena sensus* (Latin: 'pain of the senses', e.g. fire); the second, the more grievous turning from God and His grace, is punished by *poena damni* (Latin: 'pain of loss', the pain derived from the knowledge that one is eternally cut off from the grace of God).

107.30–1 *Saint Thomas . . . the angelic doctor*: St Thomas Aquinas (1224/5–74), Dominican priest, teacher, and philosopher theologian; his teachings were at first condemned (and he was not canonized until 1323) but six centuries later were made the basic texts for study in Catholic seminaries; sought to bring together Aristotelian philosophy and Catholic doctrine; author of the *Summa contra Gentiles* and the *Summa Theologiae* (left unfinished at his death); he was called 'the Angelic Doctor not only because of his legendary chastity but also because of his interest in those immaterial beings' called 'angels' (Ralph McInerny (ed.), *Thomas Aquinas: Selected Writings* (London: Penguin, 1998), 368). For 'dominican' see 130.14 n.

107.31–9 *worst . . . for ever*: Arnall borrows from Pinamonti who cites Aquinas (*Hell* in *T* 180); from *Summa Theologiae*, Part III, Query 98 'Of the Will and Intellect of the Damned', esp. Article 8: 'Whether the Damned Will ever Think of God' (trans. Shapcote, ii. 1077).

108.2–3 *The soul tends . . . her existence*: from Aquinas, *Summa Theologiae*, Part II, Query 1, Article 8: 'Whether Other Creatures Concur in that Last End' (trans. Shapcote, i. 615) (in *Hell* in *T* 180).

108.18 *pœna damni, the pain of loss*: Latin, as translated; see 107.22–7 n.

108.20 *pain of conscience*: the next 'consideration' (*Hell* in *T* 180) (see 98.33–5 n.).

108.23–4 *the worm . . . triple sting*: Pinamonti cites Innocent III (b. 1161, pope 1198–1216) on the triple wound of conscience: 'in his book of the Contempt of the World: "The Memory will afflict, late repentance will trouble, and want of time will torment"' (*Hell* in *T* 181).

109.5–8 *saint Augustine . . . God Himself*: (354–430), Doctor of the Catholic Church, Bishop of Hippo Regius (now Annaba, Algeria); Pinamonti adapts for his own ends Augustine, *City of God* (413–27) XXI.ix, 'The nature of eternal punishment' *(Hell* in *T* 180; *G*).

109.13–14 *sacraments and graces and indulgences*: on 'sacraments' see 100.25 n; on 'grace', see 87.20–3 n. 'Indulgence': 'the remission of punishment in purgatory, still due for sins even after sacramental absolution . . . now ordinarily confined to the pope' (*OERD*).

109.37 *pain of extension*: the inalleviable extent of the remorse of the damned; cf. *Hell* in *T* 182.

110.36–8 *blood of the innocent Lamb of God . . . insists upon*: the justice required by Christ sitting at the Last Judgement; after *Hell* in *T* 183.

111.1 *eternity of hell*: the last of the seven 'considerations'; see 98.33–5 n. The image of hell elaborated here originates in Pinamonti: 'Let us . . . imagine . . . a mountain of this small sand [as in an hourglass], so high as would reach from earth to heaven' (*Hell* in *T* 183).

111.38–9 *holy saint . . . vision of hell*: remains a mystery.

112.6 *beatific vision*: the sight of God, only of course possible for the blessed in heaven.

112.29–30 *hideous malice of mortal sin*: 'Mortal sin' is thought to be a malicious killing of the soul which deprives it of divine grace. (Pinamonti sprinkles his text with 'malices' (*Hell* in *T passim*).)

112.31 *venial sin*: sins which are not 'mortal sins': they corrupt the soul but not irreparably, but they are still sins. Arnall is trying to stress that just because they are not 'mortal sins' does not mean that they are not to be taken seriously.

112.39–113.2 *A sin . . . glory*: see 99.7 n.

113.6 *hanging for three hours on the cross*: according to Matt. 27: 45 and Luke 23: 44.

113.9 *spit upon that face*: as did the Roman soldiers, Matt. 27: 30 and Mark 15: 19.

113.12 *awful winepress of sorrow*: cf. Isa. 63: 3 and Rev. 19: 15.

113.13 *wound in His tender side*: see 100.14–20 and n. and John 19: 33–4.

113.13–14 *thorn piercing His head*: see 100.14–20 and n. and Matt. 27: 29, Mark 15: 17, John 19: 2.

113.24 *act of contrition*: prayer intended to draw the penitent's mind to Christ's suffering and his heart to sorrow for his sins. The prayer that follows (114.3–26) is a traditional 'Act of Contrition'.

113.25 *He is there in the tabernacle*: see 61.11 n.

114.3–26 *O my God! . . . amend my life*: see 113.24 n. As G points out, one phrase is missing: 'Who art so deserving' should read 'Who *for thy infinite goodness* art so deserving'; contrition should arise from an awareness of God's infinite goodness.

114.30 *viscid*: from the Latin *viscum*: 'birdlime'; 'having a glutinous or gluey character; sticky, adhesive, ropy' (*SOED*).

115.4 *plenipotentiary*: 'a person invested with full or discretionary powers, especially in regard to a particular transaction' (*SOED*), so 'spiritual plenipotentiary': one who would have the power to deal with sin (a priest); but in one sense the evasiveness through obscure language is exactly the point.

115.26–8 *He had sinned . . . God's child*: after the parable of the prodigal son: 'I will arise and go to my father, and will say unto him, Father, I have sinned against heaven, and before thee, And am no more worthy to be called thy son: make me as one of thy hired servants' (Luke 15: 18–19).

115.31–3 *he had dared . . . corruption*: see 88.8 (and n.), 93.6–8.

116.4–24 *A field of stiff weeds . . . Help!*: cf. Joyce's 'epiphany', no. 6 (*PSW* 166).

117.4–14 *He once had meant . . . guide us home*: virtually verbatim from Newman, 'The Glories of Mary' (*Mixed Congregations*, 359).

117.33 *that part of the body*: in this particular instance, the penis.

117.34 *serpent, the most subtle beast of the field*: see 99.25 n.

118.8 *angel guardian*: in Catholicism, everyone has an angel assigned to them to help them away from evil and towards good.

118.10–12 *his own soul . . . his own body*: a catechetical definition of 'actual sin'.

118.37 *Consciousness of place*: see 107.16–17 n.

119.4 *Church Street chapel*: Capuchin Franciscan friary (see 119.34 n.); and see *PWJ*: 'All through Ireland it is customary to call a Protestant place of worship a "church", and that belonging to Roman Catholics a "chapel"' (143); cf. 'Findlater's church' (135.7).

119.28–9 *those whom Jesus . . . His side*; the disciples, whose trust was 'simple' as they were common men, not men of rank.

119.34 *brown habit of a capuchin*: the Capuchins (founded 1529): a branch of the Franciscans (the Order of Friars Minor, founded in 1209 by St Francis of Assisi (*c.*1181–1226), a preaching and missionary order which originally included a vow of complete poverty); the strictest of three Franciscan orders; they take their name from the long cowl they wear in addition to the usual Franciscan brown, white-belted habit (from Italian *cappucio*: 'cowl') (*OERD*).

120.25 *God's yoke was sweet and light*: Matt. 11: 28–30: 'Come unto me, all ye that labour and are heavy laden, and I will give you rest. Take my yoke upon you, and learn of me; for I am meek and lowly in heart: and ye shall find rest unto your souls. For my yoke is easy, and my burden is light.'

120.27 *God loved little children . . . to Him*: Mark 10: 14: Jesus to his disciples: 'Suffer the little children to come unto me, and forbid them not: for of such is the kingdom of God.'

121.6–7 *prayed of the priest to bless him*: see 106.33 n.

121.8 *Confiteor*: see 65.25 n.

121.8 *my most grievous fault*: words of the *Confiteor*; Stephen stops about a third of the way through (after 'through my fault, through my fault, through my most grievous fault'), before beseeching the Blessed Virgin and saints to intercede with God for him and before asking for forgiveness.

121.10 *your last confession*: sins must be confessed at least once a year (hence, at 201.15–16, Stephen's 'easter duty'); a necessary part of confession is a statement of the length of time since one's last confession.

121.27 *sins of impurity*: see 83.2 n.

122.4–5 *weary and old*: cf. 'Portrait' (*PSW* 212 and n. 7).

122.27 *grave words of absolution*: in Latin: '*Absolvo te in nominis Patris et Filii et Spiritus Sancti, Amen*' ('I absolve you in the name of the Father and of the Son and of the Holy Spirit').

122.28 *token of forgiveness*: the priest is blessing Stephen with the sign of the cross.

122.30 *say his penance*: the priest would have required that Stephen repeat particular prayers as a sign of his penitence.

123.8 *And life lay all before him*: cf. Milton, *Paradise Lost*, xii. 645–7, of Adam and Eve on their expulsion from Eden: 'Some natural tears they dropped, but wiped them soon; | The world was all before them, where to choose | Their place of rest, and Providence their guide.'

123.19 *ciborium*: 'a vessel with an arched cover used to hold the Eucharist' (*OERD*).

123.20–3 *Corpus Domini nostri . . . In vitam eternam. Amen*: Latin: 'The body of our Lord'; 'Unto eternal life. Amen.' The first and last words spoken by the priest as he administers the Eucharist.

CHAPTER IV

124.1–5 *Sunday . . . Blessed Virgin Mary*: Stephen has ordered his life in accordance with the plan for devotions outlined in *The Sodality Manual; or a Collection of Prayers and Spiritual Exercises for Members of the Sodality of the Blessed Virgin Mary* (Dublin: 'Messenger' Office, 1886), 'Devotions for Every Day of the Week', 301–13 (Sullivan, 135–6).

124.7 *heroic offering*: one made for the benefit of others, as here, the pope.

124.8–9 *the sovereign pontiff*: the pope.

124.11 *interleaved prayerbook*: one between the pages of which devotional cards and notices have been inserted; see 51.27 n.

124.13–14 *two candles . . . old and the new testaments*: those standing at either side of the crucifix on the altar.

124.15 *catacombs*: in Rome, subterranean galleries used by the early Christians for the burial of their dead; Roman law made every burial place sacrosanct; the Christians exploited this and so were able to worship there undisturbed (*OERD*).

124.16–17 *ejaculations*: suddenly uttered words of prayer.

124.17–18 *stored up ungrudgingly . . . quarantines and years*: *JSA* suggests that Stephen here is following the 'bank balance' theory of indulgences whereby grace is stored up and may be used to relieve the suffering of souls in purgatory; 'quarantines': 'the remission of as much punishment as would be obtained by forty days of canonical penance' (*JSA* 248). See 95.16 n.

124.23–4 *purgatorial fire . . . everlasting*: hellfire is eternal, unending; purgatorial fire no less real but less long-lasting. See 95.16 n.

124.26 *supererogation*: the performance of more than duty requires.

125.3 *rosaries*: see 64.8 n.

125.7–8 *three daily chaplets*: 'chaplet': one-third of a rosary (or the 55 beads (one-third of the total 165) used to count that number of prayers said); see 64.8 n.

125.8–9 *three theological virtues*: as Stephen goes on to suggest, 'faith, hope and love [or charity]' after 1 Cor. 13: 13: 'And now abideth faith, hope, charity, these three.'

125.12–13 *Mary . . . glorious mysteries*: Mary's glorious mysteries, the contemplation of which is to be the occupation of one reciting the rosary, are divided into three (corresponding to each of the three chaplets): (1) the five joyful, (2) the five sorrowful, and (3) the five glorious mysteries (*G* lists them).

125.15 *seven gifts of the Holy Ghost*: Wisdom, Understanding, Counsel, Piety, Fortitude, Knowledge, Fear of the Lord; after Isa. 11: 2.

125.16 *seven deadly sins*: see 89.20–1 n.

125.19 *wisdom and understanding and knowledge*: see 125.15 n.

125.26 *Paraclete*: from Greek: παράκλητος in John 14: 26, meaning, strictly, 'advocate', but usually translated 'Comforter'; one of the names of the Holy Spirit.

125.26–7 *Whose symbols . . . mighty wind*: the 'dove' after e.g. Matt. 3: 16: 'And Jesus, when he was baptized, went up straightway out of the water: and, lo, the heavens were opened unto him, and he saw the Spirit of God descending like a dove, and lighting upon him'; the 'mighty wind' after Acts 2 (which gives an account of the Pentecost, when the Holy Spirit descended on the Apostles), esp. v. 2: 'And suddenly there came a sound from heaven as of a rushing mighty wind, and it filled all the house where they were sitting.'

125.27 *a sin . . . beyond forgiveness*: see Mark 3: 29: 'But he that shall blaspheme against the Holy Ghost hath never forgiveness, but is in danger of eternal damnation'; the exact nature of this sin *has* been a source of much debate.

125.29–30 *offered up mass . . . tongues of fire*: at the feast of the Pentecost (Whitsunday, the seventh Sunday after Easter), priests wear red robes; see Acts 2: 3: 'And there appeared unto them cloven tongues like as of fire, and it sat upon each of them.'

125.37 *incomprehensibility*: as in the Athanasian creed (*c.* 4th–5th cent. AD): 'And the Catholic faith is this: That we worship one God in Trinity, and Trinity in Unity; neither confounding the Persons: nor dividing the Substance . . . There are not three incomprehensibles, nor three uncreated: but one uncreated, and one incomprehensible.'

126.38 *constant mortification*: to bring the body, the flesh, the passions into subjection by self-denial and discipline.

127.11 *twigging*: 'twig': 'to beat with or as with a twig' (*SOED*); here, with a brush or broom made of twigs.

127.20–1 *all the fasts of the church*: of which there were many: Lent (40 days), Ash Wednesday, every Friday, vigils of important Holy Days, Ember Days (12).

127.27 *except at the gospels*: when it is obligatory to stand.

128.9–10 *actual reception of the eucharist*: the taking of communion at mass.

128.12 *visit to the Blessed Sacrament*: Stephen's individual visits to church to pray before the altar (other than at mass).

128.13–14 *book written by saint Alphonsus Liguori*: probably *Visitations to the Blessed Sacrament* by St Alphonsus Liguori (1696–1787), founder of the Congregation of the Most Holy Redeemer ('Redemptorists', 1732), a missionary order. Liguori does quote the passages extracted here from the Song of Solomon (or in the Douay, Canticle of Canticles).

128.14 *foxpapered*: pages that have been discoloured with brownish marks are said to be 'foxed'.

128.17 *canticles*: see 128.13–14 n.

128.18–22 *telling her names . . . commorabitur*: cf. Joyce's 'epiphany', no. 24 (*PSW* 184).

128.19 *bidding her arise as for espousal*: S. of S. 2: 13: 'Arise, my love, my fair one, and come away'; Cant. 2: 10: 'Arise, make haste, my love, my dove, my beautiful one, and come' (this latter quoted in Liguori, 'Eighth Visit' (repr. London: Burns and Oates, 1960), 35).

128.20–1 *Amana . . . the leopards*: 'Amana': a mountain near Lebanon; from S. of S. 4: 8: 'Come with me from Lebanon, my spouse, with me from

Lebanon: look from the top of Amana, from the top of Shenir and Hermon, from the lions' dens, from the mountains of the leopards'; cf. Cant. 4.8.

128.22 *Inter uber mea commorabitur*: Latin: 'He shall lie betwixt my breasts' (S. of S. 1: 13).

129.13–14 *bidden by his confessor ... past life*: because no one has completed penance for past sins until the end of his or her life or time in purgatory, confession of past sins is urged.

129.21–2 *Perhaps that first ... had not been good?*: it would have been 'good' only if made in 'perfect contrition'.

129.23–5 *surest sign ... amendment of his life*: an almost exact quotation from the *Maynooth Catechism* (1883): 'The surest sign that our confessions were good and that we had sincere sorrow for our sins is the amendment of our lives' (*A Companion to the Catechism* [including *The Catechism ordered by the National Synod of Maynooth*] (Dublin: M. H. Gill, 1886), 302).

129.27 *director*: the director of studies at Belvedere.

130.14 *dominican and franciscan*: 'dominican': the Order of Friars Preachers, founded (1216) by St Dominic (*c*.1170–1221), Spanish priest and friar; often called 'Black Friars' after their black cloaks; devoted to preaching and to study, to education and missionary work; historically, champions of Catholic orthodoxy. For 'franciscan', see 119.34 n.

130.15–16 *friendship between saint Thomas and saint Bonaventure*: St Thomas Aquinas, Dominican (see 107.30–1 n.) and St Bonaventure, Franciscan (see 101.24–6 n.) taught at the same time at the University of Paris.

130.16 *capuchin dress*: see 119.34 n.

130.18 *dubitative*: '*literary*: of, expressing or inclined to doubt or hesitation' (*OERD*).

130.20–2 *some talk ... other franciscans*: the Capuchins always wore their traditional robes, even in public; other Franciscans wore theirs only within the confines of the community.

130.23 *cloister*: from Old French *cloistre* from Latin *clostrum*, 'enclosed space': the enclosed space of a convent or monastery.

130.34 *Les jupes*: French: 'The skirts'.

131.7 *Stradbrooke*: see 53.5–9 n.

131.18 *craft of jesuits*: the Jesuits 'took the lead in opposing the Reformation in Europe and became known for the uncompromising zeal with which [they] spread Catholic beliefs' (*OERD*); indeed, they came to be thought to be capable of guile and deceit in the pursuit of good ends, of being 'too worldly', even of casuistical behaviour; also, because of their devotion to education, they have been accused of being too clever by half. Stephen finds no evidence for any of this in his actual experience.

131.30 *muff*: a beginner.

131.31–2 *his equivocal position in Belvedere*: Stephen was a 'free boy'; he paid no fees.

131.35 *obedience*: see 49.26 n.

132.3–5 *Lord Macaulay ... mortal sin*: Thomas Babington, 1st Baron Macaulay (1800–59), English historian and essayist; the comment here is misguided on the one hand, ludicrous on the other: Macaulay was Protestant and largely anti-Catholic (Lord Acton, himself Catholic, remarked of his *Essays Critical and Historical* (1834) that they were 'A key to half the prejudices of our age'); there is no such thing as a non-deliberate mortal sin. Cf. 'In the opinion of his director, Saint Robert Bellarmine, and three of his other confessors, [St Aloysius Gonzaga] never in his life committed a mortal sin' (Alban Butler, 'St Aloysius Gonzaga', *Lives of the Saints*, rev. edn. (New York: Kenedy, 1956), quoted by *A*).

132.6 *Victor Hugo*: (1802–85), French poet, novelist, and dramatist; only his early *minor* work is overtly Catholic, unlike the later work on which his entire reputation rests.

132.12 *Louis Veuillot*: (1813–83), French journalist, editor of *L'Univers*, a political Catholic paper which 'supported the temporal power of the Pope and the church's right to interfere in civil affairs'; his prose style was that of 'a first-rate journalist' (*JSA* 249).

132.29 *a vocation*: a strong feeling of fitness for a particular career, here, the equivalent of a divine call to the priesthood.

133.3–4 *prefect . . . sodality*: see 88.4–5 n.

133.12 *power of the keys*: the power to hear confession and to give absolution; after Matt. 16: 19: 'And I will give unto thee [Peter] the keys of the kingdom of heaven: and whatsoever thou shalt bind on earth shall be bound in heaven: and whatsoever thou shalt loose on earth shall be loosed in heaven.'

133.29 *thurible*: see 34.8n.

133.30 *chasuble*: a loose, sleeveless, usually ornate outer vestment worn by a priest celebrating mass or the Eucharist (*OERD*).

133.32 *the second place*: deacon, one who assists the priest at mass.

133.36 *minor sacred offices*: the deacon, and the deacon's assistant, the sub-deacon.

133.37 *tunicle of subdeacon*: short vestment worn at Eucharist or mass.

133.39 *humeral veil*: from 'humerus': the shoulder: a veil or scarf worn on the shoulders of the sub-deacon during mass and in which the sacred vessels are wrapped when he holds them.

133.39 *paten*: plate used to hold the Eucharist.

134.1–2 *a dalmatic of cloth of gold*: 'dalmatic': wide-sleeved, long loose vestment, open at the sides, worn by deacons over their white vestment (or 'alb') at Eucharist.

134.3 *Ite, missa est*: Latin: 'Go, it is a dismissal [the mass is ended]', words comprising the Dismissal, what the priest says at the end of mass.

134.15–16 *sin of Simon Magus . . . sin against the Holy Ghost*: from Acts 8: 9–24: Simon Magus (or 'Simon the Sorcerer') offered the Apostles money in exchange for the power of bestowing the gift of the Holy Spirit through the laying on of hands; from him the word 'simony' derives: the buying or selling of ecclesiastical privileges; in medieval writers, his story is elaborated to include sins against the Holy Ghost (see 125.27 n.)

134.18 *children of wrath*: Eph. 2: 3: 'Among whom also we all had our conversation in times past in the lusts of our flesh, fulfilling the desires of the flesh and of the mind; and were by nature the children of wrath, even as others.'

134.22 *ordination by the imposition of hands*: priests are ordained through the blessing conferred on them (the Sacrament of Holy Orders) by the 'laying on of hands' (Acts 6: 6) by the bishop; Catholicism maintains that the priesthood had been so conferred from Jesus to Peter and from Peter to the Apostles and so on in an unbroken line.

134.26–7 *eat and drink damnation . . . body of the Lord*: 1 Cor. 11: 27: 'Wherefore whosoever shall eat this bread, and drink this cup of the Lord, unworthily, shall be guilty of the body and blood of the Lord.'

134.29 *order of Melchisedec*: Melchizedek: King of Salem, 'the priest of the most high God' (Gen. 14: 18); Jesus is described as 'a priest for ever after the order of Melchisedec' (Heb. 5: 6); following the line of authority outlined above (134.22 n.), this makes Catholic priests priests 'after the order of Melchisedec'.

134.32 *novena*: from Latin: *novem*: 'nine': a nine-day devotion consisting of special prayers or services devoted to a particular saint or to the Virgin Mary for a particular purpose: here, that Stephen might know whether or not he has a vocation.

134.32 *your holy patron saint, the first martyr*: see 6.26 n.

134.36 *Once a priest always a priest*: true, in Catholic doctrine; though he may have his right to celebrate the sacraments removed because of unworthiness.

134.36–9 *Your catechism . . . never be effaced*: in Catholic doctrine, baptism, confirmation, and holy orders can neither be repeated nor effaced.

135.7 *Findlater's church*: Presbyterian church in Rutland (now Parnell) Square.

135.22 *novitiate*: the probationary period after entering an order and before taking holy orders; the house where those in the novitiate ('novices') live.

135.37–8 *fainting sickness of his stomach*: from fasting the night before entering the novitiate.

136.4 *S. J.*: 'Society of Jesus', signifies a Jesuit.

136.12–13 *Lantern Jaws . . . Foxy Campbell*: nicknames for one of the Belvedere teachers; see *U* 40.

136.14–15 *the jesuit house in Gardiner Street*: the house attached to the Jesuit church of St Francis Xavier in Gardiner Street Upper, central Dublin.

136.36 *bridge over . . . Tolka*: Tolka: river in north Dublin which flows to Dublin Bay; the bridge: Ballybough bridge.

136.39 *hamshaped encampment of poor cottages*: the original 'Tolka cottages', made of mud and straw, have been destroyed.

137.16 *second watered tea*: i.e. tea that has had a second pot of water poured on to the leaves (to save tea).

138.1 *Oft in the Stilly Night*: first line of a poem by Thomas Moore (see 151.14 n.): 'Oft in the stilly night, | Ere Slumber's chain has bound me, | Fond memory brings the light | Of other days around me; | The smiles, the tears, | Of boyhood's years, | The words of love then spoken', etc.

138.14–17 *Newman . . . children in every time*: in Newman's *An Essay in Aid of a Grammar of Assent* (1870) about Virgil (Publius Vergilius Maro, 70–19 BC, Roman poet, author of *Eclogues* and the *Aeneid*): 'his single words and phrases, his pathetic half lines, giving utterance, as the voice of Nature herself, to that pain and weariness, yet hope of better things, which is the experience of her children in every time' (London: Burns, Oates & Co., 76). Cf. 'Portrait', where are echoed passages of Newman's *Grammar* (*PSW* 211 and n. 5). (As Atherton discovered, 'all the passages which Stephen quotes from Newman's work . . . are given in a one-volume anthology, *Characteristics from the Writings of John Henry Newman*, William S. Lilly, London, 1875' (*JSA* 249).)

138.19–20 *Clontarf Chapel*: 'Clontarf': from Gaelic: *Cluain Tarbh*: 'bull's meadow' (*O* 13), on Dublin Bay east of Dublin; the chapel: Catholic St John the Baptist on Clontarf Road, Clontarf.

138.26 *the university*: University College, Dublin; opened as Catholic University (1854) with Newman as rector; reorganized as University College (1880) in affiliation with the Royal University (a misnomer: really an examining board; established by the University Education Act of 1879); became Jesuit (1883); reorganized and finally merged (by the 1908 Irish Universities Act) with the Queen's Colleges in Cork and Galway, into what will become the National University of Ireland (*F* 419, 607, 611). See 75.1 n.

138.28 *the Bull*: a sea-wall running from the shore at Clontarf into Dublin bay.

138.30 *police barrack*: near Clontarf chapel.

139.7–8 *to escape by an unseen path*: cf. Dante's and Virgil's escape from hell by way of 'an unseen path' in the *Inferno*, xxxiv. 127.

139.10–13 *notes of fitful music . . . an elfin prelude*: for one explanation, see *G*.

139.19–21 *Newman . . . everlasting arms*: Newman, *The Idea of the University Defined and Illustrated* (1852), Discourse I, 'Introductory' (ed. I. T. Ker (Oxford: Oxford University Press, 1976), 29); Newman borrows his phrases from Ps. 17: 34 (Douay) and Deut. 33: 27.

139.28 *Dollymount*: area just north of Clontarf.

139.30 *christian brothers*: see 59.32 n.

140.14 *the commandment of love*: cf. Luke 10: 27: 'And [Jesus] answering said: Thou shalt love the Lord thy God with all thy heart, and with all thy soul, and with all thy strength, and with all thy mind; and thy neighbour as thyself.'

140.19 *A day of dappled seaborne clouds*: a slightly adjusted quotation from Hugh Miller (1805–56), *The Testimony of the Rocks; or, Geology in Its Bearings on the Two Theologies, Natural and Revealed* (Boston, 1857) in the context of his thinking about Satan's being unable to understand divine creation: 'a day of dappled, breeze-borne clouds' (both *G* and *JSA* give fuller contexts).

140.30–1 *lucid supple periodic prose*: cf 'Portrait': 'For the artist the rhythms of phrase and period, the symbols of word and allusion, were paramount things' (*PSW* 214).

141.2–3 *slowflowing Liffey*: 'slowflowing' because at this point an estuary, so subject to the ebb and flow of tides; see 79.2–3 n.

141.5–6 *seventh city of christendom*: for a discussion of the possible origins of the phrase, see *G*.

141.8 *thingmote*: place of Scandinavian council of law (from Old Norse *þing*: a public meeting or assembly, especially a legislative council, and *mote*: a mound, especially as the seat of a camp, city (*SOED*)); when Dublin was ruled by the Danes (mid-ninth to early eleventh centuries), there was just such a huge mound in the centre of town (demolished late seventeenth century).

141.9–10 *clouds, dappled and seaborne*: see 140.19 n.

141.21 *Stephanos*: Greek: στέφανος 'crown' or 'wreath'.

141.26–7 *Bous Stephanoumenos! Bous Stephaneforos!*: 'Bous Stephanoforos': Greek: βους στεφανοφόρος: the ox as garland-bearer for the sacrifice (Bous: βους: 'ox'); 'Stephanoumenos': a wreathed ox; also a nonce word that the boys have invented: 'Stephen's ox-soul'.

142.4 *Norfolk coat*: a man's loose-belted jacket with box pleats (*OERD*).

142.16 *ghost of the ancient kingdom of the Danes*: see 141.8 n.

142.18 *fabulous artificer*: Daedalus; see note to epigraph.

142.36 *O, Cripes, I'm drownded!*: like Icarus; see note to epigraph.

143.2–3 *cry of a hawk or eagle on high*: see 189.2 n.

143.13–15 *His soul ... of his soul*: cf. Gabriele D'Annunzio (1863–1938), Italian playwright, poet, and novelist), *Il Fuoco* (*The Flame*, 1900), the end of Part I, when the hero is 'reborn' after a night with his beloved, and vows 'to create with joy'! (trans. Susan Bassnett (London: Quartet, 1991) 114, 120). *G* traces the pervasive influence of this novel and of *Il Piacere*, 1889 (*The Child of Pleasure*) on *Portrait* (*G* 260–1) and *WD* contains relevant excerpts from *Il Fuoco* and a third work, *Le Vergini del Rocce*, 1895 (*The Virgins of the Rocks*), the influence on Joyce of which Stanislaus Joyce remarks in *My Brother's Keeper* (166) (*WD* 269–79).

143.18 *stoneblock*: a bathing place off the Bull.

143.25 *Howth. The sea ...*: Hill of Howth, tall headland on the north-east coast of Dublin Bay. Cf. this entire scene of Stephen at the sea with 'Portrait' (*PSW* 215).

144.8 *to queen it*: 'to act or rule as queen' (*SOED*).

144.9 *cerements*: grave-clothes.

144.15 *girl stood before him in midstream*: cf. Ethan Brand's meeting of a young woman (also apparently looking out at the water) following close upon his refusal to enter the church (Henrik Ibsen (1828–1906), Norwegian dramatist, *Brand* (1866)). *G* traces the parallels between *Portrait* and *Brand* more fully (129–30).

144.19–20 *Her thighs ... almost to the hips*: a daring display for the time.

144.22 *slateblue*: cf. blue as the Virgin Mary's colour.

145.7–8 *angel of mortal youth and beauty*: cf. Dante's description of Beatrice at the beginning of his *La Vita Nuova*.

145.8 *an envoy from the fair courts of life*: cf. 'Portrait' where the exact phrase is used, though there about a prostitute (*PSW* 216).

145.27–31 *Glimmering . . . deeper than other*: cf. Dante's vision at the end of the *Paradiso*, xxxiii. 115–20.

CHAPTER V

146.8–9 *Daly or MacEvoy*: assumed names.

146.22 *The dear knows*: *PWJ*: 'The expression *the dear knows* (or correctly *the deer knows*), which is very common, is a translation from Irish of [a substitution of a harmless word for a forbidden one]. The original expression is *thauss ag Dhee* (given here phonetically), meaning *God knows*; but as this is too solemn and profane for most people, they changed it to *Thauss ag fee*, i.e., *the deer knows*; and this may be uttered by anyone. *Dia* [Dhee] God: *fiadh* [fee] a deer' (69).

146.27 *blue*: a kind of washing powder to whiten clothes.

147.22 *nuns' madhouse*: St Vincent's Lunatic Asylum (run by the Sisters of Charity) on Convent Avenue, Fairview, in north-east Dublin.

147.34 *The rainladen trees . . . evoked in him*: cf. 'Portrait' (*PSW* 215 and n. 45).

147.35 *Gerhart Hauptmann*: (1862–1946), German dramatist, novelist, poet whose women are fairly feeble; Joyce translated his *Von Sonnenaufgang* (*Before Sunrise*, 1889) and perhaps *Michael Kramer* (1900) in the summer of 1901. (The former has been published as *Joyce and Hauptmann: Before Sunrise: Joyce's Translation*, ed. Jill Perkins (San Marino, Calif.: Huntington Library, 1978).)

147.38–9 *the sloblands*: from the Gaelic: *slab*: mud, mire, filled land; known as Mud island, a tidal flat where the Tolka enters Dublin Bay.

147.39–148.1 *the cloistral silverveined prose of Newman*: Newman is renowned for his eloquent prose (silver signifying this eloquence, as in 'silvertongued'); hence thoughts of his prose counterbalance the mud-flats.

148.1 *North Strand Road*: road running from the mud-flats, across the Royal Canal towards the centre of Dublin.

148.3 *Guido Cavalcanti*: (1259–1300), Italian poet, friend of Dante, famous for the poetic expression of lonely love. For his 'dark humour', see the story Stephen alludes to in *U* 45.

148.4 *Baird's stonecutting works*: D. G. Baird and J. Paul Todd, Talbot Place, behind the Custom House in central Dublin.

148.4 *spirit of Ibsen*: the only overt mention in *Portrait* of Henrik Ibsen (see 144.15 n.); the young Joyce championed him in 'Ibsen's New Drama' (1900), an essay on Ibsen's *When We Dead Awaken* (1899) whose hero, Rubek, shares much with Stephen (*CW* 47–67 and *KB* 30–49). Cf. *U* 570: 'Stephen thought to think of Ibsen, associated with Baird's, the stonecutter's in his mind somehow in Talbot Place.'

148.6 *marinedealer's shop*: Ellen Smith, sailor's outfitter, waterproof and flag maker, Burgh Quay on the south bank of the Liffey.

148.7–8 *Ben Jonson . . . wearier where I lay*: Ben Jonson (1572–1637), English dramatist and poet; the lines here come from Aurora's Epilogue in *The Vision of Delight* (1617), ll. 237–42: 'I am not wearier where I lay | By frozen Tython's side tonight, | Than I am willing now to stay, | And be a part of your delight; | But I am urged by the Day, | Against my will, to bid you come away.'

148.10 *Aristotle or Aquinas*: Aristotle (384–322 BC), Greek philosopher, student of Plato, in many ways the founder of philosophy with his develop-ment of the inductive method of reasoning and the empirical approach to understanding of the natural world, whose works Aquinas attempted to integrate with Catholic theology (see 107.30–1 n).

148.14 *waistcoateers*: 'low-class prostitutes' (*SOED*).

148.15 *chambering*: 'sexual indulgence' (*SOED*).

148.19 *garner . . . Aristotle's poetics and psychology*: Aristotle's *Poetics*; there is no work titled 'psychology' though Aristotle does address the subject in various places, e.g. *De Sensu* and *De Anima*. Stephen here admits that his reading has been only 'a garner of slender sentences', that is, that probably he has read Aristotle only in anthologized form (as he may have read Newman: see 138.14–17 n.). Cf. 'Portrait': 'He had interpreted for orthodox Greek scholarship the living doctrine of the *Poetics*' (*PSW* 218). Joyce read Aristo-tle in a French edition (in Paris in 1903) and copied his own translations into a (now lost) notebook; some phrases survive; for a full list and biblio-graphical information as well as an exhaustive discussion of Joyce's develop-ing aesthetic, see Aubert.

148.20 *Synopsis Philosophiæ Scholasticæ ad mentem divi Thomæ*: Latin: 'A Synopsis of Scholastic Philosophy for the Understanding of St Thomas'; Aubert has identified this as a work edited by Apud A. Roger and F. Cher-noviz (2nd edn. Paris, 1892): 'a mechanical digest for seminary students . . . not only an outline of Thomistic philosophy but also a detailed and system-atic criticism of lay philosophies, especially modern ones'; 'no internal evi-dence suggests that [Joyce] used it extensively despite a few verbal echoes'. Aubert reproduces two pages of the *Synopsis* (Aubert, 100–1, 110–11, 167).

148.26–7 *in revery . . . nobility*: cf. 'Portrait': '[he] who, in revery at least, had been acquainted with nobility' (*PSW* 213).

148.33 *the bridge*: Newcomen bridge, which crosses the Royal Canal.

149.3 *Hopkins' corner*: Hopkins and Hopkins, gold and silver smiths, on the corner of Lower Sackville (now O'Connell) Street and Eden Quay.

149.6–7 *social liberty and equality . . . classes and sexes*: cf. Francis [Sheehy-] Skeffington's demands in his 'A Forgotten Aspect of the University Ques-tion' which he published in a pamphlet together with Joyce's 'The Day of the Rabblement' (1901) both of which had been refused by the college magazine (see *CW* 68–72 and *KB* 50–2). Skeffington advocated equal status for women (and changed his name to Sheehy-Skeffington on marrying Hannah Sheehy) and was an ardent pacifist. Ironically, he was shot by a

British army officer during the 1916 uprising. He had tried to stop the Dublin poor from looting, was arrested and summarily shot (*E* 399).

149.7–8 *United States of the Europe of the future*: cf. William Thomas Stead (1849–1912), *The United States of Europe* (1899).

149.15–16 *nominal definitions, essential definitions*: Aristotle's distinction (from *Posterior Analytics*, B. II, ch. 8): 'nominal': the definition of a thing in terms of the effects it produces; 'essential': the definition of a thing in terms of cause ('essence' being here the feature of a thing which provides the fundamental account of its other genuine properties) (see 'Aristotle', *The Oxford Companion to Philosophy*, ed. Ted Honderich (Oxford: Oxford University Press, 1995), 54).

149.17 *favourable . . . side by side*: standard teaching method especially of the Jesuits (cf. Aquinas's mode of analysis in any of his analytical works).

149.20 *the green*: St Stephen's Green, south of the Liffey, central Dublin; University College sits on its south side.

149.25 *Cranly*: appears again in *Ulysses*, though only in Stephen's memory (*U* 7, 32, 176, 177, 180, 203). Compare Joyce's 'Trieste Notebook' (*c*.1907–1909) for his comments on the actual persons who were models for Cranly, Lynch, and Davin (*WD* 92–3).

149.28 *a severed head*: not unlike St John the Baptist, seen as Jesus's precursor (Matt. 3), who is beheaded (Matt. 14: 1–12); see 209.20–8.

150.21–2 *Ivory . . . ebur*: English, French, Italian, and Latin for 'ivory'.

150.23 *India mittit ebur*: Latin: 'India sends ivory'.

150.24 *Metamorphoses of Ovid*: see note to epigraph.

150.27–8 *a ragged book written by a Portuguese priest*: text on Latin grammar and prosody, *Prosodia*, by Emanuel Alvarez, SJ (1526–82); went through hundreds of editions and was standard item in Jesuit curriculum (cf. *WD* 102).

150.29 *Contrahit . . . vates*: Latin: as it stands, on its own: 'The orator abridges; poets elaborate in song', but it comes from Alvarez's *Prosodia* (see above) and in context means something quite other: *Si mutam liquidamque simul praeeat brevis una, contrahit orator, variant in carmine vates*: 'If a mute and liquid syllable both precede one short syllable it is short in prose but long or short in verse' (*JSA*).

150.31 *in tanto discrimine*: Latin: 'in such a great crisis'.

150.33 *implere ollam denariorum*: Latin: 'to fill the earthenware pot with denarii'; Stephen translates it in the next line. 'Denarii': Roman coins.

150.35 *Horace*: Quintus Horatius Flaccus (65–8 BC), Roman poet, author of *Satires* and *Odes*, these latter celebrating friendship, love, wine, the country life; also wrote a treatise on poetry, *Ars Poetica*.

151.4 *vervain*: variety of Verbena, a herbaceous plant with small blue, white, or purple flowers.

151.10 *Trinity*: Trinity College; see 75.1 and 138.26 nn.

151.13 *fetters of the reformed conscience*: i.e. the mind under the influence of Reformation thought: Trinity was founded to promote just such thought (see 75.1 n.).

151.14 *droll statue of the national poet of Ireland*: 'national poet': Thomas Moore (1779–1852), Irish (sentimental) poet; the epithet is more English than Irish, though he was immensely popular; left Ireland in 1798 for England. The statue, which stands just outside the gates of Trinity College, is 'droll' because it depicts Moore wearing a classical toga.

151.18 *Firbolg*: supposed early primitive inhabitants of Ireland, characteristically short and dark.

151.19 *Milesian*: supposed invaders of Ireland led by Mileadh of Spain, characteristically poets and artists.

151.19 *Davin*: Stephen thinks of him here because of his ardent support of all things Gaelic.

151.25–6 *formal in speech with others*: Christian names would seldom be used outside the family.

151.27 *Grantham Street*: just west of University College.

151.34 *Michael Cusack, the Gael*: (1847–1907), founder of the Gaelic Athletic Association (see 51.13 n.); Joyce uses him again in *Ulysses* where he is the model for the 'Citizen' in 'Cyclops'.

151.37 *curfew was still a nightly fear*: in the early eighteenth century, then even more strongly under the Coercion Acts (passed between 1800 and 1921 for the administration of Ireland), curfew was imposed; it required both that people be indoors and that lights be extinguished.

151.39 *Mat Davin*: Maurice Davin (1864–1927), athlete and founder (with Cusack) of the Gaelic Athletic Association (see 51.13 and 151.34 nn.); he and his brothers Pat and Tom held several world athletic records during the 1870s.

152.3 *fenian*: see 32.4 n.

152.7 *the cycles*: Irish epics or legendary stories of Irish heroes, which are grouped into 'cycles': the Ulster and Fenian cycles, the cycle of the Kings, the Mythological cycle. Cf. Joyce in 'James Clarence Mangan' (1902) (*CW* 81–2 and *KB* 59).

152.12 *the foreign legion of France*: supposed romantic destination for young men; a military force in North Africa under French officers, comprising a rag-bag of expatriates, exiles, and French nationals.

152.14 *tame geese*: as opposed to the 'wild geese', the name given to those Jacobite Irish soldiers who, after William III's reconquest of Ireland, were allowed by the Treaty of Limerick (1691) to become exiles to France (see 96.38–97.1 n.).

152.23 *streets of the poorer jews*: see 84.14 n.

152.26 *disremember*: *PWJ*: 'Disremember: to forget. Good old English; now out of fashion in England, but common in Ireland' (248).

152.32 *Buttevant*: small market town some 30 miles north-east of Cork city.

152.33 *hurling match*: old Irish game, revived by the Gaelic Athletic Association; a cross between hockey and lacrosse with a stick called a *camann* (see 152.39 n.); fifteen players to each side.

152.34 *Croke's Own Boys and the Fearless Thurles*: typical of the teams formed under the Gaelic Athletic Association's encouragement; 'Croke': The Most Reverend Thomas William Croke (1824–1902), made (1875) archbishop of Cashel, south of Thurles (in Tipperary), highly political (in fact, advised by Pope Leo XIII to take a less active role in politics), first patron of the Gaelic Athletic Association (*F* 418).

152.36 *stripped to his buff . . . minding cool*: *PWJ* distinguishes this particular usage (i.e. not 'to strip naked' but 'to strip to the waist') as coming from Munster (227); 'minding cool': Gaelic: *cúl*: goal in ball games (*O* 336).

152.36 *Limericks*: after the town west of Thurles (see 152.34 n.) in County Limerick (things get a bit confused geographically in Davin's description of who's playing for whom).

152.38 *wipe*: *PWJ* 'Wipe: a blow: all over Ireland: he gave him a wipe on the face. In Ulster, a goaly-wipe is a great blow on the ball with the *camaun* or hurley: such as will send it to the goal' (351).

152.39 *camann*: Gaelic: *camán*: crook: stick used in playing hurley (*O* 336).

153.1 *aim's ace*: *PWJ*: 'Aims-ace; a small amount, quantity, or distance. Applied in the following way very generally in Munster:—"He was within an aim's-ace of being drowned" (very near). A survival in Ireland of the old Shakesperian word *ambs-ace*, meaning two aces or two single points in throwing dice, the smallest possible throw' (209).

153.7 *yoke*: *PWJ*: 'Yoke; any article, contrivance or apparatus for use in some work' (352).

153.8 *mass meeting*: political gathering, the political strategy of holding mass (or 'monster') meetings to show support for particular causes or candidates was especially exploited by Daniel O'Connell (see 21.18 n.).

153.8–9 *Castletownroche*: village in County Cork, 5 miles from Buttevant.

153.9 *the cars*: see 16.4 n.

153.12 *Ballyhoura hills . . . Kilmallock*: a 15-mile walk north into County Limerick.

153.15–16 *redden my pipe*: *PWJ*: 'Redden; to light: "Take the bellows and redden the fire." An Irishman hardly ever *lights* his pipe: he *reddens* it' (311).

153.29 *Queenstown*: see 77.20 n.

153.34 *There's no one in it but ourselves*: 'There's no one in but ourselves'; *PWJ*: 'When mere existence is predicated, the Gaelic *ann* (*in it*, i.e., "in existence") is used' (25).

154.1 *Clane*: see 14.22 n.

154.6 *first handsel*: 'a gift or present (expressive of good wishes) at the beginning of a new year [or day] . . . deemed to ensure good luck' or 'the first money taken by a trader in the morning' (*SOED*). Cf. Joyce in his Trieste notebook (*WD* 94).

154.22 *a student of Trinity*: stereotype: a Trinity student would be assumed to have money since going there was presumed to indicate one's membership of the Anglo-Irish Protestant 'ascendancy' (by comparison with poorer Catholics who would attend University College); see 75.1 n.

154.22–3 *Grafton Street*: street in central Dublin with fashionable and expensive shops.

154.24–5 *slab was set ... Wolfe Tone*: Theobald Wolfe Tone (1763–98), founder of United Irishmen (see 7.33 n.), nationalist whose republicanism was secular and patriotic, raised support in America and in France, accompanied abortive French expeditions to Ireland in 1795 and 1798 (the 1798 Rebellion), captured, committed suicide on being refused soldier's death (see *F* 175). A slab to the memory of Tone (and to commemorate the centenary of the 1798 Rebellion) was placed at the north-west corner of Stephen's Green (15 Aug. 1898); the sculpture was left unfinished and the slab eventually removed to widen the street (1922).

154.27 *tawdry tribute*: perhaps; *G* quotes the *Irish Times* describing immense and enthusiastic crowds and stirring speeches (by W. B. Yeats and John O'Leary among others) and Maud Gonne's finding the ceremony 'dispiriting and disappointing'.

154.27 *four French delegates*: since Tone raised French sympathy for the Irish cause.

154.27–8 *a brake and one*: 'a large carriage frame with no body, or a large wagonette' (*SOED*, s.v. 'break').

154.29 *Vive l'Irlande!*: French: 'Long live Ireland!'

154.30 *Stephen's Green*: see 149.20 n.

154.36 *Buck Egan*: John Egan (*c*.1750–1810), politician, violently opposed to the Act of Union (1800).

154.36–7 *Burnchapel Whaley*: Richard Whaley, Protestant and vehement anti-Catholic who gained the nickname 'Burnchapel' from the arson he purportedly committed in the Rebellion of 1798. He had a large house built (at 86) on St Stephen's Green (*F* 188) (later taken into the University College buildings).

155.3–4 *was the jesuit house extraterritorial*: i.e. was their allegiance not to Ireland, but 'extraterritorial', i.e. to Rome (Jesuits take a special oath to the pope). Cf. Joyce in his Trieste notebook (*WD* 102).

155.5 *Ireland of Tone and of Parnell*: heroic, yes, but also republican Ireland; see Ch. I and 5.23–4, 33.8, and 154.24–5 nn.

155.24 *a levite of the Lord*: Levites, under Judaic law, acted as assistants to the priests. Cf. *WD* 102.

155.26 *canonicals*: the canonical dress of the clergy.

155.27 *ephod*: Jewish priestly vestment.

155.29 *waiting upon wordlings*: see 131.18 n.

155.31 *prelatic beauty*: 'prelate': historically, an abbot or prior; now a high ecclesiastical dignitary (*OERD*).

155.33 *sweet odour of her sanctity*: 'odour of sanctity': 'A sweet or balsamic odour stated to have been exhaled by the bodies of eminent saints at their death, or when exhumed, and held to attest their saintship; hence, figuratively, reputation for holiness; occasionally used ironically (*SOED*).

155.33–4 *mortified ... its obedience*: see 126.38 n.

156.5 *Pulcra sunt quæ visa placent*: Latin: 'Those things are beautiful which please the eye'; Stephen adapts Aquinas (*Summa Theologiae*, Part I, Question 5, Article 4, 'Whether Good has the Aspect of a Final Cause'):

'*pulchra enim dicunter ea quae visa placent*': 'beautiful things are said to be those which please when seen' (trans. Shapcote, i. 26); Joyce copies this first Latin line into his Pola notebook (1904) (and translates it slightly differently) (*CW* 147); see, too, Aubert, 101–5.

156.10 *Bonum est in quod tendit appetitus*: Latin: 'The good is comprehended in that which is desired'; an adaptation of Aquinas, who in *Summa Contra Gentiles*, B. III, Ch. III, develops the opening statement of (the Latin translation of) Aristotle's *Nicomachean Ethics*: '*bonum est quod omnis appuent*' ('the good is that which all things desire') (see Aubert, 101–5); Aquinas uses a similar phrase in *Summa Theologiae* (Part I, Question 5, Article 4), whence the statement in 156.5 n. above derives. See, too, Joyce in his Pola notebook (*CW* 146).

156.19 *Like Ignatius he was lame*: Ignatius Loyola *was* lame, having been wounded in war (see 46.34 n.).

156.20–1 *legendary craft of the company*: see 131.18 n.

156.23–4 *he used the shifts . . . greater glory of God*: see 131.18 n. 'for the greater glory of God' is the English for the Jesuit motto *ad majorem dei gloriam* (see 46.35–6 n.).

156.26 *obedience*: see 49.26 and 131.35 nn.

156.28–9 *Similiter atque senis baculus*: Latin: Stephen's translation, 'Like a staff in an old man's hand', is accurate; from Loyola's *Summarium Constitutionum* (1635) of the Jesuits, founded to give aid to the pope when needed (Sullivan, 120).

156.39 *cliffs of Moher*: spectacular cliffs on the west coast of Ireland.

157.5–6 *no such thing as free thinking . . . its own laws*: a standard Catholic refutation of free thought (thought free from the shackles placed upon it by organized religion and its attendant dogma).

157.15 *Epictetus*: (*c*.55–*c*.135), Greek philosopher, preached common brotherhood of man and the Stoic philosophy, referred to himself as 'the old man'; his teachings were preserved by his student Arrian (b. *c*.89) and posthumously published.

157.18–19 *An old gentleman . . . soul is very like a bucketful of water*: 'old gentleman': Epictetus as 'the old man' who did so liken the soul ([Arrian's] *Discourses of Epictetus*, iii. 3. 20 (ed. Christopher Gill, trans. Robin Hard (London: Dent, 1995), 158).

157.20–4 *put an iron lamp . . . instead of the iron lamp*: again, Epictetus (*Discourses of Epictetus*, i. 18. 15 (ed. Gill, 44–5)).

157.37–8 *literary tradition . . . marketplace*: Samuel Taylor Coleridge (1772–1834), English poet and aesthetic philosopher, makes a similar distinction in his *Biographia Literaria* (1817), ch. XXII.

157.38–158.1 *a sentence of Newman's . . . company of the saints*: Newman, 'The Glories of Mary' (in which he is translating very literally Ecclus. 24: 16 (Vulgate: '*et in plenitudine sanctorum detentio mea*'; *JSA* and *A*): 'And I took root in an honourable people, and in the glorious company of the Saints I was detained' (*Mixed Congregations*, 358).

158.15 *tundish*: English (not Irish): 'a shallow vessel with a tube at the bottom fitting into the bung-hole of a tun or cask, forming a kind of tunnel used in brewing; hence, generally, funnel' (*SOED*).

158.19 *Lower Drumcondra*: northern suburb of Dublin.

158.25 *prodigal*: from the parable of the prodigal son (Luke 15: 11–32) in which the elder and consistently faithful son is angry at his father's forgiveness of and largesse toward the younger 'prodigal' son who has squandered his father's goods and only latterly returned to the fold.

158.26 *clamorous conversions*: the Oxford Movement (*c.*1833–45), led by Newman among others, which aimed at restoring to the Anglican Church traditional Catholic teaching and practice; it emphasized ceremony, set up Anglican religious communities, supported social work and scholarship; formed the basis of Anglo-Catholicism. Newman, of course, subsequently converted to Catholicism.

158.29–30 *tardy spirit*: one who has come late to the truth.

158.31 *serious dissenters*: 'dissenters': in England, those who were neither Catholic nor Anglican, but belonged to a nonconformist religion; they too had a history of persecution in England.

158.32 *pomps of the establishment*: the elaborate rituals of Catholicism or High Church Anglicanism.

158.34–5 *six principle men . . . supralapsarian dogmatists*: Each of these is a (particularly peculiar) dissenting Baptist sect. See *G* and *A* for descriptions.

158.37 *insufflation*: blowing or breathing on a person to symbolize the influence of the Holy Spirit (*OERD*).

158.37–8 *imposition of hands*: like the 'laying on of hands' of Jesus and the apostles: to transfer the authority of the priesthood or bestow the Holy Spirit (see 134.22 n.).

158.38 *procession of the Holy Ghost*: the doctrine that the Holy Spirit 'proceeds' from the Father to the Son and thence to the Church.

158.39–159.1 *disciple . . . receipt of custom*: Matthew, the tax collector, as described in Matt. 9: 9: 'And as Jesus passed forth from thence, he saw a man, named Matthew, sitting at the receipt of custom: and he saith unto him, Follow me. And he arose, and followed him.'

159.2 *chapel*: in England, nonconformist churches are commonly called 'chapels', those of the Established Church 'churches' (unless they happen to come attached to larger institutions like colleges or castles, when they are called 'chapels'); in contrast to Ireland (see 119.4 n.).

159.11 *Ben Jonson*: see 148.7–8 n.

159.12 *language in which we are speaking is his before it is mine*: i.e. English, with all that that means given the history of the English in Ireland, though see 170.35–9.

159.18 *the beautiful and the sublime*: a distinction drawn by various aesthetic philosophers, most famously in English by Edmund Burke (1729–97, an Irishman, educated at Trinity College, who became a lawyer in England), in his 'A Philosophical Enquiry into the Origin of Our Ideas of the Sublime and the Beautiful' (1757).

159.33 *Per aspera ad astra*: Latin cliché: 'Through hardships [literally, rough things] to the stars'.

159.35 *first arts' class*: class for preparation towards one of the four examinations ('First Arts' taken in the second year) required for a degree at University College (Sullivan, 158).

160.1 *Loyola*: see 46.34 n.

160.1 *halfbrother of the clergy*: cf. Joyce in his Trieste notebook, where of the Jesuits he writes: 'They flatter the clergy their half brothers' (*WD* 102).

160.3 *ghostly father*: a spiritual father (i.e. confessor), after the Holy Ghost.

160.3–7 *this man . . . the lukewarm and the prudent*: see 131.18 n.

160.8–9 *Kentish fire*: 'rapturous applause, or three times three and one more. The expression probably originated with the protracted cheers given in Kent to the No-Popery orators in 1828–29', i.e. during the time of the debate over Catholic Emancipation (*Brewer's Dictionary of Phrase and Fable*, 620).

160.22 *Leopardstown*: racecourse in south Dublin.

160.28 *Are you as bad as that?*: a juvenile joke: has Stephen been caught so short he needs toilet paper?

160.30 *In case of necessity*: an even worse joke; see 89.33–5 and 89.29 n. ff.

160.34–5 *atheist freemason*: strictly a contradiction in terms, since Masons require that all members believe in 'The Great Architect of the Universe', but here 'atheist' because non- (and presumed by many to be anti-) Catholic.

161.3 *W. S. Gilbert*: William Schwenck Gilbert (1836–1911), English dramatist, most famously paired with the musician Arthur Sullivan (1842–1900) to write fourteen light operas (1871–96).

161.5–7 *On a cloth . . . billiard balls*: from the final act of Gilbert and Sullivan's *The Mikado* (1895), where in the reign of the benevolent Mikado wrongdoers will be brought to particular forms of justice; here, the billiard sharp will have to play 'extravagant matches | In fitless finger stall | On a cloth untrue, | With a twisted cue | And elliptical billiard balls'.

161.15–16 *sabbath of misrule*: like the medieval Feasts of Misrule, licensed carnival festivities (see *Brewer's Dictionary of Phrase and Fable*, 625).

161.16 *the community*: see 7.37 n.

161.20–1 *mental science*: as opposed to 'moral science', the study of the general rules that govern human behaviour (1860, first use cited in *SOED*).

161.21 *case of conscience*: more usually within the domain of 'moral science'.

161.34 *platinoid*: an alloy of nickel, zinc, copper, and tungsten (*SOED*).

161.35 *F. W. Martino*: not Martino, but Fernando Wood Martin (b. 1863), an American chemist who did develop platinoid and wrote several chemistry textbooks.

162.15 *Ulster*: one of the original four Irish provinces (see 52.3 n.); here, the Protestant-dominated north-east part of Ireland.

162.21 *pound of flesh*: now proverbial, from Shakespeare, *The Merchant of*

Venice, I. iii. 147–52, where Shylock demands that should Antonio not repay his debt, the forfeit will be 'an equal pound of your fair flesh'.

162.27 *Belfast*: main city in Ulster; Stephen reads MacAlister as what he thinks of as a typical Ulsterman (more practical than imaginative) whose father would have done better to send him to Queen's University, Belfast (by implication more vocational than University College) and save himself the rail fare.

162.36 *Epictetus*: see 157.15 n.

162.37–8 *pronounce the word science as a monosyllable*: a comment on the Ulster accent.

163.7 *two photographs*: of the Tsar Nicholas II (1868–1918, r. 1894–1917) and Tsarina Alexandra Feodorovina (1872–1918; r. 1894–1917) of Russia; Nicholas issued a 'Peace Rescript' in 1898 which resulted in the Hague Peace Conference of 1899 (which Sheehy-Skeffington attended (see 149.6–7 n.) which led not to 'general disarmament' but to the setting up of an international war tribunal.

163.19 *Ego habeo*: schoolboy Latin: 'I have'.

163.21 *Quod?*: schoolboy Latin: 'What?'

163.24 *Per pax universalis*: schoolboy Latin: 'For universal peace'.

163.33–4 *Credo ut ... humore estis*: schoolboy Latin: 'I believe you are a bloody liar and your expression shows that you are in a damned bad humour'.

163.37 *No stimulants and votes for the bitches*: parody of the demands of those like Sheehy-Skeffington (see 149.6–7 n.).

164.1–2 *he pours his soul so freely into my ear*: cf. John Keats's (1795–1821) 'Ode to a Nightingale' (1820) where the bird 'pours his soul abroad' and see 99.28–9 n.

164.6 *A sugar!*: Joyce to his translator: 'A euphemism used by Cranley [*sic*] in as much as it begins with the same letter for a product of the body the monosyllabic term for which in English is sometimes used as an exclamation and sometimes as descriptive of a person whom one does not like. In the French language it is associated with Marshal Cambronne and the French (the females at least) sometimes use a similar euphemism employing the [word] miel instead of the word used by the military commander' (*LIII* 129–30).

164.7 *Quis est in malo humore ... ego aut vos?*: schoolboy Latin: 'Who is in a bad humour, me or you?'

164.16 *Elizabethan English*: examples of which are still to be found spoken in parts of Ireland; Stephen is thinking of the Irish rural eloquence in which the twin strains of Gaelic and Elizabethan English persist.

164.19 *sacred eloquence of Dublin*: that of the famous Irish eighteenth-century orators.

164.20 *Wicklow pulpit*: see 28.29 n. and 174.10.

164.25 *the progressive tendency*: socialism.

164.34 *handball*: ball for the traditional Irish version of the game, revived by the Gaelic Athletic Association (see 6.13 and 51.13 nn.).

165.10 *Czar's rescript*: see 163.7 n.

165.11 *Stead*: William Thomas Stead (1849–1912), crusading, anti-war journalist.

165.11 *general disarmament*: see 163.7 n.

165.11–12 *arbitration in cases of international disputes*: see 163.7 n..

165.12 *signs of the times*: after Jesus to the Pharisees and Sadducees in Matt. 16: 3: 'O ye hypocrites, ye can discern the face of the sky; but can ye not discern the signs of the times?'

165.12–15 *the new humanity ... greatest possible number*: cf. Frances Hutcheson (1694–1746), English philosopher, *Concerning Moral Good and Evil*, §3, 8: 'The action is best, which procures the greatest happiness for the greatest number', and Jeremy Bentham (1748–1832), English Utilitarian, in *The Commonplace Book*: 'The greatest happiness of the greatest number is the foundation of morals and legislation'; now a near cliché.

165.21 *Marx ... cod*: Karl Marx (1818–83), German political philosopher and economist; Temple's slang: 'Marx is only a bloody joke'.

165.27 *Socialism was founded by an Irishman*: extraordinarily oversimplistic and chauvinist claim; at a very long stretch, one possible candidate is James (Bronterre) O'Brien (1804–64), who wrote on the state of the working class, propounded schemes for land nationalization, 'came closer than any of his peers to formulating a coherent social policy' (*F* 365), and coined the terms 'social democrat' and 'social democracy'; another is William Thompson (1775–1833), who published *An Inquiry into the Distribution of Wealth* (1824) and an *Appeal* (1825) for the equality of the sexes, willed his property to the co-operative movement (though his family wrested it back), was quoted by Marx, who was himself described by Sidney (1859–1947) and Beatrice (1858–1943) Webb (English socialists) as 'Thompson's disciple', atheist and vegetarian (*F* 307–8).

165.28 *Collins*: Anthony Collins (1676–1729), born at Hexton, Middlesex, English theologian, deist, wrote *Discourse of Freethinking* (1713), 'freethinker' (see 157.5–6 n.).

165.35–6 *Lottie Collins ... lend her yours?*: Lottie Collins was an English music-hall star of the 1890s; popularized 'Ta-Ra-Ra-Boom-De-Ay' (a street rhyme) in *Dick Whittington*, a pantomime, in 1891; the rhyme continues 'She is going far away | To sing Ta-ra-ra-boom-de-ay' (Iona and Peter Opie, *Lore and Language of Schoolchildren*, 107).

166.1 *five bob each way*: 'five bob': five shillings; 'each way': a bet as in a horse race, five shillings to win, five to place, five to show. Joyce to his translator: 'He means nothing except that he affects to consider the Middlesex philosopher as the name of a racehorse' (*LIII* 130).

166.16 *Pax super totum sanguinarium globum*: schoolboy Latin: 'Peace over all this bloody globe'.

167.3 *Nos ad manum ballum jocabimus*: schoolboy Latin: 'Let's go play handball'.

167.16–17 *like a celebrant attended by his ministers*: as a priest about to celebrate mass.

167.28 *prefect of the college sodality*: see 88.4–5 n. and 133.3–4.

167.32–3 *matric men . . . first arts men . . . Second arts*: respectively, first-year, second-year, and third-year students (Sullivan, 158).

168.3 *I'll take my dying bible*: 'I'll swear on my dying words'.

168.20–1 *Jean Jacques Rousseau*: (1712–78), French philosopher and writer, believed in the fundamental goodness of human nature and the corrupting influence of civilization, author of *Émile* (1762), in which he suggested that education should allow free individual development, and *Social Contract* (1762), in which he argued for the right of the people to revolt against any government which had broken its 'social contract' (i.e. if its policies ran counter to the general will).

168.25 *super spottum*: schoolboy Latin: 'On the spot'.

169.1–2 *go-by-the-wall*: a slippery individual.

169.19 *tame goose*: see 152.14 n.

169.29–30 *Long pace, fianna! . . . salute, one, two*: 'fianna': Gaelic: soldiers or warriors (from the name of the army of Fionn Mac Cumhail, the hero chieftain of the later Irish heroic cycle); it also became associated with the 'fenians' (whence their name); the entire phrase here: instructions from the Fenian handbook. See 32.4 n.

169.34 *rebellion with hurleysticks*: a 'sneerer's' comment on the failed Fenian Rising of 1867 (training having taken place not with guns but with camann (see 152.39 n.).

169.35 *indispensable informer*: another snide comment, this on the long-established practice of the betrayal of nationalist groups by informers.

170.1 *office of arms*: office (in Dublin castle) which had charge of coats of arms and genealogies.

170.4 *league class*: Gaelic League class in the Irish language (see 51.13 n.).

170.14–15 *address the jesuits as father*: as opposed to the polite Dublin convention of addressing them as 'sir'.

170.18 *Harcourt Street*: street running south from St Stephen's Green.

170.36–7 *days of Tone to those of Parnell*: see 155.5 n.

171.1–2 *Our day will come*: Fenian slogan.

171.8 *nationality, language, religion*: cf. 'Portrait' where a slightly different tetrad throws its nets: 'social limitations, inherited apathy of race, an adoring mother, the Christian fable' (*PSW* 214).

171.8 *nets*: cf. William Blake (1757–1827), English poet and radical, *The Book of Urizen* (1794), plate 25, ll. 15–16, 19–22: 'Till a Web dark & cold, throughout all | the tormented element stretch'd . . . | None could break the Web, no wings of fire // So twisted the cords, & so knotted | The Meshes: twisted like to the human brain // And all call'd it, The Net of Religion.'

171.21 *Your soul!*: Joyce to his translator: 'A form of procope for "Damn your soul"' (*LIII*, 130).

171.25 *Let us eke go*: Joyce to his translator: 'Cranly misuses words. Thus he says "let us eke go" when he means to say "let us e'en go" that is "let us even go". Eke meaning also and having no sense in the phrase, whereas even or e'en is slight adverbial embellishment. By quoting Cranly's misquotation Lynch gives the first proof of his culture. The word yellow (the second [proof]) is his personal substitution for the more sanguine hued adjective, bloody' (*LIII* 130). On 'proofs of culture' see 'Portrait': 'they recommend themselves by proofs of culture' (*PSW* 218).

171.33 *second proof of Lynch's culture*: see preceding note.

171.35 *swear in yellow*: see 171.25 n.

171.38 *Aristotle has not defined pity and terror*: not directly in the *Poetics*, which is where he says that 'tragedy . . . is the imitation of an action . . . with incidents arousing pity and fear' (vi. 1449^b 24–8; *Complete Works of Aristotle: The Revised Oxford Translation*, ed. Jonathan Barnes, 2 vols. (Princeton: Princeton University Press, 1984), ii. 2320); cf. xi. 1452^a 38 (ii. 2324); though Aristotle does define them in relation to his conception of catharsis in e.g. *Rhetoric* ii. 5 and ii. 8 (ii. 2202–4, 2207–9). See, too, Joyce in his Paris notebook (1903): 'Now terror is the feeling which arrests us before whatever is grave in human fortunes and unites us with its secret cause and pity is the feeling which arrests us before whatever is grave in human fortunes and unites us with the human sufferer' (*CW* 143).

172.29–30 *Venus of Praxiteles in the Museum*: nude statue of Venus by Praxiteles (Greek sculptor of the fourth century BC) a plaster cast of which stood in the National Museum in Kildare Street.

172.32 *carmelite school*: school run by the 'Carmelites', the strict Catholic Order of Our Lady of Mount Carmel (founded *c*.1156).

173.26 *Rhythm . . . esthetic relation*: cf. Joyce in the Paris notebook (*CW* 145), 'Portrait' (*PSW* 211), and Aubert's discussion of the significance of the concept to Joyce (89–93).

174.1 *canal bridge*: bridge over the Grand Canal (forming a southern circular boundary of central Dublin).

174.10 *Wicklow*: see 28.29 n and 164.20.

174.27 *Pulcra sunt quæ visa placent*: see 156.5 n.

174.35–6 *Venus of Praxiteles*: see 172.29–30 n.

174.37–8 *Plato . . . splendour of truth*: Plato (*c*.429–*c*.347 BC), Greek idealist philosopher, pupil of Socrates, tutor of Aristotle; Ellmann and Mason claim that Joyce takes this rather epigrammatic version of a typical Platonic statement from a letter (18 Mar. 1857) to Mlle Leroyer de Chantepie from Gustave Flaubert (1821–80, French novelist, author of *Madame Bovary* (1857)): 'la forme, la beau indéfinissable résultant de la conception même et qui est la splendeur du vrai, comme disait Platon' (quoted at length in *CW* 141 n.): 'form, the indefinable Beauty resulting from the conception itself, which is the splendour of truth, according to Plato' (translated (with date 11 Mar. 1857) in *WD* 248). Cf. Joyce's use of the same phrase in 'James Clarence Mangan' (1902) (*CW* 83 and *KB* 60).

175.5–8 *Aristotle's . . . book of psychology . . . to the same subject*: Stephen means Aristotle's *Metaphysics*, only in part a 'book of psychology'; the 'statement' comes from Book IV (Γ), iii. 1005^b 19–20: 'The same attribute cannot at the same time belong and not belong to the same subject in the same respect' (ed. Barnes, ii. 1588).

175.24 *eugenics rather than to esthetic*: Stephen makes the same distinction as does Bernard Bosanquet: 'sexual preference is . . . contrasted with aesthetic selection, real beauty is distinguished from beauty which only has reference to desire' (*The History of Aesthetic* (1892; repr. London: Macmillan, 1904), 62) quoted by Aubert who argues throughout the significance of Bosanquet to Joyce (84 and *passim*). Bosanquet is adapting Aristotle, *Problems* lii. 896ᵇ 10–30 (ed. Barnes, ii. 1389).

175.26 *The Origin of Species*: (1859) by Charles Darwin (1809–82), whose theory of 'natural selection' proposed that organisms that are best adapted to their environment are most likely to thrive and to reproduce; their genes get passed on and their kind become predominant; the 'fittest' will 'survive'; but Darwin stressed that this was a long-term process, not something which could be easily seen within the life of a given individual.

175.36–7 *sir Patrick Dun's hospital*: hospital near the canal, built in 1803 from the estate of Sir Patrick Dun (1642–1713), Scots-Irish physician.

176.15 *applied Aquinas*: the remark seems perverse, since Aquinas's aim was to elucidate Catholic doctrine, not to produce an aesthetic (see, on this point, William T. Noon, *Joyce and Aquinas* (New Haven: Yale University Press, 1957), 4, 9, 126, and *passim*); though for a full discussion of what this might mean for an aesthetic theory, see Aubert (4–6, 100–9). See, too, Joyce, 'Holy Office' (1904): 'So distantly I turn to view | The shamblings of that motley crew, | Those souls that hate the strength that mine has | Steeled in the school of old Aquinas' (*PSW* 99).

176.26–7 *Pange lingua gloriosi*: Latin, in full, *Pange lingua gloriosi corporis mysterium*: 'Tell, my tongue, of the mystery of the glorious body of Christ', Aquinas's hymn sung on Maundy Thursday (day before Good Friday) to celebrate Jesus's institution of the Eucharist at the Last Supper (an English translation is given in Liguori, *Visitations*, 98); by Fortunatus (see below), not Aquinas.

176.30 *Vexilla Regis of Venantius Fortunatus*: Latin, in full, *Vexilla Regis Prodeunt*: 'The King's Banners Advance'; as Stephen says, a hymn by Venantius Fortunatus (*c*.530–600), bishop of Poitiers and Latin poet, which is sung during Passiontide.

176.32–5 *Impleta sunt quæ concinit . . . Regnavit a ligno Deus*: Latin: 'The mystery we now unfold, | Which David's faithful verse foretold | Of Our Lord's kingdom, while we see | God ruling nations from a tree'; another stanza of the *Pange lingua*.

176.37 *Lower Mount Street*: leads north towards the centre of Dublin from the Grand Canal.

177.3–5 *Griffin was plucked . . . the Indian*: Griffin failed at the civil service exams; Halpin and O'Flynn passed the exams for places in the civil service within the United Kingdom; Moonan ranked very highly in the exams for a place within the British administration in India; O'Shaughnessy did well in the same.

177.6 *Irish fellows*: if 'nationalists' is meant, odd that they should be celebrating the success of Irish men in the British civil service exams; more likely, those serving in the Irish civil service (which was, of course, British, not nationalist).

177.11 *a question of Stephen's*: 'Who came top in the matric [first-year] exams?'

177.23 *Glenmalure*: valley in County Wicklow.

177.30 *Goethe and Lessing*: Johann Wolfgang von Goethe (1749–1832), German poet and dramatist (author of *Faust* and of the 'Wilhelm Meister' novels which developed the genre of the *Bildungsroman*); Gotthold Ephraim Lessing (1729–81), German critic and dramatist, author of *Laocoön* (see 177.32 n.).

177.31 *the classical school and the romantic school*: these comments are little more than clichés; the two writers did not write *about* the 'classical' and 'romantic schools' (as though they were political movements one might or might not support).

177.32 *Laocoon*: (1766), Lessing's analysis of the limits of poetry and painting, based on the Graeco-Roman statue of Laocoön and his sons wrestling with the serpents; argued that the limits of the two kinds of art (poetry in time and sculpture in space) make straightforward comparisons between the two impossible. Stephen quotes Lessing on this point in *Ulysses*, 'Proteus' (*U* 37).

177.33 *idealistic, German, ultraprofound*: nonsense.

178.5 *Merrion Square*: Georgian square in central Dublin.

178.10–11 *Aquinas says: ad pulcritudinem tria requiruntur, integritas, consonantia, claritas*: Latin: Stephen's definition is accurate; he paraphrases Aquinas, *Summa Theologiae*, Part I, Question 39, Article 8: 'For beauty includes three conditions: *integrity* or perfection, since those things which are impaired are by that very fact ugly; due proportion or *harmony*; and lastly, brightness, or *clarity*, whence things are called beautiful which have an elegant colour' (trans. Shapcote, i. 211, italics added).

178.24–6 *esthetic image . . . is presented in space*: after Lessing's distinction (see 177.32 n.).

179.1–8 *claritas . . . reality of which it is but the symbol*: Joyce to his translator: 'A reference to Plato's theory of ideas, or more strictly speaking to Neo-Platonism, two philosophical tendencies with which the speaker at that moment is not in sympathy' (*LIII* 132).

179.16–17 *radiance . . . whatness of a thing*: in his emphasis on the object as it is apprehended (or 'conceived in [the artist's] imagination'), Stephen shifts Aquinas's meaning slightly; for the latter *claritas* is not a matter of how a thing is perceived, it is a characteristic of the thing itself, its form, hence its *quidditas*.

179.19–20 *the mind in that mysterious instant Shelley likened beautifully to a fading coal*: Shelley, 'A Defence of Poetry' (80.33 n.): 'A man cannot say, "I will compose poetry." The greatest poet even cannot say it; for the mind in creation is as a fading coal, which some invisible influence, like an inconstant wind, awakens to transitory brightness; this power arises from within' (*The Prose Works of Percy Bysshe Shelley*, ed. Richard Herne Shepherd, 2 vols. (London: Chatto & Windus, 1912), 32). Joyce uses the phrase in both his essay (1902) and his lecture (1907) on James Clarence Mangan (*CW* 78, 182 and *KB* 57, 133) and in *U* 186.

179.25–6 *Luigi Galvani*: (1737–98), Italian physiologist, Catholic hero of sorts since he resigned his position at the university in Bologna rather than risk compromising his religious beliefs.

179.27 *the enchantment of the heart*: Galvani uses the phrase to describe the effect of the insertion of a needle into a frog's heart (it briefly ceases beating).

179.38–180.4 *art . . . relation to others*: Victor Hugo in his 'Preface' to his play *Cromwell* (1827) also distinguishes the lyrical, epical, and dramatic, but on historical and cultural, rather than formal grounds. Cf. the young Joyce's use of the distinction in his Paris notebook (6 Mar. 1903) (*CW* 145). Aubert contends that 'Joyce's actual inspiration' is S. H. Butcher, who in discussing Greek drama suggests that '*mimesis* [has] three objects . . . *pathos*, *ethos* and *praxis*—or, in his reformulation, the immediate lyrical experience born from *pathos*, the epical mediation as staging an *ethos*, and dramatic *praxis* as the truly symbolic act as of the subject' (Aubert, 88; Butcher, *Aristotle's Theory of Poetry and Fine Art* (1895; rev. edn. London: Macmillan, 1902)).

180.10–13 *Is a chair . . . why not?*: compare Stephen's questions with those of Joyce in his Paris notebook (*CW* 146).

180.11 *Mona Lisa*: the famous painting (*c.* 1503–5) by Leonardo da Vinci (1452–1519) of Lisa, wife of Francesco del Giocondo.

180.12 *Sir Philip Crampton*: Crampton (1777–1858): famous Dublin surgeon; the bust stood above a drinking fountain outside Trinity College; the inscription is self-critical, saying that the statue 'but feebly represents' Crampton's gifts (*JSA* quotes in full (255)).

180.20 *Lessing . . . statues*: see 177.32 n.

180.35 *Turpin Hero*: yes, an old English ballad, sometimes called 'Dick Turpin' after the eighteenth-century highwayman who was hanged in 1739; various versions exist, at least one of which moves from first to third person; most are in the third person throughout.

181.1 *lambent*: playing lightly and brilliantly over (from Latin *lambere*: 'lick').

181.5–8 *The artist . . . paring his fingernails*: cf. Flaubert's comparison of the artist to the god of creation in his 1857 letter (see 174.37–8 n.): 'L'artiste doit être dans son oeuvre comme Dieu dans la Création, invisible et tout-puissant, qu'on le sente partout, mais qu'on ne le voie pas' ('An artist must be in his work like God in the creation, invisible and all-powerful, everywhere felt but never seen') (*CW* 141 n. 1 and *WD* 248).

181.11 *the duke's lawn*: small park near Leinster House, originally Kildare House, built (1745) by James Fitzgerald, 20th Earl of Kildare, later (1766) Duke of Leinster (J. T. Gilbert, *A History of the City of Dublin*, 3 vols. (Dublin: McGlashan and Gill, 1859), iii. 275–7).

181.11 *the national library*: west of Leinster House in the same complex of buildings.

181.18 *Kildare house*: most previous editions have 'royal Irish academy'; but Joyce sent a letter to Harriet Weaver in 1917 when she was collating corrections to be made to the next printing of *Portrait* asking her to make the change; it is correct in the 1918 and 1924 editions, which resolves the conundrum noted by several previous annotators: the 'royal Irish academy' is not on the route Stephen and Lynch are taking, but some 300 yards away—an absolutely uncharacteristic geographical mistake by Joyce. By changing it to 'Kildare house' (see 181.11 n.) Joyce corrects his 'mistake' (British Library Add. MS 57345, fo. 126; Joyce to Harriet Weaver, 16 Nov. 1917).

181.34 *Liverpool*: nearest large English city to Ireland; has a considerable Irish population.

181.35–6 *Half a crown cases*: 'half a crown': two shillings and sixpence; so, charity cases.

181.39 *stewing*: slang: dogged study by someone not naturally gifted.

182.4–5 *Ego credo . . . in Liverpoolio*: schoolboy Latin: 'I believe that the life of the poor is simply frightful, simply bloody frightful, in Liverpool'; perhaps, but not a patch on the 'life of the poor' in Dublin. See F. S. L. Lyons, *Ireland Since the Famine*, 2nd edn. (London: Fontana, 1973), 277–8, for a description of the Dublin slums of the time in which 30% of Dubliners then lived.

182.8–14 *The quick light shower . . . skirts demurely*: cf. Joyce's 'epiphany', no. 25 (*PSW* 185).

182.9 *quadrangle*: between the arcades of the National Library and the National Museum.

182.25 *seraphim*: the highest order of angels (see 95.36–9 n.).

182.29 *An enchantment of the heart*: see 179.27 n.

182.37–183.1 *In the virgin womb of the imagination . . . made flesh*: cf. *Ulysses*: 'In woman's womb word is made flesh but in the spirit of the maker all flesh that passes becomes the word that shall not pass away' (*U* 373) and Joyce to Nora Barnacle Joyce: 'thinking of the book I have written, the child which I have carried for years and years in the womb of the imagination as you carried in your womb the children you love, and of how I had fed it day after day out of my brain and my memory' (21 Aug. 1912 (*SL* 202–3)).

183.1–2 *Gabriel . . . virgin's chamber*: the archangel Gabriel (having been promoted by Stephen) came to announce to Mary (the 'annunciation') the forthcoming birth of Jesus (Luke 1: 26–38), which announcing represents the moment that 'the Word was made flesh' (John 1: 1) (see 100.7 n.).

183.6–7 *lured . . . falling from heaven*: Stephen at his most arcane, picking up on various medieval heresies which suggest that Lucifer and his cohort fell as a result of lusting after Mary.

183.12 *villanelle*: nineteen-line poem comprising five three-line and one final four-line stanzas; the first line of the first stanza is repeated as the last line of the second and fourth stanzas and as the penultimate line of the last stanza; the last line of the first stanza is repeated as the last line of the third and fifth stanzas and the final line of the entire poem; all of which Stephen's poem does; often regarded as a precious, self-conscious poetic form.

184.18 *Sacred Heart*: one of the representations of Jesus: exposing his heart as an emblem of his love; first seen in a vision by Saint Margaret Mary Alacoque (1647–90), a French Visitandine nun.

184.23–4 *sad and sweet loth to depart*: a song typically sung on taking leave of friends.

184.24 *victory chant of Agincourt*: 'The Agincourt Song', a popular fifteenth-century song celebrating the victory of the English over the French at the Battle of Agincourt (1415). (*G* quotes.)

184.24–5 *air of Greensleeves*: sixteenth-century ballad sung to lady Greensleeves who has 'wrongly' and 'discourteously' refused the love of the singer.

184.28 *called by their christian names*: see 151.25–6 n.

184.31–5 *She passed now dancing . . . on her cheek*: cf. Joyce's 'epiphany', no. 26 (*PSW* 186).

184.32 *carnival ball*: one given just before the beginning of the Lenten season.

185.7–9 *a heretic franciscan . . . Gherardino da Borgo San Donnino*: Gherardino (d. 1276) led the 'Spirituals', a group within the Franciscans desiring to return the order to its original strictness (see 119.34 n.), condemned as a heretic. Cf. 'Portrait' (*PSW* 214).

185.13 *her Irish phrasebook*: from her 'league class'; see 170.4 n.

185.22 *scullerymaid*: the lowliest of servants.

185.28 *handsel*: see 154.6 n.

185.30 *By Killarney's Lakes and Fells*: ballad from *Inisfallen*, an opera by Michael Balfe (1808–70).

185.30–2 *a girl . . . shoe*: cf. Joyce in his Trieste notebook: 'girls laughing when he stumbled in the street were unchaste' (*WD* 94).

185.32 *Cork Hill*: side street running alongside City Hall.

185.34 *Jacob's biscuit factory*: W. and R. Jacob & Co., Steam Biscuit Bakery, west of St Stephen's Green.

186.7 *latticed ear of a priest*: because pressed against the lattice separating the one confessing from the one receiving the confession in the confession box.

186.10 *a potboy*: one who serves pots of ale in a pub.

186.10 *Moycullen*: village in County Galway.

186.12–14 *priest of the eternal imagination . . . everliving life*: see 182.37–183.1 and 183.1–2 nn., though note that Stephen substitutes the alchemical 'transmutation' for the Eucharistic 'transubstantiation' and cf. 'Portrait': 'Like an alchemist he bent upon his handiwork, bringing together the mysterious elements, separating the subtle from the gross' (*PSW* 214).

186.22 *The chalice flowing to the brim*: cf. D'Annunzio's image in his *Il Fuoco* (see 143.13–15 n.) of a woman momentarily blinded by the impact of a painting; she has experienced 'a filling up of the chalice to the brim' (*G*). Cf. *The Flame* (ed. Bassnett), 5, and *WD* 277.

186.32 *great overblown scarlet flowers*: cf. D'Annunzio's image in his *Il Piacere* (see 143.13–15 n.) where the hero faces a similar image: 'some men were taking down the hangings from the walls, disclosing a paper with great vulgar flowers, torn here and there and hanging in strips' (*G*).

187.4 *tram; the lank brown horses*: see 57.33 ff. and n.

187.25 *strange humiliation of her nature*: her menstrual period; its characterization as 'humiliation' has a long history in Western religion. Cf. Joyce in his Trieste notebook (*WD* 95).

188.4–22 *Tell no more of enchanted days*: cf. this villanelle with the one written by Joyce (*c*.1898) and dubbed by his brother Stanislaus 'The Villanelle of the Temptress' (*PSW* 72); 'he' in 'Portrait' also writes 'tributary verses' (*PSW* 216). See 'Introduction' n. 48.

188.23 *the library*: National Library in Kildare Street.

188.24 *ashplant*: the ash was, in Celtic mythology, the plant from which spears were made (Robert Graves, *The White Goddess* (New York, 1948), 22).

188.25 *Molesworth Street*: runs west from Kildare Street.

188.32–3 *odd or even in number . . . thirteen*: in numerology, odd numbers are masculine, even feminine, and the number thirteen unlucky (though differently associated—with water and the maternal—by Agrippa in his *Philosophy of Natural Magic* (see 189.16 n.).

189.2 *temple of air*: in Roman divination, the 'augur' (the official who observed and interpreted the meaning of natural signs) marked off the ground to correspond with the sky above (the 'temple of air'), then observed (the number, kind, behaviour of) the birds overhead; from this the gods' approval or disapproval of a proposed event was deduced.

189.3–4 *squeak of mice behind the wainscot*: cf. Tennyson's 'Mariana' (who waits in vain for the arrival of one who 'cometh not'), sixth stanza: 'the mouse | Behind the mouldering wainscot shrieked'.

189.15 *augury*: an omen; see 189.2 n.

189.16 *Cornelius Agrippa*: Heinrich Cornelius Agrippa von Nettesheim (1486–1535), German physician, philosopher, and suspected magician; he discusses augural divination in chs. 53–6 of his *De Occulta Philosophia* (*The Philosophy of Natural Magic*, 1531).

189.17–18 *Swedenborg*: Emmanuel Swedenborg (1688–1772), Swedish scientist, philosopher, and mystic; concerned to show by scientific means the spiritual structure of the universe; influenced theosophists and poets alike. (*G* notes that his nickname was *Daedalus Hyperboreus* ('Daedalus of the North').) He wrote about augural divination in various places; *JSA* suggests one source, *G* another. Cf. Joyce in his essay on William Blake (1912): 'Swedenborg, who frequented all of the invisible worlds for several years . . .' (*CW* 221 and *KB* 181) and 'Portrait' (*PSW* 214).

189.25 *curved stick of an augur*: the *lituus* with which the augur marked off the ground.

189.26–7 *the hawklike man*: Daedalus.

189.28–9 *Thoth . . . cusped moon*: Thoth: the Egyptian god of wisdom, justice, writing and patron of sciences; most usually represented in human form with the head of an ibis surmounted by the moon's disc and crescent (*OERD*).

189.33 *an Irish oath*: *O* draws the comparison with the Gaelic *tat* (a call to sheep about to turn the wrong way) and *tot* (noise, clamour); neither is really an oath, though the first might have been mistaken for one (*O* 336). See, too, '*thauss*' in 146.22 n.

190.4–7 *Bend down your faces . . . loud waters*: opening lines of Cathleen's farewell speech to her nurse, Oona, and her poet-friend, Aleel, in *The Countess Cathleen* (1892) by W. B. Yeats (1865–1939), Irish poet and dramatist; she has exchanged her soul for bread to feed her people who are dying in a famine.

190.19 *Symbol of departure or of loneliness*: i.e. do the birds he's seen (coupled with the verses he's recalled) signal that he will leave or that he will find no beloved?

190.21 *the opening of the national theatre*: the first production of the Irish Literary Theatre (precursor of the Irish National Theatre Society, which came to be known as the Abbey Theatre) was Yeats's *Cathleen* (May 1899); it was greeted with extreme protest: 'a libel on Ireland' because in it the country was shown as poverty- and famine-stricken, her people willing to sell their souls to the devil for food. See 'The Day of the Rabblement' for Joyce's response (*CW* 68–72 and *KB* 50–2).

190.29 *Made in Germany*: from the title of Ernest Williams's *Made in Germany* (1896) which suggested that the effect of oversubsidized and shoddy German goods on the British economy was wholly detrimental; here, because Germany represents the source of Protestantism (or anti-Catholicism).

190.34 *budding buddhists*: after the popular reaction against the interests of various Irish (and English) artists in theosophy and other occult Eastern religions.

191.6 *The Tablet*: English Catholic weekly journal (then very conservative).

191.10 *Pawn to king's fourth*: conventional opening in chess.

191.16 *Diseases of the Ox*: apparently the title of a chapter in a book (see *A*).

192.4 *sir Walter Scott*: (1771–1832) Scottish novelist and poet, established the form of the historical novel in English.

192.6–7 *Bride of Lammermoor*: (1819) Gothic novel by Scott involving crossed love, curses, and the extinction of an ancient family line.

192.12–13 *genteel accent . . . marred by errors*: he lacks the education to go with his class.

192.15 *incestuous love*: folklore about one of 'dwarfish stature' (191.27).

192.17 *game of swans*: 'game': collective noun for a flock of swans kept for pleasure (*SOED*).

192.29 *Bantry gang*: the Sullivan brothers (Timothy Daniel (1827–1914) and Alexander Martin (1830–84)) and their nephew Timothy Healy (1855–1931), all from Bantry (on the south-western tip of Ireland), all ostensibly pro-Parnellite but regarded as Parnell's betrayers; this is especially the case with Healy, who led the majority against Parnell in the fateful meeting in Committee Room 15 (see 26.18 n.).

193.8–9 *a touch*: 'to have sexual contact with' (*SOED*).

193.10 *riding a hack to spare the hunter*: 'riding the workhorse to spare the good one'.

193.13 *your intellectual soul*: one of Aristotle's three parts of the soul, the others being the vegetable and the animal.

193.17 *Forsters are the kings of Belgium*: everything Temple says about the Forsters here and in what follows is nonsense (see *G*); it parodies the then current national/cultural interest in claiming Irish heritage.

193.29 *Clanbrassil*: Gaelic: *Clann Bhreasail*: children of *Breasal* ('red'), the clan-name of the MacCanns of Armagh (*O* 336).

193.35 *Giraldus Cambrensis*: Latin: 'Gerald of Wales': Geraldus de Barri (*c.*1146–1220), Welsh ecclesiastic who visited Ireland with Henry II's son, Prince John, and wrote two books on Ireland: *Topographia Hibernica* (*The Topography of Ireland*, *c.*1185) and *Expugnatio Hibernica* (*The History of the Conquest of Ireland*, 1169–85), apologist's histories meant to justify the Anglo-Norman invasion; found nothing admirable in the Irish.

194.1 *Pernobilis et pervetusta familia*: Latin: 'A very noble and ancient family'; Gerald uses the phrase to compliment the family of Fitz-Stephen (literally, 'sons of Stephen') for its role in the Anglo-Norman conquest.

194.11 *paulo post futurum*: Latin translation of the Greek phrase ὁ μετ᾽ ὀλίγον μέλλων: literally, 'the future after a little'; the 'name of a tense of the passive voice of Greek verbs, used chiefly to state that an event will take place immediately', but figuratively, 'a future which is a little after the present; a by-and-by (1848)' (*SOED*).

194.22 *law of heredity*: much discussed in the wake of Darwin's *Origin of Species* (see 175.26 n.).

194.26–7 *Reproduction is the beginning of death*: exact source unknown, but despite its being spoken by Temple, it is neither nonsense nor an uncommon sentiment in the wake of Darwin.

195.16 *dual number*: grammatical term: 'the inflected form expressing two or a pair' (*SOED*); used in Latin, Greek, and even Old English, but not in modern English.

195.22 *an iron crown*: 'the ancient crown of the kings of Lombardy, so called from having a circlet of iron inserted (reputed to have been made from one of the nails of the Cross)' (*SOED*).

195.32 *Malahide*: for 'Malahide' see 105.37 n.; and cf. 'Portrait' (*PSW* 211).

196.7 *Darkness falls from the air*: a misquotation (as Stephen later realizes: 197.12 n.) of a line in the third stanza of 'A Litany in Time of Plague' (1592) by Thomas Nashe (1567–1601), English poet and playwright: 'Beauty is but a flower | Which wrinkles will devour; | Brightness falls from the air; | Queens have died young and fair; | Dust hath closed Helen's eye. | I am sick, I must die | Lord, Have mercy on us!' Cf. Yeats's use of the line in his 'The Symbolism of Poetry' (1900).

196.8–9 *A trembling joy . . . like a fairy host around him*: cf. Virgil's *Aeneid*, II. 682–4, where Aeneas's son Ascanius [Iülus] is shown to be favoured of the gods: 'a tongue of flame seemed to shed a gleam and, harmless in its touch, lick his soft locks and pasture round his temples' (trans. H. Rushton Fairclough, 2 vols. (London: Heinemann, 1978), i. 341).

196.14 *Dowland and Byrd*: John Dowland (*c*.1563–1626), English lutenist and composer; William Byrd (1543–1623), English composer.

196.14 *Nash*: Thomas Nashe: see 196.7 n.

196.16–17 *softness of chambering*: see 148.15 n.

196.18 *slobbering Stuart*: James I of England (1566–1625; r. 1603–25) and VI of Scotland (r. 1567–1625), whose reign is typically seen as darkness in the wake of the brilliance of that of his predecessor Elizabeth I (1533–1603; r. 1558–1603); he was not popular and a common contemporary description of him focuses on a tongue too large for his mouth.

196.19 *ambered wines*: those perfumed with ambergris (*SOED*).

196.20 *proud pavan*: sixteenth-century dance.

196.21 *Covent Garden*: in London; originally the 'convent garden' of the Abbey of Westminster; later a piazza, laid out by Inigo Jones in 1630 (the first square to be laid out in London); by 1670 it had become a market, mainly for fruit, vegetables, and flowers, which it remained until 1974 (*OERD*); but Stephen's thoughts are slightly anachronistic.

196.22 *wenches*: MS has 'wenchers' and so, briefly, men appear in Stephen's reverie (*JJA* 10: 1131).

196.24 *clipped*: embraced (*SOED*).

197.3–4 *curious phrase from Cornelius a Lapide ... sixth day*: Cornelius a Lapide (1567–1637), Flemish Jesuit biblical commentator; in his *The Great Commentary on the Bible* he suggests (in comment on Gen. 1: 25: 'And God made ... every thing that creepeth upon the earth after his kind: and God saw that it was good') that actually God didn't make lice and the like but rather that they 'spontaneously generated' from other substances (like maggots from bad meat).

197.12 *Brightness falls from the air*: see 196.7 n.

197.25 *ferrule*: 'a ring or cap of metal put round the end of a stick to strengthen it or to prevent it from splitting and wearing' (*SOED*).

198.12 *ipso facto*: Latin: 'by that very fact'. Joyce to his translator regarding this passage: 'Translate this word for word. It means and is intended to mean nothing' (*LIII* 130).

198.15–16 *the Adelphi*: hotel not far from the National Library.

198.24 *I suffer little children to come unto me*: see 120.27 n.

198.32–3 *why does the church ... hell if they die unbaptised*: doctrinally, unbaptized children go not to hell, but to limbo, which borders on hell, where they will be sad but will not suffer; they cannot go to heaven because they have been born in 'original sin'.

199.6–7 *Saint Augustine ... going to hell*: Augustine argues in various places that the gravity of 'original sin' means the unbaptized must be punished; in *Enchiridion*, however, he remarks that 'the mildest punishment of all will fall upon those who have added no actual sin to the original sin they brought with them' (ch. 93). For Augustine, see 109.5–8 n.

199.8 *limbo*: literally, Latin: 'at the edge'; see 198.32–3 n.

199.11 *a sugan*: Gaelic: *súgán*: hay- or straw-rope (*O* 336).

199.23 *spouse of Satan*: Sin; Milton propounds the allegorical espousal of Satan and Sin (from which union comes Death), though he also makes Sin Satan's daughter; see *Paradise Lost*, ii. 747–67 and Jas. 1: 15.

199.32 *Roscommon*: county (and town) in the west of Ireland.

200.8 *Come away*: cf. 'Portrait' (*PSW* 214) and Joyce's poem 'O, it is cold and still' (1902) (*PSW* 90).

200.12–13 *bird call from Siegfried*: in Richard Wagner (1813–83), *Siegfried* (1876), third opera in the tetralogy *Der Ring des Nibelungen* (composed 1848–74), in which the birds' song is a significant leitmotiv; in Act II, scene ii, Siegfried attempts to understand the song of the birds: he fails at first but after slaying the dragon Fafner (whose blood he absent-mindedly licks off his finger) he understands: they tell him of the hidden Rhinegold, of the Tarnhelm that makes its wearer invisible, and that whoso masters the Ring will rule the world.

200.17 *Adelphi hotel*: see 198.15–16 n.

200.18 *Kildare Street*: on the west side of the National Library.

200.18 *Maple's hotel*: small, respectable hotel on Kildare Street.

200.22–3 *patricians of Ireland*: the Anglo-Irish, Protestant 'ascendancy'.

200.23 *army commissions*: traditional career for the sons of Anglo-Irish gentry.

200.24 *land agents*: managers of the tenanted estates owned, largely, by the Anglo-Irish (often absentee) landlords.

200.26 *jarvies*: drivers of hackney coaches.

200.29–30 *before their squires begat upon them*: cf. 'Portrait': 'To those multitudes, not as yet in the wombs of humanity but surely engenderable there, he would give the word' (*PSW* 218).

200.39 *Let us eke go*: see 171.25 n.

201.15–16 *easter duty*: see 121.10 n.

201.20 *I will not serve*: see 99.10 n. and 208.16.

201.21 *That remark was made before*: at least twice; see 99.10 n.

201.32 *believe in the eucharist*: i.e. do you believe in 'transubstantiation'—held not only by the Church but by the British government to be the litmus test of whether or not one was a Catholic (see 38.36–7n.).

202.9 *Depart from me, ye cursed, into everlasting fire*: see 96.6–8 and 105.3–4 n.

202.12 *day of judgment*: see 95.19 and *passim*.

202.16–17 *bright, agile, impassible . . . subtle*: supposed characteristics of the risen bodies of saints.

203.25–6 *lap of luxury*: cliché.

204.1 *a mother's love*: see 11.6 n.

204.9 *Pascal*: Blaise Pascal (1623–62), French mathematician, philosopher, Jansenist (a harsh and morally rigorous—and ultimately condemned as heretical—Catholic movement in seventeenth-century France); his sister (in her life of him) reportedly said that he refused to allow his mother to kiss him (*G*).

204.12 *Aloysius Gonzaga*: see 11.6 and 46.38–9 nn.

204.18–19 *Jesus, too . . . scant courtesy in public*: after e.g. Mark 3: 31–5 and

John 2: 1–4, where Jesus seems to ignore, or speak harshly to, his mother in public.

204.19 *Suarez*: Francisco Suarez (1548–1617), Spanish Jesuit theologian, who attempted to excuse Jesus's behaviour to his mother by suggesting that in the original Aramaic 'woman, what have I to do with thee?' (John 2: 4) was courteous. Cf. Joyce's essay on William Blake where he describes Suarez sardonically as a 'most orthodox church philosopher' (compared with the 'undisciplined and visionary heresiarch' Blake) (*CW* 216; cf. *KB* 176).

204.21–4 *Jesus was not what he pretended to be. . . Jesus himself*: supposedly in showing self doubt (see Matt. 27: 46).

204.27 *whited sepulchre*: see 96.16–17 n.

204.30–1 *a pervert of yourself*: in the strict sense of one who has been turned away from a right religious system (from the Latin: *pervertere*: 'turn the wrong way, corrupt') (*SOED*).

205.1–2 *more like a son of God than a son of Mary*: as Stephen will later argue with his mother: Jesus's relations with his father (God) are of greater significance than those with his mother (Mary) (see 210.2–3).

205.3 *communicate*: strictly, to take communion.

205.4–6 *host . . . not a wafer of bread*: see 38.36–7 n.

205.17–18 *sacrilegious communion*: one taken when in mortal sin, itself a mortal sin: Stephen's first mortal sin is what Cranly judges to be his apostasy.

205.24 *penal days*: see 28.22 n.

205.29–30 *an absurdity . . . incoherent*: cf. Joyce in 'Ireland, Island of Saints and Sages' (1907): 'perhaps . . . we will see an Irish monk throw away his frock, run off with some nun, and proclaim in a loud voice the end of the coherent absurdity that was Catholicism and the beginning of the incoherent absurdity that is Protestantism' (*CW* 169; cf. *KB* 121).

205.31 *township of Pembroke*: on the south-eastern edge of Dublin.

205.37 *Rosie O'Grady*: song by Maud Jerome, the refrain of which begins 'Sweet Rosie O'Grady, | My dear little rose, | She's my steady lady | Most everyone knows' and ends as Cranly repeats at 206.16–19.

205.39 *Mulier cantat*: Latin: 'A woman sings'.

206.10 *Et tu cum Jesu Galilæo eras*: Latin: 'Thou also wast with Jesus of Galilee' (Matt. 26: 69); said to Peter after Christ's crucifixion, the occasion for the first of Peter's three denials of Christ; it forms part of the sung mass on Palm Sunday and is sung by a woman.

206.12 *proparoxyton*: in poetic metre: a word having the accent on the ante-penultimate syllable (as in the Latin *Galilǽo*).

207.11 *Harcourt Street station*: see 170.18 n.

207.15 *Sallygap to Larras*: on either side of the Wicklow mountains, the shortest route being over the mountains (on a road built by the British army in the 1798 rebellion (*G*)).

207.33 *Juan Mariana de Talavera*: (1536–1623), Spanish Jesuit historian who argued that killing or overthrowing a tyrant was justified by any man (in his *De Rege et Regis Institutione* (1599), described by Joyce as 'written for the stupefaction of posterity[,] a logical and sinister defence of tyrannicide' (*CW* 216; cf. *KB* 176).

207.38–9 *the secular arm*: the civil (as opposed to the ecclesiastical) authorities.

208.16 *I will not serve*: see 99.10, 201.20 nn.

208.20 *silence, exile, and cunning*: Stuart Gilbert suggested to Ellmann that Stephen's motto might come from Honoré de Balzac (1799–1850, French author of ninety-one interconnected novels), *Le Médecin de campagne*, where the hero's motto is the Latin: '*Fuge . . . Late . . . Tace*' (see *E* 354). *G* suggests another Balzac novel, *Splendeurs et misères des courtisanes*, as source for the same motto. Translated it means: 'flight, subterfuge, silence'.

208.22 *Leeson Park*: gives on to Leeson Street bridge over the Grand Canal.

208.28 *Yes, my child*: as the priest says to the one confessing.

209.16 *coursingmatches*: 'coursing': greyhounds chasing hares; cf. Stephen's memory in *U* 32.

209.22–3 *Elisabeth and Zachary*: parents of John the Baptist (Luke 1: 5–25).

209.23 *precursor*: Stephen imagines Cranly as John the Baptist, 'precursor' to his Jesus; see 149.28 n.

209.24 *locusts and wild honey*: what John the Baptist ate (Matt. 3: 4).

209.25–6 *stern severed head . . . veronica*: John the Baptist condemned King Herod's marriage to Herodias (his brother's wife); when Salome (Herodias's daughter) dances exquisitely for Herod's birthday, he promises to give her whatever she wants; she demands (and gets) the head of John on a platter. A 'veronica' is a cloth bearing an image of Jesus's face, after St Veronica, who is said to have offered a cloth to Jesus to wipe the sweat and blood from his face; the cloth is said to have retained the image of his features (*OERD*).

209.26–8 *Decollation . . . saint John at the Latin gate . . . decollated precursor trying to pick the lock*: 'decollation': the beheading of John the Baptist; celebrated by 'the fold' (i.e. the Church) on 29 August. 'Saint John at the Latin gate': not John the Baptist, but St John the Apostle, who was saved by divine intervention when being persecuted by Romans near the Latin Gate (in Rome); he is referred to as 'the disciple whom Jesus loved'. Stephen has thought first of Cranly as this second John (the Beloved) but now thinks of him as the first John (the precursor).

209.29–30 *Let the dead . . . marry the dead*: see Luke 9: 59–60: Jesus to a potential follower: 'And Jesus said unto another, Follow me. But he said, Lord, suffer me first to go and bury my father. Jesus said unto him, Let the dead bury their dead; but go thou and preach the kingdom of God'; and Matt. 22: 29–30: 'Jesus answered and said unto them, Ye do err, not knowing the scriptures, nor the power of God. For in the resurrection they neither marry, nor are given in marriage, but are as the angels of God in heaven.'

210.1 *B.V.M.*: Blessed Virgin Mary.

210.2–3 *relations between Jesus and Papa . . . lying-in hospital*: see 205.1–2 n. and compare *U* 199.3–9.

210.11 *Bruno the Nolan*: Giordano Bruno of Nola (1548–1600), Italian Dominican, philosopher, proponent of doctrine of universal love, condemned as a heretic and burned at the stake. Cf. Joyce's essay 'The Bruno Philosophy' (1903) (*CW* 132–4 and *KB* 93–4) and 'Portrait' where Bruno is included among the 'heresiarchs of initiation' (*PSW* 214).

210.14 *risotto alla bergamasca*: Italian: 'risotto from Bergamo'.

210.18 *Stephen's, that is, my green*: St Stephen's Green.

210.20–2 *quartet of them . . . overcoat of the crucified*: see John 19: 23–4, of the Roman soldiers who crucified Jesus.

210.26–8 *Blake wrote . . . I wonder if William Bond . . . very ill*: third and fourth lines of William Blake's poem 'William Bond', the eponymous hero of which has love problems too. See, too, Joyce's essay on William Blake (*CW* 214–22; cf. *KB* 175–82).

210.30 *diorama in Rotunda*: 'Rotunda': group of buildings in corner of Rutland (now Parnell) Square which housed a theatre, concert hall, assembly rooms (and now a cinema and maternity hospital, the latter of which was partly funded by the proceeds of the earlier activities); 'diorama': a precursor of the cinema: 'a scenic painting in which changes in colour and direction of illumination simulate a sunrise, etc.' (*OERD*).

210.31 *William Ewart Gladstone*: (1809–98), British Liberal prime minister, introduced a number of social and political reforms (including elementary education and the Third Reform Bill extending the franchise); he was manœuvred by Parnell into support for Irish Home Rule but didn't deliver; his withdrawal of support for Parnell over the O'Shea divorce Joyce described as 'complet[ing] the moral assassination of Parnell with the help of the Irish bishops' ('Home Rule Comes of Age' (1907) (*CW* 193; cf. *KB* 142)); cf. 'The Shade of Parnell' (1912) (*CW* 223–4; cf. *KB* 191) and 'Portrait' (*PSW* 212) and 26.18 n.

210.32 *O, Willie, we have missed you*: penultimate line of a song by Stephen Foster (1826–64), American songwriter.

210.36–7 *A long curving gallery . . . vapours*: cf. Joyce's 'epiphany', no. 29 (*PSW* 189).

211.9 *Still harping on the mother*: cf. Polonius, remarking on Hamlet: 'Still harping on my daughter: yet he knew me not at first' (*Hamlet*, II. ii. 190–2).

211.9–12 *A crocodile . . . eat it or not eat it*: answer: assuming a crocodile who keeps his word, 'eat it'.

211.13–14 *Lepidus . . . operation of your sun*: the drunken comment of Lepidus, one of the triumvirate that includes Julius Caesar and Mark Antony, in Shakespeare's *Antony and Cleopatra*: 'Your serpent of Egypt is bred now of your mud by the operation of your sun; so is your crocodile' (II. vii. 29–31).

211.17–18 *Johnston, Mooney and O'Brien's*: Dublin biscuit-makers and teashop proprietors.

211.21 *Shining quietly behind a bushel of Wicklow bran*: Joyce to his translator: 'An allusion to the New Testament phrase "The light under a bushel"' (*LIII* 130); Jesus in the Sermon on the Mount: 'Ye are the light of the world. A city that is set on an hill cannot be hid. Neither do men light a candle, and put it under a bushel, but on a candlestick; and it giveth light unto all that are in the house' (Matt. 5: 14–15).

211.22 *Findlater's church*: see 135.7 n.

211.24–5 *shortest way to Tara was via Holyhead*: 'Tara': the ancient seat of Irish kings; 'Holyhead': port in Wales where ships from Ireland landed; hence, the shortest way to the heart of Ireland is departure. Cf. Joyce in his Trieste notebook: 'The shortest way from Cape of Good Hope to Cape Horn is to sail away from it. The shortest route to Tara is via Holyhead' (*WD* 101).

211.30 *how he broke Pennyfeather's heart*: Joyce to his translator: 'In rowing. Compare Rower's heart. The phrase of course suggests at once a disappointment in love, but men use it without explanation somewhat coquettishly, I think' (*LIII* 130); 'rower's heart': heart enlarged from exercise which is then thought to be vulnerable if exercise stops.

212.3 *Michael Robartes remembers forgotten beauty*: original title of Yeats's poem 'He Remembers Forgotten Beauty' (1899).

212.4–5 *when his arms . . . loveliness which has long faded from the world*: after the opening lines of 'He Remembers Forgotten Beauty': 'When my arms wrap you round I press | My heart upon the loveliness | That has long faded from the world . . .'.

212.8–15 *Faintly, under the heavy night . . . what tidings?*: cf. Joyce's 'epiphany', no. 27 (*PSW* 187).

212.19 *tundish*: see 158.15 n.

212.25 *west of Ireland*: supposedly the 'true' Ireland, at least its more rural side.

212.25 *European and Asiatic papers please copy*: as though an obituary of one of great importance has been composed.

212.33–4 *It is with him I must struggle . . . till day come*: cf. Jacob's wrestling with the angel in Gen. 32: 24–30.

212.37 *Grafton Street*: see 154.22–3 n.

213.3–4 *spiritual-heroic refrigerating apparatus . . . Dante Alighieri*: cf. Dante's carefully poised, platonic, admiration of Beatrice in *La Vita Nuova*.

213.16–22 *The spell of arms . . . terrible youth*: cf. Joyce's 'epiphany', no. 30 (*PSW* 190 and *LII* 79).

213.27–8; *to forge in the smithy of my soul . . . conscience of my race*: cf. Ethan Brand's determination in Ibsen's *Brand* (see 144.15 n. and *G*).

213.29 *Old father, old artificer*: Daedalus, again. Note that this makes Stephen Icarus.

JANE AUSTEN	**Emma**
	Mansfield Park
	Persuasion
	Pride and Prejudice
	Sense and Sensibility
MRS BEETON	**Book of Household Management**
LADY ELIZABETH BRADDON	**Lady Audley's Secret**
ANNE BRONTË	**The Tenant of Wildfell Hall**
CHARLOTTE BRONTË	**Jane Eyre**
	Shirley
	Villette
EMILY BRONTË	**Wuthering Heights**
SAMUEL TAYLOR COLERIDGE	**The Major Works**
WILKIE COLLINS	**The Moonstone**
	No Name
	The Woman in White
CHARLES DARWIN	**The Origin of Species**
CHARLES DICKENS	**The Adventures of Oliver Twist**
	Bleak House
	David Copperfield
	Great Expectations
	Nicholas Nickleby
	The Old Curiosity Shop
	Our Mutual Friend
	The Pickwick Papers
	A Tale of Two Cities
GEORGE DU MAURIER	**Trilby**
MARIA EDGEWORTH	**Castle Rackrent**

GEORGE ELIOT	Daniel Deronda
	The Lifted Veil and Brother Jacob
	Middlemarch
	The Mill on the Floss
	Silas Marner
SUSAN FERRIER	Marriage
ELIZABETH GASKELL	Cranford
	The Life of Charlotte Brontë
	Mary Barton
	North and South
	Wives and Daughters
GEORGE GISSING	New Grub Street
	The Odd Woman
THOMAS HARDY	Far from the Madding Crowd
	Jude the Obscure
	The Mayor of Casterbridge
	The Return of the Native
	Tess of the d'Urbervilles
	The Woodlanders
WILLIAM HAZLITT	Selected Writings
JAMES HOGG	The Private Memoirs and Confessions of a Justified Sinner
JOHN KEATS	The Major Works
	Selected Letters
CHARLES MATURIN	Melmoth the Wanderer
WALTER SCOTT	The Antiquary
	Ivanhoe
	Rob Roy
MARY SHELLEY	Frankenstein
	The Last Man

The Oxford World's Classics Website

www.worldsclassics.co.uk

- Information about new titles
- Explore the full range of Oxford World's Classics
- Links to other literary sites and the main OUP webpage
- Imaginative competitions, with bookish prizes
- Peruse the Oxford World's Classics Magazine
- Articles by editors
- Extracts from Introductions
- A forum for discussion and feedback on the series
- Special information for teachers and lecturers

www.worldsclassics.co.uk

American Literature

British and Irish Literature

Children's Literature

Classics and Ancient Literature

Colonial Literature

Eastern Literature

European Literature

History

Medieval Literature

Oxford English Drama

Poetry

Philosophy

Politics

Religion

The Oxford Shakespeare

A complete list of Oxford Paperbacks, including Oxford World's Classics, Oxford Shakespeare, Oxford Drama, and Oxford Paperback Reference, is available in the UK from the Academic Division Publicity Department, Oxford University Press, Great Clarendon Street, Oxford OX2 6DP.

In the USA, complete lists are available from the Paperbacks Marketing Manager, Oxford University Press, 198 Madison Avenue, New York, NY 10016.

Oxford Paperbacks are available from all good bookshops. In case of difficulty, customers in the UK can order direct from Oxford University Press Bookshop, Freepost, 116 High Street, Oxford OX1 4BR, enclosing full payment. Please add 10 per cent of published price for postage and packing.